I0760619

N. C. HAYES

THE REDFERN LEGACY:
BOOK ONE

The Wayward Prince
The Redfern Legacy: Book One

For Jaren

Part One

Prince of Nothing

Chapter One

The bells ringing in the distance signaled the news my village had been waiting to hear for weeks: the king had finally died.

When King Mal of Nautia had first fallen ill, the Grand Palace had tried their best to keep the sickness a secret. However, my neighbors, many of whom worked in the palace itself, possessed an unquenchable thirst for gossip. Within days, talk was everywhere. I was in the garden when I heard the chimes, and my attention turned to the road leading to the palace square, where children ran and parents walked swiftly behind to hear the official announcement.

"Shaye, are you coming?" I turned to see Finn, the neighbor boy who like to help Uncle Gideon repair fences and do other small chores in exchange for copper pieces. His sandy hair hung in his eyes as he leaned against my front gate, but the toothy smile that normally consumed most of his face was absent today. Finn would be twelve years old this summer, though tall enough to pass for nearly fifteen, and was just old enough to understand the solemn mood that hung over our village.

"No, you go ahead," I told him, my spade deep in the garden bed I was turning. Harvest had come and gone, and while wet leaves still clung to the ground, the icy chill of early winter was starting to show itself in the air. It would be a few more weeks until frost truly set in, but a head start now meant less work later in the harsh cold. "I still have work to do here. Be back before sundown, or your mother will be after you."

"I know, I know," he said. "Does your uncle still need help hauling that wood in the morning?"

"I think so. Stop by after breakfast tomorrow and he'll find something for you to do, I'm sure."

"See you then!"

I wiped the sweat from my brow as he took off down the road. On the other side of it, in front of a small house nearly identical to the one I shared with my uncle, stood Cait, Finn's mother. She watched too as he ran toward the square, followed by his brothers and sisters that poured out of the house after him. We made brief eye contact before she gave me a curt nod, wiped her hands on her apron, and turned back inside.

Cait and I had been playmates in school, but like all girls in Nautia, we could no longer attend once we were fifteen and old enough to marry. While her parents arranged a courtship with the miller's son, Uncle Gideon continued my education at home. Cait gave birth to Finn when we were just sixteen. Now, at twenty-eight, she was a mother of five, the wife of a respectable tradesman, while I was a spinster, unmarried and ruined.

Or so they said. I would rather be kept company by my books than by a husband, least of all the options available to me here. To hear folks discuss their marriages, hardly anyone even liked their spouse. Why sign up for a life of discontentment when I could spend my days as I pleased, caring for Gideon and studying whatever subject might pique my interest?

The village was quiet now, with most of its residents in the city square, mourning King Mal and celebrating the new king, the barely fifteen-year-old Callum. Most of my neighbors' homes still flew the Nautian flag, a solid bloodred banner with a pair of crossed battle-axes in the center, near their doors in recognition of Nautia's one hundred and forty-fifth anniversary. The aggressive sigil of House Thandreil was a constant reminder of our nation's brutal beginnings.

The gate creaked as Uncle Gideon stepped into the garden. I had been meaning to grease those hinges. Perhaps Finn could do it for me tomorrow.

"How was your day?" I asked as I put my gardening tools away in their basket.

"It ended a while ago," he said. There was a smudge of soot on his cheek, and his coat and vest were both partially unbuttoned, revealing the white shirt beneath. Even from where I knelt, the symbol of the royal blacksmith was visible against the black of his vest, stitched in red just over his heart. "When the bells started ringing, they told the staff to go home. It took me all this time just to fight through the crowd." He took my basket as I stood, and we started toward the house. "Crown Prin—er, King Callum is going to address the people in a few minutes."

I wondered how Callum must be feeling. Still a child, now the king of a small nation because his father was dead. His mother the queen had died during his birth. Mal's younger brother, Prince Gram, was the only living family the young king had left.

"The boy has just lost his father. What could he possibly have to address so urgently?"

"Promises of stability through the transition of power," Gideon speculated. "Calming concerns about strikes from the Old Ones during an uncertain time in the kingdom."

I shook my head. "Can't they give him a day? Poor thing."

Gideon kept his grip tight on the basket handle, but his usual stoic look did not tell me any of his thoughts.

"I'm sure some advisor or another has a plan. He's a good boy. Quiet, polite, the few times I've seen him. He'll be all right." He opened the front door and stepped aside to hold it for me. I entered and, with a frown, watched my uncle walk toward his bedroom to clean up before dinner, unsure of why a knot was forming in my gut.

A few hours later, Gideon was reading by a lamp in the sitting room while I washed the dinner dishes. When finished, I would join him to continue my latest read, a volume on the history of mushroom foraging, which had turned out to be much more interesting than it seemed at first glance.

The sitting room was my favorite place in our house. Being just the two of us, Gideon and I had allowed the space to become a den of organized chaos framed by our interests. In the center of the farthest wall sat our fireplace, while each other wall was lined by bookcases and makeshift shelves. The only places not blocked by books were the spots where Gideon had hung his maps—antique curiosities from before the war, some depicting pre-revolutionary Nautia, back when we were still a territory of Medeisia, the kingdom of sorcerers. Others depicted the lands across the Lucent Sea: Keotis and Sewyth, the elf kingdoms, and Auperene, the faelands. The maps were of course contraband, but they had been up on the wall my entire life and had yet to draw any attention.

To the left of the fireplace was Gideon's stiff armchair, covered in a tough blue fabric that had survived my jumping on it as a child, alongside the various spills I had caused—not to mention the ones Gideon had done himself. Next to it was a small table with a collection of pens and notebooks cluttering its top, some of the papers already marked with the telltale signs of teacup drips. To the right, the setup was similar, except that my chair was far more comfortable. A deep burgundy velvet covered the surface, soft though worn in some spots from overuse. Finn had delivered it to our doorstep one morning about a year ago, stating that his mother no longer had use of it. My armchair at the time had stuffing coming out of the seams and a loose spring that poked, and I sent Finn home with two apple-and-fig pies and a large loaf of honey bread to give Cait my thanks, though I never heard another word from her about it.

I was just hanging a skillet on its hook above the stove when three sharp knocks rang out from the front door. Gideon made to stand, but I was already halfway there, wiping my hands on my apron. I opened the door to a figure in a hooded cloak. He must have seen my eyes widen because he quickly put down his hood, revealing his face. He was handsome, with brown skin and black hair and eyes nearly the same color. Unkempt curls too long to be tamed hung around his face, the ends just reaching his squared jaw.

"Hello," he said after a silent moment, and I realized I had been staring at him.

I frowned. "Can I help you?"

"Yes, er, is this the home of Gideon Eastly?"

"It is," I replied slowly. My eyes trailed from the urgent set of his shoulders to the gold clasp at his neck, holding his fine black cloak shut. Too fine, I realized, to have come from any tailor in Nautia. "Is there something I can—" Gideon appeared next to me, jaw clenched beneath his graying beard. I stepped aside, expecting him to send the man on his way.

"Come in. Sitting room is this way," my uncle said gruffly instead, turning back into the house. I tried to keep from gaping as I watched the stranger follow my uncle into the next room.

A few minutes later, I arranged what might have passed as a tea service on the one serving tray we owned. I could not remember ever hosting a guest and had to dig in the back of a cabinet to even find a third teacup to serve him with. If I were being honest, I was grateful for the few minutes to stall and regain some composure. Gideon's reaction to the man was unsettling, as if this was someone he knew and did not particularly want to see. It was not often that Gideon looked so unnerved.

My uncle and the stranger were talking in soft tones, until I entered the room and they stopped, leaving a heavy silence in the air. I set the tray on Gideon's table, which had been cleared and shifted between them, but before I could lift the pot to serve them, my uncle said, "That's fine, Shaye. You've had a long day. You should go get some rest." I glanced at our visitor, who gave me a tight-lipped smile as he took the teapot himself.

"I'm fine," I replied. "I wouldn't want to be rude to our guest—"

"Leave us, Shaye." My face heated with embarrassment as I locked eyes with my uncle, startled by his stern words. He clenched his jaw again as I stood a bit straighter and smoothed my skirt.

"Well," I said to the cloaked man. "Good night, then."

He inclined his head. "Good night."

I said nothing to Gideon as I walked past him and down the hall to my small bedroom. I shut the door soundly behind me and raged quietly at the humiliation of being ordered around like a child. Gideon had never spoken to me in that way. Even when I was young, he spoke to me as an equal, giving me the courtesy of an explanation even if I didn't like the decision. Yet now he sent me away with nothing more than an order and a look of fear in his eyes. What had this stranger brought to our home that would make my uncle behave this way?

I stretched out on my bed without changing out of my dinner clothes, counting the minutes, and hoping I would get a knock on the door and an explanation. As time passed and I felt myself dozing off, I knew the likelihood of it happening before morning was slim. I fought to keep my eyes open, but try as I might, sleep eventually overcame me.

Chapter Two

A loud bang from the front of the house woke me. My eyes snapped open and I scrambled to my feet. A pause, then more banging came, joined by the muffled sounds of men yelling. I stumbled out of my room and swiftly made my way toward the sitting room. Gideon and the man were standing a few feet from the door as the pounding outside continued. A loud voice rang out, "King's Guard. Open up!"

"This is exactly what I told you would happen," the cloaked man told my uncle sternly. "They know. They *have* known. We need to go now."

"What's going on?" Both of their heads turned toward me as I stood staring from the hallway. Sweat was beading at Gideon's forehead.

"Shaye," he said, "go pack a bag—"

"There's no time," the stranger said. "We need to get her out of here."

"This is your final warning," the voice from the other side of the door called out. "If you do not open this door in three seconds, we will break it down and you will not be met with mercy." The following crash against the door indicated that our time had already run out. Gideon approached it as a second impact slammed into the wood. The stranger placed his hands on my shoulders and moved me further into the hallway. He pressed my back against the wall.

"Stay hidden," he murmured before sweeping back into the entryway. Where I expected the third and final *bang* or the sound of our door being broken down, I instead heard a high-pitched squeaking of hinges, followed by Gideon's voice.

"Hello, gentlemen," my uncle said with false courtesy. "How can I be of service to you?" The men did not reply, but there was a sound like a brief scuffle, then boots stepping onto the creaky wooden floors. The door slammed shut behind them.

"I was under the impression that the guards of the Grand Palace had at least some sense of decency." Our visitor's tone was casual, almost sarcastic compared to the anxiety in his voice a moment before. "Last I checked, soldiers couldn't simply barge into citizens' homes."

"We will take any measures necessary to protect these realms and the rule of law," one of the guards spat.

"Charming."

"We have been told explicitly by the palace witches that there is sorcery flowing from this shack, and we intend to take its source before the king," said a second guard, and I nearly recoiled. It was well known that there had not been sorcery in Nautia in one hundred and forty-five years. All Nautians were taught that no sorcerer had stepped foot on our side of the border since the revolution, when Calvin Thandreil led an army of rebels against the Old Ones—the sorcerers of Medeisia—who'd once ruled over us. The only magic permitted in our land now was from the king's witches, who'd allied with us against the Medeisians. But how could they have sensed sorcery here?

"Witches," the man scoffed. "Spoiling the fun, as usual." I crept to the end of the hall and peeked around the corner. "My friend and I will not be going anywhere. Go back to your palace and tell your witches that their spells are faulty."

"Not a chance, boy," the guard grunted. "Either you give up the sorcerer, or we take you both and burn this dump to the ground." He took a step forward, sizing him up for a fight. He was short, with cropped blond hair and a ruddy complexion. The second guard was taller, but bald and much older than his companion. Our stranger sighed.

"You had to do this the hard way."

Faster than I could blink, a broadsword appeared in his hand and swung down at the blond guard, who caught it just in time, blocking the blow with his own blade. The two swung again, swords clashing and clanging so loudly, my ears rang. The bald guard and my uncle gaped at the fight for a few seconds, and then, as if just remembering the other, both scrambled for weapons. The cloaked man whistled and tossed Gideon a second sword seemingly pulled from nowhere, which he used to parry a strike. Swords flashed as my uncle, with a considerable amount of skill, fought the guard into a corner. I had never seen Gideon use a weapon beyond a bow and arrow to hunt rabbits in the woods, but now I watched with one hand at my throat as he battled a soldier in our house and a stranger defended us from the other. It was only seconds later that the guard thrust his blade forward, slicing Gideon along the side of his body. He fell back.

"*Gideon!*" I shrieked and darted from my hiding place. Both guards whipped around, but before either could react, the blade disappeared from the cloaked man's grasp and he raised his hands. Balls of strange, blue light glowed in his palms. He launched them into the soldiers' chests, and the pair fell to the floor, still.

My uncle sat up, clutching his side. "I'm all right," he told me as I knelt beside him. "It's a surface wound. I'm fine." Tears pricked behind my eyes as dark blood began seeping through the fabric of his shirt. Yet he stood, and I followed. He gripped the sword in his hand, placing the other on the side of my face, the way he'd done when I was a child—comfort, and a way of holding my full attention. I heard horses snorting and screaming in the distance and the sounds of armored men approached from the village road.

"We need to go," the man said from beside us. "There are more coming, and when they see their comrades here . . ." He did not finish, and when I looked again at the men, I realized they were not simply knocked out as I originally thought. Gideon swallowed, and the man added, "I'm sorry. I thought there might be more time."

"Shaye, you need to go," my uncle said. "With him."

"What—just me?"

He nodded firmly. "I can't come with you. I'll hold you back, and you must reach your destination quickly."

"No. I don't understand. I'm not just going to leave you here—"

"You have to." The horses grew louder. "Go with him. You'll be safe." The words sounded like an order when paired with the sharp look my uncle threw in the man's direction.

"No harm will come to her, Sir Gideon," he promised. Gideon inclined his head. Then he sighed, still holding my cheek.

"You look just like Brina," he said. My mouth went dry. He'd never said my mother's name out loud before. Gideon's eyes scanned my face as if to memorize it, while his own was ashen and swimming with regret. "I never told you. I never told you a lot of things. I'm sorry for that."

"It's all right." I choked back tears. "Where are we going to—" Men's voices bellowed from what must have been just outside our garden gate. We were out of time. How would we go anywhere now? There would be no getting past the soldiers.

"I'll send word when I can," Gideon told me over the sound of guards marching through our garden and up the walkway. He pressed a kiss to my forehead. "Go."

I watched my uncle ready his sword, and as the door flew open, nearly exploding off the hinges, the man beside me gripped my hand. My stomach dropped, and we disappeared into darkness.

Seconds later, we were standing in a vast field with a bright moon hanging over us in the sky. I yanked my hand back and staggered away as a quiet sob ripped from my throat. He swore from behind me. The field we stood in was empty; not a house or even a road was anywhere in sight.

"What did you just do?" I asked. "Where are we?"

"It's called effuging. A way of transporting oneself quickly across long distances," he replied. "As far as the where of things . . ." He looked around once again, apparently recognizing our location despite the lack of landmarks. "I intended to take us to my home, in Sylvanna, but it looks like the Nautian witches' wards work both ways. I'd say we're about a mile from the border. We'll have to walk and cross into Medeisia on foot."

"*Medeisia?*" I gasped. "I can't go to Medeisia. That's where—the Old Ones—" I stopped at the man's loud sigh. He shook his head and knelt before digging through a knapsack I hadn't noticed before. He pulled out a canteen. "What?" I asked.

"I haven't heard anyone call us 'the Old Ones' in decades, my lady." He handed me the canteen. "Take a drink."

"What do you mean 'us?' You . . . you're—" I fumbled as the realization washed over me and my voice came out thinner. "You're not like the stories."

He conjured a ball of blue light once again. "What do you think this is, if not sorcery?" I stared.

"It didn't really occur to me what you were doing. I'm very . . . confused." I took the canteen and drank quickly before handing it back, unsure if declining an offered refreshment would be seen as an insult. I had once poured over books that Gideon insisted be kept secret—contraband, like his maps—some of which detailed the history and geography of the continent before the revolution, while others told stories of nobles and royals among the Medeisians. The most documented figures in these tales were those who had committed monstrous acts against mortals and other sorcerers alike. I vaguely remembered a footnote somewhere noting that insulting a sorcerer was a dangerous act.

"I can't go with you," I blurted out. "I don't even know your name. I have to go back and help my uncle—if I just explain—"

"My name is Aydan, my lady." He closed the canteen and shoved it back into the knapsack. "There is no good that can come from you going back anywhere near that village." I glared at him. "I am sorry, Lady Shaye. I know this must be very overwhelming—"

"I'm not a lady," I snapped. "You keep calling me that. My uncle is a blacksmith. We aren't *titled.* We barely make ends meet."

Aydan blinked a few times, then ran his hands over his face and up through his shaggy hair, sighing again in frustration. "You truly don't know anything? Gideon never told you about your past? Your connections? Your *parents*?"

"I-I . . . he told me that my mother died giving birth to me, and that my father was killed before then. I'd never even heard him say her name before tonight," I stammered.

Aydan stared at me again, shaking his head. He swore under his breath, then turned away and paced a few times before saying, "There is . . . much to tell you, then. I'm sorry, my la—*Shaye*," he corrected himself. "I will explain what I can on our way to Medeisia."

"Why must we go there?" I asked. "Surely, Nautia would be safer—"

"It isn't," Aydan said. "You may become the most wanted woman in Nautia before the night is through. There is nowhere in the world more dangerous for you right now. If they find you after a pair of their guards were killed by magic . . . if he's kind, the Nautian king would simply execute you."

"I don't understand," I said. "I'm nobody. What would the king want with me?"

"He will want to know how a sorceress was raised from infancy in his capital, without his knowledge." My stomach dropped.

"He will believe you to be extraordinarily powerful, regardless of what power you do or do not contain. The Grand Palace knows sorcery has been in that cottage. We need to make sure you're as far away from it as possible."

"I'm not a sorceress." I could barely form the word.

"I can assure you, Shaye, you most certainly are." I gaped at him, sure somehow that he spoke truth. There was no way to know, but the knot in my stomach had transformed itself into a fluttering ball, urging me forward. "I'll explain what I can." Aydan placed his hand on my back and guided me into the darkness.

Chapter Three

We walked in silence for a time as I worked to find my footing in the dark. Though the moon hung brightly over our heads, it was difficult to see where we stepped, and while the field had at first looked to be just grass, the terrain was rockier than I'd anticipated. I found myself stumbling more than once over sizable boulders; meanwhile, Aydan walked smoothly beside me, as if the magic he held also kept him poised at all times.

"Your mother's name was Brina Eastly," my new companion started after a couple of minutes. "When the King of Medeisia was exiled during the Nautian Rebellion, he and his court were forced to retreat west to a smaller territory called Ayzelle. There were a few dozen mortal families who stood by the royal family and followed them to this new territory, taking up residence in the villages alongside the sorcerer commoners who fled the capital. The Eastly family was fiercely loyal to the Crown. Every man in their family from the time of the Rebellion served in the King's Guard, or on the battlefield. Brina was the first woman in the Eastly family to join the army. Enlisted the day she came of age if I remember correctly."

"You knew her?" Gideon was the only person I'd ever known who knew my mother when she was alive. Aydan shook his head.

"Our paths never crossed. I was an emissary at that time, living in Sylvanna. But the gossip traveled the way it always does in those circles. An Eastly woman, not yet twenty years old, joining the ranks. Rumor had it your grandfather threw a fit," he added. "But she must have known what she was getting into, since her brother Gideon had gone before her."

"Gideon, a soldier—" I began with a laugh, but Aydan continued over me.

"For a time, yes. But then he joined the King's Guard and was knighted. He served his term and retired to Xarynn before Brina began training. Within a few years, she was climbing the ranks, and by her mid-twenties, she was made a commander and leading her troops into battle when the king's new home was attacked. Those who knew her well tell me she was quite remarkable."

I shivered and crossed my arms over my chest. It was a strange thing, to hear someone—a stranger, a *sorcerer* of all people—tell me things about my family that my uncle could never bring himself to. Silence hung in the air for another moment while I let his words settle, then I asked, "And my father?"

He sighed. "I did know your father, for a time. It is his immortal blood that has passed to you."

"Are you . . . taking me to him?"

"He's dead." Aydan stopped and looked at me. "You said Gideon explained this to you."

I ducked my head. "I just thought, I don't know, maybe he was lying. You're telling me my father was a sorcerer. The stories all say it's nearly impossible to kill them."

Aydan mumbled something about mortals and their legends and then said to me, "The mortals like to tell tales that make our kind seem more fearsome than we are. Before the Rebellion, it was because they worshiped us. Now it's because they fear us."

We kept walking, and I looked him over out of the corner of my eye. He was the first immortal I'd ever met. I had assumed he was my age, but now . . .

"How old are you?"

"One hundred and sixty-eight," he said.

I faltered, then asked, "How old were my parents?"

"I'm not quite sure about Brina. But Lord Ronan would have been nearing his nine-hundredth birthday when they wed." I swallowed. *Nine hundred years old.*

"How did he die? Was he a soldier as well?"

Aydan's jaw shifted as if he were biting the inside of his cheek. "No," he finally said. "He wasn't a soldier."

"What killed him, then?" I pressed.

He was quiet again, then opened his mouth but I turned away from him, suddenly overcome with a strange sensation. It was a prickling on my skin, like I'd just barely run my hands over the top of a thornbush. My palms hummed and my fingertips twitched while I stared down at them. "What in the world—"

"We're about to cross the border." I looked to where he pointed, not seeing any physical landmark, but sensing it apparently in my very skin and bones. I felt drawn to it, like I should walk faster. I did. "Can you feel it?" Aydan asked as he sped up to keep pace with me, hand hovering near my elbow in case my overeager feet led me to step on a loose stone.

I nodded. "What *is* that?"

"Magic calls to magic. Your blood is drawn to it."

I stopped just before the edge and looked to Aydan, who stood a few feet back from me. I turned back toward the invisible boundary.

"You'll be fine," he said from behind me.

I didn't have much of a choice but to believe him as I stepped over the line, into Medeisia. It felt familiar. My palms hummed more urgently, like crossing over had given whatever lay beneath the surface permission to show itself entirely. I looked at my hands, opening and closing them, and then glanced at Aydan, who was watching me.

"What is this?" I asked.

"You haven't been in Medeisia since you were a baby, so your power has never been exposed to the ancestral magic here. You're waking up."

My blood suddenly ran cold. Medeisia. I was *in* Medeisia. The enormous weight of it all began hammering down upon me. I had just chased magic over the border of Medeisia, while traveling with an apparent sorcerer. He knew about my family—knew Gideon well enough to seek him out—and said *I* was . . . one of them. A sorcerer. But it was impossible. It had to be a lie, a trick of his magic, somehow. Sorcerers were the villains in every story at school; they were mentioned in every decree. Every announcement made by the palace warned of the imminent danger of sorcery. How could I have sat there and listened to it all, *agreeing* with it, if I were tied to Medeisia somehow? How—how would I get to Gideon? How would he contact me, or know where I was going? Did Aydan tell him? How would I—

"Lady Shaye." Aydan's hand was on my shoulder and I realized my breathing had gone ragged as I swallowed air in deep gulps. My eyes burned and blurred with tears. "Shaye. I need you to find your breath and get ahold of yourself." His voice was firm but not unkind. "I imagine this is very difficult, but I need you to stay calm for a few more moments. It is late. We need to find a safe place to camp. You'll feel better when you've had some rest."

I didn't quite believe him, but I nodded anyway. A place to camp. Yes. Okay. I rubbed my eyes with the heels of my palms and exhaled shakily.

The only useful light was the moon above us, but soon we found a flat enough spot. Aydan rummaged around in the knapsack again, and I realized the bag must have been enchanted. It looked like it might hold the canteen and some simple provisions if you packed it tightly, but Aydan produced a small tent and two bedrolls. He began setting up the tent by hand.

"Wouldn't it be . . . easier to use magic?" I asked in a slightly shaking voice, both horrified and curious at the thought of seeing magic at work again. At least my breathing was calming down.

"Yes, it would." Aydan staked the tent into the soft ground. It was a low shelter that felt safe even without much cover around. "But unfortunately, I'm not welcome in this part of Medeisia, so I mustn't use magic if I can help it. I'm being tracked."

"Is that why we aren't effu . . . whatever it was you did back there?"

"Effuging. Yes, it is," he said. "The people tracking me would be able to tell I was here, and it could cause problems for my lord and lady. I'm not eager to be on their bad side, considering I already went on this mission without their knowledge." My interest piqued, and I cocked an eyebrow. I felt a bit better with the distractions around me.

"Why aren't you allowed here?"

"Sorcerers have very long memories. We're prone to grudges."

"That's not an answer."

"You ask a lot of questions," he said without looking up. "I can't be expected to answer all of them. Get some sleep, Lady Shaye." He opened the tent flap for me. His bedroll was spread out just a couple of feet from the tent's opening, near enough for me to not feel alone but far enough to give the illusion of privacy.

I mumbled a tired "good night" before crawling into the tiny tent, not bothering to even remove my shoes. I lay on the soft bedroll and took a deep breath. Two. And before I remembered taking a third, sleep overcame me.

Chapter Four

Just a few hours later, I woke as the sun was rising, the light on my face enough to pull me from sleep. I blinked a few times, remembering where I was and what had happened the night before. The image of Uncle Gideon as he held my face flashed in my mind, and my chest ached.

Go with him. You'll be safe.

I swallowed, knowing Gideon would say this was not the time to be emotional. There would be plenty of time to recover and figure out what to do next when we got to wherever it was we were going.

I crawled out of the tent and brushed damp grass from my skirt, wishing I'd had time to pack something else. This would have been easier in my gardening trousers. With a deep breath of crisp morning air, I looked around and couldn't help but gasp at the view before me:

Lush, green fields as far as the eye could see. No hills or villages, nothing to block the view of the sprawling, ancient trees along the horizon, with branches reaching toward the heavens. They formed a perfect line stretching for miles.

Aydan appeared next to me, holding a tarnished kettle. I jumped. "Sorry," he said. "Do you drink tea?"

"Sure." I noticed a small fire for the first time. Aydan must have built it before I woke. My stomach growled and I found myself hoping there might be more than tea for breakfast. I moved to take advantage of the fire's warmth, slowly shuffling, my body stiff and aching from sleeping on the ground. I sat on Aydan's bedroll while he set the kettle over the flame. From the knapsack, he produced a pair of teacups and a small wooden box.

"Only bags, unfortunately." He pulled two from the box. "But it's better than nothing." We both watched in silence as the kettle heated, and once it began to whistle a bit, Aydan poured water over the tops of the bags and passed my cup to me. I let it steep for another minute, blowing on the steaming tea.

The taste was weak, but I gulped it down, grateful for the temporary warmth. Aydan handed me an apple from the bag and kept another for himself. "How can you fit all of this in there?" I asked. "I mean, obviously it's magic, but . . . *how*? A spell?" I bit into the fruit.

"We don't use spells," he replied. "Our magic doesn't need them. Sorcery is a gift from the gods. The power exists within us and we simply learn to wield it." He chewed and swallowed before adding, "The bag is standard-issue for soldiers in Sylvanna."

"You're a soldier, then?"

"No, I'm not a soldier. Not anymore, at least. I borrowed this from a friend. He thought I might run into trouble while trying to locate you and did not want to send me on this mission unprepared." He took another bite of apple.

"A friend sent you to find me?"

"Yes."

"Why?"

"Why what?"

I huffed. "Why did this person decide that last night was the right time to come? They must have known your presence would attract the attention of the palace. My uncle is wounded and probably sitting in a prison cell right now. I'd like to know who decided his freedom was a fair price to pay," I said, angrier than I'd realized.

"My presence didn't attract the attention of the palace, Shaye." He poked a stick into the fire. "Those guards were coming whether I arrived or not. You've been pouring out magic for months." I blinked. "I'm just glad I got there in time."

"The palace witches . . . they were detecting *me*? How? I've never used sorcery." Suddenly the meager breakfast sat heavy in my stomach.

He shrugged. "Our powers usually start emerging as we reach adulthood. Sometimes they can arrive early, like they did for my sister and me. Sometimes they arrive late, as they seem to have done with you. Some believe it has something to do with bloodlines, or the land, but really, no one knows for sure. My best guess would be that being hidden away amongst mortals kept your magic below the surface a bit longer than most." Aydan stood and tossed his apple core behind him. "Once they arrive, there's not much you can do to hide your abilities until you've mastered them. Magic calls to magic—clings to it—and if it isn't released, it will fill you up until it bursts from you with no warning."

I thought of the past few weeks and every time I thought I'd misplaced something, only to turn around and find it. Every time I'd haggled in the marketplace and gotten my way, or when I turned up a copper short and the fishmonger told me not to worry, giving me my order free of charge. Each time, I would return home to tell Gideon of my luck and he'd frown, saying nothing. I scowled at the memories but didn't reply. Instead I asked, "So, will we arrive at our destination today?"

"No." Aydan stuffed our supplies back into the pack, taking my now empty teacup from me and shoving it in as well. "We'll be walking for a few days still. Once we pass through this territory, I can effuge the rest of the way without being detected."

"And where exactly *is* our destination?"

"Sylvanna," he said. "My home is there." I wracked my brain, trying to remember the maps from Gideon's library. Sprawling Medeisia with Xarynn to the north and Sylvanna to the west, its palace matched only by the grandness of its Nautian twin. The books called it—

"The garden city?"

Aydan nodded. "I served as emissary there for quite some time, and now I'm a council member, advising my lord and lady."

"Priamos and Solandis," I recalled. According to the stories, Lord Priamos and Lady Solandis had ruled the city-state of Sylvanna for the last thousand years. "Why don't they know that you've come to collect me?"

"Better to ask forgiveness than permission," Aydan replied, unconcerned. "They've kept their territory safe these past centuries by being cautious and strategizing well. There wasn't time for caution or strategy in this mission."

"I'm sorry to have put you in such a position," I said. "I don't want you to be punished for helping me." He waved me off.

"It's nothing. We just have to be careful that we aren't seen for now, and once we arrive in Sylvanna, I'll meet with my lord and lady and explain everything. If anything, it will be a slap on the wrist.

They have a bit of a soft spot for me." I opened my mouth to question him further, but Aydan stood and threw the pack over his shoulder. "We need to get moving," he said firmly. I joined him in taking down the tent and rolling the bedrolls to fit inside the pack. He extinguished the fire and covered what remained in dirt, removing any evidence of our stay, before he pointed toward the tree line and started walking. I followed.

Aydan had not been exaggerating when he said we would be walking for days. It took hours to get from our campsite to the tree line, and from there we walked along it, stopping only when the sun went down. On our second night together, he told me we could not light a fire for fear of being seen by anyone patrolling the area. Each night, we took our shares of cold rations and went to bed in the dark, me in the tent and my new companion on his bedroll a few feet from the entrance. He told me it was better not to talk much in case we were overheard by passersby or potential Ayzellen trackers looking for us, but I suspected whatever patience he'd had for my questions had run out. Now he rarely spoke at all, usually only to indicate when it was time to stop for the night.

On the fifth day, still hours from sunset, Aydan decided to stop early.

"It's going to storm," he said. I looked at the sky. Clouds gathered, but it remained bright blue. "I'd rather set up camp now than when rain is pouring down on us." I nodded, too tired to question. "We can light a fire for a bit before the sun goes down," he added. "There's not much chance of anyone seeing the flame while it's light out."

That perked me up. "I'll gather some wood," I offered. The thought of real warmth excited me. Each night had grown colder since we fled Nautia, and my clothes were proving inadequate. My once-blue apron dress was filthy, the hem looking like it had been dyed black. There'd been no time for grooming, other than a quick splashing of water on our faces when we stopped to fill the canteen. I was fairly certain that my braid was becoming a long, single knot. Hygiene was the least of my frustrations, however. My body ached and my mind had begun to wander for most of the day, wondering where Gideon might be, if he was alive. Wondering if Aydan could even be trusted, or if I was being led into even worse danger. But mostly, I just wondered when we would be done walking.

"Stay close to the tree line. It's easy to get turned around in there if you're unfamiliar."

"I'll just be a few minutes," I told him. He started unpacking and setting up my tent, which he had been kind enough to do for me each night, despite the fact that he did not deem it necessary to say more than a handful of words to me during the day.

I made my way beyond the tree line and into the darkened forest. It was not as dense as it appeared from the outside, but the branches of the towering trees blended into one another to block out most of the light that should have been pouring in at that time of day. The rocks on the forest floor were covered in bluish-green moss, quite like the rocks in Nautia. We must not have been so far away from my village that plants grew differently. I wasn't sure if that was a comfort or not.

I took my time there, gathering large sticks and small branches, tucking them beneath my arm. It was maybe ten minutes before I heard a twig snapping from a short distance away and I ducked behind a tree. I pressed my back into it, hoping that it was indeed wide enough to hide my body. My chest heaved as I waited, counting the seconds and listening for more footfalls, hoping that whoever was there would pass by without incident. After nearly a minute, I peered around the side of the trunk and gasped at the source of my fear. In a clearing, perhaps fifteen yards away, stood a doe. Her head was bent low as she nibbled on what must be the last few bits of greenery she would find before winter set in.

I watched her for several minutes. Deer were hard to come by in Nautia; most of us simply trapped rabbits or raised hens if we wanted a supply of meat. I had never seen one alive, only ever catching glimpses of my neighbors' kills the few times they'd been lucky enough to get one. I wondered if her den was nearby, but my thought was interrupted by my own shriek when an arrow flew from the other end of the clearing and struck the doe just behind the shoulder. She fell, dying instantly, and a man emerged from some shrubbery, walking swiftly toward me. I realized I had both dropped my firewood and stepped out from my hiding spot, and was standing in plain sight on the edge of the clearing.

"Miss, are you all right?" he called when he had nearly reached me.

"Yes," I said breathlessly. "I just wasn't expecting your arrow."

"I'm sorry to have startled you." He slung his bow over his shoulder. I crouched to gather my wood back into my arms, and he bent to help me. Once we'd gathered all that I'd dropped, I turned to take my leave.

"I'll leave you to your task, then," I told him. "Thank you for your help."

"You know, it's not a good idea for a woman to be out here alone. I can escort you back to your camp." His words were polite, but his tone and the way he looked at me then made me tense.

"I'm not alone," I started, only to be interrupted by a sharp voice from behind me.

"*Shaye*." Aydan approached swiftly. His hood was up and I noted a small dagger in his hand. "Are you hurt?" he asked, looking me over.

"I'm fine."

"I heard a scream."

"That was my fault, I'm afraid," the hunter said. "The lady was watching the deer and I shot it. Startled her, it seems." His eyes landed on the dagger. Aydan sheathed it.

"Let's go," said my companion. I'd just turned to follow him when the hunter grabbed my arm.

"Miss, if you don't want to go with him—"

"Let go of me—" I tore my arm from his grip. Aydan was there in an instant, standing between us. The movement caused his hood to fall back, revealing his face and the mop of wavy black hair on his head. The hunter's eyes widened.

"Collect your kill," Aydan demanded roughly, "then go home."

"Yes—yes, of course. Of course." The hunter bowed his head slightly. Aydan pulled a coin purse from his pocket and let it jingle a few times.

"For your discretion," he said, pressing it into the man's hand. "Go." The hunter pocketed the money and turned back toward his deer. Aydan took my hand and led me through the trees, back to the spot where he had started to set up camp.

Once we were there, he immediately started throwing supplies into the knapsack, rolling up bedrolls and dismantling the tent. I silently packed away the kettle and canteen.

"Aydan, I-I'm sorry—" I started quietly.

"We need to put a few miles between us and that hunter."

"Is something wrong?"

"He knew my face. He's probably on his way to alert the King's Guard of my location." Aydan put the bag over his shoulder.

"You paid him off," I said.

"They'll double it," he replied. I wondered what he had done, to find himself hunted so fiercely by the Medeisian king. "Come on, we'll have to skip the fire. We can cover more ground before the sun goes down." I cast one last mournful look at my pile of firewood and followed.

We were able to walk for another hour before the rain started pouring down upon us and we had to do exactly what Aydan had been trying to avoid: set up camp in the rain. I helped him hammer tent stakes into the ground while freezing water dripped into my eyes, blurring my vision. When we finished, Aydan tossed the knapsack inside and we both clamored in. We wiped the water from our faces, shivering as we caught our breath. We took a minute to settle ourselves before we both seemed to realize that we were about to share the tent for the night.

"When the weather calms down a bit, I'll be happy to return to a spot outside—"

"Oh, don't be such a martyr." I rolled my eyes, though in the darkness he could not see me. "Just take your boots off. I don't want you getting mud everywhere." Without another word, Aydan obliged and laid his socks flat on top of them so they could have a chance of drying overnight. He placed everything neatly by the entrance and laid out his bedroll beside mine. We each crawled into our respective spaces and, despite our miserable conditions, tried to fall asleep.

Chapter Five

The storm woke me a few times during the night with lightning cracking overhead and thunder booming after. It was past midnight when the rain stopped and finally allowed me to sleep soundly. When I felt myself being shaken awake in the tent, I didn't hold back my string of curses as I rolled to face the tent wall.

"Wake up," Aydan hissed at me, jostling my arm again. This time I sat upright, startled. It was bright outside. Too bright. We'd slept too long. Aydan was hastily shoving his feet back into his boots.

"What?" I asked, reaching for my own and following suit.

"Listen to me," he said, voice low and serious. "Everything is going to be fine. Let me do the talking." He waved a hand over my head, and I felt cold spreading from my crown, down my body, to my feet. "That should disguise you well enough to start." I grabbed my braid and saw that I was now blonde. But if he was using magic, that must mean—

"By order of King Zathryan, come out with your hands where I can see them," called a male voice from outside the tent. "Keep calm, and please note that magic will be met with silver."

Aydan swore softly. "Do you trust me?" he breathed.

Did I? He was a sorcerer. Everything I had ever been taught about Medeisians told me that they should never be trusted, that they were dangerous, and a constant threat to the well-being of mortals. The knowledge that every word he'd said to me so far could be a lie sat in the back of my head, whispering to me each night as I went to sleep, and yet, when I looked at him now, his eyes filled with concern as he waited for my answer—despite all logic, I realized that, yes, I did trust him.

And even if not, what other choice did I have?

I nodded and Aydan leaned forward, placed a hand on either side of my face, and kissed my forehead. This time, tingling warmth followed the path from my head to my toes, followed by a slight stinging sensation, like I'd rolled naked through a patch of nettles. It subsided quickly enough, but there was no time to ask what had been done this time, as the voice came again. "Sir, you are *commanded* by His Majesty to show yourself—"

"All right, all right," Aydan called, tone flippant and unfamiliar. He emerged from the tent. "Can't give a man a moment to get his pants on."

"Your companion as well, sir," I heard the man add.

He reached a hand back through the flap for me and said, "Come out, my dear. No need to be frightened by these brutes." I let him pull me into the bright sunlight, where, when my vision cleared, I saw no fewer than twenty armed guards surrounding us, half of whom were on horseback. They wore gold armor bearing a rampant winged lion and carried multiple swords, some even with bandoliers of daggers strapped across their chests. My eyes flicked to Aydan, who was smirking at a handsome, tawny-haired young man standing a few feet before us.

Was he about to fight all of these guards? Guards who were armed to the teeth, not to mention what magic they must wield . . . Could Aydan take them all on?

"The king requests your presence at Castle Ayzelle immediately—"

"Request denied," Aydan cut him off. "It was kind of you to deliver the message, captain, but we'll just be on our way." He took my hand just as a guard grabbed my other arm and slapped my wrist into a cuff, which immediately locked. Almost instantly, it began to itch, irritating my skin, which erupted in hives. I yanked at it, but the cuff would not budge.

"Stop!" I gasped.

"Remove it," Aydan growled.

"His Majesty has ordered that unauthorized travelers be brought before him. I'm sure he'd be quite curious to see who was traveling with *you*—"

"His Majesty must be terribly bored if he wishes to start his day with the interrogation of peaceful travelers." Aydan glared at the captain, who held his stare. Without looking away Aydan said to me,

"It seems we'll be paying King Zathryan a visit after all, my dear." He clenched his jaw, then added, "Lead the way, captain."

The guard stepped between us before removing the cuff and gripping his own hand over my wrist. My stomach swooped and instantly we were standing before a tall gate. I twisted, searching for the rest of the guards, but we were alone. Before I could take my hand back, he fastened the cuff back in place. I blinked and more guards appeared, Aydan in tow. He stared wide-eyed at the gate, then at me—at the cuff on my wrist. I saw he now had a cuff as well.

The last of the guards arrived, minus those riding horseback, the captain gripping the arm of the man next to him. He approached the gate and knocked three times, and it swung open with a slow creak. A stone path lay before us and, in the distance, what must be Castle Ayzelle.

It was not as large or ornate as the Grand Palace of Nautia, but a castle all the same. High, towering masses of dark gray stone, albeit there were no stairs leading to watchtowers or clear windows at any high points on the building. Somehow, knowing that there was only one floor made this castle less intimidating than the Grand Palace at first glance. But inside this castle was the King of Medeisia. The king of sorcerers. I froze.

The guards shoved me forward and I almost lost my balance before Aydan was beside me, catching me under the arm. He kept his hand on mine. "We're going to be fine," he murmured.

"I'm sorry," I whispered, trying not to move my lips too much. "I never should have talked to that man—"

"It's not your fault. Whatever you do now, try not to speak. If we're lucky, the king will ignore you and focus on me."

"What's he going to do to you?"

"Nothing I can't handle." He squeezed my hand as we walked. "It's going to be fine."

"You know, the more you say that, the less I believe you," I said. He huffed a humorless laugh while I scratched at the cuff on my wrist. "This thing *burns*."

"It's silver," he explained quietly. "Inhibits the use of magic." I scoffed. Aydan cocked an eyebrow.

"I thought that was a myth—"

"Quiet, you two," the guard next to me snapped. Aydan scowled at him, but we both stopped talking. He squeezed my hand again.

We were escorted down a stone path, surrounded by the armed guards. We'd only been walking for a few minutes when we reached the entrance to the castle: a great stone arch with beautiful carvings depicting the same winged lion from the guards' armor—seated with a regal air, then rampant, then salient, with a pair of fighting lions meeting in battle at the apex of the arch. If I hadn't been so terrified, I might have stopped to study them more closely. We passed underneath and found ourselves inside the entrance hall. The walls and floors were made with the same dark stone. The floors were covered with enormous rugs in deep blues and golds, while the walls held intricately woven tapestries on opposite sides of the corridor. To my left was the sun, and directly across from it, the full moon.

"Halt," said the captain. We stopped outside of a huge door. The captain opened it and entered, leaving it ajar. We stood with the other guards, waiting for instruction. Aydan reached for my hand once again, and I wasn't sure if he was comforting me or himself this time. The captain appeared again and said, "Enter."

Chapter Six

My legs were made of wet sand. A hand pushed me forward and I forced myself not to stumble. Aydan let go of me as we stepped into the great hall. It was enormous; my and Gideon's entire house wouldn't take up even a quarter of the space. The walls were windowless, decorated instead with more long tapestries of more winged lions, and sunlight poured through three skylights spaced along the high ceiling.

People lined the room. I could feel their magic, I realized. Defensive, like they were all preparing for an attack. Hundreds of Medeisian men and women dressed in finery crowded the walls. Men in tailored jackets embellished with fine embroidery, ladies in layered skirts that ballooned out around them in shades of brown, gray, and green. Several powdered wigs were dotted throughout the crowd, accompanied with makeup so heavy, it looked as though it might crack if one managed a smile. As we moved forward in the room, I felt the power come in waves. It dawned on me that I must be sensing the magic of the sorcerers, and lack thereof from the mortals, as we passed each row of people. Those watching remained silent as we were marched toward what—or rather, *who*—awaited us on the other end.

Upon a dais at the far end of the great hall was a solid white marble throne, and upon that sat King Zathryan of Medeisia. He glared as we approached, the armor of our entourage clanking loudly in the echoing hall. We stopped before him, and I did my best to keep my gaze low.

Though I knew he was a sorcerer, I had not expected the king to look so young. There were no wrinkles to be seen on him; I couldn't spot a single gray hair from where I stood. Had he been mortal, I would have assumed we were the same age. He sat up straight, as dashing and handsome as any mortal knight I'd ever seen, with thick golden hair that reached his collar and smooth, lightly tanned skin that looked as if he spent his days riding horses through the countryside rather than sitting upon a throne. His shapely lips pulled into a sneer. I felt sweat beading at my brow and my palms went clammy as the silence stretched.

Finally, the king spoke.

"Captain Whittaker, you have succeeded once again," he said without looking at the man. The captain bowed deeply.

"It is an honor to serve the Crown, Your Majesty."

"Tell me, what was he doing on my lands?"

"We have not yet interrogated him, Your Majesty, but at first glance, he appeared to be just passing through."

"Is that right, boy?" King Zathryan addressed Aydan. "Thought you'd take a shortcut through *my* lands after you were *banished*—"

"Banished?" Aydan scoffed. The king's face went beet red. "The last correspondence I received from this court was an order to return."

"Which you defied, resulting in your permanent banishment from the capital," he said through gritted teeth.

"Ah," said Aydan, "I must have missed that letter. Apologies, Your Majesty. A simple clerical error. Call off your guards and I'll be happy to go back to where I belong." Gone were the nerves Aydan had displayed to me as we approached the hall; my companion sounded practically bored. One hand was shoved into the pocket of his trousers and he gestured flippantly with the other. If this posture and tone were intended to anger the king, it certainly seemed to be working. I just hoped his charade wouldn't get us killed.

The king chuckled darkly. "You petulant little roach. You'd like that, wouldn't you? Doing what you wish, free from responsibility or consequence, then traipsing back to Sylvanna to play in the gardens with lowborns and bastards—" He stopped. Aydan shifted his body in front of me, but it was no good. Zathryan looked right into my eyes. "Speaking of lowborns." He grinned. "Who do we have here?"

Captain Whittaker spoke first. "She was traveling with him, Your Majesty. They shared a tent."

"Ah." The king looked back to Aydan. "Do you often drag whores along on your travels, or was this a special occasion?" I flushed at the insult. Aydan did not react.

"I was escorting the lady back to Sylvanna, to be reunited with relatives there," he lied flatly. Zathryan stared at him for a moment before looking back at me. He started to say something but cut himself off, emotionless for several seconds. Then he did something I did not expect.

He laughed.

Booming laughter rang out in the otherwise silent hall as the courtiers stared, not knowing if they too should be laughing with their king.

"*Excellent* try, boy." He grinned as Aydan's face remained neutral. "You nearly had me fooled. Now, remove her glamours. I want to see my guest."

"I don't know what you're ta—"

"I don't have time for these games." With a wave of his hand like clearing the air, the icy sensation that had moved down my body in the tent an hour before moved up this time, up my legs and stomach, back over my face and head. I crossed my arms over my body, shivering a bit as the feeling wore off. Whispers rose from the crowd as they took in my true appearance, ratty and dirt-smudged. I looked back up at Zathryan, whose humor had vanished, and I stared, not knowing what else to do. After several moments, he said softly, "Who are you."

Aydan stepped in front of me. "Your Majesty, I—"

"Shut up," he snapped at him. He flicked his wrist and Aydan fell to the side as if he'd been shoved. "Your name, girl," Zathryan said, his voice dripping with command. The look in his eyes was wild, like a flame. I threw Aydan a panicked look and he nodded once, mouth tight.

"I'm growing impatient, girl." A bluish glow came off the king's hands as they gripped the arms of his throne.

"I-It's Shaye, Your Majesty," I said and curtsied hastily.

The crowd murmured again.

"Your family name?"

My mouth went dry as I held his gaze. I felt the urge to lie, but I wasn't sure why. It didn't take a scholar to realize he already knew the answer. "Eastly, Your Majesty."

Before I could react, the king was on his feet, storming toward me. Balls of blue light engulfed his hands as he raised them in my direction. I stumbled back and Aydan darted between us, arms outstretched. "I can explain—"

"*You!*" Zathryan snarled at Aydan. "You brought this cursed wench into my court!"

"She doesn't know *anything*. She didn't even know his *name* until I told her," Aydan insisted.

"And you believed her like a fool," scoffed the king. "I'm sure she spread her legs far enough for you to believe anything—"

"Father!" Aydan said sharply. My head snapped up. *Father?*

King Zathryan glowered, then looked around the hall at his court. Then at me. He picked at the sleeve of his jacket and brushed a stray piece of hair from his eyes.

"Captain Whittaker, this woman is under arrest," he said. The captain stepped forward. "Take her away while I decide what to do with her." My heart sank.

"Father," said Aydan, "she has broken no laws—"

"Perhaps I will spare us all this trouble and have her executed now," Zathryan said and snapped his fingers. The guards surrounding us drew their swords in unison. Aydan looked around at all of them.

Finally, he sighed and spread his hands. "If there's no stopping you . . ." He stepped out from in front of me. "At least give her the dignity of a quick death."

My mouth filled with ash. Zathryan's blue lights were gone now, but his fists remained balled at his sides. He nodded at the guard closest to me and the guard grabbed me roughly by the arm.

"Oh," said Aydan, "just one small thing. I almost forgot." The king glared. "Lady Shaye is blood-shielded." The crowd grew louder, murmurs bouncing intensely off the walls. I could barely hear the king's reply over it and the blood rushing in my ears. I had no idea what he was talking about, and I wasn't sure I would live long enough to find out.

"You're lying."

"Maybe." Aydan shrugged. "But are you willing to test it?" The men stared at each other, silent, until the king said:

"There are plenty of prisoners awaiting execution who would do the job well."

"Yes, but does the shield effect only them? Or will it also respond to the man who ordered her death?" Aydan smirked. "It's been so long since a blood shield was tested in Medeisia. Perhaps we should find out."

"Are you threatening your king?" Captain Whittaker asked, stepping closer.

"Not at all," Aydan answered dryly. "I'm protecting him, by warning him of certain dangers."

The king started to speak, but he was interrupted by a girlish voice calling out from behind the dais.

"Your Majesty?"

My eyes darted to the dais, as did Aydan's. A beautiful woman with sharp features stepped down and walked toward us, her footsteps echoing delicately on the stone. She wore a well-tailored, green gown that complemented her skin, the same warm brown tone as Aydan's, and in her shiny black curls was a small gold tiara encrusted with diamonds and emeralds. Large emeralds hung from her ears as well, dangling low to swing just above her shoulders with each step. She stopped when she reached the king's side. "Your Majesty, perhaps there is another solution to this problem."

"What do you suggest, princess?" he asked. I swallowed. *Princess.*

"If these two remain here, under house arrest, then we can study the Eastly girl before the Sylvannians get their hands on her. See if she's any threat to us."

"I am telling you now, she is no threat—" Aydan said.

"Quiet!" Zathryan snapped. He spoke in a low tone to his daughter. "How will studying her reveal her true nature? Would it not be prudent to simply take care of the problem now?"

"Perhaps, Your Majesty," the princess said, voice hushed. "But showing her mercy to start will go a long way with the courtiers. Besides." She glanced at me. "If she doesn't betray us, perhaps we can use her."

Zathryan considered. It was the longest few moments of my life, watching the King of Medeisia decide my fate.

"Fine," he grit out, then called loudly, "Captain Whittaker, escort these two to the prince's quarters. The prince and Miss Eastly will remain here at my pleasure. They will not leave the castle." He gestured and a tingling sensation rushed down my spine, and I knew the king's power would hold me in this castle until he decided otherwise. I was at his mercy.

King Zathryan leaned in, his lips almost brushing my ear. "If I hear even a whisper of your betrayal, or any attempts to escape . . . blood shield be damned, I will have your head on a spike."

"Yes, Your Majesty." I dipped my head to hide my trembling.

The king turned on his heel and stormed away, past the dais and through a door. The princess followed, as did a dozen other men, while the rest watched as Captain Whittaker led us back to the castle's grand entrance. Aydan and I followed in silence as we were turned to the left and down a long corridor to a new wing. At the end was an ornately carved door with no handle, where the guards stopped and stared at Aydan. The door hummed with magic that told me to walk away from it.

"Go ahead," Captain Whittaker said. Aydan raised his wrist, which still held the silver cuff. The captain sighed and used a key to remove it, then mine. My skin was an angry, blistered red.

"Thank you," said Aydan. He placed a palm against the door and the magic seemed to dissolve. A brass knocker appeared. "Now leave us."

The captain's mouth tightened before he gave a grudging bow, mumbled, "Your Highness," and turned away to march back down the corridor.

Chapter Seven

We stepped inside and the hum of magic returned around the door as soon as it shut behind us. I took a sharp breath, having expected a modest-sized bedroom, maybe a bathroom. Instead, I was met with a lavishly decorated foyer, complete with ornately carved wooden furniture and beautiful wine-red rugs. Aydan stood in front of me with his back turned. One hand rested on his hip while the other combed back through his shaggy black hair. He stared across the room quietly for a moment, then suddenly cried out, "*Fuck*."

I jumped.

He stormed into the next room, and I followed quietly behind him. He started snapping his fingers—once, twice, four times—as he tore through desk drawers, searching their contents.

As he looted the room, figures began to appear in the center. Two women and two men stood before us while Aydan continued his search for who knows what. One of the confused-looking women stepped forward.

"Elise," Aydan said, "where is my stationery? I can't even find a damned pen in this place."

"In the study, I believe, sir. Let me—"

"No need." He left to fetch it himself. The woman, Elise, had honey brown hair and a pale complexion. Like everyone else I had seen in the past few days, she appeared to be quite young, but there was something in her eyes and the way she carried herself that told me I was mistaken. She nodded in greeting, and I did the same. Seconds later, Aydan returned with stationery and pen in hand. He hunched over a small desk and scribbled a note. When he finished, he folded the page and waved his hand over it, a blue seal appearing. He placed the note in Elise's hand.

"Take this to Lady Solandis. Tell anyone who stops you that you've been ordered by me to place this letter directly into the lady's hand. When you see that she has read it, return here." Elise nodded and disappeared as quickly as she'd come. He turned to the others and said, "I'm sorry to say, we'll be taking up residence here for an unexpected stay." He gestured to me, his first acknowledgment of my presence since entering the dwelling. "This is Lady Shaye. She'll be staying with us. Isolde, if you could please prepare a room for her, then perhaps we can offer her something hot to eat. She's been traveling for a while now. I'm sure she's tired of cold rations." In unison, the group bowed before going their separate ways to carry out his orders.

The prince.

My head pounded as I tried to wrap my mind around these last few hours. Aydan was staring at me expectantly, and I realized he had been saying something.

"I'm sorry, what?"

"I said, I'm going to get this taken care of," he repeated. "We'll be on our way to Sylvanna soon. I just need to figure a few things out."

I didn't respond and instead looked him up and down. He wore the same plain black tunic and pants he'd been wearing when he arrived on my doorstep a week ago, which were now filthy. His tattered boots looked like they might fall apart as soon as he pulled them off, and his shaggy, dark hair was as dirty and tangled as mine. Yet the way he carried himself, his demeanor and tone, had changed since arriving at the castle—or had I simply imagined that? His quiet, serious presence had been odd but welcome as we traveled, but in the great hall just now, he'd been an entirely new character, practically mocking the king—his father—to his face.

"Are you all right?" he asked.

"You lied to me."

"Yes." I found myself a little stunned at his blunt honesty.

"Why didn't you tell me that you're a prince? *The* Prince of Medeisia?"

"Because of what you saw there." Aydan waved his hand toward the door. "I am prince of nothing, my title means nothing, and I have no intention of staying in my father's court. The plan was to wait until we were safely in Sylvanna to explain everything, to keep from overwhelming you—"

"Why do you get to decide what will overwhelm me?" I snapped before I could stop myself. I pursed my lips while he seemed to consider my words. *Does he have his father's temper?* I wondered.

Finally, Aydan said, "There is a room for you down the corridor." He pointed behind me. "Second door on the right. It will have everything you need to get cleaned up and comfortable. When you've had a bath and a moment to rest, we'll sit down for lunch and I'll tell you everything."

"Everything?"

"Everything you want to know. I promise."

I considered for a moment. "I don't have any other clothes." My dress, which had once been periwinkle blue, was now dingy and gray. "I will need to wash this."

"There are clean clothes waiting for you in your room," he said. "The servants will see to your dress in the morning."

I hesitated, but finally turned and headed down the corridor he'd indicated. When I reached the second door on the right, I paused, then entered. It was a modestly sized bedroom with a larger bed than I'd ever slept in, topped with a white quilt with a hand-embroidered pattern at the edges that resembled the rugs in the foyer. I wondered if the pattern was common in Ayzelle, or if it was one that Aydan had simply liked. Would he have even been the one to select such things? On the wall opposite the bed, there was a wardrobe, a desk, and even a bookshelf with a few volumes sitting on it. To the left was another door, which I opened to find a bathroom with a deep porcelain tub already filled and steaming. I pulled off my boots and my ruined stockings as carefully as I could. My feet were sore and swollen, raw from days of walking. I managed to peel my dress from my body. Upon closer inspection, I couldn't see how anyone, sorcerer or not, could save the filthy thing and resolved to throw it away. I untied my braid and only then did I look in the mirror.

I looked horrible.

A week of traveling with few provisions and sleeping on my uncomfortable bedroll in a tiny tent hadn't done much for my appearance. It was clear that I hadn't been eating enough, my ribs practically visible, and dark circles had formed under my eyes from lack of sleep. I sighed and turned back to the tub, eager to be clean and warm.

I climbed in and tried to keep from groaning too loudly as I leaned back. I closed my eyes, savoring the heat and the moment of relaxation, but fought the urge to fall asleep. I needed to get washed and dressed so I could finally get some answers. Reluctantly, I sat up, found the bar of soap, and started scrubbing.

Chapter Eight

Despite my attempts to make quick work of the bath, it took me two thorough washings to scrub the dirt from my body. Had I been more confident in how exactly to do so, I would have refilled the bath with clear water halfway through. As it was, I let the murk drain and wiped the stains from the tub after I toweled myself dry.

Now thoroughly clean and wearing the new dress that had been laid out for me, I found my way back to the parlor where I'd left Aydan. It was empty.

I waited for a moment, admiring the details of the room. Small tables spaced between the furniture held various baubles: gold frames containing charcoal portraits of beautiful faces I had never seen, a working grandfather clock in miniature that had me wondering if it had been built that way or shrunk down by magic, and hand-painted vases filled with flowers that were certainly enchanted to remain fresh and beautiful.

Muffled chatter and banging rang out from behind a door on the far wall of the parlor. I pushed it open to reveal a busy kitchen where the two male servants were now cooking. Both were tall and tan; one had sandy blond hair, and the other's was so light, it looked silver as the sun shone through the window above the table. They did not see me and instead continued their conversation in a language I couldn't understand. I watched, fascinated by how they worked in unison, chopping and dicing, kneading and pulling, without ever breaking their pattern. A few moments passed before the door on the opposite wall swung open and the other woman marched in. She stopped abruptly when she saw me standing in the doorway.

"My lady," she gasped, placing her hand on her chest. "My apologies. Have you been waiting long?" Her face and hair were nearly identical to the silver-haired man's, and her accent was heavy, though I couldn't place it. The cooks both stopped and inclined their heads to me, wide-eyed.

"We did not see you, my lady," said the silver-haired man. His accent was thick as well. "Our deepest apologies." The second man whispered something in the other language, but the first simply shushed him.

"Oh," was all I could think to say. "No, I wasn't waiting long. And please, don't apologize. I was enjoying watching you."

"Can I help you with something, my lady?" the woman asked.

"I was just looking for the prince. He told me to meet him in the parlor after I'd changed, but he wasn't there."

"Elise returned a few moments ago. I'm sure he is discussing the response from Lady Solandis with her," she said. "May I show you to the dining room, my lady?"

"Er, yes, thank you. But please, call me Shaye." She nodded politely and led me through the door behind her. I waved over my shoulder to the men, who bowed one last time before returning to their work. "What are their names?" I asked. "And yours?"

"My name is Isolde, Lady Shaye," she said as we entered the dining room. "They are Zale and Tory. My apologies for Tory; he cannot speak the common tongue very well."

"Where are you from? Outside of Medeisia?"

"We are from Xarynn, Lady Shaye."

Xarynn: Medeisia's window to the world, I remembered from my reading. The continent was vast and rich with different cultures in each territory, but if you wanted to see what lay across the sea, Xarynn with its ports was the only exit point.

The door opened behind me and I turned to see Aydan, now bathed and changed into a clean set of clothes.

"Ah, there you are," he said. "I hope the dress is suitable."

"It is." I ran a hand along the skirt. It was soft, comfortable, and a lovely shade of forest green, which complemented the slight auburn of my hair nicely. "Thank you, Your Highness."

Aydan scoffed. "Don't start with that. Just Aydan."

"Fine. Thank you, *Aydan*."

He smirked, then looked over my shoulder. "Thank you, Isolde. I think Elise might need some help preparing the rest of the rooms."

"Yes, Your Highness." She curtsied and left swiftly through the swinging door into the kitchen.

"Who is staying in the other rooms?" I asked when she was gone.

"The servants," he replied, pulling out a chair and gesturing for me to sit.

"Are there no servants' quarters in these chambers?" I let Aydan push the chair in for me. He began pouring wine from a bottle that had not been there a moment before and handed me a glass.

"There are." He settled in the seat opposite me. "There are also six bedrooms in these chambers that would otherwise remain empty. I didn't take you for a snob, Lady Shaye." I flushed.

"I-I didn't mean it like *that*," I stammered, embarrassed. "I just didn't think a *prince* would want—" Aydan cut me off, laughing.

"I'm teasing you," he said, still chuckling. "Even they get flustered about it." He gestured to the kitchen. "Fifty years of working with me and Isolde still heads straight for the servants' quarters."

Fifty years.

"Are all of your servants from Xarynn?"

"No, Elise is from Sylvanna," he said. "The other three arrived at the Sylvannian border half a century ago, looking for work in the villages. They couldn't find anyone to take them on, and eventually ran into Elise, who brought them here. They came to Sylvanna to build a better life, so I took them on. It's worked out for us so far."

"That was kind of you," I said.

"Elise needed help, and they were there, ready to work. It wasn't exactly charity," he said. "They keep busy enough, taking care of my household."

"You have a large family, then?"

"You could say that." I must have looked confused, because he added, "My friends . . . other council members, they live in my home in Sylvanna. Most of the time, anyway. They have their own chambers in the Grand Palace but prefer to stay with me."

The door opened again suddenly and there was Isolde, carrying a large tray with covered dishes. She set them before us and lifted the lids. A rich rabbit stew filled large bowls to the brim. Isolde placed a platter with freshly baked bread between us. My mouth watered at the smell.

"Lovely," said Aydan. "Thank you, Isolde. That will be all."

She curtsied and left, the door swinging behind her. I heard her call out in Xarynnea to her brother and his husband before it closed.

Ravenous, I took a huge bite and nearly groaned. Aydan reached for the bread and placed a thick slice on a small plate for me before taking one himself. I could only gesture a thank you with my mouth full, but he wasn't looking anyway. It seemed a week straight of walking with nothing but cheese, apples, and tea had gotten the best of both of us.

After a second bowl, we both had our fill. Aydan had gone to the kitchen himself for our second helping, much to the protest of the servants who were eating their own lunch. Once our dishes were piled together, Aydan waved his hand over them and they vanished from the table. He topped off both of our wineglasses and sat back in his chair.

"So," he said. "I promised you answers. What do you want to know?"

"Well." I considered, my thoughts now slightly hazy with my stomach full. "Before anything else, will you tell me what a blood shield is?"

"Oh," he said, "that." He set his glass down. "A blood shield is an ancient type of protection magic. Only members of royal bloodlines can tap into it, so it is very rare to come across—and makes it dangerous to attack members of the royal family."

"But what does it do, exactly?"

"For as long as the person who created the shield is living, the person being shielded will be protected by their power against any attack, even a weapon made of silver. If someone were to injure or kill the person being shielded, the injuries would simply reflect back on them." Aydan motioned for my hand. "Look," he said, producing a pin from nowhere. He pricked the tip of my finger, drawing blood.

"*Ouch*." I jerked back. "You could have warned me—" He held up his own finger, showing a trickle of blood sliding down from an identical puncture. "Well, that's not exactly protection." I flushed, hiding my wounded hand beneath the table. "I'm still bleeding."

"A deterrent, then." He chuckled. "A piece of the shielder's power covers the one being shielded, and any attacks are mirrored back onto the attacker. It doesn't take long to realize that the person you're harming is shielded, and then you must decide if you're willing to part with your life to make a point. Most are not."

"You gave up a piece of your power to protect me?"

"A very small one," he confirmed. "Hardly noticeable."

"I—um, thank you." He waved me off.

"It's nothing. We were headed to hostile territory. I had a way to help." He took another drink. "Anything else?" I sighed, wringing my hands.

"Is silver truly the only thing that can kill you?"

"No," he replied, his voice flat but not unkind. "That is another story from the younger mortal generations. Plenty of things can kill us—most of the same things that kill mortals, actually. We simply have magic in our veins to heal ourselves should the need arise. The only thing that cannot kill us is time. Illness and injury come for us all eventually, but our bodies will not age after we've reached maturity. Silver simply inhibits our magic. A useful weapon, but certainly not the only one." Aydan gestured for me to continue with my questions.

"I suppose . . . I suppose we should just start at the beginning. My beginning, that is. Who am I? Who was my father and why does the king want me dead?"

"All right," he said. "Well, you know, your mother was a mortal woman named Brina Eastly. She was a commanding officer in the Ayzellen army. She met your father at a ball here in this castle. His name was Lord Ronan Redfern, the king's Chief Advisor." Aydan paused to take another drink. I did the same.

"I knew Lord Ronan for most of my childhood, before I moved to Sylvanna. He was a tough man, but fair. He taught me much about my powers and how to wield them. Ronan was one of the most powerful sorcerers to ever live. In fact, after centuries by my father's side, and especially after the mortal rebellion, there were some who looked to Ronan as the true leader of Medeisia while my father warmed the throne.

"His courtship with Brina was a whirlwind, as I understand. Love at first sight, that sort of thing. Within a month of meeting, they were married. Less than a year after that, they announced that Brina was with child."

"Are marriages between sorcerers and mortals forbidden?" I asked.

Aydan shook his head. "Not at all. It is certainly warned against by some. Watching a spouse grow old and wither away while you stay forever young would be excruciating, in my opinion. But plenty of couples make it work. Brina and Lord Ronan were apparently committed to doing so." I drummed my fingers on the table nervously, waiting for him to continue. "You're sure you want me to go on?"

I nodded. "I want to know."

"No one is quite sure when his descent began, but some suspect that it started years before he met Brina. You see, Ronan was one of the most powerful sorcerers to ever live, yet somewhere along the way, he began consulting with witches."

"What's wrong with witches?" I asked as Aydan reached for the bottle and topped off both our glasses. The witches of the mortal palace held high status in Nautia and were not to be crossed. It was considered an honor to be received by them, and deadly if they deemed you undesirable. They mostly stayed behind the palace walls. I had seen the witches of the Grand Palace only once, when they'd accompanied King Mal during an appearance in the capital square. They stood behind him, stoic and silent, observing the crowds. I remembered feeling the power surging from them, knowing that something ancient lay beneath the surface. Perhaps it was my own magic sensing theirs.

"Witches are born mortal," Aydan said. "They use unnatural means to gain their power, and many would say that it is an affront to nature to harness magic that was not yours to begin with; that the magic of the sorcerer is a divine gift from the gods, which is why we can wield it at will, without relying on spoken spells or potions."

"Do you think that?"

Aydan shrugged. "Whether it is the will of the gods or simply an accident of nature, our power appears to us and theirs is forced. I've never heard of a witch with good intentions, but I'd be curious to meet one who claimed to have them."

I felt my stomach turn as Aydan continued.

"One day, I received word in Sylvanna that Lord Ronan had been arrested for treason. I thought it was a joke. Ronan had always dismissed any talk of him being the 'true leader' of Medeisia as ridiculous. He'd had men flogged for even suggesting it. But, after further investigation, it seemed Lord Ronan had been practicing witchcraft in secret to further expand his power, amass an army, and usurp my father's throne.

"My father was devastated. Ronan was his oldest, dearest friend. To learn of this betrayal, which was so sinister . . . it nearly destroyed him. He insisted on multiple trials; he wanted to hear Ronan's confession. But Ronan remained silent through all of them."

"He wouldn't admit his crimes?" I asked.

"No. That was the strange thing. My father was offering mercy in exchange for a confession, but Ronan would not say a word. Not until Brina was brought up." He traced the rim of his glass with a finger. "When the interrogators brought up the subject of your mother, who was being held in their home under house arrest, Ronan began to speak. He insisted that Brina knew nothing of his activities. When she was questioned, Brina pleaded with the interrogators to let them go, to not harm her baby, and to understand that this was all for the greater good."

"So my mother must have been in on it as well, then," I said.

"Some think so. Others believe, and I'm inclined to agree with them, that she was . . . well, a victim in his plot." Aydan elaborated, "If Ronan was trying to take the throne, he would have had a stronger claim if he already had an heir in place. A mortal wife would be easier to control and would be out of the way sooner or later, while his heir would be immortal and just as powerful as him. His bloodline would be secure. It is likely that Brina was bewitched that night at the ball. Their swift marriage and pregnancy all but confirm it."

I swallowed thickly. The wine in my glass cast a bloody shimmer on the table before me, seeping into the polished grain and churning my stomach.

"I was monitoring the situation as well as I could from within Sylvanna. Lord Ronan had requested several meetings with me in the year prior to his death. They all wound up postponed or canceled for one reason or another. We corresponded often, but he never told me why he needed to meet in person. I now suspect that he was going to request my support for his claim."

"You're the heir to the throne. Why would he think that you would support such a thing?" I asked.

"I'm not the heir," he said. I raised my eyebrows but he either didn't see or didn't care to acknowledge my surprise. "But I am considered a senior member of the royal family, regardless of what my father thinks of me. If I were to support Ronan's bid for the throne, many on the continent would have supported the claim. I never would have considered such a thing, of course, but the risk would have been worth the potential gain in his eyes.

"One week after his final trial, Lord Ronan was executed. When asked if he had any last statements, he stood before my father and every courtier in Ayzelle and declared: 'Beware the jackal among the pride.'"

I blinked. "What does *that* mean?"

"Who knows?" Aydan shrugged. "Some final dig at my father, apparently. He didn't resist as they brought him to the chopping block." I shuddered.

"How do you know all of this, if you weren't here?"

"Irsa wrote to me," he replied. "It devastated her. Ronan was our mentor, and she was . . . well, rather infatuated with him when we were younger. She was the one who discovered him practicing witchcraft."

I bit the inside of my cheek while Aydan sighed and said, "A few weeks after Lord Ronan's execution, you were born. Brina had been under house arrest for more than a month by then and was unwell. She didn't trust any of the servants or healers sent to help her, wouldn't take any remedies she was given, and barely ate. She tried to deliver you by herself. By the time the healers arrived and figured out what had happened, it was already too late to stop her bleeding. She died later that night."

My eyes burned as I asked, "So your father, what, just *gave* me to Uncle Gideon?"

"No," he said. "I don't know what he planned to do with you, but you were immediately taken to Castle Ayzelle. You were left in a cradle, and when the guards returned with the king, you were gone. My father ordered for you to be found, but after years of searching every territory in Medeisia, he must have given up. No one knew what happened to you until my friend discovered your location a few weeks ago."

I stared at the table, watching myself fold and unfold my hands as I listened to his story.

"Are you all right?" Aydan asked after a moment's silence.

"I'm just digesting, I suppose. It's not every day you learn you're a traitor's daughter."

"Listen. You are not responsible for his choices. I don't care what anyone in this court, including my father, has to say. Lord Ronan did terrible things, broke his vows to not just his king but all of Medeisia. He was the Chief Advisor, the right hand to the king, which means he took an oath to serve the Crown, and instead he tried to take it for himself. You share blood with him and nothing else. I haven't known you for long, Lady Shaye, but I do know you are a loyal companion and an honest woman."

I let it sink in for a moment. Aydan's words might have been reassuring if I hadn't just witnessed his father's disdain for me. It did not seem that the prince's trust in me would get me very far beyond these chambers. "So Zathryan thinks I'm here to, what, finish Lord Ronan's work?"

Aydan sighed, leaning back in his chair. "Probably. I'm sure now that we've been seen together, he'll insist that Sylvanna has declared war. That's why I alerted my Lady as quickly as I could. They're preparing for an attack from this court as we speak." My eyes widened. "It's unlikely that Ayzelle will attack Sylvanna," he clarified upon seeing the worry on my face. "My Lady just prefers not to take chances."

"How did you come to be a council member in Sylvanna?" I asked.

"That is a very long story," Aydan said.

I was about to press further when loud voices rang out from the other room. Aydan frowned and stood, and I scrambled to my feet to follow him through the door, toward the commotion.

Upon entering the parlor, we could see that Princess Irsa was standing in the foyer near the door with her arms crossed, arguing with Elise.

"Your Highness, I cannot allow you—"

"*Allow* me? I've never—"

"Irsa, will you please stop accosting my servants?" Aydan stepped into the foyer to join his sister and Elise, while I remained near the door to the kitchen.

Irsa scowled at him, while Elise's face remained indifferent. He turned to her and said, "Thank you, Elise. I'll take it from here." She curtsied and swiftly left the room.

"She is very rude," said Irsa once Elise was gone.

"She was following my orders," Aydan replied.

"Well, then *you* are very rude." Irsa sniffed before walking past him and into the parlor. Aydan followed.

The princess looked around, touching the picture frames and knickknacks around the room as she walked by them, then finally lowered herself onto one of the cream-colored sofas. Aydan produced a goblet of wine and handed it to her. She raised it in thanks before taking a long drink.

"You certainly know how to make an entrance," she said, smirking at him. He rolled his eyes. "The Wayward Prince has finally returned to court."

"Lady Shaye, allow me to formally introduce you to my sister, Crown Princess Irsa of Medeisia," he said. I bowed my head hoping my face didn't reveal my surprise at hearing her title. Nautia did not allow women to inherit the throne; it hadn't crossed my mind that the princess would be first in line before Aydan. Irsa acknowledged me briefly with a curt nod.

"Father is irate, I hope you know." She turned her attention back to her twin, cradling the goblet with delicate fingers, the dark polish of her nails gleaming against the metal.

"The death threats hinted as much," Aydan said. He motioned for me to sit in one of the cushioned chairs while he took the space next to Irsa on the sofa. "If he would call off his dogs and stop tracking me, we would have been in Sylvanna and out of his hair a week ago." Without looking, Aydan handed me a new goblet of wine, then summoned a tumbler for himself filled with amber liquid.

"He has his reasons." Irsa's shrewd eyes trailed over me. "I suppose you were telling the truth and Miss Redfern here truly knows nothing?"

"I just told her the story," Aydan said, "and it's Lady Eastly. She doesn't use Redfern."

"She won't use 'lady' either," Irsa said after another sip. "Father just revoked her title. Sorry." She added flatly in my direction.

"She's committed no crime," Aydan said incredulously. "He didn't even revoke Lord Ronan's title after being charged with *treason*, and he revokes the one sliver of privilege this woman has?"

"He's being decisive. Ronan's trial was difficult for him. It was a lot to unravel."

"He's grown cruel since last I saw him."

"He's not cruel, he just—" She paused, considering her words. "He, the council—and myself, frankly—are concerned that the appearance of Lord Ronan's long-lost daughter could stir up more unrest."

"More?" Aydan frowned. "Ayzelle is struggling with rebels? *Again*?"

Irsa sat up, looking defensive as she set her goblet on a nearby end table. She smoothed out her skirts and turned to face Aydan fully, "Yes, *again*, Aydan, likely because *our* military is under lock and key in a rebellious territory insistent on warding out their own *king*."

Aydan raised his eyebrows at the change in tone. "I had nothing to do with the decision, and you know that my Lady did not make it lightly."

My attention darted between them as they stared each other down in silence. Nearly a full minute passed, and then Irsa suddenly rose to her feet. Aydan stood as well and I followed suit. The princess crossed the parlor with Aydan close behind, while I remained standing, unsure of whether I should stay or leave and let them finish in private. Irsa entered the foyer and spun abruptly to face her brother.

"If you want to know about the state of this court, I suggest making an inquiry more than once a century," she snapped.

"I'll take that into consideration," Aydan said as he opened the door for her. "Good night, Irsa." Her face turned an impossible shade of red before she stormed out of the chamber and down the corridor. Aydan shut the door and sighed.

"Sorry about that," he said. "Though, I think that might be record length for a peaceful conversation with my sister."

"I'm sorry to have caused all of this tension with your family," I said. Aydan laughed.

"*You* are certainly not the cause of any tension with my father and sister. There are many decades of bad decisions and broken promises responsible for that."

"Is that why you went to Sylvanna?" I pried. "To get away from them?"

He sighed and gestured back toward the parlor. "Let's sit. I'm already drunk, I may as well tell you my story too."

Chapter Nine

I took a seat in the armchair once again, tucking my legs up underneath myself as I did so. Elise appeared in the doorway.

"Would you like any tea this evening, Your Highness? Lady Shaye?" Was it that late already? The day seemed to fly by and drag on all at once.

"No thanks, Elise." Aydan raised his glass to indicate he had all he needed. I'd lost track of how much alcohol he'd had in the last few hours, but it seemed he had no plans of stopping tonight.

"I'd love some, please," I told her. "And it's just Shaye. Thank you." Elise nodded and left toward the kitchen.

Aydan and I sat in silence for a moment while he tapped his fingers nervously on the arm of the sofa where he sat. He opened his mouth as if to speak, and then shut it again. He took a long drink from his glass and made it disappear.

"My father, King Zathryan, came to the throne two hundred and fifty years ago, shortly after his six-hundredth birthday," he started. "His father, my grandfather, had died in the middle of quite the political mess, leaving him to pick up the pieces.

"Sylvanna has had a strained relationship with the Crown for centuries. When Lady Solandis conquered the Tyrant Prince Niklaus, the people of Sylvanna wanted to make her their queen. She refused the title but accepted the responsibility of leading her people as requested. She governed the people of Sylvanna while still taking guidance from the Crown and remaining under Medeisian rule." I knew most of this from my reading, but to hear it from Aydan directly had me more captivated than any wrinkled page of text could have.

"My great-grandparents, and eventually my grandfather, spent their lives fighting this, and declared Sylvanna a rebel state. There wasn't much anyone could do without declaring an all-out war, since Sylvanna is on the other end of the continent from the old capital and had a stronger standing military than even the king himself." The old capital, where the mortal King Callum now sat. It was a source of great pride to the people of Nautia that a militia of just a few hundred mortals, led by Calvin Thandreil and allied with the nearby covens, had overthrown such a powerful regime and started the Thandreil dynasty. I had read about it for years, fascinated by the story. Now I found myself on the other side of it.

Aydan went on. "A centuries-long feud ensued, resulting in Sylvanna isolating from the other territories. When my father inherited the throne, my grandfather had just been in the middle of some negotiations with an emissary from Sylvanna. The Lord and Lady were extending an olive branch, hoping for peace and to expand trade, allowing travel between the Sylvanna and the other territories. My grandfather had been gravely ill for some time and was especially hostile during these negotiations. My father, only Crown Prince at the time, had no choice but to sit and watch while his father ruined an opportunity for peace and prosperity between the Crown and Sylvanna. The Sylvannians nearly withdrew their offer when my grandfather died, and my father rushed to reduce the damage." Aydan paused as the kitchen door swung open and Elise hurried in with a large tray filled with a tea service.

She quickly and quietly set down the tray and bowed out of the room faster than I could thank her. I poured a cup, noticing she'd brought two despite Aydan's refusal. He waited patiently while I stirred in honey and milk, and I sat back with my saucer in hand.

"And so, Zathryan did what no king or queen had done in nearly eight hundred years: he traveled to Sylvanna. To negotiate a peace treaty in person.

"It took nearly a year to organize, but after several arguments with his extended council and personal advisors, my father found himself effuging to the Sylvannian border. He was escorted inside by an armed guard, and then greeted in the great hall by Priamos, Solandis, and their daughter: my mother, Astra."

I felt my eyes widen. Oh. *Oh*.

Aydan nodded, confirming that I had heard him correctly.

"To hear my mother tell it later, their bond was instant. That night at the ball thrown in his honor, my father kept finding his way back to her. They danced for most of the night, and on each day he spent in Sylvanna, they would walk through the gardens together. He found reasons to extend his stay, though the treaties and trade agreements had long been signed.

"Eventually, my father had to return to the capital. There was a nation to govern, after all. Yet the woman he loved would have to remain in Sylvanna, thousands of miles away from him. My father approached the Lord and Lady and asked their permission to propose marriage to my mother. Solandis refused. She said her daughter was preparing to lead Sylvanna someday, not to be shipped off as a political pawn. My father tried to convince them of his love for my mother, but it wasn't until Astra herself stormed into the room and pleaded with her parents to allow the marriage that they agreed. My father fell to his knees right there and asked her to marry him.

"My parents' marriage, despite being a love match, was an enormous political victory, and their wedding day was celebrated in every town and village in Medeisia. The celebrations in the capital are said to have lasted the entire week. Peace had finally been achieved, and prosperity soon followed as trade lines opened between Sylvanna and the other territories of Medeisia. However, what was a time of peace and celebration throughout the continent soon turned into a time of anguish for my parents.

"You see, my father desperately loved my mother. He would have done anything for her, overcome any obstacle to ensure her happiness. But the one thing he couldn't simply snap his fingers and present to her was the one thing she wanted most in the world: a child. They tried, for years. They saw every healer, took every remedy. After a handful of miscarriages, my mother finally was able to carry a pregnancy to term—only for the child to be stillborn. A boy."

Aydan sighed and reached for the teacup. He poured his tea, added nothing, then leaned back into his sofa.

"Losing that child nearly destroyed my mother. She disappeared from her public duties for over a year. My father couldn't help her, though he tried. He told me once that she was stuck. She would wake up in the night, wailing, looking for the child, wandering in the darkness. Solandis herself came to stay in the Grand Palace for a time to try and help. Nothing and no one could save Astra from that nightmare.

"Then, one day, she simply became unstuck. She was herself again; she attended public events, performed her duties as she did before. She never spoke of the lost baby again, and she seemed to give up hope that she would ever have a child of her own.

"Decades passed and one day, without explanation—and after eighty-two years of marriage—my mother found herself pregnant once again.

"My parents made no public announcements. They were anxious the entire pregnancy—how could they not be? Not only would their child be an answered prayer for *them*, but they would also be the future of Medeisia, the heir to a five-thousand-year dynasty," he said.

"That's a lot of expectation for someone who hadn't even been born yet," I commented as Aydan paused to drink his tea.

"It is," he replied, "but that is the reality of our bloodline. We have remained powerful and maintained our claim to the throne because of it. The power that lies in the royal bloodline, and especially the power that lies in the anointed monarch . . . only they can tell you what that weight truly feels like." He set his cup back on the tray and continued.

"My mother labored for twenty hours before delivering a healthy daughter, my sister Irsa. She cried and rejoiced, and my father was called into the labor suite to celebrate with her. Then, just as Irsa was handed off for my father to hold, my mother felt intense pain once again, and only six minutes after delivering my sister, she delivered me as well. A surprise twin."

"They must have been overjoyed," I said.

"Under different circumstances, they would have been," Aydan said.

"What do you mean? They waited so long for a child and then had *two*. That's about as close to a miracle as I've ever heard."

"Well, my mother would agree with you. She doted on us, suspended her public duties, even refused the standard nannies and wet nurses that would have been expected of a queen to hire. Had my father not been king, I believe he would have felt the same way.

"You see, the ancient laws of succession were written to state that the firstborn child of the monarch would inherit the powers of the monarch upon their anointment. They referenced even more ancient scrolls that indicated that the first child was the most magically powerful in a sorcerer's bloodline, and therefore the firstborn would be best suited for the throne. Never, in the history of my family's reign, had the firstborn been a girl."

"If the girl is the most magically powerful, wouldn't the law be on her side?"

"Yes, the *law* would be on her side, but the foolish hearts of the men who govern these lands were not," Aydan said. "If my sister had been born alone, then there would be nothing to argue. She would be heir apparent and titled Crown Princess when she came of age. However, because I was born alongside her, many in my father's council felt that he should simply declare that I had been born first. He could not bring himself to ask my mother to go along with such a lie, but he did instruct his scholars to search for a legal loophole. After years of scouring nearly every library in Medeisia, they found it. The Heirs' Duel.

"The rules were simple: if a younger member of the line of succession felt that *they* were in fact more powerful than the heir apparent, they could publicly request the Heirs' Duel once they were of age. The two would duel with no weapons other than their magic, and the winner would be named the Crown Prince or princess.

"My father couldn't publicly appear to be preparing me for such a thing, but after our ninth birthday, my and Irsa's power began to reveal itself, and suddenly our joint schooling stopped. We were sent to separate tutors, the explanation being that Irsa needed different types of tutors to prepare her for the throne. Meanwhile, I was being trained, with a new tutor added to the team each time a new power revealed itself. My father told me there was an accident when we were born, that *I* should have been the first born, and how my training for the duel was our secret—mother and Irsa couldn't know. That someday I would be king, and it was my duty to be prepared for such a day. So, every day except Yule, for nine years, I trained, and Irsa and I grew apart.

"I bought into every word he said. I was the prince, the son of the most powerful sorcerer in Medeisia. I nearly matched him, even as a child. I beat out my tutors in every practice duel, excelled in every task they presented to me. I was a star pupil, the best my tutors had ever seen, so they told me. Why would my father tell me that I was better than my sister if I wasn't? Why would I have been given every tutor, every opportunity to hone my abilities, if I wasn't truly *destined* to be the next King of Medeisia? In my mind, the Heirs' Duel was just a technicality—a bump in the road on the way to my destiny.

"The day of our eighteenth birthday, there was a feast. Every lord and lady in Medeisia was there, even Priamos and Solandis. Every courtier dressed in their very best to celebrate the next generation coming of age and, they thought, the official titling of Irsa as Crown Princess.

"I made my grand entrance an hour after the feast started. Barged through the doors, knowing all eyes would be on me—*loving* the idea of the surprised look on their faces. I strode confidently across the great hall in the Grand Palace of Nautia and declared to my father that I was requesting the right to challenge my sister to the Heirs' Duel.

"What I didn't expect were the looks of betrayal on my mother's and sister's faces. Irsa looked like I had slapped her. My mother looked like she would cry, and when my father granted permission, she did. She begged him not to allow it, insisting that one of us would kill the other. He would not yield. After a century of marriage, this was the first time he gave my mother an order: control herself or leave the room. She couldn't bear to watch, so she left.

"Within minutes, a space in the great hall had been cleared and Irsa and I stood facing one another. She looked terrified, enraged, and betrayed. But she stood her ground and did not try to get out of the duel. My father explained the rules and what would be granted to the winner, and then it was time to begin." I felt my fingers dig into the arm of my chair.

"I allowed her to take the first shot. She hit me and I knew instantly that it would be much more of a challenge than I had anticipated. That perhaps, despite what poison had been fed to me for the previous nine years, my sister wasn't inherently weaker than me due to her sex. That being the *prince* might not get me as far as I thought it might. I got in the next few blows, even knocked Irsa off her feet once, but within minutes, she unleashed the enormity of her, and nothing—*nothing*—could have prepared me for the raw power that emerged from my twin." Aydan sighed.

"I woke in an infirmary room three days later, with almost no memory of the duel. I had been defeated—badly. My ability to heal had been diminished by Irsa's power, so a long stay in the infirmary was ahead of me. My mother sobbed at my bedside, thanking the gods that I had finally woken up. Then she yelled at me for being an insolent fool, for nearly making a murderer of my sister, and for forcing my father's hand in allowing the duel to begin with—"

"He didn't tell her the truth, even after all of *that*?" I cut him off.

"No. He explained to her that he didn't want to bruise my ego, and allowed the duel, not realizing it would go as far as it did. She believed what she wanted. Irsa was named Crown Princess that night.

"After I had been awake for a few days, my father finally came to visit. He entered the room and stared at me in bed. I thought—I thought maybe he was trying to come up with the words to apologize. To say that he was sorry for putting those ideas in my head, for allowing me to make a fool of myself in front of every courtier and nobleman on the continent. Or at least to tell me he was happy that I was alive.

"Instead, he told me that I had humiliated him, myself, and our entire bloodline. That my training had been a waste and that he should have spent his time training Irsa instead of me, since nine years' worth of the finest tutors money could buy were not enough to win against an eighteen-year-old woman with no formal dueling experience. He called me a disgrace, said that he was glad that I would never sit upon his throne, that clearly he had been wrong about a woman's ability to rule and that the gods had shown him the error in his thinking in the form of my pitiful display." My stomach clenched.

"He assigned me to my new position as an emissary of his court. I would be away from the Grand Palace for most of the year, visiting other territories. I would come home for a week, make my appearance in court, and then be sent away again to negotiate some deal, or to simply be the king's representative across the continent. The courtiers at the Grand Palace coined me the 'Wayward Prince' following my scandal, and that was what I became. Aloof, cocky, without direction or a plan. At first, I pretended not to care—I fed into it. It was just a role I played to make visiting the Grand Palace more bearable, but after a while, it was hard to know where Aydan Aevitarus ended and the Wayward Prince began.

"It wasn't all terrible. I visited my grandparents in Sylvanna often, and I experienced parts of the continent I had never seen before and would never have been allowed to explore on my own had I been named Crown Prince. But knowing what I had done to my sister, to my mother—and how I had disappointed my father—

stuck with me everywhere I went. Knowing that I had thrown away any chance of a truly close relationship with Irsa was a difficult pain to bear.

"For five years, this carried on. Then one morning, I awoke in a suite in the Duke of Xarynn's manor to the news that a mortal rebellion had broken out in the night. The rebels, allied with witches, had attacked my family home, armed with silver weapons. They overtook the Grand Palace and killed my mother, countless courtiers, and other guests before forcing my father and sister and what was left of the Nautian court to flee to Ayzelle, to this castle that we sit in tonight." Aydan was staring at his hand, pulling at some lint on the arm of the sofa.

"I tried to come to court here in Ayzelle as soon as I received the news, but my father would not receive me. It was Lord Ronan who informed me that I had been relieved of my position as emissary and banished to Sylvanna. I was no longer welcome at court.

"You see, I had been in the middle of peace negotiations with the leaders of the mortal territories. They were seeking more independence and my father would not allow it. I had been in a meeting with Thandreil and his men three days before the attack, and my father blamed me for not keeping their rebellion at bay."

"You couldn't have known their plans," I said gently, noticing the haunted look in Aydan's eyes.

"I know," he said softly. "It just . . . maybe I *should* have. Maybe there were signs that I didn't read, something I missed. I think about that meeting often and wonder if there was something I could have done to save my mother's life." He rubbed the back of his neck. "It's been a long time since I've told that story."

"Thank you for telling me," I said. Aydan remained quiet, staring at the arm of the sofa once again, trying to pick at that invisible piece of lint. I watched, unsure of what to say or if I should say anything at all. After a few minutes, the clock chimed in the foyer, breaking Aydan's concentration as he glanced up at it.

"It's getting late," he said. "You must be exhausted."

"I am," I admitted with a sigh. "Today was . . ."

"A lot," he finished for me. "Are you hungry? I could have a plate sent to your room."

"No, I think I'd rather just get some rest," I replied, standing to leave.

"I'm going to stay up a bit longer, I think. If you need anything don't hesitate to ask."

"Thank you," I said. "Good night, Aydan."

"Good night, Lady Shaye."

"I'm not a lady, remember?" I joked. "If I have to disregard your title, then you have to disregard mine."

"Fine." He chuckled, if somewhat reluctantly. "Good night, Shaye."

"Good night, Aydan."

Chapter Ten

The next day, I woke with a pounding headache. I took my time sitting up, taking in my surroundings. The bedroom—mine for the time being, I supposed—now contained a few more comfort items than had been present the previous evening. I noted a hand-painted pitcher and matching cup on a small table near the entrance to the bathroom, as well as a small arrangement of fresh flowers on the vanity. The shelves and books had all been dusted. I wondered if this had been done magically from outside the room, or if I had been sleeping so deeply that I didn't notice Isolde and Elise coming in.

I'd fallen asleep without changing out of my dress, and now I crossed the room to the wardrobe to select something fresh to wear. I found a comfortable-looking dress of deep blue cotton. I changed into the new frock and left the old one spread out on top of the bed, then sat in front of the vanity. Sleeping in a real bed had done wonders for my appearance, or at least the bags under my eyes, even after just one night. I quickly ran a brush through my hair before braiding it back and leaving the room.

Isolde and Elise were busy rearranging cushions on the parlor sofas when I entered. They both stopped and curtsied when they noticed me. I gave them an awkward smile, still uncomfortable with their formal treatment. I certainly didn't feel deserving of a curtsy.

"Good morning," I said.

"Good morning, my lady," said Isolde. "Would you like something to eat?"

"Yes please," I replied over the sound of my stomach growling. Isolde set down her work and led me to the dining room where Aydan and I had shared dinner the night before. She pulled out a chair and gestured for me to sit as a tea service appeared on the table before me.

"I will tell the kitchen you are ready for breakfast. Do you have any requests, my lady?"

"Oh." I'd never had much of an option to choose from. "Perhaps just some porridge." Isolde stared. "Or maybe . . . an egg?" She blinked, then smiled politely.

"I will tell the kitchen," she said.

I sipped on my tea while I waited, and in just a few minutes, Isolde brought out a large tray filled with toasted bread, pastries, fruit, a platter of fried eggs and sausages, and in the center, a bowl of porridge topped with berries and a drizzle of honey.

"Is there anything else you require?" she asked.

"No," I said, a little overwhelmed. "No, this is incredible. Thank you, Isolde." She began to leave when I added, "Will the prince be joining me?"

"His Highness left before the sun was out this morning, my lady. He had an audience with the king and the Crown Princess."

"Oh," I said. "Well, thank you, Isolde."

She curtsied and left me to my breakfast.

I spent the remainder of the day resting in my room, emerging only to eat dinner at the table when Isolde came to collect me. Aydan did not return before I fell asleep that night, and again the next morning, he was gone for another audience with Zathryan and Irsa.

This routine continued for nearly a week, with me being left alone for most of the day. Elise and Isolde were kind enough, but they always seemed to have their hands full and I quickly felt that I was in their way if I made any attempt to have a conversation. I finally kept myself awake long enough to hear Aydan enter the chambers on the sixth day I had been a resident of Castle Ayzelle. I'd forced myself to keep my eyes open, reading a volume on the history of the Medeisian territories and the wars that formed them, until I heard the door open and close, followed by low voices down the corridor. I came out from my room and padded my way to the foyer, where Elise was taking Aydan's jacket.

"Thank you, Elise," he said, exhaustion in his voice.

"Would you like me to bring tea to your room, Your Highness?"

"No tea," he said. "But a plate of whatever was served at dinner would be lovely. My father elected, yet again, to serve mutton this evening."

"What's wrong with mutton?" I asked. Aydan looked up, a bit startled.

"I've always hated it, and my father knows that," he said. "What are you doing awake? It's nearly three in the morning."

"I haven't seen you since my first night here." I realized now how silly I must seem. "I haven't heard anything about my uncle. And there are only so many books one can read in a week before boredom sets in."

He sighed, but it did not seem to be out of frustration. "Are you hungry? I was just going to eat something."

"No thank you," I said. "But if you don't mind the company, I'll sit with you."

"Please do."

Elise brought tea out for me when she arrived in the dining room with a steaming plate of the roast chicken Zale and Tory had prepared earlier that night. Aydan was less ravenous than he'd been during our last meal together, eating at a slower pace tonight.

"I'm sorry I've left you alone so much," he said after a few minutes. "I've been trying to strike a deal with my father to get us to Sylvanna faster."

"Let me guess." I smirked. "We're leaving in the morning?"

"Not quite. But I did convince him to allow us outside of the castle, to walk the grounds."

"The height of privilege," I said. He huffed a laugh. "Has there been any word from Gideon?"

"I've sent out inquiries to every contact that might be able to help. There has been no response yet."

I fiddled with my napkin on the table. "Thank you. It's kind of you to use your resources to help me."

"It's nothing," he said. "Gideon bought us enough time to get out of that house safely. It would be bad form to leave him in the hands of Nautian captors if it can be avoided." I took a drink of my tea. "I have no plan for tomorrow. Would you like to join me on a walk around the grounds? I'd be happy to show you the garden." He finished his plate and made it vanish.

"Actually," I said, noting the change in subject. "I was wondering if you could teach me *that*." I pointed to where his plate had been just a second before.

"What, how to clear a table?"

I rolled my eyes at his joke. "Magic. I have this power and don't know how to use it. Can you teach me?"

Aydan considered, leaning back in his seat. "I suppose you'll have to learn some time," he said. "As long we keep it to ourselves, I don't see why not."

"Really?"

"We'll start after dinner tomorrow." He nodded. "We should both get some rest."

"Thank you, Aydan." I stood and pushed my chair in. "I'll see you tomorrow."

Chapter Eleven

The next night, I lay in bed, tossing and turning, unable to sleep.

Our first lesson, following an indulgent dinner of roast duck with plum sauce, was a disaster to say the least. We'd sat in the parlor on opposite sofas while Aydan began his instruction: "The way we're all initially taught, once we've tapped into our power, is to remind ourselves that this magic, the extended life, the abilities, it's all a gift from the gods. The ability to bend our surroundings to our will is their gift, and we should use it wisely." He rolled up his sleeves, revealing a tattooed left forearm. "Now, whether it's really the gods, or the land, or simply an accident of bloodlines, we can never truly know, but this is what we are taught." He placed a full bottle of wine in the center of the table, next to an empty glass. He made a waving gesture toward it, and the bottle uncorked itself without him laying a hand on it. "Pour a glass," he said. I stared at it, then looked up at him.

"How?"

"Decide that you want it. *Will* the wine to do what you want. Hold the glass in your hand if you'd like. Let that power you've felt beneath the surface trickle out and do your bidding." I nodded and snatched the glass from the table. I held it before me for what felt like an hour, urging that tingling to show itself. For a moment, I thought I felt it, then it was gone. I sighed.

"I don't think I'm doing it right."

"Keep trying," he said quietly. I fixed my gaze back onto it and threw my mind toward it.

There it was—that tingle, the vibration right there under the surface, ready to show me the extent of my power, the extent of the force that lingered within me, enough to frighten kings both mortal and sorcerer—

The glass shattered.

One second, it was in my palm, my mind urging the bottle to come to me, to fill the glass to the brim, to overflow and stain the parlor carpets. The next, the glass practically exploded, sending tiny shards flying in every direction. I blinked at my empty hand now smeared with blood.

"What happened?"

Aydan motioned for the shattered glass, and it reappeared whole in my hand, which was healed as well.

"It's normal," he told me. "This time, focus on the bottle. Ignore the glass." I nodded, determined.

I shattered the glass eight more times before I got frustrated enough to quit for the night. Aydan assured me again that it was normal, that no one gets their first lesson right, and that we'd keep working on it. I excused myself for bed.

That was hours ago, and all I'd done in the meantime was lay here. My eyelids finally drooped, and I grew excited in hopes of falling asleep—until I felt the urge to relieve myself. Irritated, I hauled my body to the attached bathroom. Once I'd finished, I decided I was thirsty as well, but when I went to pour some water from the pitcher on the vanity, it was empty. Now fully awake, I took the pitcher and left the room, shuffling in the direction of the kitchen.

Quietly I passed through the corridor, not wanting Elise or Isolde to wake and decide they needed to wait on me. I thought for a second that I might be too late because ahead of me, past the foyer and through the parlor entrance, a figure stood in near total darkness. It was too tall, now that I had a better look, to be either of the women. Zale or Tory, then.

"Hello?" I called, taking up a nearby lantern. It was already lit. Strange. No response from the parlor. Again I said, "Hello?"

The figure turned, and I nearly dropped the lantern and pitcher both.

Gideon.

Uncle Gideon stood before me, in the prince's private chambers. He looked just the same as I saw him coming back from town that last day—tanned, healthy, with some dirt smudged across his cheek.

"Gideon," I breathed, taking a step forward. "What are you doing here? Where have you been? How did you . . ." His eyes were wide, staring me up and down.

"Shaye," he croaked. "You must . . . you must . . ." His voice was barely a whisper.

"What is it?" I wavered, wanting to reach out and touch him. "Can I get you anything?"

"You must go—with him. You'll be safe. Go." He choked.

"We can't go," I said, tears streaming now. "King Zathryan has taken us prisoner. He and the Crown Princess want to keep us here—"

"Go, Shaye." When he reached for me, I saw in the faint light of the lantern that his arm was covered in blood. Red pooled from beneath his shirt, the stain growing and appearing in different spots, until blood poured from his mouth, his eyes, blood-streaked tears streaming down his face. "*G-Go!*" He heaved, a terrible gurgling sound, and grabbed my arms. I screamed. He shook me violently, bloodied face inches from mine, wailing my name over and over—

"Shaye!"

I was in bed, being shaken. I heard myself crying—screaming.

Aydan leaned over me, holding me by the shoulders as I looked around wildly, thrashing my head, searching for Gideon—

"You're all right. You're in your room, in Ayzelle. You're all right," he repeated. I took a breath and nodded. Of course I was. It was just a nightmare. Aydan let go of my arms and sat up straight on the edge of my bed, giving me space. I put a hand on my forehead, then pulled my knees to my chest and buried my face into the blanket. It and my nightdress were completely soaked with sweat. "Thank you, Elise," Aydan said softly. I looked and saw her standing in the doorway in her nightdress, a shawl pulled tightly around her and golden-brown hair loose around her shoulders, her eyes wide with fright.

"Thank you," I mumbled. "I'm all right now." She shut the door gently and we were alone. Embarrassed, I looked over at Aydan, resting my head on my knees again.

He was bare-chested and barefoot, clothed only in a pair of loose trousers. The surprising part was not his exposed skin but the tattoos covering his left arm. I had seen them briefly before, but I'd not realized their extent—traveling from his wrist to his shoulder, drifting up toward his neck. The swirling, vine-like shapes were nearly floral, not quite filigree, and formed no definite image but were stunning nonetheless.

"Those are pretty," I said. He followed my gaze to the black swirls covering his brown skin.

"They're from my time in the Sylvannian army. We expand upon them as we rise in the ranks."

"You said you're not a soldier."

"I said I'm not a soldier *anymore*," he corrected. "I served my time and retired to join my grandparents' council."

I did not respond. Instead, I closed my eyes, attempting to banish my nightmare from my mind's eye. "I'm sorry," I mumbled.

"For what?"

"Disturbing your household."

"It's not a disturbance," he said. "If you . . . if you need to talk about it—"

"I don't."

Silence.

After a few moments, I felt him stand from the bed. "If you change your mind, you know where to find me." I looked up again as he shut the door behind him, leaving me alone in the darkness.

The next morning, I woke to sunlight pouring through the curtains and hitting my face. Odd. I had been waking much earlier over the past days. Still groggy, I slowly dragged myself from bed and dressed, braided my hair with cloudy eyes, and wondered if there was any breakfast left for me, or if it was already lunchtime.

I strode down the corridor to the parlor and stopped, surprised to see Aydan in the middle of the room with Elise, holding a short stack of papers and muttering to her urgently.

"I thought you were meeting with your sister this morning?" I asked. Aydan looked up, startled.

"We finished a little while ago." I looked up at the clock. It was well past noon.

"I didn't realize I was so tired." Aydan said nothing, his expression rather tight as he stared at me. "What?"

He exhaled. "You may want to sit down." Slowly, I sat in one of the armchairs. He dismissed Elise, who left without a word.

"What's wrong?" I asked suspiciously. He straightened the papers before passing them to me. As I began to read, the prince spoke:

"This is a letter from a Sylvannian spy—a mortal man who owed me a favor. He went to Nautia at my direction and was able to find out what happened to Gideon." His words became muffled.

The prisoner was belligerent, refusing to answer questions during interrogation, and spitting on an officer of the Guard, the page read. *He had suffered several concerning injuries while fighting his arrest. Even so, once it had been determined that Gideon Eastly was of no use to them, the Nautians escorted him to the gallows—*

"Shaye, I don't know what to say. I'm so sorry."

Aydan was standing over me, hand hovering at my shoulder like he was unsure how to comfort me.

No time to be emotional, my uncle would say.

I blinked, and the tears welling in my eyes spilled over the brim.

"His survival was a long shot," I finally said, my voice tight but surprisingly steady. "We saw the soldiers at the house. He was never going to fight them all off." I gave the papers back to Aydan. My hands shook. "He died protecting me. They were interrogating him about me."

"Protecting you was all he cared about. He told me as much that night, before the first soldiers arrived." I wished Aydan's kind voice made a difference in the ache spreading through my chest.

I stood, brushing away the tears that streamed down my face. "I think I'll spend the afternoon in my bedroom."

"Of course," he said as I walked past him and back down the corridor. When the door shut behind me, I let a sob choke out before crawling back beneath my blankets.

Hours later, there was a soft knock on the door. I called to whoever it was to enter, and Elise walked in silently to set a tray on my bedside table. I thanked her in a soft voice and sat up slowly when the door clicked shut again. On the tray was a covered plate, a simple tea service for one, and a folded note sealed with blue wax stamped and with an elegantly styled *A*. My stomach ached from crying, and so I ignored the plate but fixed the tea with honey and milk before cracking the wax seal and unfolding the thick, cream-colored paper. A white flower fell from it. The note read simply:

Please accept my deepest condolences.
–A

I folded it and placed it in the table drawer, then sat on the bed, fiddling with the flower between my fingers. After a few moments, I reached for one of the books on the shelf on the opposite wall and pressed it between the pages, before returning to bed and burying myself beneath the covers again.

Chapter Twelve

Over the next month, I began having nightmares more frequently.

Each time, they would begin like the first—so real, so normal—before devolving into horror. I had not woken up screaming again since the night I dreamt about Gideon but had started to wake standing next to my bed. More than once, I vomited out of sheer fright, and nearly every day since I dreamt of my uncle, I found myself emitting sparks from my fingertips at random. At first I assumed the dreams were a response to my uncle's death, but now they felt heavier, carrying a weight I did not know how to bear for much longer.

Despite the horrors taking place at night, my days were fairly mundane. Some mornings I ate breakfast with Aydan, and on others he would be called away to meet with his father or sister. The prince returned absolutely fuming to the chambers on more than one occasion. One day, Elise had just alerted me that lunch was being served, and as I stood from one of the parlor sofas where I'd been reading, Aydan stormed in, removing his jacket with jerking motions. Elise hurried over to ensure he did not tear it.

"What's wrong?" I asked.

"My sister." Before I could ask if he wanted to elaborate, he raged off toward his bedroom.

Halfway through lunch, he came to the dining room and sat across from me. "I'm sorry for my outburst," he said.

"Are you all right?" I asked.

"I'm fine," Aydan replied as Isolde entered with a plate for him. He thanked her and picked up his fork. "Just more of the same with Irsa. What you saw the other night was us getting along."

"And you're not getting along now?"

He shook his head while chewing, then swallowed and said, "I think my father would have given up keeping us here by now if she wasn't so insistent that we stay."

"Why does she care if we're here?" I asked. "Certainly she'd prefer to have you out of her hair if she dislikes you so deeply."

"You would think so," he said. "But I suspect Irsa just enjoys making me miserable now. I don't entirely blame her. I tried to steal her crown. It was my father's idea, but I was old enough to know that what we were doing was wrong."

"You know," I sighed. "Someday you might consider forgiving yourself for all of that." A ghost of a smile emerged on Aydan's face. My fingers sparked, but I shoved my hands in my lap quickly enough that the prince didn't see. Something about the strange outburst of power felt wrong; I had not yet told Aydan about it.

"I'm sorry, it seems all I've done lately is complain about my family while you've been cooped up inside. Do you want to walk the grounds with me?" he asked before taking another bite of his meal.

"That sounds nice." I wiped my mouth with my napkin and placed it on the table. Rather than let Isolde come for it, I raised my hands overtop to try and make it vanish.

"Focus on where it needs to go," Aydan offered once he realized what I was doing. "That's all it is. A dirty dish belongs in the scullery. Try to send it there." I focused all my attention on this tiny task, and after a long moment, the napkin vanished and the plate cracked in half. I swore. Aydan waved his hand so the plate formed back into a single piece. "Try again."

I tried a few more times before eventually making the plate disappear, only to hear it shatter on the kitchen floor where I had sent it instead of the scullery. I winced, then followed the sound into the kitchen and apologized to Zale and Tory before cleaning up my mess and giving up for the day.

To reach the castle grounds, Aydan had to take me past the great hall, where many courtiers and council members were gathered, socializing. A pair of sorceresses, nearly identical save for their hair color—one light and one dark—sneered, making eye contact with me from where they stood.

"The Floinn sisters," Aydan whispered in my ear. "They've had that look plastered on their faces for decades." Their brows furrowed simultaneously at the sight of Aydan leaning in so closely to speak to me. I made it a point to let them see me tighten my grip on the prince's arm.

"Careful." He chuckled. "You have enough enemies here."

"Miss Eastly," cried a familiar girlish voice before I could respond. I turned to see Irsa approaching with a sickly-sweet diplomatic smile spreading across her face. I curtsied.

"Your Highness," I replied with a tight smile of my own.

"Coming out to play, are we?" The Crown Princess asked in a tone that sounded like it was reserved for speaking to children and dogs. "I'm sure you're feeling rather shut in. It will be nice to get out for a walk."

"Yes, Your Highness."

"She wouldn't feel so shut in if you would stop filling our father's head with suspicions of treason," Aydan chimed in. I felt my face grow red.

"I'm not filling his head, I'm reminding him of dangers that he may not have considered," she said sweetly. "When he is convinced that Miss Eastly isn't a danger to our great nation or the Crown, you two can scurry off to the garden city and never be seen again." She turned her attention back to me. "It's starting to get cold outside. I hope you've brought a shawl. Although." Her eyes landed on my hand tightly gripping Aydan's arm. "You already look rather cozy." I didn't have time to respond as Irsa turned on her heel and, with her ladies, strode past us, cutting off the conversation. I curtsied belatedly and, when she was out of sight, let go of Aydan. He placed my hand back on top of his arm.

"Ignore her," he said. "I don't mind looking cozy." My face heated but I did not take my hand away as he led me out of the castle, over the drawbridge, and into the gardens to walk the stone path.

That night when we returned to the chambers, I was properly exhausted. Aydan had led me around the entire perimeter of the castle grounds, which was several miles in length. He pointed out places where he liked to play as a child when his family would come to this castle for holidays, spots that he was still convinced might be haunted, and his favorite flowers growing off the path that reminded him of Sylvanna and his mother.

When I went to my room for the night, too tired to sit for dinner, Elise arrived with a tray containing tea, finger sandwiches, and a crisply folded page of Aydan's stationery. I ate two of the small sandwiches while Elise drew a bath and shoved a third in my mouth before opening the note.

Same time tomorrow?
–A

I couldn't help smiling to myself as I scrawled my reply.

We walked each afternoon for the next few days. It was nice to get out of the chambers, but I found myself enjoying Aydan's company more than I cared about walking the paths. He told me about his friends and life in Sylvanna, how those friends had become more like family over the decades than his own. They had all been writing him letters while we were locked away by Zathryan, eager for him to come home and, apparently, to meet me as well.

Meanwhile, I shared stories about growing up in Nautia with Gideon. How it hadn't always been easy between us, but my uncle had been fair and kind in his way. Aydan listened to an hour or more of stories about life in my village, chuckling at the prudish nature of my mortal neighbors when I told him they considered me a ruin to my uncle's good name, and doubled over in laughter completely when I explained that they thought this because of a few conspicuous romances in my teenage years. Even through his teasing, it was easy to talk to Aydan. At night, when my vision began to blur at the edges and I let my thoughts wander while I lie in bed, I would smile to myself, realizing that for the first time in a long while, I had a real friend.

On our fifth walk together, Aydan took me to a small pond on the southern end of the grounds, where I sat against a tree while he lay at the water's edge with his eyes closed and hands behind his head, enjoying a rare sunny afternoon after weeks of nothing but the gray skies of winter, which had fully set in since my arrival. It was still cold enough to require a coat, but the sunshine had melted the remaining snow on the ground this morning; Aydan and I agreed that we should take advantage of the sunlight while we had the chance.

"Did you come here as a child?" I asked over the top of my book. All the other spots he had shown me were childhood favorites.

Aydan hummed without opening his eyes. "I used to come here and daydream about the type of king I would be."

"Oh?" I pried. "And what kind of king were you, in your daydreams?"

"Loved. Feared. Victorious in every endeavor, with a beautiful consort and loyal heirs to support my whims." He chuckled, then added, "Though if I were smart, I would have an anointed queen."

"A what?"

"An anointed queen rules as an equal to her king, until the day she dies. My great-grandmother, Queen Euna, was the first anointed queen. Her husband, King Cavell, died ten years into their reign and so she ruled alone for centuries. She is widely regarded as Medeisia's greatest monarch, which isn't surprising."

"It's not?"

"My lady, I have spent the last century and a half observing and advising different leaders throughout Medeisia, and something I learned very quickly is that men are not nearly as impressive as we like to think we are. We're usually better off leaving the running of things to the women." I stifled a laugh and he smirked, keeping his eyes shut.

"And what endeavors did you have in mind for your reign?" I asked, enjoying the game. Aydan pondered seriously for a moment.

"My dream was always to quell the unrest that simmered near the capital. I tried, on my father's behalf, during my negotiations with the mortals in the days before the rebellion."

"What are your dreams now?" I asked. "If you could snap your fingers and have anything?"

"Peace," he said. "I want peace between Sylvanna and the Crown. Between the Crown and Nautia. I'd like to see the Eternity Throne restored to my family . . . It's an impossible dream."

"It's lovely," I said. I opened my mouth to speak again but shut it when I heard a rustling in the bushes beside my tree. I jumped to my feet. "What the hell is that?"

"Not sure," Aydan replied, on his feet now, stepping closer to the shrubbery as I moved backward. He reached his arm in.

"Be *careful*," I scolded. As soon as the words left my lips he snatched his hand back, swearing and bringing a bleeding finger to his lips. "What happened?"

"Bastard got me," he said before reaching back in. I started to tell him to leave it, but before I could get the words out, Aydan pulled a squirming, scrawny kitten from within the thorn bush. He held it to his chest as it chewed on his fingers, more playful than defensive. "Where did you come from?"

"It's cute." I took a closer look. It was slate gray with curious bright orange eyes. It meowed at me when I approached, and Aydan placed it in my hands. "I've never held a cat," I told him as the kitten began to purr.

"Never?"

I shrugged. "They're all feral in my village. The only people who had cats around were people who had barns. We didn't, so there was no use for one."

"Not even as a pet?"

"Pets are for rich people."

"Well, it needs to go somewhere, and there's no sign of a mother around," Aydan said. "Do you want it?"

"I don't know how to take care of a cat."

"Feed it, pet it, give it a place to sleep." My hesitation was muted by the purring kitten falling asleep as I held it against my chest.

"I suppose I could take care of it," I said, adjusting so it was cradled in my arm like a baby.

"Her," Aydan corrected upon second glance. "Let's get her back inside, it'll be getting cold soon." He offered me an arm, but I declined, using one arm to hold the kitten, and the other to pet her stomach. I had never experienced such instant attachment to an animal. "She'll need a name," he said after a few moments. When we approached the drawbridge, he produced a cloak and placed it over my shoulders, hiding the kitten from view.

By the time we arrived back in the chambers, I had decided to call her Catchfly, after the flowers that grew along the garden gate at my and Gideon's home. Aydan removed the caked dirt from her fur with a wave of his hand while Isolde brought a saucer of milk. Despite our efforts to play with her, all she seemed to want to do was go to sleep. I held her in my lap, even through dinner.

"Thank you," I told him when he walked me to the door of my bedroom.

"An early Yule present." He winked, scratching Catchfly's ears; she stirred, squeaking out a small meow. "I'm glad you like her." I smiled down at the kitten, then looked back to Aydan, standing before me in the doorway to my bedroom.

"Well," I said. "Good night, I suppose." Aydan hesitated, and for a second, I thought he had something else to say, but instead he simply cleared his throat and bid me good night as well.

That night, I curled my body around Catchfly, slipping into sleep with the vibrations of her purring against me.

I woke to the sound of glass breaking somewhere in the chambers. Catchfly was gone, and the door to my bedroom was open. I sighed, realizing she must have broken something in the kitchen. Dragging myself out of bed and into the darkened hall, I conjured an orb of dim light and sent it above my head to light my way without disturbing the household, a trick Aydan had taught me only a few days before. I glanced around the parlor to see if Catchfly was hiding under any furniture but could not find her. A muffled thud from behind the kitchen door sent my eyes rolling as I cursed the tiny kitten under my breath. I pushed on the swinging door and let out a scream.

Aydan lay sprawled on the kitchen floor, his belly sliced open from navel to sternum, gore spilling from the wound. His handsome face was twisted in fear, dark eyes staring into nothingness. Blood covered everything: his body, the floor, my bare feet. I dropped to my knees.

"*Aydan!*" I yelled, grabbing at his cold body, "Aydan, *please*—please wake up—" I choked. I shook him over and over, "*Someone help him*! Aydan! Can you hear me?

"Aydan!

"Aydan!

"AYDAN!—"

"Shaye!"

"Someone, PLEASE—"

"SHAYE, OPEN YOUR EYES!"

My eyes snapped open at the command. I was on my feet, back to the wall with strong hands pinning me there by my shoulders. Aydan's eyes were wide, nostrils flared, and his hands engulfed in that blue light I hadn't seen since the first night we met.

"Put it out, Shaye," he said sternly. I looked down and saw that my own hands were engulfed in flames, orange and blazing in the darkness. My eyes shot back up to meet Aydan's, and the flames went out before I could even ask how to extinguish them. My face was hot with tears and I heaved out a sob as he let go of me and I threw my arms around his neck, squeezing tightly to prove to myself that he indeed stood before me, alive and well. He squeezed back, one hand rubbing up and down my back. "You're all right," he said in my ear. "We're safe, we're in Ayzelle."

"What's happening to me?" I whispered, my voice trembling.

He didn't answer, but instead murmured, "Let's get you back to bed." I let go but he kept an arm around my shoulders while we walked slowly down the hall to my bedroom.

We entered, and Catchfly was fast asleep on her pillow. Aydan guided me to my bed, where I sat, still shaken, and he poured me a glass of water from the pitcher. I drank it while he lowered into an armchair that had been across the room a second before, and now sat beside the bed. I drained the glass and played with the empty cup in silence, staring at my lap as his gaze burned into me. When I finally lifted my head, he had his chin propped on his fist, looking me over, waiting for me to say something. I opened my mouth and closed it again. Where would I begin?

"Are you all right?" he finally asked.

I sighed. "No." He sat up straight.

And then I told him everything. Every nightmare I'd had since the first about Gideon, every bit of tingling beneath my palms, the involuntary sparks—and that they were all getting worse. I told him what I saw in my nightmare that night.

"It's so *real*," I said, digging the heels of my hands into my eyes. "It's not like a regular dream. I feel like myself in them, everything feels normal, and then I see such horrible things." I swallowed. "I've woken up outside of my bed before, but tonight is the first time I've left this room." Aydan continued to look me over, digesting the story I had just told him. "Please say something."

"Well," he said as he went back to propping his head on his fist. "We can almost certainly do something about the nightmares.

I'll consult a healer in the morning." I let out a relieved sigh. "The sparks, the flames—you've never experienced this before we met?"

"I never experienced magic before meeting you." He considered.

"That will be more difficult to conceal, but we will need to keep this to ourselves for now." I nodded dully. Untamed sparks flying from my fingertips would certainly not encourage the king to lift our house arrest.

"Thank you," I said. "I'm sorry to wake you. Again." Aydan waved me off.

"Try and get some sleep, Shaye. I'll stay and make sure you don't wake again." I started to protest, but Aydan repeated gently, "Sleep."

Rather than argue that he should not sleep in an armchair on my behalf, I yawned and rearranged the covers, pulling them to my chin and rolling over to face Catchfly. I placed my hand on her tiny warm body, a touchstone in the darkness.

"Thank you," I said.

He did not reply.

Chapter Thirteen

I woke the next morning to Catchfly pawing at me, demanding to be fed. Groaning, I picked her up and set her on the floor despite her protests.

"Give me a minute," I mumbled, running a hand over my face. The previous night played in my mind's eye: the pond, the nightmare, and all that came after. I looked over at the armchair and saw that it was empty. The table beside it, however, held a tray with covered dishes and a folded sheet of stationery with my name scrawled on it. I reached my hand out and attempted to summon the tray to me as I sat up in bed. A moment of concentration and the letter drifted into my hand while the tray crashed to the floor.

I swore, and Catchfly pranced over to the spilled tray looking for a treat.

"Don't choke," I warned her as I peered over the end of the bed and watched her snatch a slice of ham nearly the size of her body. She looked proud of herself as she dragged her prize off to a corner tore into it. I turned my attention to the letter in my hand, my name written in careful, neat loops. I opened it and read:

> *Shaye,*
>
> *I am sorry to have left you so early this morning. I have been summoned by my father to weigh in on a diplomatic matter in Irsa's place while she addresses trade in Xarynn.*
>
> *The king has insisted on placing Captain Whittaker in the foyer to keep watch over you. He has been instructed by me to leave you alone. Please use my study should you need a place to read privately. I will return as quickly as I can.*

Fondly,
–A

I folded the letter and left it on the bed while I dressed. Today, I chose a simple gown of pewter gray, then gathered my hair and pinned it at the nape of my neck. I stooped down to gather the spilled food back on the tray. Catchfly was now snoozing in the corner, her ham unfinished but her belly swollen. I laughed and shook my head before scooping up her leftover breakfast and taking it with the rest of the tray.

The kitchen was busy. Elise and Isolde had joined Zale and Tory rather than making their normal rounds throughout the chambers. The women were chopping vegetables and tossing them into a large pot that I guessed would soon contain lunch. Zale and his husband seemed to be starting their preparations for dinner. I placed the tray in the large sink and began separating pieces of ruined food from the dishes and threw them in the garbage. Isolde tried to take the dishes from me, but I waved her off and moved on to washing, placing each item on the wooden drying rack next to the sink. When I finished, I opened a cupboard and fished out an apron.

"How can I help?" I asked as I tied it on. Isolde and Elise shooed me out of the kitchen, insisting they did not need it, that I should go relax, and they'd bring me lunch when it was ready. I protested but soon gave up, taking the apron off and placing it on the counter.

Instead, I now glanced through the shelves in my bedroom, looking for something interesting to read. I found a novel on the shelf beneath a stack of some neglected-looking volumes—a romance, by the sound of the title. It would have to do.

Rather than retreat to Aydan's study, I decided to brave the parlor, to show Captain Whittaker that he would not be intimidating me today. I walked swiftly into the room, made myself comfortable on a sofa, and cracked the volume open. I glanced up once, to find the tawny-haired captain staring in my direction. He was mortal, to be sure, and young—not much older than myself. I scoffed, not caring if he knew my disdain for his presence and turned my attention to the book in my lap.

It did not take long for me to become engulfed in the story. Hours passed, and I was swept away in the tale of a daring princess and her quest to free her subjects from the rule of an invading tyrant, all while she fell in love with the prince of the enemy kingdom. Isolde tried to call me into the dining room for lunch, but I was too enthralled to leave the world of the story. After I ignored her twice, she brought in a lunch tray and left me to my own devices. The soup went cold and when Isolde came back to retrieve the tray, she mumbled something about me wasting away if I did not stop to eat at some point. When the clock chimed for six o'clock, I looked again in the captain's direction. He still stared.

"May I offer you something to eat, captain?" I asked more coldly than I meant to.

"No thank you, Miss Eastly," he said stiffly. If he had an opinion of me beyond the orders set by his king, I could not tell. His face was utterly unreadable.

"I'm sorry that you won't have anything more interesting to report back to His Majesty tonight," I said.

"I'm not," he replied coolly. "I'm not particularly eager to report nefarious plots to my king."

"It's a good thing I'm not doing anything nefarious, then." I held up the book and tapped the cover. A smirk appeared on the captain's face.

"Well, that's debatable." He chuckled darkly. "That book is a crime against literature, to be sure." I scowled at him.

"I *like* it, thank you very much," I said. "And it's not as if I have a wide variety of choice here."

"If you'd like to change that, perhaps you'd like to tell the king what Sylvanna's plans are with you."

"What are you talking about?"

"Did you really expect anyone to believe that shit your prince was—"

The front door opened, and Aydan walked through, looking irritable. He paused when he registered the captain in the doorway, then me sitting with a book in my lap and a scowl on my face. His eyebrows rose at my expression.

"You're dismissed, Captain Whittaker."

"Your Highness." The captain inclined his head just long enough to pass for formality, then turned on his heel and marched out the door without another glance. Aydan lifted a hand toward the door, and I felt a hum beneath my skin as his wards reset themselves for the night.

"Was your day as terrible as mine?" he asked.

"Only the last few minutes," I replied, then held up my book. "I read for most of the day." Aydan glanced at the title and grinned.

"*Enchanted, Enchanting*?" He chuckled. "Where did you find *that*?"

"On a shelf in my room," I said defensively. "*I* rather enjoyed it."

"My apologies," he teased. "I'd never hope to insult you, my lady."

"What made your day so terrible?" I asked.

"Besides being stuck in a chamber with my father's council?" I pursed my lips as he added, "Only being the subject of every snide remark regarding past relations with mortals . . . I would have thought they'd have a better insult than *Wayward Prince* after all this time, but Lord Declan isn't exactly known for his creativity."

"Mortals?" I stood and set the book on the side table. "Why is Zathryan asking you to weigh in on issues with mortals? I thought the mortals here were loyal to the Crown."

"They were." Aydan sighed. "But generations of them have come and gone, and many of the families whose ancestors followed my father here to Ayzelle are now experiencing the same frustrations as those who led the last rebellion. My father has changed almost nothing and will not negotiate. The council tries to reel him in, but they're too scared of him to argue much."

"What will happen now?"

"For the next few days, I'll be in and out of meetings with the council, standing in until Irsa returns at the end of the week. With any luck we can keep the mortals at bay."

"Will the captain be monitoring me the whole time?" I asked.

"Unfortunately." Aydan replied as he removed his jacket and made it vanish. "But if I can play along with my father and quell this unrest, he may be convinced to lift his hold on us." Excitement fluttered in my chest.

"We're going to Sylvanna?"

"With any luck, yes. But let's not get ahead of ourselves. I'm starved. All they ever serve at those meetings is *mutton.*" He grimaced. "Let's get ready for dinner."

That night, after Aydan and I had had our fill of Zale's venison pie, we sat at the table, drinking wine while I practiced the magic Aydan had shown me and he told me more about the grand council and the troubles with the mortals. They were represented by a handful of men from the surrounding villages and had submitted a list of requests to Zathryan and his council with the signatures of nearly two thousand mortals in and around Ayzelle.

"I didn't know there were two thousand mortals in Medeisia," I said.

"Oh yes." Aydan unbuttoned the collar of his shirt and leaned back in his chair. It was nice to see him so genuinely casual. "It was only a thousand or so that followed my father from the capital after the Rebellion, but there are mortal populations scattered throughout the continent. Entire mortal-only villages exist in Xarynn, and I hear in the lands beyond the sea there are mortal republics looking to ally themselves with sorcerers, if they can get equal footing with us. There is a lot of opportunity for benefit there. I hope I can make my father see that."

"What does the council say?" I asked as I practiced creating balls of light in my hand, letting each one go out just as I produced another in the opposite palm, never letting the room get dark.

"The grand council is too scared to challenge him much beyond gentle suggestion. He hasn't had a proper Cabinet in decades. The only person he will listen to is Irsa. I've already sent word to her to return early. We'll see if she responds. In the meantime, I'm willing to challenge him, but I must tread carefully and not push him too much. If he feels his power being threatened, he'll shut down the meetings and ruin the opportunity to negotiate."

"His power being threatened? Why have a council at all if they only tell you what you want to hear?"

"From what I've heard, my father has become increasingly difficult to reason with in recent years. Immediately after the Heirs' Duel and my assignment to the emissary position, there was a change in him—more defensive of his hold to the throne. It got worse after the Rebellion, and apparently came to a head following Lord Ronan's execution. He was the only one who could truly challenge my father's decisions. Aside from Irsa, that is." Aydan drained his glass and it vanished.

"Couldn't Irsa step in?" I asked, giving up on my light practice and simply sending both balls to the ceiling to illuminate the room. Aydan looked impressed by my work but shook his head at my question.

"Even if she wanted to, no." He drummed his fingers on the arm of his chair, "Once one takes the title of Crown Prince or

Princess, they are magically bound to follow the anointed monarch's orders." A knot formed in my stomach at the thought of what might happen if this negotiation went poorly. "Oh, I nearly forgot," Aydan added, reaching into his inner jacket pocket and pulling out a glass bottle. "I spoke to my favorite healer today, Jemma, and she gave me this for your sleepwalking."

"Is that what we're calling it?" I asked, eyebrows raised as I took the bottle and examined it. It was filled with a lavender liquid and had a tiny dropper in the lid.

"I figured that would be a better than telling her about your extra abilities," he replied. "It would be a good idea not to mention that to just anyone, by the way."

"You've already said that. I wasn't exactly planning on handing out a newsletter."

"Just thought I'd mention it," he quipped, drumming his fingers again. "Jemma said a drop under your tongue at bedtime should stop you from sleepwalking. Two will stop the nightmares as well, but you won't have any dreams at all."

"Fine by me." I pocketed the bottle. "Thank you for that."

"My pleasure." He looked at the clock. "It's getting late. I'm afraid I'll have to call it a night."

"I'd better do the same," I said, moving to stand. Aydan followed suit. "Will I see you in the morning?"

"Most likely. The council isn't meeting until lunchtime."

"Good," I said. Aydan smirked.

"Did you miss me?"

"Shut up." I pushed the chair in sharply and Aydan's grin grew. I strode down the corridor to my room and his laughter followed me to my door.

"Good night, Shaye," he called after me. Heat rose in my cheeks and my fingers sparked at the teasing in his voice. I closed the door and ignored it.

Chapter Fourteen

Jemma's tincture worked. I did not have a single dream that night; instead, I'd sunk into a comforting pool of blackness and didn't come out until Elise entered the room to wake me the next morning, offering to help me dress for the day. She was pushing the final pins into my hair when we heard abrupt voices coming from the front of the chambers. We exchanged a glance and both stood.

Aydan was talking to someone in the foyer.

"—cannot arrive unannounced at my private residence." He said in a voice I didn't recognize. The voice, I realized, of the Wayward Prince—dripping with the sort of lazy authority that the court had come to expect from him. As I approached, I saw that he stood before Captain Whittaker.

"Your Highness, with all due respect, I take my orders from His Majesty," said the captain. "He has ordered me to stand guard over your household while you assist in the council, and to let you know that they are starting an hour earlier than scheduled."

Aydan paused; eyes narrowed. Then he twisted and said, "Apologies, my lady, but it seems I must postpone our meeting." He turned back to the captain, "Captain Whittaker, you may take your orders from my father, but let me make one thing clear—if you spend your time here trying to intimidate, interrogate, or otherwise harass the members of my household, I will personally see to it that your life becomes very difficult." He stared deeply into the captain's eyes, and the captain, to his credit, held the prince's gaze. Aydan turned to me, sketched a bow, and was gone. The captain was watching me now. His icy blue eyes bore through me, and I tried not to look intimidated, instead turning my back on him as I retreated to the kitchen.

I spent the day in between the kitchen and Aydan's study. Not reading—I'd finished *Enchanted, Enchanting* the previous night after dinner while I waited for the tincture to kick in. No, today I wanted to practice my magic, and see what I could do without instruction. I started with the handful of skills Aydan had taught me. Then, I decided to stack books on his desk. Willing the action, I gestured for the top shelf and waved my hand toward the desk to force the book to stack itself where I told it to. The volume wound up lying about eight inches from where I'd intended it to, but it was *there*, without me touching it. I continued, making a stack that was ten books high before I started shivering and I realized the fireplace was completely cold. I bent to add some fresh wood when I paused. An idea crossed my mind, and I wasn't sure it would work.

Using all the intention, all the will in my being, I closed my eyes and pushed both hands in the direction of the fireplace. Power tingled beneath my skin, startlingly warm and nearly alive. I faltered, and nearly let it go when I realized the warmth wasn't just coming from me. I opened my eyes to a roaring fire in the hearth. I loosed a satisfied sigh, and grinned to myself, feeling quite a bit of pride in my own progress.

Such pride was short-lived, however.

When Aydan returned that evening and dismissed Captain Whittaker, I carefully asked, "Can I show you something?" I led him to the study, where I had put the fire out before Aydan was due home that day.

I repeated what I had done earlier, and another huge grin split across my face when fire crackled on the hearth once again. Aydan took a step back, his eyes widened slightly.

"What do you think?" I asked, wilting a little when he wasn't nearly as excited as I was.

"That is . . . impressive, Shaye," he replied carefully.

"Have I upset you?" I asked.

"No," he said. "Just . . . maybe keep the fire to yourself for now." I opened my mouth to ask why, but Aydan quickly excused himself to prepare for dinner. He retreated to his bedroom, leaving me standing alone and confused in the study.

The next two days were more of the same. Aydan would leave early to attend meetings with the grand council while Captain Whittaker stood at his post in the foyer, watching the servants and me go about our day until Aydan returned for dinner. Irsa had finally returned from Xarynn and was assisting in the negotiations with the would-be rebels.

On the third day, I was sitting in the parlor, flipping through an uninteresting book about cheesemaking, debating whether I should go retrieve *Enchanted, Enchanting* from my bedroom, even though I'd already finished it twice over. I felt the captain's gaze burning into me from across the room, so I sighed and placed the book in my lap.

"What?" I asked.

"Nothing, Miss Eastly, just keeping an eye on things."

"That's bull and you know it," I snapped. "So, out with it. What does the king want from me? What does he want to know?"

"It's not hard to reach the conclusion that you have some connection to Sylvanna, Miss Eastly." The captain stared down his nose at me. "His Majesty wants to know what it is."

"And if I told you that I didn't even know that I was a sorcerer, or who my father was until the prince brought me here?" I asked. "Let alone have a connection to Sylvanna, on the other side of the continent?"

"I would not be inclined to believe such a story unless I was presented with sufficient evidence."

"So I'm guilty until proven innocent, then?" The captain didn't answer. I glared at him. "How did you even come to be a captain? You can't be older than, what, twenty-five? And a mortal. Why would the king ever give you such a position?"

"It wasn't *given*, it was earned," he snapped. "Every man in my family has served in the King's Guard for two hundred years. My great-grandfather saved King Zathryan's life the night of the Rebellion at the Grand Palace. I have been working since childhood toward this position."

"What is your first name?"

"Why?"

"It seems I'll be here awhile, since I don't have any information you want." I opened my book and began aimlessly flipping through the pages again. "I'm curious to know the name of the man openly spying on me." He continued glaring. "Suit yourself." I stood and placed the book on the table, then started toward the kitchen.

"It's Stefan," he said, but I didn't look back as the door swung shut behind me.

An hour later, I was covered in flour, kneading away at a ball of dough by myself in the kitchen. I'd asked Zale and Tory if I could have some privacy and got to work making bread. I hadn't been able to cook a thing since I'd left Nautia and punching into a risen dough ball was all I could think to do to relieve some of the aggression I felt following my discussion with Captain Whittaker. I scattered some flour on the tabletop and pushed and pulled at the dough until it stopped sticking.

"Rough day?"

I looked up and Aydan, dressed in a black tunic and matching pants, was leaning against the doorframe with his arms crossed, watching me as I continued to beat the dough.

"Oh, just more of the same," I said. "Being treated like a monster, ready to strike at any moment, so I *must* be kept in my cage until my keepers decide what to do with me." I threw the dough back into the bowl and gripped the edge of the table. "I'm never going to get out of here." In an instant, Aydan was standing next to me.

"We're leaving, Shaye," he said. "Very soon. We reached an agreement today. A treaty will be drafted before the end of the week."

"What? That's . . . that's wonderful," I said, breathless. "How?"

"Zathryan finally saw the benefit of negotiation, it seems." Aydan laughed lightly. "I never thought I'd see the day. He came to the council chambers today and announced that he wanted a treaty and granted the mortals most of their demands. He had to deny a few, of course, but—"

"The captain has indicated that the king wants more from me," I told him, hope deflated following my conversation with the open spy in Aydan's foyer. "That he thinks I'm working for Sylvanna. He said that I'm not going anywhere until the king is satisfied with his investigation."

"My father has told me himself, today, that you and I will be released upon signing the treaty." Aydan brushed a stray curl from my face before taking my hands in his own. Heat flooded my cheeks, and my chest grew tight, "I know. I know this has been unbearable, and it's my fault. I am sorry you've had to endure so much these past weeks. It's all coming to an end. We'll soon be in Sylvanna, and your new life can begin."

"Would you think less of me if I told you I was a little scared to go to Sylvanna?" I asked.

"Of course I wouldn't." He squeezed my hands. "Though, if you are trying to tell me you'd rather I drop you off in Xarynn, I'll have to decline the request. Kenna will have my head if she doesn't meet you soon."

"Will they like me, your friends?"

"What's not to like?" He smiled down at me for a moment before releasing me. He looked at the table, and my mess of flour and dough. "Can you teach me?" he asked.

"You want to know how to make bread?"

"I've never cooked," he replied, removing his jacket and throwing it onto a nearby chair. "Unless you count warming rations on a campfire." He rolled up his sleeves and reached for the bowl. I snatched it away.

"If you're going to learn, you're going to do it right," I said. "This is nearly ready to go in the oven. You're going to start from the beginning. Get a clean bowl."

Aydan's eyes sparkled and a grin spread across his face as he turned to look for a bowl in the cupboard.

Aydan and I spent the rest of the evening in the kitchen as I taught him how to make a loaf of bread, and he told me about Sylvanna, and what I should expect when he could finally show me the city. We talked about Gideon, and I told him more stories about my childhood in Nautia while he told me stories about misadventures he'd had while in the army. Halfway through waiting for the dough to rise, Aydan opened a bottle of wine and by the time the loaf was ready to slice we were both slightly drunk and covered in flour. We spent the rest of the night talking and laughing as we ate his creation with leftover cheeses and fruit from the day before.

It was well past midnight when Aydan walked me to my bedroom and bid me good night by kissing me swiftly on my cheek. I hoped that he didn't see me blushing in the dim light of the orbs Elise left on the ceiling before I stepped into the room and quickly shut the door behind me. Catchfly lay sleeping on her pillow and I sighed, realizing how tired I was.

After a much-needed bath, I took my tincture and crawled into bed, excited for the next few days to pass. Of course Captain Whittaker would be trying to get into my head; he was irritated that I was not intimidated by his presence, so he was trying to upset me. *Just a few more days,* I thought as sleep began to overtake me, and I would finally be free to start a whole new life.

Chapter Fifteen

Hours later, I was torn from sleep by the sounds of crashing and screams from somewhere in the castle. I sat straight up, fumbling to my feet in the pitch black of my bedroom until I formed a ball of light and sent it to the ceiling. The door flew open and Aydan rushed in, hands and arms consumed by blue light. He was breathing hard and sweat beaded at his forehead.

"You need to hide," he said.

"What's happening?"

"We've been fooled. The mortals have infiltrated the castle. They have silver, they're slaughtering courtiers in their beds." He crossed the room in two strides and peered through the curtain. "Our forces are assembling as we speak. I'm going to join them." My eyes widened and I opened my mouth to protest, but Aydan stopped me. "Get dressed. Stay here, in your room. Elise and the others will be here too, they know what to do. I'll be back soon."

"Aydan, don't go—"

"People need help." He placed a hand on my cheek, and I felt the wards strengthen around me. Then, as quickly as he arrived, he effuged from the spot in front of me.

For an instant I stood frozen, then I flung open the doors of my wardrobe and threw on the first dress my fingers touched before running to the window. I could hear yelling and clashing of metal against metal mixed with explosions of magic, and as I peered around the curtain, my heart dropped into my stomach.

It was a full-fledged battle.

The mortal forces clearly had the element of surprise. Medeisian soldiers were fighting to form lines, but it was too late.

Weapons clashed at all angles. Utter chaos. I spotted the captain—Stefan—taking on two mortal soldiers himself, roaring as he brought down his sword, cutting through the air, through flesh, blood spattering his skin and armor. On the other side of the yard, a blue flash erupted. King Zathryan himself stood on his castle grounds, engulfed in light. Aydan and Irsa stood on either side of him, aflame as well. They worked in tandem, the blue glow soon turning into what looked like lightning as the three royals, all at once, shot their power forward into the oncoming mortal forces. Men shrieked and fell where they stood.

I watched with my hand at my throat. Irsa shouted something, pointing toward the castle. Both Aydan and Zathryan nodded and she effuged away. They turned back to the field and began knocking soldiers out of the way with their power. Even from my window, I could see Aydan faltering. He'd told me once during our lessons that this power, the power that lay only in the royal bloodline, tired him more quickly than other uses of his magic. Like a drain on his life force.

A sword appeared in his hand and Aydan swung at a charging man who, by his ornate helmet, looked to be a commander of the mortal army. He was well matched and the two carried on their fight for three terrifying clashes before Aydan finally shot him down with the lightning. Aydan yelled something at his father and the two stood shoulder to shoulder to face what remained of the mortal forces descending upon the battlefield with weapons raised. The blue light once again began to form, not at their hands, but within the chests of both men, expanding and crackling like a violent storm until—

Light exploded from them in every direction, and what remained of the attacking forces became nothing but mist on the wind. Aydan hit his knees, gasping for air. Then he turned, and when he looked to his father, my eyes followed.

King Zathryan lay sprawled on the ground, an arrow sticking out of his chest. Aydan was at his side in an instant, pulling the arrow out in a single motion, but when he examined the tip, his eyes went wide. He gathered his father in his arms and effuged away without a trace.

I stepped back from the window and turned to see all of Aydan's servants standing behind me in their bedclothes. Tory and Isolde held hands while Zale gripped his husband's shoulder. Elise was stone-faced and pale.

"He's okay," I said with a confidence I didn't feel. "You'd better get dressed." Elise nodded and swept from the room while the rest of them trailed out more slowly. Once they were gone, I started gathering some of my belongings—an extra dress, fresh stockings, a shawl, a few toiletries, and the now dog-eared copy of *Enchanted, Enchanting*—and threw them in a knapsack I found in the bottom of the wardrobe. Catchfly stood by dutifully. Once I was satisfied, I set the bag on the floor by my bed, and the tiny kitten curled herself on top of it. I sat between it and the window with my back to the wall, waiting for whatever came next.

I didn't realize I was asleep, until I felt myself being shaken.

Aydan crouched before me, hands on my shoulders. His shirt and hands were caked in blood. His fathers or his own, I couldn't know. I scrambled to my feet.

"What's happening? Are you all right? Are you hurt?"

"I'm not hurt," he said tightly.

"I saw, from the window. Is—"

"Irsa is dead," he choked. "She fell after she left my father and I to help inside the castle." My heart sank and I reached for Aydan's hand.

"Aydan, I'm so sorry—"

"My father was shot with a silver-tipped arrow." He seemed to struggle to get the words out, "He lives, for now. His healers tell me he will not linger for long."

"What—"

"The king has named me Crown Prince, Shaye." Silver lined Aydan's eyes now. "He has ordered me back to Sylvanna." I nodded.

"Okay," I breathed, reaching for the knapsack. "We can go when you're ready—"

"No," Aydan took my hands and squeezed them. His breathing was shallow, and his palms were clammy as he explained, "My father has lifted his hold on me. Just me. I'm supposed to have gone already, but I-I couldn't just leave without—" It dawned on me what he was trying to say.

"You're leaving me here?" I asked in horror.

"Only— only for a short while," he gasped. "The healers, they say it will not be long. They say they can't keep him going longer than a week or two." I stared. The breathing, the cold sweat. I remembered now what Aydan had told me a few days before, how the heir to the throne was bound to follow the king's orders. He was disobeying, to say goodbye.

"What do I do?" I gripped his hands as they held mine. "What will they do to me if you're not here?"

"Nothing," he said firmly. "The wards on this place are strong. Your blood shield still stands. Elise and the others will stay with you. You'll stay in these chambers and wait, and when the healers can't keep my father alive anymore, I'll return for you."

And Aydan would be King of Medeisia.

I looked at him. His breathing was labored. "I'm so sorry, Shaye," he whispered.

"It's okay. I'll be okay." My voice was shaking. Tears began to spill over onto my cheeks. Aydan wiped one away and held his hand there for a moment.

"Two weeks," he said again. "I'll see you in two weeks." I closed my eyes as he bent down and kissed the top of my head. He let go of my hand, and when I opened my eyes, I saw that I was alone.

It took two days for the banging to begin on the door to the chambers.

First, it was just the voice of a single guardsman, knocking, ordering me to open the door. As hours, and then days passed, the banging increased, as they attempted to use various tools, then magic, and on the eighth day I heard a man call for a battering ram.

When it first began, Isolde had nearly fainted, but after a couple of days, we grew accustomed to it. I asked the servants to try and go about their days as normally as they could. At night, however, the banging continued, and we all decided to sleep in the same room, just in case.

Today was day ten, and with only a few more days until Aydan was expected to return, I could not help but feel slightly more cheerful than I had since our holdout began. That is, until I heard the commotion outside the front door. I walked to the foyer, and from what I could tell, the battering ram had started once again. Paired with it today was a blinding green light that poured in through the perimeter of the door. The wood splintered and I jumped, gasping. The air around me felt like it had begun to crack as well. It seemed that they had found the right person to break through Aydan's wards. I called out for Elise. She came quickly to my side, the other servants following close behind. The door rattled again as the battering ram hit. Dust fell from the ceiling. I gripped Elise's hand.

"You need to go," I said.

"My lady, I will not leave your side."

"You will," I looked over her shoulder at Zale, Tory, and Isolde as well, "You all will. Go back to Sylvanna."

"My lady—"

"The Crown Prince has blood-shielded me. I'll be all right. I cannot guarantee that you will be. Please, go home."

"Lady Shaye, we have been ordered by the Crown Prince—"

"To stand by my side and do my bidding?" Zale nodded. "Then this is an order: go home to Sylvanna. Let the Crown Prince know what has happened. I'll see you all in a few days. Now go."

The men each bowed deeply, with mumbles of "my lady," before they effuged from the chambers. The battering ram crashed into the door again, and I felt the wards come down completely. Isolde wrapped me in a tearful hug before disappearing. Elise looked at me and squeezed my hand once more before finally following my order, leaving me standing alone in the foyer. Catchfly appeared by my feet, and I scooped her into my arms just as the door came crashing to the ground.

Swords came first, then the guards who held them. They rushed in and surrounded me where I stood, my shoulders straight and Catchfly clutched to my chest. I refused to flinch.

Captain Whittaker marched toward me. "Miss Eastly." He nodded. "I've been instructed by His Majesty to escort you to your new quarters."

"And where would that be?" I asked coldly. "The dungeon?"

"Not quite. His Majesty has granted you mercy yet again. Follow me, please."

"Do I have a choice?"

"There's always a choice, Miss Eastly," I heard one of the guards say behind me as his sword poked into my back. "You just might not like the other option."

"Enough," the captain snapped at him. I scowled and marched forward, following the guards through the corridors whose paintings were now torn to shreds after the attack. The castle was still in disarray, as if the king would not allow repairs to begin until I had been captured.

I was led to a door, which the captain opened and entered. I stared until a guard nudged me forward, and I stepped into the tiny bedroom that would now apparently be mine.

"You will remain in this room unless someone comes to collect you. Meals will be left at the door three times per day. You'll be allowed to walk the grounds once per week, with an escort." I looked around at the dingy room. There were no windows along the bare, dark walls. There was a small stiff-looking bed in the corner topped with a thin, folded blanket, an empty table, and a chamber pot on the wall furthest from the bed. Not even the dignity of a bathroom. I turned back to the captain and was surprised to see his face filled with what looked almost like pity. He added quietly, "It was the best I could do."

I scowled. "You tried to help me?"

"It seemed like the right thing to do. The king . . . he is not well. I can check on you, make sure you have the things you need—"

"I'll be fine," I snapped. Aydan would be back in a few days. Catchfly and I could handle a small room.

"Fine, then," the captain replied. He called to his men, "Move along." And then left the room, shutting the door behind him.

I gathered Catchfly into my lap and crawled into bed, ready to await the death of the king.

Part Two

Long Live the King

One Year Later

Chapter Sixteen

I could see my breath on the air as I plunged my scouring brush back into the bucket of water to my left. It had taken nearly the whole day, but I was finally coming to the end of my task: scrubbing the floors of the great hall by hand. Cleaning these floors would take any other sorcerer servant half a second, but I hadn't been permitted to use magic since the attacks on Ayzelle. Each time my water became too filthy, the guard assigned to me would escort me to the servants' quarters, where I would dump the soiled water and refill from the pump on the wall before carrying it back across the castle. The work was tedious and tore at my hands, but there were much worse ways I could spend my days.

We were fast approaching the first anniversary of the mortal attacks on Ayzelle. The first anniversary of the death of Crown Princess Irsa, and the onset of King Zathryan's condition. He had not left his chambers since that night, and now spent his days in bed, cursing the mortals who dared lay siege to his capital. "Two weeks," the healers had said after the attack, and yet he lingered, his commands carried out by the grand council and the few courtiers who remained. Many had perished that night, and more than half of the survivors had fled for their family homes, no longer finding safety in the castle.

I sighed and tossed the brush into the bucket for the final time before hauling myself to my feet. "I'm finished," I said to the guard. He grunted, just enough to acknowledge me, and followed as I made my way to a door in the wall and pushed to reveal a hidden corridor. Several of them had been built into the castle upon its erection, to allow servants to come and go without disturbing the courtiers. Couldn't interrupt such important work as standing around and gossiping, after all.

Over the drain, I rinsed the grime from the bucket and brush and tossed them into a closet, all with the guard on my heels. It wasn't hard to see why none of the other servants would speak to me; none could get near enough to do so. Not with the constant escort, anyway. A few would offer tight-lipped smiles if they made eye contact, but quickly turned their heads if anyone saw. I couldn't blame them. I was tainted.

The Redfern name hung over me like a shadow, and the prince's attention last year had done me no favors either. Whispers followed wherever I went, especially when I was assigned to work in the private quarters of nobles and courtiers. Some would sit and smirk as I scrubbed their floors and changed their linens, while others followed behind me, knocking things over as I straightened them or simply pondering aloud why I had not yet been executed. I often wondered the same thing.

I turned to my guard—a tall, fair-haired boy today—and asked if I could return to my room for the night. He nodded and left without a word, seemingly as eager to be done with this assignment as I was. This was a recent privilege, walking alone at the end of the day. Up until now every second of time spent outside my tiny bedroom had been supervised. The king himself had apparently granted this small kindness, and I was not going to have it revoked by openly questioning his motives. Despite the freedom, I moved swiftly along the path to my room, keeping myself in view of at least three people the whole way. Any missing time could turn into an accusation that would land me back in an interrogation cell, or worse.

Finally, I shut myself inside my chambers and leaned back against the door with a sigh. The room was small and somewhat bare, though I had managed to collect a few trinkets to keep myself from staring at nothing but empty stone walls. I was permitted to pick flowers on my weekly walks around the grounds, and now several wreathes of dried dandelions and sunroots hung around the room. They were nothing compared to the vibrant vases of fresh-cut blossoms of the prince's chambers, or even the more modest arrangements from my home garden, but it was better than nothing. The room also contained a wardrobe and a bed, from upon which an enormous gray cat with rusty orange eyes stared at me expectantly.

"Hello, Catchfly," I said sweetly. "Have you been working hard today? Are you just absolutely starved?" A small meow escaped her as I reached into my apron pocket and pulled out a folded handkerchief. She jumped lightly from the bed, an impressive feat given her size, and began weaving herself in and out of my legs. I crouched and set the treat before her, a few pieces of bacon I'd swiped during breakfast, and scratched her fluffy, gray head before turning to wash my face at my makeshift vanity: a small table with a bowl and pitcher and a tiny hand mirror I'd propped against a stack of books.

I was patting my face dry with a clean cloth when a sharp knock came. Catchfly growled but went back to her bacon when I shushed her.

"Come in," I called out. The door opened and a familiar, friendly face peered around it. I gasped. "You're back!" Two steps to cross the room and I threw my arms around the neck of Stefan Whittaker.

"It was only two days." He chuckled, returning the hug with a quick squeeze before pulling away. "I told you, we just needed to drop in on Xarynn and come straight back. How have you been? You look like you had a long day." I rolled my eyes.

"You really know how to compliment a woman. I was scrubbing the great hall, so excuse my appearance."

Stefan's brow furrowed. "Did they light a fire for you?"

"You know they didn't," I said. "They're not going to waste firewood on me."

"I'll talk to His Majesty," Stefan said before bending down to pat Catchfly's head. She swatted at him. "You'll like me someday." He laughed lightly. Catchfly retreated under the bed in response. Stefan sat atop it, motioning for me to follow suit, and I slipped off my shoes to settle next to him. He pulled my aching feet into his lap to examine their condition. My shoes were nearly worn through and pinched my feet horribly, causing sores and blisters where the rough material constantly rubbed. I had no money or access to a cobbler to buy a new pair, and no way to let the wounds heal. Stefan had been discreetly making inquiries on my behalf but hadn't had any luck.

My ankle too was an absolute mess. After the mortal attack last year, I had been interrogated about my suspected involvement in the mortal siege. When they found that I had committed no provable crime, I was returned to this room, and Stefan was charged with locking a silver cuff on my ankle. Instead, in an act of kindness, he had locked a cuff of steel around me, polished well enough to shine if anyone caught a glimpse. So far no one had come close enough to notice, but a year straight of metal chafing my skin had rendered it raw. Stefan had been providing me with balms and ointments stealthily procured from the castle healers, which I suspected was preventing some much more serious problems.

"You probably shouldn't mention the fire to the king," I said after a few minutes, pulling my feet away and tucking them underneath myself. "It's really not that bad, and I wouldn't want to . . . aggravate his condition."

"I don't want you freezing to death."

"I'm hard to kill," I teased. He frowned.

It was true. I'd learned only too well the type of damage a sorcerer's body could take, and it would be a long time before I ever forgot. The memories rang in my ears:

"Don't hurt her."

"Leave. Now."

"Please . . . no more . . ."

"I'm sorry."

"I'm sorry—"

"Shaye." I heard Stefan say my name and shook away the dread in my chest.

"Hm?" I tilted my head, pretending I'd simply been daydreaming. Stefan worried about me enough as it was.

"I asked if you wanted to take your walk tonight," he said. As Captain of the Guard, Stefan oversaw my weekly walks around the grounds—the only time I was allowed to go outside. It was during these walks that Stefan first tried to talk to me like a person instead of a prisoner. It wasn't until after the interrogations stopped that I listened to anything he had to say.

"I don't think so," I sighed, disappointed. "As much as I'd like to get out, I don't want to hurt my feet further and not be able to sleep tonight." Sleep was my one escape from the hell of my waking hours, aside from talking with Stefan and the little bit of reading I was able to do.

"In that case, I need to head out for a while so I'm not here when your dinner arrives." I understood. The Captain of the Guard lounging on the bed of the Crown's most dangerous prisoner would not bode well.

"Will you be back tonight?" I asked.

"I'll try," he said. "I have an audience with His Majesty to report on the Xarynn visit, so that may take some time. If I'm not back in"—he looked the small clock on my table—"two hours, go ahead and sleep. I'll see you tomorrow." We stood, and Stefan hugged me briefly again before he left. When the door clicked shut behind him, I breathed out slowly, taking in the silence.

It was true that I'd come to rely on Stefan in the past year. Despite my initial distaste for him, the captain had not only become my ally, but a cherished friend. His loyalty to King Zathryan ran deep, and although it made my blood boil to even hear the man's name, I knew Stefan was doing his best to help me where he could. He made sure that Catchfly and I both ate regularly, that we had the things we needed.

But it wasn't only that. Stefan and I talked for hours most nights, about our families, our childhoods, our dreams for the future. For me, that mostly meant dreaming of a day when I could leave Ayzelle and live a life outside of Zathryan's grasp. Stefan, on the other hand, didn't think much beyond his career as captain. He hadn't always wanted to follow in his father's footsteps and become a soldier but did so in his honor when the last Captain Whittaker died in service to the Crown. He joined the Guard on his eighteenth birthday and quickly climbed the ranks, becoming the youngest Captain of the Guard in Medeisian history at age twenty-two. He'd held his position for nearly six years, and the ambush that killed Princess Irsa was the first time anyone had been able to breach Stefan's guard system. When he told me about it, months later, the devastation on his face was enough to break one's heart.

While I waited for food, I decided to read. My now tattered copy of *Enchanted, Enchanting* lay under my bed, waiting for me to continue it for what was now the fifteenth time. Books were hard for Stefan to acquire for me since only the nobility were permitted to use the library. But he had managed to sneak into my previous quarters sometime after the Guard and Ayzellen Council had torn through the place, finding *Enchanted, Enchanting*, along with a couple of history books. The histories were set aside in favor of the romance novel most nights. I got enough of Medeisian court during the day.

My dinner arrived—a sad, watery excuse for beef stew and a slice of stale bread—and I ate it as I read. After a while, I looked at the clock and found that it was nearing midnight. Stefan was not coming. I sighed and closed the book before calling Catchfly up to join me. Under my bed once again, I found the bottle of lavender liquid I'd been taking for nearly a year now, placed two drops beneath my tongue, and tried not to think of who gave me the tincture to begin with as I let sleep embrace me for the night.

Chapter Seventeen

The second I opened my eyes the next morning, I knew I was late. Catchfly lounged on the foot of the bed, staring at me. I leapt to my feet and muttered, "You could have woken me, you know," to her as I quickly dressed. Her response was to stand and stretch before turning the other way, curling into a ball and closing her eyes. I splashed some cold water on my face and tore a brush through my limp, tangled hair until it was manageable enough to braid. As I shoved my feet into those awful shoes, I told her, "You'll have to catch a mouse or something today." She didn't bother looking at me, but I could have sworn I saw her let loose a sigh as I practically ran out the door.

The normally busy corridor was empty. Maybe no one would notice my tardiness. There was no guard to escort me or assign me my duties, so I headed toward the servants' quarters, where perhaps someone was waiting for me. If not, Mr. Vyne, the steward, would have an assignment for me, I was sure. As I walked my normal path, it became clear that something unusual was happening. The corridors were all empty, not just the one near my room. No servants, no courtiers or noblemen to pause and curtsy to as they sneered in my direction. Instead, as I grew closer to the servants' quarters and thus the great hall, I heard the low rumble of dozens of voices trying to speak softly all at once.

I peeked inside, then carefully entered the hall, staying at the perimeter of the room. It was fuller than it had been since the king shut himself away, with likely every living person in the castle standing in unorganized clusters as they murmured to one another. They were all dressed finely, as if for a feast.

I spotted a group of women in aprons and weaved through the gaggles of noblemen and their gossiping wives. A young mortal servant named Amelia smiled tightly at me.

"Sorry to interrupt"—I nodded toward the others, who ignored me—"but what's going on?"

"Didn't you hear?" Amelia whispered. "King Zathryan has taken a turn for the worse."

"Oh," I said flatly. The king had taken many turns for the worse over the last year.

"That's what I said," Amelia continued, "but his healer, Jemma—well, she's friendly with my mother, and she—well, everyone knows she's just the *best* healer anyone could hope for. Once, when I was little, I fell out of a tree and broke my arm—"

"Sorry," I said, "what's happening with the *king*?"

Amelia lowered her voice. "He's asked for the Wayward Prince. A message was sent to Sylvanna this morning. The Crown Prince is on his way right now." I coughed and a cold sweat broke out on my forehead.

"Y-You're sure?" I asked. She nodded.

"A guardsman effuged over to Sylvanna this morning and delivered the message. The captain sent out notices to the rest of the castle." She gestured toward the doors on the other end of the great hall, behind the dais I'd once been presented to. They were opened and Stefan walked through, a somber look on his face. None of the courtiers took notice, so I bid Amelia farewell and approached to fall into step beside him.

"Is it true?" I murmured.

"Yes," he replied. "I'm sorry, I can't talk here." He picked up his pace and headed for some council member whose name I couldn't remember. I stopped and stood where I was, my stomach filling with a sort of cold dread while I debated if I should go back to my room for now.

But then the herald took a step into the hall and cried out, "His Royal Highness, Crown Prince Aydan of Medeisia, has arrived."

The crowded room fell silent, and in an instant, the courtiers and council members, nobles and servants, all scattered to the perimeter of the great hall. I found Amelia and her friends once again and positioned myself behind them. Standing on my toes to get a better look, I held my breath, sure I'd hear a pin if it fell to the floor. Several sets of footsteps echoed as they approached, then the Crown Prince entered the great hall, flanked by four people I had never seen.

He looked different.

His once shaggy hair was cropped short and neatly combed. He wore all black: a well-tailored jacket embroidered with Zathryan's winged lion crest in gold on the breast, fitted pants, and shining boots, with a short cape pinned to his shoulders. The Crown Prince's mouth was a hard line. He and his entourage stopped as Stefan stepped forward and bowed deeply.

"Your Highness, allow me to escort you to the king's—"

"I know where I'm going. Thank you, captain," he said curtly. "But please, join us. I know your presence is a comfort to my father." Stefan bowed again and fell into place behind them as they crossed the hall, eyes fixed forward as they made their way to the door on the other end. As soon as it shut, the crowd exploded into whispers.

My stomach knotted. I muttered something about breakfast as I pushed my way toward the exit, but no one so much as glanced at me. I left the hall and, for the first time, walked through the castle freely. I didn't quite know what to do with myself and wound up wandering the corridors in a daze until I found myself in the kitchens, where the cooks had not yet abandoned their posts to join the others. One of them was called Henry, a sorcerer with dark curls and deep dimples when he smiled. He wasn't smiling now, instead looking rather grim, but he picked up a plate when he saw me and piled it high before placing it in my hands and shooing me out of the kitchens.

I couldn't think of anything I'd rather do than lie in bed, so I headed back to my room and did just that. Once I'd returned to the familiarity of my quarters, I found that my stomach had settled, and I was grateful to have so much food in front of me. Catchfly was grateful for both the roast chicken and sliced ham I tossed to her. She ate greedily before coming to snoop around my plate for anything I'd left, which wasn't much. She pawed at it a few times and I relented, setting it on the floor for her to lick clean.

"You're disgusting," I said over her slurping. She ignored me. I spent the next few hours reading before I eventually fell asleep, napping for most of the afternoon. When I woke, there was still not a soul to be seen outside my door, so I returned to the great hall.

Everyone was still there. Tables with food and wine were set out, as if it were a party. It crossed my mind that for some, it very well might have been. All of us, however, were witnessing history. Medeisian kings didn't die often.

Another hour passed, and it was fully dark outside. I overheard some people say they might turn in for the night. Then the door opened.

Stefan marched out and stood in the center of the room, his face hardened and pale. And then he said, "The king is dead. Long live the King."

"Long live the King!" the courtiers echoed. My heart was in my throat. The hall fell silent once again as footsteps sounded, and the herald cried out:

"His Majesty, King Aydan of Medeisia."

Nearly in unison, the crowd dropped down to one knee. I peeked up and saw King Aydan approach Stefan, who knelt. Stefan unsheathed his sword and presented it to the new king.

"Your Majesty, I offer you the protection of my blade." His head remained low. "May it guard your body, your throne, and your realm, all the days of my life."

"Captain Whittaker, you served my father well, and I trust you will continue to do the same for me. You knelt before me a captain. Rise and face me as a lord of my court." Stefan stood, looking shocked when King Aydan shook his hand. The king turned his attention to the crowded, silent hall. "My father, King Zathryan, served Medeisia well. Tomorrow night we shall lay him to rest upon his pyre and honor his reign with a feast. Until then, I shall retire to my chambers." He did not look at anyone else before turning on his heel and walking back through the doors.

Chatter erupted in the hall as the nobles began gossiping. Some of the ladies cried quietly into handkerchiefs, comforting one another. I looked across the room at Stefan, who made eye contact with me for half a moment, looking bewildered. I turned to leave the hall, knowing he would get the message.

Back in my darkened room, I leaned against the door, smiling. Zathryan was finally dead.

I rubbed my hands together and willed a ball of light to form in my palm before sending it to the ceiling to illuminate the room. For the first time in a year, I was not scared of being found out. My heart fluttered, and Catchfly rubbed herself excitedly on my legs.

"It finally happened, Catchfly," I whispered. "He's finally gone." And *he* had returned. The door opened behind me, and I stopped trying to imagine what life would look like under the new king's reign. Stefan entered, grief-stricken.

"Hi," he croaked, and I wrapped my arms around him.

"Stef," I murmured. "I'm so sorry." A lie.

I pulled him down to the bed, where he lay his head on my shoulder. We stayed like that for a while, and whether he cried or not, I didn't see.

"Did you do that?" he asked suddenly. Stefan was pointing to the ceiling where my ball of light remained.

"Yes," I replied cautiously. He pushed himself off me.

"Are you *insane*?" he hissed. "Do you not remember what the consequences are for using magic?"

"I remember."

"Then why would you risk—"

"Because King Aydan taught me to use my magic in the first place." Stefan's brow furrowed. "He knows the truth about me, my intentions. He's not going to hold me to Zathryan's standards."

"You can't know how he'll be as king. That kind of power, it—sorcerer kings are not the same as lords and princes, Shaye. They're chosen by the gods."

"Maybe so, but King Aydan was . . ." I wanted to say *my friend*, but instead I said, "He was a fair man when I stayed with him—" We both jolted at a sudden knock. "Does anyone know you're here?" I asked softly.

"Of course not," he said. Another knock.

I motioned for him to stand away from the door as I stepped forward and grabbed the knob. I took a deep breath before cracking the door to peek through the opening. I gasped and threw it open wider.

Elise stood before me, her hands folded neatly in front of her. An eager smile spread across her face. She looked the same as I'd last seen her: golden-brown hair pinned neatly at the nape of her neck; dress crisply ironed. Tonight, she wore no apron, but had a small golden brooch in the shape of a winged lion pinned to her front.

"Elise," I breathed. "I-I can't believe it's you."

"Good evening, my lady." She smiled. "It's lovely to see you again." She glanced at Stefan, who had emerged from his corner, then back at me. "I am so sorry to interrupt. However, I have been sent here to ask if you might feel up to an audience with His Majesty."

I swallowed. "He wants to see me?"

"Yes, my lady, if you're not otherwise occupied."

"I'm not. I mean, I am available, that is. To meet with His Majesty." I gripped the door. "Could I have just a moment to freshen up?"

"Certainly, my lady." Elise inclined her head. "I'll wait in the corridor. Take your time."

"Thank you."

"Why does the king want to see you?" Stefan asked the second the door shut.

"How would I know?" I replied, sitting at my vanity. I splashed a little of the cold water on my face and patted it dry.

"I don't understand," Stefan continued, then chewed the inside of his cheek. "Zathryan isn't even cold yet and the king wants to see you privately."

"Well," I said, wrapping my hair back into a long braid, "I'll be sure to tell you all about our mundane conversation when I return." I stood and turned toward the door, but Stefan gripped my wrist.

"Be careful, Shaye," he warned. "He's not the Wayward Prince you thought you knew—he's a king now." I took my hand back.

"I'll be fine. I'll see you later." I opened the door and joined Elise in the corridor.

Chapter Eighteen

Elise led me through a servants' passage to the north end of the castle, as the great hall was still crowded and she didn't want to cause me any discomfort.

"Thanks for that," I told her. The idea of those people watching me enter the new king's private chambers mere hours after his arrival made my blood run cold.

I'd never been allowed past the doors leading to the king's chambers, let alone inside the dwelling. Similar to the private residence of the prince, it was intended to be a family home within the castle and not to be entered unless by direct invitation. Zathryan and Irsa had lived there alone together for more than a century. Part of me felt sorry for the late king, mourning his dead daughter while fighting for his life, surrounded by servants and guards, yet utterly alone. Just a small part.

We arrived at the chamber door, which matched the ornately carved doors to the great hall and to the chambers I'd stayed in all those months ago. Elise reached out to push one, and it opened without hesitation.

"His Majesty reworked the wards so I could come and go as needed," she explained as she guided me through the door.

The foyer of the king's chambers was grandly decorated, the walls painted a dark shade of green and covered in ancient, beautiful portraits. I had seen the works of many skilled painters throughout the castle since my arrival, and not one of them came close to what I saw here. It was hard to contain my awe as I looked around, trying to study each one as I passed.

"There's more in the parlor, if you'd like to follow me, my lady," Elise said, gesturing in the other direction. I followed, craning my neck to see the frames that sat up high, some nearly at the ceiling.

In the parlor, as promised, dozens of paintings filled the walls of the enormous room. Where the foyer had been portraits, I assumed of long-dead members of the royal line, here the walls were covered in landscapes. I looked around at the other décor: the beautiful furniture, the extravagant pottery and floral arrangements that covered every table. I suddenly felt very underdressed.

"If you'll excuse me, my lady, I'll go and tell His Majesty that you've arrived." She curtsied and left me there alone.

I couldn't shake my nerves. I paced the parlor twice, sat on one of the sofas, then quickly stood when I realized it was probably not polite to sit in a king's presence.

Swift footsteps echoed from the corridor where Elise had disappeared. I watched expectantly, assuming she was returning to collect me and bring me to—

Aydan himself appeared in the parlor, walking both quickly and restrained, like a child whose mother told him to stop running indoors. I took a step toward him, then another, and met him in the middle of the room. Gone was the hardened expression I had seen in the great hall, replaced with the soft eyes I remembered and a half smile as he greeted me.

"Shaye," he said. "It is . . . very good to see you."

I jolted, remembering myself, and curtsied. "Your Majesty." He scoffed.

"Very funny," he said. Then, realizing I wasn't joking, added, "You know how I feel about titles."

"You're the king," I offered as explanation.

"I'm still just Aydan." His face didn't change, but I felt his mood shift to concern. "Are you—erm, how are you? Are you all right?"

"I'm fine." I wiped my hands on my skirt, but it didn't do anything to help the heat growing beneath them. "This is all just very strange," I admitted.

He chuckled darkly. "I understand. Here." He walked over to a nearby table which held wine and glasses and poured one for each of us.

"Thank you." I accepted it and drank deeply. I hadn't tasted wine in some time. "Why did you make Stefan a lord?" I blurted. I expected Aydan to laugh, but instead he raised an eyebrow.

"He and the rest of the Guard made it clear they were loyal to my father. I needed to ensure they are also loyal to the Crown. The captain presented his sword to me in front of every courtier in Ayzelle. The rest of the Guard will follow his lead. It seemed like a logical choice." He drank from his own glass. "You call him Stefan now." It was not a question. I flushed.

"We've developed a friendship in the last few months."

"I see." He paused, and seemed to be studying me as I stood before him.

I looked around again at the paintings. "These are lovely."

"They are. As soon as I'm settled in here, these will all be taken down and placed in the public galleries of Medeisia."

"You don't like them?"

"I love them," he said, "but my father had a bad habit of keeping beautiful things locked away. These have been here for more than a century now. The people deserve to see them." I nodded and he followed my gaze to a particularly simple piece: a field of purple wildflowers. "Do you like that one?"

"I do."

"I'll make sure it goes somewhere you can see it often, then." He took another drink, then asked, "Would you like to meet my friends?"

Aydan led me down hall, further into his new home. At the end we met an oak door, and I heard voices chatting away happily on the other side. The king pushed it open, revealing another huge, lavishly decorated room. The walls were a creamy shade of white that, despite the lack of windows, when paired with the high ceiling made this room appear much brighter than the foyer and parlor. On one end was an enormous wooden table, long enough to seat at least twelve people. On the other was a sitting area with plush furniture arranged around a fireplace, a mirror of the parlor room outside. Lounging in a high-backed armchair was one of the men who had accompanied Aydan into the great hall. He was sharply dressed, still wearing the black ensemble he'd arrived in. It was quite like Aydan's, minus the embroidered breast. Golden hair fell to his shoulders with half of it tied back into a knot, and he was laughing, a low, warm sound, while one of the women from their entourage stood near a table filled with decanters and glasses, pouring from a bottle of amber liquor.

I was immediately self-conscious of my old, worn-down dress and frizzy braid. Her black hair was a mass of tight, shiny coils that lay down her back, with the front pulled away from her face with gold pins. Her slate gray gown was simple and elegant, with sleeves trimmed in white lace that stood out against her dark skin. I watched as she rolled her eyes at the blond man's laughter and shook her head.

"You can*not* beat her," she said, handing him a tumbler.

"Of course I can, I'll show you tomorrow." He took a drink. "You know she won't turn me down."

"That's because Kenna delights in your suffering." She drank as well. Aydan cleared his throat and they both looked up, surprised.

"Aydan darling, who would win in an arm-wrestling match, me or Kenna?" The man recovered first.

"Kenna. Every time." The blond looked deeply offended, while the woman laughed. Aydan gestured to the pair. "Shaye, this is Gerridan Hollick, my oldest friend and newly appointed emissary." I inclined my head in greeting. "This is Lady Shaye Eastly."

"Just Shaye," I corrected as I fiddled with the now empty wineglass in my hands.

"Glad to meet you, Shaye," Gerridan replied before bowing his head. The woman approached and took my glass from me.

"May I?" The corners of her eyes crinkled as a wide, warm smile spread across her face.

"I, um, yes—thank you," I said, even though she was already pouring. She brought it back to me filled, and I smiled and took a sip as Aydan spoke again.

"Princess Hannele is a strategy expert and will be working closely with my generals," he said. Upon hearing her title, I swallowed and coughed, curtsying quickly. I had allowed a princess to serve *me*. Aydan and Gerridan were chuckling—not at me, but at the look on Princess Hannele's face as she shoved Aydan's arm. He laughed and batted her away. I could only gape.

"Don't *do* that!" Hannele scolded. Then to me, "My family has not held any real power in centuries. The title is a formality."

"Quite the high-ranking formality," I observed. Gerridan smirked while Hannele glared at him.

"My grandfather aided Solandis in her rebellion and turned against his brother Niklaus. Solandis allowed his line to keep the title and some lands . . . I'm sure it's more complicated than that, but it's been a few decades since anyone told me the whole story." She paused to drink.

"So, you're both from Sylvanna?" I asked. The pair nodded.

"We serve on the council," said Hannele.

"Or we did," Gerridan said, "before dear Aydan begged us to join *his* Cabinet."

"I asked," Aydan said dryly. "And I believe I'm paying you double what you made serving in Sylvanna."

"Oh, you certainly are." Gerridan winked at the king.

Aydan leaned in and explained, somewhat apologetically, "We tend to keep things casual between us."

"I can see that."

Gerridan huffed a laugh as a door on the opposite wall opened. In walked a serious-looking man holding a tumbler of his own. It was the other man that had accompanied Aydan to Ayzelle. He'd abandoned the armor and broadsword he'd been wearing upon arrival, now in a simple pair of black trousers and a thick dark blue knitted sweater that complemented his golden brown skin and stretched over his broad muscled chest and shoulders. His hair was cropped short, and his neck was covered in the same vine-like tattoos Aydan wore, though his were less floral. He looked up, registering Aydan first, but when his eyes landed on me, he jumped, dropping his glass. It shattered on the floor, spilling liquor all over the rug.

No sooner than the glass shattered, Hannele waved her hand lightly. The liquid soaking the rug vanished, and the glass reassembled itself before my eyes.

"Shaye, this is my Lord General, Alastair Greenwood," said Aydan in the silence that fell. "Al, this is Lady Shaye Eastly, though she claims she'd rather you just call her Shaye."

General Greenwood inclined his head. "I'm sorry if I startled you, Shaye."

"It's all right," I replied. "Hannele's cleanup was rather impressive. I haven't seen magic up close in some time."

"Have you been able to practice your abilities at all?" Aydan asked.

I shook my head. "Zathryan forbade it." I lifted the edge of my skirt an inch or so off the floor, revealing the cuff around my swollen ankle. Aydan's eyes widened.

"Gods, Shaye, why didn't you say something?"

"It's not silver," I said. "Stef—the captain had one made in secret. It's polished steel. No one ever came near enough to realize." Aydan's face was livid.

"I'll see what I can find," Hannele announced and left the room before I could assure her that I was fine.

"How have you been able to hide your abilities?" Gerridan's eyes were keen. "Surely you haven't been able to keep from doing magic all this time?"

"I would do little things here and there. Small tasks, to let some out." I glanced at Aydan and took a deep breath. "Also, I can . . . I can still do the fire thing," I said softly. "My room gets cold and there's no fireplace, so—well, here." I looked around and found an unlit lantern on the other end of the long table. I raised my hand and focused for a couple of seconds before a flame flickered to life on the wick. I turned back and saw that Gerridan had risen to his feet and was staring intently at the flame. Alastair frowned deeply as the emissary crossed the room and lifted the lantern, examining it himself.

"What do you think?" Aydan asked him.

"I think you were right about the lady, Aydan," Gerridan said quietly.

"Right about what?" I crossed my arms again as the four of them stared at me. "What is so extraordinary about lighting a lantern?"

"Let's sit." Aydan gestured toward the sofas. "There are some things you should know."

By the time we had all made ourselves comfortable in the sitting area, Hannele returned with a key to unlock the cuff. She carefully removed it, and my ankle was bruised and angry looking where the steel had rested. As she knelt, I noticed the princess eyeing my torn, ugly shoes, but before I could hide them from her, she tapped once on each shoe and then stood, insisting she fill my drink for me once again. I tried to say that I didn't need anything, but it was too late. My shoes looked brand new, and I flushed as Hannele pressed a fresh glass into my hand. I thanked her and set it aside, my head already swimming from the alcohol after having had none for so many months.

"What do you know of elemental magic, Shaye?" Aydan asked.

"Nothing," I replied. "I know almost nothing about any type of magic. Just the things that you showed me last year. Casting light, duplication, that sort of thing."

"Medeisians are not capable of elemental magic," Hannele said carefully. I furrowed my brow.

"The old texts say that when the gods gifted the early Medeisians our abilities, they knew they must give us limits." Aydan said as he reached for a flickering candle on the table beside him. He balanced the candlestick flat on his palm before taking his hand away. It remained, hovering where Aydan willed it to stay. "I cannot alter the flame itself," he said, allowing the candlestick to set itself back on the table, "but I can manipulate its vessel all I want.

"I . . . forgive me, I still don't understand." I looked around at the king and his friends. Alastair had not said anything this whole time but continued to stare at me. "If our sorcery cannot conjure the elements, how am I doing so?"

"By using another source of magic. From the Children," Gerridan replied. Aydan shot him a sharp look. I gaped at him.

"From what?"

"The Children of the Onyx Temple. They're a coven, located somewhere in the Creg'tam mountain range. They practice elemental and psychic magic. It's widely believed that Lord Ronan Redfern sought out the Children when he was looking to expand his powers and usurp Zathryan."

My vision blurred. I was going to be sick.

I stood quickly—too quickly, I realized as I swayed. In an instant, Aydan was on his feet with his hand under my elbow.

"I'm *not* a witch," I choked out, praying they would believe me. "I've never even—the first time I ever used magic was *here*, in Ayzelle. I've been a prisoner here this entire time, how could I have found a *coven*—"

"We don't think you're a witch, Shaye," Aydan said. "Not in that way."

"*How* are you an emissary?" Hannele asked, whipping around to scold Gerridan. "That was the *worst* possible way to say that—"

"What is it you think I am?" I asked Aydan. It was Alastair who replied.

"Magic calls to magic," he said. "Before your father, there had never been a sorcerer who sought out the power of witchcraft, and certainly never one who then produced a child." I sat back down and began wringing my hands in my lap. "We believe that Ronan's power passed to you, as all Medeisian magic passes from parent to child. It stands to reason that the power he developed from the Children, from practicing witchcraft, entangled itself with his natural abilities and has been passed down to you as well."

I propped my elbow on the arm of the sofa and rested my temple against my fingers, closing my eyes. I wanted to stand up and storm out of the room, wanted to call them all liars cruelly tormenting me for some prank, some joke they were playing on the servant girl just because they wanted to. Because they were powerful and bored, and they could. And yet, as soon as the words had met my ears, I knew. I knew in the very core of my being that what they said was true. Of course it was.

I opened my eyes and looked at Alastair, who was studying me closely, before turning back to Aydan. "What does this mean for me?"

"I don't know," he answered. "It may take years for your powers to fully emerge, or they could all appear to you tomorrow after breakfast. But I do know that whatever you have brewing beneath the surface will eventually pour out of you one way or another. You must learn to control this now, or someday you won't be able to."

"If you are right, and I am a—whatever I am, how can I possibly learn to control it?"

"You're sitting with the most powerful sorcerers in all of Medeisia, my lady," said Hannele. "Between us, I truly think we can help you."

"We'll figure it out together," Aydan assured me. Before I could reply, I heard the door to the king's chambers open and slam shut again, followed by footsteps stomping down the corridor.

A pale, petite woman with hair like wildfire strode into the room in a huff, heading straight for the drink cart to pour herself a glass of wine. She drank deeply without turning to look at or greet anyone.

"Having fun, Kenna?" Gerridan grinned from his armchair.

"Don't even get me started," Kenna spat before pouring another. She glared at Gerridan. "The men in this court are damnable."

"And the women?"

"They're even worse. The women wouldn't even *look* at me."

"That's quite an accomplishment," Gerridan teased, "since you make a spectacle of yourself wherever you go."

She ignored his comment. "I thought I had caught the attention of two of the men in that damned hall, but once we were alone, they decided they'd rather indulge in one another than pay me any attention."

"Watching can be fun," Gerridan countered with a wink. Kenna scoffed.

"Voyeurism is boring. I left. Hello." Kenna looked me up and down, cocked an eyebrow, and smirked. "Oh, she's fun." She offered her hand. Alastair and Aydan both opened their mouths to object, but I had already taken it. A few seconds passed and Kenna scowled slightly, then patted my hand with her free one.

"Kings will fall to their knees before you," she said quietly.

"I'm sorry?" I blinked.

"Shaye, allow me to introduce Kenna Vesper, my seer," Aydan explained. "She delights in the delivery of cryptic messages."

"Cryptic? *Me*? Never." Kenna smiled into her wineglass.

Soon the Cabinet began to talk amongst themselves. Aydan remained in his seat next to me on the sofa as we watched Kenna and Gerridan bicker about whether Kenna was a habitual cheater when it came to chess. The clock chimed, and I saw that it was close to midnight.

"It's quite late," I said to no one in particular. "I should probably head back to my quarters."

"I'll have Elise show you the way," Aydan replied.

"I think I can find my way back. But thank you."

"You have a new suite. I hope you don't mind. I've had your belongings moved."

"Why?"

He frowned. "I didn't think it would come as a surprise that I've reinstated your title. You are a lady of Medeisia once again. The suite was empty anyway. You're not kicking anyone out, if that was your concern."

My brow furrowed once again and I asked, "May I be frank with you?"

"By all means."

"Why am I here?" I felt the eyes of Aydan's friends all turn to me. "Your father hasn't even sat upon his funeral pyre and the first thing you do is summon a grimy servant girl you used to know—for what? To be paraded around to your powerful friends like some traveling curiosity?"

Aydan looked taken aback. "Shaye, I assure you that I never intended to make you feel badly. I wanted to see for myself that you were all right. I wanted my friends to meet you because I knew they would have some insight into my suspicions surrounding your abilities. I also wanted to ask a favor of you, but it can certainly wait until the morning if you're not feeling up to discussing it."

"What would that be?"

"Do you remember when you asked what sort of king I thought I'd be?" Lying on the grass by the pond, watching the clouds pass over a winter sky. A year and a lifetime ago. "The vision I told you about that day—of Medeisia reconciled with Nautia, the Eternity Throne returned to my family's name. It's still my vision. I will need help to achieve this, which means I need a strong Cabinet. I have these four already." He gestured to his friends, who were still watching us. "I still need a Chief Advisor, and I'd like to ask you to fill that position."

"You're joking." I turned to the Cabinet. They weren't laughing.

"I assure you, my lady, I am not," Aydan said. "I need an advisor who can see both sides of our quarrels. You grew up in the mortal realm, in the heart of Nautia. You know what the common people want, and what they've been deprived of by the current owners of the Eternity Throne."

"I thought it might be a bad idea too," Gerridan chimed in. "Until Aydan told me about your history with the mortals. You could have great value here."

"I don't know what to say." I gulped. Chief Advisor. Lord Ronan's position under Zathryan.

"Take some time." Aydan nodded. "It's been a long day. Think about it. When you know your answer, send a note with Elise. She'll be tending to your new suite."

"I—thank you. I should—I should go to bed." I stood, as did Aydan and the other two men. "It was lovely to meet all of you," I said to the Cabinet, and ignored Aydan's troubled expression to add, "and to see you again."

"Lady Shaye." He inclined his head, and Elise appeared beside me to guide me out.

I woke the next morning to an urgent knock on the door.

The night before, when Elise brought me to my new suite, I had entered to find all my belongings, few as they were, placed neatly in appropriate spots around the bedroom. Catchfly greeted me happily on our new bed, which was large and inviting.

"Is there anything else I can do for you tonight, Lady Shaye?" Elise had asked from the doorway.

"Just one thing, if you don't mind," I said as I opened the drawer to a writing desk near the wall and pulled out stationery and a pen. I scrawled a quick note and folded it before placing it in her hand. "Would you please take this to Captain Whittaker?"

"Of course." She dipped her head. "Do you need help dressing for bed?"

"No, thank you. Good night, Elise."

"Sleep well, my lady."

The knocking continued as I hauled myself to my feet and found a shawl. I opened the door and Stefan stormed in past me, looking around the room.

"What happened?" he asked.

"Good morning to you too," I said as I closed the door. He looked me up and down, and then around my suite as though the walls had personally offended him.

"What is this?" he asked. "Why are you here?"

"King Aydan has reinstated my title. I'm a lady of Medeisia again. The suite was empty, so he gave it to me."

"In exchange for *what*, exactly?" Stefan asked.

"What do you mean? He didn't ask for anything," I said. "He introduced me to some of his friends, gave me the suite, and offered me a job." Stefan ran a hand over his face.

"Shaye . . . you don't understand how these people work, do you?"

"Why are you acting this way? He made you a lord last night, it's not like you aren't benefiting from him as well."

"Yes, after I declared my loyalty to him publicly. I'm Captain of the King's Guard, it's expected. But you . . . what have you promised him?" Stefan asked.

"I haven't promised him anything. I told you, he gave me the suite and offered me a job. That's it." Something in my gut kept me from telling Stefan of the Cabinet's suspicions about my abilities.

"You have a job," he said. I scoffed.

"Indentured servitude isn't a job, Stef." He grew quiet.

"I'm sorry," he said. "I'm just worried. I've spent a long time trying to keep you safe, and I just . . . I don't want anything bad to happen to you. I don't want to see you hurt again." I took his hand.

"*I'm* sorry, Stef. For worrying you. But the king *has* been kind to me. He helped me, in the past."

"What's the job?" he asked.

"He's asked me to take the Chief Advisor position," I said. His eyebrows shot upward.

"You're not serious."

"That's what I said. He told me to take some time and consider it." Stefan put his hand under my chin, tilting me up to meet his gaze.

"Shaye, you are in very dangerous territory. The king has spent most of his life behind the walls of Sylvanna. No one knows what happens there. Their borders have been closed for nearly a century, they even warded out King Zathryan and the Crown Princess after your father's execution. Solandis and Priamos are ruthless. They have the most powerful standing army in Medeisia. You don't keep that much power locked away for a thousand years without being as fearsome as they come."

"Aydan wasn't like that when I knew him."

"You knew him for a few weeks, nearly a year ago. I doubt you ever saw his true colors. He may have been grown when he sought refuge with his grandparents, but he's spent more time under their influence than with his own parents. You must tread lightly. They did not call him *wayward* for nothing. The things he's done, how far he's strayed . . . Aydan is brilliant and vicious. There must be some sort of alternate plan. He wouldn't have offered such a high position to someone with so little experience, especially with your family history." I flushed at that last remark.

"If you don't think I should take the offer, I won't," I said. "I'll send a note and be done." I ignored the pang of disappointment in my chest. Until I said the words, I hadn't been sure if I wanted to take the job.

"You can't *turn him down*," Stefan said incredulously. "If you thought you were a prisoner before—"

"He's not like that," I interrupted, repeating my earlier sentiment with some frustration. "The king wouldn't make me a prisoner for saying no. He tried to prevent my imprisonment to begin with."

"I've heard stories about the Wayward Prince my entire life, Shaye," Stefan countered. "Now that he's king . . . I don't know what will happen to our positions here if he starts looking to settle scores." He gripped my arm tightly enough to hurt, and I pulled away.

"Well, I'd better take his offer, then." His face paled. I placed my hand on his cheek. "I'll be careful, I promise." He nodded.

"I just want you safe," he said softly.

"I know." I hugged him quickly, then asked, "Would you like to accompany me to the funeral feast tonight?"

"You know I can't, Shaye."

"Well," I started. "Our friendship isn't a secret anymore. Not from the Crown, anyway."

"What are you talking about?" he asked sharply.

"It was mentioned last night. Aydan didn't seem to have a problem with it," I explained. Stefan's eyes flashed.

"Why the hell would you do something so stupid?"

"I was making conversation," I said defensively. "I didn't think it would be so upsetting to you. Zathryan is dead, the danger is gone—"

"No, the danger has only just begun," Stefan snapped. "Aydan and his *Cabinet* are some of the most powerful sorcerers in the world. They want you close to them, for reasons we don't know, and you've just revealed me as a weakness."

I wanted to explain myself, but instead I just said, "I'm sorry." Stefan shook his head. I reached for his hand, but he stepped back, and without a word, he walked out the door and slammed it behind him.

Tears welled in my eyes and my face grew hot with embarrassment. Catchfly wove herself around my ankles, but it did nothing to comfort me. Another knock rang out from the door, and I rushed to open it, hoping I would find Stefan come to let me apologize. Instead, Elise stood on the other side, smiling broadly. Her smile disappeared when she saw my face blotchy with tears.

"Good morning, Lady Shaye. Are you all right?"

"I'm fine, Elise. Good morning."

"His Majesty has asked that I attend to you," she said. "I came to see if you'd like any tea this morning. Or perhaps some help dressing?"

"No, thank you, I think I'll just sit in the bath for a while." I turned for the bathroom, but Elise beat me to it and began filling the tub with steaming water. In a cupboard on the wall she found jars of salts and oils, which she poured in as well. A floral perfumed scent mingled with the steam. She shut them back in the cupboard, then wiped her hands on her apron.

"If you need any help, give a shout. I'll be cleaning the bedroom," she said before leaving the bathroom and shutting the door behind her. I didn't bother telling her that nothing but the bed had been touched since she left me the night before; I knew she'd find something worth lingering for.

I tossed my nightdress on the floor and climbed into the tub, leaning my head back against the cool porcelain as I tried to forget the argument with Stefan. He had never been angry with me before, nor I with him.

After a few minutes of mulling the conversation over, I called out for Elise, unsure if she was still in the next room. She opened the door but did not look inside.

"Yes, my lady?"

"Would you please bring me something to write with? I need to send a message."

"Of course." The door shut, and a second later, a pen and piece of stationery appeared on a small table sitting next to the tub. I didn't bother to leave the warmth of the water. I only needed to write three words: *I'll do it.*

I folded the note and placed it back on the table before calling through the door, "The king said I could send a note with you. Would you mind?"

"Not at all, my lady." I heard her snap her fingers from the bedroom, and the note disappeared. With a deep breath, I closed my eyes and lay my head back once again, trying my best to enjoy my soak.

Half an hour later, I emerged to find an empty, spotless room after Elise had made her departure. I took a towel to my hair before sitting at the vanity and brushing the long waves. It had been a long time since my hair had been washed properly, so I left it down to dry and began inspecting the bottles and jars arranged neatly on the table before me. A proper lady's vanity. I was intrigued, though I didn't know what half of these creams and potions did. I supposed Elise would be able to tell me. I'd just opened one of them to sniff its contents—it smelled of rosemary and lavender, and as far as I could tell was meant to be spread on one's face—when Elise returned, holding a note with a blue wax seal. Without speaking, I broke the seal and unfolded the message:

Lady Advisor,

I'm glad to hear it, and I am grateful. The day is yours. The pyre will be lit at sunset.

Fondly,

–A

I folded the note and set it aside. "Yesterday, I was little more than a slave," I said. "Today, I'm supposed to be a lady of the court. The Chief Advisor." I made eye contact with Elise in the mirror, and she reached for a brush. "I feel like a fraud. What if I mess it all up? The last Chief Advisor—"

"The last Chief Advisor was a traitor. You are not. If you do your job with the interest of the people in mind, then you will be ten times the leader Lord Redfern was." Elise began separating my hair into sections. "The king would not have offered you the job if he thought you would do poorly. He enjoys your company, yes, but he is not frivolous."

"I haven't seen him in a year," I said, more to myself than her.

She pursed her lips. After a moment's silence, she said, "I don't know much about leading a court, or advising a king." She ran the brush through my hair. "But I do know how to make you look like a lady. Looking the part is half the job." She winked at my reflection, and I nearly smiled.

Chapter Twenty

Hours later, I arrived without escort to the pyre outside on the grounds. No one seemed to notice I was there, and I was grateful. It felt strange to be standing amongst the courtiers, dressed in fine clothes like theirs, rather than the grimy dresses I was so used to wearing. Despite my best efforts, the two maid uniforms I owned held an oily layer of soot and grease that could not be washed out. Tonight Elise had selected a charcoal gray gown for me, trimmed with black lace at the neck and wrists. Elegant, and simple enough to be put on alone. The varying fashions worn by the noble women of Ayzelle—many-layered skirts, wide pannier dresses with intricate, decorative laced backs, as well as single-layered dresses with collars up to the throat and elaborate embroidery across the entire gown as if the fabric was a canvas and thread was paint—all seemed to share the feature of needing several servants to dress and undress each day. I wasn't sure that I would ever be comfortable enough to allow Elise or Isolde to see me unclothed, and despite my new status, it did not feel right to ask them for something I could do easily enough by myself.

The courtiers were gathered near the pyre itself, many of the same weeping women from the night before placing small bouquets at the base, dropping handkerchiefs and other mementos nearby, as if a small piece of them would travel with their king to what lay beyond. I fought the urge to spit.

Standing further back was another group, who by their attire, I guessed were residents of the nearby villages come to pay their respects as well. I could see from where I stood that many of them had their own bouquets and mementos to drop along the pyre's edge.

Most seemed hesitant to cross paths with the weeping ladies. I couldn't say I blamed them.

After a moment of watching, I felt a hand meet my elbow. Stefan stood beside me, looking grim.

"You look nice," he said stiffly. He wore mourning clothes instead of armor tonight.

"So do you," I replied hesitantly. "Stef, I—"

"I'm sorry," he cut me off. "I shouldn't have reacted that way. I just . . . you mean a lot to me, Shaye. I don't want you to get hurt because of me."

"You mean a lot to me too, Stefan." I took one of his hands in my own. "You've been a friend to me these past months. I wouldn't have survived without you." He squeezed my hand, then opened his mouth to speak, but before any words came out, the herald called out Aydan's arrival.

Aydan and his Cabinet approached the pyre in a similar fashion to their arrival the previous night; Aydan led the way, with Kenna and Hannele flanking him, followed closely by Alastair and Gerridan. Elise must have known what the rest of them would be wearing, as my charcoal gown closely resembled the gowns of the ladies in Aydan's entourage. The men wore black, and Aydan was the only one of them who remained unarmed. A few yards from the pyre, they stopped and Aydan turned to me, inclining his head slightly. I stiffened, gave the best curtsy I could muster, and crossed the crowd to fall in line with my new colleagues. A murmur swept past me as the courtiers began to whisper, but I ignored them, forcing myself to keep my eyes forward and my head held high. Aydan stopped, and the rest of us fell in place behind him as he turned to address the gathered sorcerers and mortals, nobles and villagers, come to see King Zathryan laid to rest.

"My father faced more challenges than any man—than any king—ought to face," he began. "Rebellion, betrayal, death. He saw it and fought it valiantly. And despite his own personal grief, King Zathryan kept his people safe and built a new capital amid such challenges. There was no choice but to move forward. To move on." Aydan swallowed.

"I am not the ruler that you all expected. This is not the role I expected for myself. Yet the gods have determined *this* to be my fate. To be the fate of Medeisia. Tonight, as we send off the king who saved us from certain destruction, I implore you all to not think of what we have lost, but what we stand to gain from what is fated.

From the unexpected. I implore you to look forward. Toward a Medeisia restored to her former glory."

A torch appeared in Aydan's hand, already lit. He turned to face the pyre but spoke loud enough for us all to hear him. "You are free from this world, Zathryan Aevitarus. Your duties are fulfilled. Go now to what lies beyond." He lowered the torch to the base of the pyre and held it there until it caught.

We watched in silence as the pyre was engulfed. It was less than a minute before the flames grew to be twice Aydan's height; I was tempted to step back, but the king and his Cabinet did not flinch, so I held my place.

When some time had passed, the Guard, save for Stefan, began the march back toward the great hall, indicating that the appropriate observation period was over, and the courtiers and councilmen followed suit. Finally, Gerridan approached Aydan from behind and gripped his shoulder to whisper something in his ear. Then he nodded to me, gesturing for me to lead the Cabinet inside. I was their leader now. I swallowed and began walking. Aydan remained where he stood, watching the towering fire carry Zathryan to the next world.

Half an hour later, everyone was seated in the great hall and Aydan arrived alone, signaling the start of the funeral feast. I sat at the head table alongside the rest of the Cabinet, several others I knew to be council members, one person I overheard Alastair referring to as a lesser general, and Stefan. In the middle was Aydan, sitting stiffly on an ornate dining chair that was all but a throne sat before a table. He looked dreadfully uncomfortable as courtiers and noblemen stood to make toasts to Zathryan's life, and the new reign of King Aydan. He barely picked at his food. I couldn't blame him; I was so nervous just sitting at the head table that I couldn't bring myself to eat more than a polite bite of each course.

When the meal was over and the speeches and toasts had finally stopped, the hall quickly filled with the buzzing of hundreds of voices talking at once as everyone began to mingle. I saw one of the council members leave his seat and bend low to Aydan's ear. He nodded at whatever the man said before he leaned over to speak to Alastair.

Someone tapped my shoulder and I looked up to find Stefan standing beside my chair.

"I think we should talk," he said.

"Is everything all right?"

"Yes, I think so," he replied. "I just . . . this is important. Could we speak in private?"

"I suppose—" Before I could answer, I felt a hand on my forearm. I turned back and saw Hannele now standing on the other side of me.

"The council has requested an urgent audience with the Cabinet tonight," she said. "We're meeting them in five minutes."

"I'll join you in just a second," I told her. Stefan's face reddened. "I'm sorry," I said. "Can we talk later?"

"Don't worry about it," he said stiffly. "I'll catch up with you when your schedule clears, Lady Advisor."

"Stef—" He turned on his heel and headed for the exit. I swallowed, then stood to join the Cabinet as we all filed from the hall to the corridor outside while Aydan bid the feast good night and proposed a final toast to his father. Kenna scoffed under her breath upon hearing it, and I suppressed my smile. I certainly shared her sentiment.

Gerridan offered me his arm as we made our way to the council room near the north end of the castle. It was a room I had been sent to clean often, huge and containing a long glass table capable of seating twenty men easily. I held onto him and tried not to look nervous as we entered. The room was empty. Aydan took his seat at the head of the table, and the rest of us fell into place in the chairs around him. Gerridan pulled out the chair to Aydan's right for me. I hesitated.

"The Chief Advisor always sits to the right of the king when he is present at council meetings," he said. "When he is not here, you'll take the head." I nodded once, then sat quickly. While we waited, I found myself tapping a fingernail on the table in front of me.

"This table was commissioned by my grandfather, King Alune," Aydan filled the silence. "He held his council meetings exclusively in Ayzelle, away from the Grand Palace. He was paranoid that his council might be plotting to kill him, and he wanted to be sure that no one was holding weapons or poison during council meetings."

"It's quite remarkable," I replied. "A pain in the ass to clean, though." Before he could speak again, the doors opened and a group of ten men filed their way into the room. I recognized one of them—a lanky, dark-haired man with an unflattering goatee—as Lord Declan. I didn't know what his role was—though I probably *should*, I realized with a flash of terror that I was now Chief Advisor and had no clue who any of the extended council members were. The men bowed in unison, and Aydan gestured for them to sit.

"Your Majesty, thank you for allowing this meeting on such short notice," said Lord Declan. "And my deepest condolences for the loss of your father. His absence will be felt throughout the continent. Even our correspondences beyond the sea will—"

"Enough, Declan," Aydan said, waving his hand dismissively toward the lord. His face was a mask of cool indifference. Hannele and the others had the same bored expression on their faces, and I tried to copy it. "My father may have enjoyed opening each meeting with twenty minutes of your sycophancy, but I have no interest in false praise. I allowed this meeting tonight because you stressed its urgency. Tell me what is so urgent."

Lord Declan cleared his throat. "Your Majesty, we felt it was prudent to urge—to *request*—that you not begin your reign with war and bloodshed."

"And what, Lord Declan, gave you the impression that I would be beginning my reign with war and bloodshed?"

"Your Majesty, it is no secret that you hold a deep desire to return to the Grand Palace, to see the capital restored there, and your eulogy seemed to suggest—"

"My lord, you're putting words in my mouth." Aydan snapped his fingers and goblets of wine appeared before each of us. "Though you are half right."

"Your Majesty?"

"I do wish to see the Eternity Throne returned to my family, but I don't plan on using violence to obtain my desires," Aydan said.

"How do you propose to complete such a task?" Lord Declan asked carefully.

"I will simply ask for it." A chuckle scattered through the men opposite us. When Lord Declan looked up and saw that no one on our end of the table was laughing, he paused.

"Your *Majesty*," he sighed. "You cannot be serious."

"My *lord*," Aydan said, matching his tone. "I am." The corner of Gerridan's mouth twitched.

Lord Declan considered his words. It seemed he had spent many years tiptoeing around the varying moods of Zathryan. I could not blame him. I had once been on the receiving end of the old king's whims. I would not soon forget the feeling. "Your Majesty, your father spent nearly half his reign here in Ayzelle. We have established a new capital here, trade lines have been open and flourishing in Xarynn and in the smaller territories and villages throughout the continent, thrilled to have direct trade with the Crown. And with your long-standing connection to Sylvanna, I'm sure it will be no time before trade is reestablished there as well."

"Agreements with Sylvanna will be reestablished shortly," Aydan confirmed. "Following my coronation—which will be at the end of this month, by the way."

"Your Majesty, it *is* traditional to wait *six* weeks—"

"It is only a tradition because that is how long Queen Euna was forced to sit in a prison cell by her own council before she took her place on the throne," Aydan interrupted, sounding bored. "I never met Euna, and therefore have no reason to honor her memory in such a way."

"As you wish," Lord Declan said. "We will send out the appropriate invitations and announcements tomorrow morning."

"Good. Now, back to your point about the capital," Aydan said. "Ayzelle has been a fine capital. This castle has served its purpose well, but *my* throne sits inside the Grand Palace—"

"Your Majesty, we simply do not have the military power—" Lord Declan started to interrupt, but Aydan snapped his fingers and Declan's mouth closed, though not by choice, it seemed.

"My lord, where are your manners?" Aydan chided. "As I was saying, the Eternity Throne, and the Grand Palace, were built by and for our kind. There is magic within those walls that even the Nautians' witches cannot wield. The new king is young, not even old enough to hold the throne without a regent. My sources believe he may be persuaded to give back what is mine by right, and rule his people from a throne built by and for mortals. My plan is not to throw the boy out into the street. It is to see the mortal and immortal realms united, my lords," he said, now addressing the other members of the extended council.

"Your Majesty," Lord Declan spoke up again having regained use of his mouth. "The amount of planning and negotiation it would take to even get a letter in the Nautian king's hand— and then to convince him to give up the Eternity Throne willingly—

forgive me, but I think you overestimate your abilities. Without even a proper Cabinet—"

"The necessary letters have already been drafted and will be sent to Nautia following my coronation," said Aydan. "And as far as your concerns regarding my Cabinet, it is complete. Just this morning, I've named Lady Eastly our new Chief Advisor." I tensed as the eyes of every man in the extended council drifted toward me. I hoped I looked aloof rather than terrified.

"You *can't* be serious." Lord Declan sneered.

"Very much so," said Aydan. Declan looked down and flipped through a stack of papers in front of him while muttering to himself. The room was quiet enough as he did so that I heard clear as day when he mumbled something about the spawn of traitors and mortals. I felt heat rise in my hands and face immediately and was too embarrassed to speak. Aydan did instead. "Lady Shaye's upbringing makes her perfect for this position, don't you think? You forget that the lady was raised in Nautia. She knows the mortals, how they live and how they want to be governed. And her despicable treatment by my father gives her some insight into what the poorest citizens of this realm want and need. She is not blinded by the wealth this council has hoarded for centuries. As far as her father is concerned, I will not hold an innocent woman accountable for the sins of a man who died before she was born. This is the last I will speak on the subject—if any of you have a problem with my choice of advisor, this is your opportunity to resign." He looked at each of them, daring someone to object. "Now, if you have nothing else to discuss, leave us. We'll meet again at the end of the week for our regularly scheduled meeting." Looking wounded, the extended council stood one by one, and bowed as they turned to leave. Lord Declan, flanked by a concerned-looking, ginger-haired man, was the last to do so, seeming confused and perhaps realizing he had achieved nothing during the meeting he himself had called.

The door finally clicked shut, and Aydan let out a long breath, slouched in his seat, and propped his head on his fist. With his other hand he reached for his goblet, which floated off the table to meet his palm. "I'd forgotten how much I hate them," he said. Gerridan clapped Aydan on the shoulder.

"You did well, sweet Aydan." Hannele and Alastair were talking in low voices about the various noblemen of the extended council, comparing notes while Kenna listened and nodded occasionally.

"Why not replace them?" I asked. "If they're supposed to be advising you as well, you should at least *like* them, shouldn't you?"

"Too much of a headache." Aydan shrugged. "Those bastards are from the most powerful—"

"—wealthiest—" Kenna cut in.

"—families in Ayzelle. The courtiers here are all the same. Replacing one with another would not likely solve any problems, and the courtiers like the council as it is. The villages don't interact with the castle, so if my citizens' lives aren't negatively affected by Declan and his cronies, I'll let them play." Aydan banished his empty goblet to wherever it was he sent the things he was finished with. "I don't answer to the extended councils. They exist to make it easier to delegate."

"Is there anyone you answer to?"

"My people, for one, and of course every person in this room. Kenna can be quite unforgiving." The seer winked in our direction.

For the next few minutes, Hannele and Alastair's conversation was taken over by Gerridan sharing bits of gossip he had picked up about the council members' families. He was recounting some scandal or another when I leaned over and said to Aydan, "By the way, I'm sorry for your loss." He furrowed his brow.

"Why would you be?"

"Your father is dead. I would imagine that it's . . . difficult, regardless of your relationship."

"You're kind, my lady, but don't spend too much time mourning the man who tortured us for the past year." Aydan turned back to listen to Gerridan's story. I didn't listen very closely for the rest of it, as I puzzled over the word, *us*.

We remained in the council room for another hour before it was agreed that we should all get some sleep. I walked with Aydan and his friends until we reached the door to my suite. They each bid me good night, Gerridan sketching a bit of a bow, and carried on down the hall. Aydan lingered, but when he started to speak, I cut him off. "Good night." I curtsied briefly, opened my door, and slipped inside before he could reply.

Chapter Twenty-One

I did not see Stefan for the next two days, until it was time to meet the others for our first official Cabinet meeting. He was speaking to the pair of guards stationed at the entrance to the north wing, where the most lavish suites, as well as the king's chambers, were located. As I approached, Stefan dismissed the guards and left, attempting to pass me without acknowledgment. I caught his arm.

"Are you going to ignore me every time I have to do my job?" I asked. "I thought we were going to talk after the funeral."

"I waited by your door until midnight. You never showed, so I left." His jaw was clenched.

"Well, I'm sorry I kept you waiting."

"You don't owe me any explanations, Shaye, it's clear where I lie on your list of priorities."

"It's been *three days*, Stef. You're being dramatic," I said.

"Am I?" He pulled his arm away.

"Stefan."

"Is there a problem?" I turned to see Alastair walking toward us, dressed in sparring clothes. "Good morning, Lady Advisor."

"Good morning, general." I smiled and Stefan straightened. "Stefan, this is Lord General Alastair Greenwood. General, this is Captain of the King's Guard, Lord Stefan Whittaker. We were just saying goodbye before I head inside."

"I'll escort you," Alastair offered. "Good to meet you, captain. I'm sure we'll be seeing more of each other." The general's words were polite but carried an air of authority. Stefan nodded curtly, then made his departure without another word to me. I watched until he disappeared around the corner, then continued on my path to the king's chambers. Alastair followed behind me, and I silently thanked the gods that he did not question me about Stefan.

Hours later, we were sitting at the long wooden table, and had nearly finished with all of the points on the agenda. The meeting had been late to start, but not because of my and Alastair's tardiness. Kenna had overslept and refused to let us begin without her. Gerridan, having overseen similar meetings on the Sylvannian Council, had offered to run the first of our Cabinet meetings so that I could observe how one might do such a thing, and I readily accepted. For all his jokes and flirting, he kept us on track with a list of suggested topics, the first being the opportunity for us all to read his draft of the letter to Nautia before he sent the final copy, and the last being the plans for reopening trade with Sylvanna.

"Solandis is prepared to sign an agreement following the coronation," the emissary said. "Her letter indicated that she would prefer to sign in person."

"I intend to make an appearance at the next eclipse festival," Aydan replied. "Tell her we'll make time then." Gerridan made a note in his book and sighed, tossing the pen in front of him and leaning back in his chair.

"Does anyone else have anything to bring to the table?" he asked.

"I'd like to supervise the extended council's plans for the coronation," Hannele said. "Declan is bound to turn it into some garish display. He'll need to be reigned in."

"Go ahead." Aydan looked to the rest of us expectantly. I opened my mouth but closed it— not quickly enough. "Lady Shaye?" I flushed.

"Oh, I don't know that this is the time. A budgeting suggestion." He looked curious, leaning back in his seat. I cleared my throat. "I think it would be prudent to raise the wages of all staff working in the castle and on the grounds. By at least double." I braced myself for my new colleagues' laughter, but it never came. They were all waiting for me to continue, intrigued. "The money is there, you can see on these account details." I pointed to one of the pages that Gerridan had set before us at the start of the meeting. "I didn't often work with the others, but from what I've overheard, most of the servants are owed back wages."

Aydan scowled while examining the totals before him. "Ayzelle isn't hurting for revenue. Why are servants missing wages?"

"No one ever spoke to me directly about it, but they seemed to have been 'forgotten.'"

"Who is in charge of distributing payments to the servants and groundskeepers?" Aydan asked, shuffling through the papers. Kenna and Hannele were doing the same thing on the opposite side of the table.

"The steward, Mr. Vyne," I replied. Aydan looked behind him and saw a servant named Alice, who I had seen many times tending to the unmarried ladies' suites, standing just outside the room. She'd been assigned to assist Elise for the day. He called her inside.

"Alice, please find Mr. Vyne and tell him that I would like to personally review his ledgers," he told her kindly. She looked shocked that the king would speak to her by name but curtsied and swiftly exited.

"Why is this your first concern?" Kenna asked me with pure curiosity in her voice.

"They're here day in and day out and go back to their villages at night completely exhausted. They don't deserve to have their families go hungry because the Crown couldn't be bothered to pay its employees," I said. "Keeping them happy and well compensated benefits us just as much as them. Growing up, my uncle and many of our neighbors worked in or near the Grand Palace. News travels fast. The servants and groundskeepers here will go home at night and tell their families and neighbors all about the generosity of their new king." Kenna nodded, and relief washed over me as the rest of them seemed to agree with my statements.

Alice reappeared in the doorway with a thick volume in her hands. She curtsied and set the ledger down in front of Aydan, who thanked her and began flipping through it immediately. A couple of pages in, Aydan summoned a pen into his hand. He began making notes in silence, clicking his tongue occasionally. After a few moments, Aydan looked up at me.

"Your name isn't listed here," he said.

"Servitude under house arrest doesn't pay a wage, it would seem," I half joked. He didn't smile but reached for a blank sheet of his stationery and wrote a few lines before folding it and waving his hand over the top to seal it. He beckoned for Alice to enter the room again.

"Please return Mr. Vyne's ledger to him and ask him to review the notes I've made. The rest of my instructions are detailed in the letter."

"Yes, Your Majesty."

"Thank you, Alice." She left and Aydan turned back to me. "The owed wages will be repaid with interest, today, and the servants' wages will be tripled, effective immediately. If there is any hint of wages being withheld, Mr. Vyne will be removed from his position."

"I—um, thank you," I said.

"Don't." He waved me off. "It was the right thing to do. Thank you for bringing it to our attention." I didn't know what to say, so I just straightened the stack of papers in front of me. Kenna was asking Hannele what she would wear to the coronation, and the group relaxed into casual conversation while pride flooded my chest.

I returned to my suite hours later, tired and satisfied with my work.

"I think I might actually have a place here," I told Catchfly while I prepared for bed. She lounged on my pillow and stared at me as I took my tincture and brushed out my hair, and I ignored her loud protests when I moved her to the side and crawled in beside her. She quickly went back to purring against me, and I fell asleep without worry for the first time in months.

Chapter Twenty-Two

The next few weeks were a blur. Between planning the coronation and trying to make sense of the final years of Zathryan's reign, there was much to do for the Cabinet. Even if Stefan and I had been on speaking terms, I would not have seen much of him. Initially Aydan wanted the Cabinet to meet formally every three days, but by the second meeting, it was clear that we would need to sit down more frequently to detangle the mess his father left behind. Strange decrees regarding the functioning of the treasury, and the extended council's ability to even tell Aydan or any Cabinet members what had been done, were tied to the power of the Crown rather than Zathryan himself, which meant they remained in place beyond his death and had become a nuisance that made governing a more difficult task than it already was. We spent several meetings simply tearing through the late king's diaries and agendas, searching for relevant information that would allow Aydan to undo his father's mess, but had yet to find anything useful.

After the meetings, now every other day, Gerridan was kind enough to spend an hour or so teaching me about the noble houses of Medeisia—which families were loyal, which were power-hungry, and who should be watched carefully. Many of these families would be descending on the castle for the coronation celebrations, and I wanted to be ready for them. In addition to his verbal lessons, Gerridan loaned me a thick volume bound in red leather with the gold words, *Houses of Medeisia: All Territories* stamped on the spine. I spent several nights devouring it, setting *Enchanted, Enchanting* aside for the first time in months.

On days with no meetings, Hannele enlisted me in helping her reign in the extended council's plan for the coronation, particularly from Lord Declan, who had unsurprisingly not warmed up to me. At his side most days was the concerned-looking man from our first meeting, who I now knew was Lord Dracus. Dracus seemed incapable of an original thought and to exist only to agree with Declan. The other lords of the extended council assisted as well, but seemed content to take orders from whoever won that particular argument, Declan or Hannele.

The ceremony itself would be performed by both a High Priest and High Priestess, in the same way it had been done for millennia—there would be no negotiations on that front. However, to call Declan's plans for the following feast and ball "extravagant" would be an understatement. I broke up several arguments myself, one being a particularly heated disagreement on the necessity of a solid gold lion centerpiece. I finally convinced Hannele to reluctantly agree to an ice sculpture so we could leave in time for dinner.

Hannele and I became fast friends during these negotiations. So much so that when we found ourselves with nothing left to do but find something to wear the day before the coronation, she insisted I accompany her to the dressmaker.

Unlike mortal dressmakers, who need weeks or even months to complete a gown for a special event, Hannele explained, Medeisian dressmakers can assemble a gown in minutes, and change details until the last second with the wave of their hand or a touch of their fingertips. She effuged us to an Ayzellen dress shop she'd once frequented before the closing of Sylvanna's borders. The dressmaker was a short man named Cecil who wore extravagant sapphire robes, embroidered with silver thread to create ocean waves near the hem that he had willed to ebb and flow like the real thing. He greeted the princess cheerfully and me only slightly less so, then busied himself with some task elsewhere in the shop, allowing the two of us some privacy. Hannele was in her element, examining the fabrics and designs of the ready-made gowns hanging around us. She pointed out a particularly extravagant piece in lavender and said, "I refuse to leave this shop until you've tried that on."

"It's beautiful." I huffed a nervous laugh. It was. The neckline was more daring than anything I'd ever worn, and the back was equally revealing. Once, a dress like that would have had me intrigued, curious to see what such a thing might look like on my body. Now, I wasn't sure if I'd ever want to show that much of my flesh. "A bit more risqué than I'd like." Hannele nodded, taking note and adjusting her decision for what I might wear to the coronation.

I was happy to let her make the selection once I had realized that I had no idea how to shop for a gown. I had never had money of my own, especially not the kind of money that was required to purchase gowns like these, until a few days ago when Elise delivered two pieces of stationery with my breakfast, which stated the balances of a pair of accounts that had been set up in my name with the treasury. When I saw the numbers on the pages, I'd nearly dropped my teacup. It was more money than Uncle Gideon had made in five years. Sure that a mistake had been made, perhaps something to do with Zathryan's other decrees surrounding the treasury, I checked three different ledgers and found that one account contained a standard months' wages for the role of Chief Advisor. The other held a years' worth of servant wages plus the interest Aydan had promised. I didn't bother asking him about it—I'd done the math, the total was correct, I had not been overpaid. Regardless, a strange, knotted feeling of guilt sat in my stomach every time the accounts crossed my mind, at the thought of the people scraping by in my former village.

"By the way," Hannele said as she continued her search, "Priamos and Solandis gave their final answer. They won't be attending the coronation." I was not surprised. Just yesterday, Gerridan had been struggling to get an answer from them, as the Lord and Lady of Sylvanna did not want to leave their territory before new treaties and trade agreements were signed.

"Is Aydan upset?" I asked.

"I haven't talked to him. Gerridan told me. If he is, he'll be over it soon enough. The eclipse festival is coming up, he'll see them then."

"Is he . . . never mind."

"What?" Hannele asked, stopping to look at me.

"Is Aydan . . . different? I mean, is he the same Aydan you've always known, or has he changed since his captivity here?"

"Why do you ask?"

"Just curious." I pretended to be interested in the sleeve of an emerald gown. "I sometimes wonder if the prince I knew last year is the same one you've known for the last century."

She considered this. "In some ways, yes, he's the same cocky, frustrating Aydan I've always known. He was certainly impacted by his most recent experience here, but not as much as you were, I expect." I froze at her words. It was like a bucket of cold water dumped on me, and I looked down to find that frost was forming on my palms. That was new. "You don't have to tell me if I'm right. But if you ever want to talk about it, I'm here to listen." I rubbed my hands on my skirts before nodding, remaining silent. Hannele's face lit up as she looked past me. "This is *it*!" she exclaimed, reaching for a dress behind me that I had not seen before. I felt myself smile a bit as she excitedly displayed the fabric to me and called out for Cecil.

Later, when Hannele and I were finally finished at the dress shop and she had effuged us back to the castle grounds, we walked arm in arm as we made our way to the north wing to meet the rest of the Cabinet for dinner. The dresses would be delivered to our rooms the next day, mine only receiving a few alterations specified by Hannele, while her gown was to be made completely from scratch. Cecil had shown her some of his designs, and I'd had to stifle a laugh when Hannele took the paper from his hands and began sketching her own. The dressmaker's eyes lit up when he saw the finished drawing, and he eagerly shooed us from the shop so he could get to work. Now I was famished and ready to dive into whatever delightful meal the cooks were preparing. We turned the corner toward the king's chambers and came to a sudden stop when we saw Stefan waiting in the hall. He immediately approached.

"I need to talk to you," he said without preamble.

"I'm busy," I replied coolly, moving past him. He grabbed my arm and Hannele's head turned so quickly, I thought she had hurt herself.

"You dare to put your hands on a lady of the King's Cabinet—" I put my hand up to stop her.

"It's fine. Go inside, I'll meet up with you in a bit."

Hannele looked at Stefan, then back at me. "If you're not inside soon, I'm sending Alastair to come find you," she said.

"No need," I assured her. "I'll be fine. Go." Hannele shot a warning glance at Stefan before walking away. I waited until the door clicked shut before I turned back to Stefan. "What do you want?"

"I just want to talk."

"Here's your opportunity." I crossed my arms. "I have dinner plans, so please be quick."

His brow furrowed. "Shaye, I am—I'm so sorry for my behavior. I-I don't know what came over me. I just, I care about you so much . . ." He stopped himself. "There is so much that you don't know yet. But you have every right to be angry with me. I would be too."

"Stef," I sighed, wondering what he meant but too tired to ask him to elaborate. "You know that I care about you too. I'm grateful for you, for your friendship. We both know I wouldn't have survived those early weeks without you." The sound of a whip cracking shot through my mind, and I did my best to ignore it. "But you can't act this way just because I'm late, or when I get tied up with my work."

"I just want to make things up to you," he said quietly, taking my hand. "Let me escort you to the coronation ball tomorrow night."

"I'm attending with the Cabinet," I replied. "We're to escort the king to the ceremony."

"The Guard is also escorting His Majesty," Stefan said. "Perhaps we can sit together during the ceremony? Then I can accompany you to the feast. We can talk more." He waited expectantly while I considered. I should have told him no, that his apology was not suitable after ignoring me for nearly a month.

"I'll go," I said instead. "But understand that I must be available to the king until the feast."

"I know. Thank you, Shaye." The door to the king's chambers opened and out walked Alastair, hands clasped behind his back.

"Princess Hannele has asked that I come to escort you to dinner," he said.

"Sorry to keep you all waiting," I replied before turning back to Stefan. "I'll see you tomorrow." He smiled and bent to kiss my cheek before walking away without another word. I touched the spot before I could stop myself, then scowled slightly.

"Are you all right?" Alastair asked.

"Yes." I turned on my heel. "And I would prefer if you'd keep what you just saw to yourself."

"I didn't see anything."

I followed behind him, glaring into his back until we reached the dining room, where Aydan sat lazily in his chair, shuffling through some paperwork that no one had forced him to put away yet. Hannele and Gerridan stood, pouring drinks and talking in hushed tones. Hannele stopped when she saw me.

"What did he say?" she asked, holding out a goblet.

"He apologized for his behavior." I sighed, taking it to sit next to Aydan. "He's going to accompany me to the feast tomorrow night." Aydan coughed suddenly, bumping his drink with his elbow and spilling it onto his papers. I snapped my fingers and the wine cleared itself from the papers and made its way back into the goblet. Gerridan snatched it from the table.

"Bravo." He peered into the cup and made a face. "A bit unsanitary for my taste, but it got the job done."

"I've been practicing," I replied before summoning a fresh drink to the table, willing it to set itself down before Aydan, who thanked me with an approving nod. "Are we waiting on Kenna?" I asked no one in particular.

"She said she had a meeting," Alastair responded as he banished Aydan's paperwork and then took the seat opposite from him, "but that was hours ago."

"Oh hush, I'm here," Kenna said as she walked through the door. Her peaches and cream complexion was brighter, glowing even, as it usually did following her visits to her various companions in court. She poured herself a drink and seated herself next to Alastair. "What did I miss?"

Gerridan pulled Hannele's chair out for her before sitting at her left and replying with a sigh, "Shaye has reconciled her friendship with Lord Stefan." Kenna's eyes widened, delighted.

"And?" She looked expectantly between me and the emissary.

"And he'll be accompanying her to the feast tomorrow night," he said flatly. Kenna's head tilted back as she cackled. I watched Gerridan reach into his jacket pocket and toss a coin purse onto the dining table. Hannele rolled her eyes.

"I'm sorry, are the two of you *gambling* on my friendship with Stefan?"

"Lighten up, it's my first win!" Kenna laughed, jingling the purse. Gerridan crossed his arms.

"They all place bets on everything." Aydan leaned in my direction so I could hear his softened voice over the sound of Kenna's one-woman celebration. "Kenna usually isn't allowed to play, being a seer."

"But since our arrival, my read on *you* has become quite unpredictable, my darling blind spot. Gerridan made an exception."

"Yes, one that I won't be making again," Gerridan countered. Kenna blew him a kiss, and he mumbled a string of expletives that sent Hannele's elbow into his ribs.

"Can we please just eat?" Alastair asked. He waved his hand and platters of food appeared before us. The teasing between Gerridan and Kenna stopped almost immediately as plates and bowls were passed back and forth.

"Why can't you see me?" I asked Kenna as I dished roasted vegetables onto my plate. She'd seemed to have such a clear, albeit strange, read on me the first night we'd met. She shrugged.

"I can't see anything related to witchcraft," she explained, taking the dish from my hands. "You may not be a true witch, but my sight doesn't know that. You'd been keeping the rest of your magic hidden up until the night we arrived. I imagine the witchcraft went somewhat dormant if you were only using it to light an occasional fire. It's not that I *can't* see you . . . Things have just been getting murky. As your abilities develop, it may get worse. Something about differing vibrations. My father once told me why, but I've long since forgotten, and frankly I wouldn't believe anything that bastard had to say anyway." Gerridan nodded over his roast beef and Kenna set the dish down with an air of finality.

After dinner, I settled in the lounge. Aydan sat beside me, watching with approval as I demonstrated some of the skills he had been teaching me when time allowed. We were alone as Kenna had another of her meetings to attend, and when Alastair had mumbled that he was turning in early, Hannele and Gerridan loudly announced that they would be taking a walk.

After he was satisfied with my ability to sort sewing needles from matchsticks without touching them, Aydan asked with mischief in his voice, "Do you want to try playing with fire?"

My mouth twitched. "I don't think I should risk burning down the king's chambers the night before his coronation."

"It'll give me a reason to go home to Sylvanna," he replied, chuckling. I fell silent, palms going clammy at the thought. "Are you all right?" He reached for my hand and I flinched, then forced a tight-lipped smile and nodded.

"Of course. Yes. I'm fine, just a bit more tired than I thought." I stood and held my hands out toward the matches. "Let's play." Aydan didn't look convinced but continued anyway.

"Light every other match, then go back to the start and put each one out." I flexed my fingers once and focused my mind.

Nothing happened.

Narrowing my eyes, I *pushed* the will of my mind into my palms.

A moment passed, and my hands began to shake. Sweat beaded on my forehead and my breathing became sharp. Aydan stood next to me. "Shaye, stop. It's fine."

"I can do it."

"You're going to hurt yourself."

"I said *I'm fine*—"

The table burst into flames.

Aydan swore and pushed me behind him. He grabbed a blanket from the back of one of the sofas, but before he could smother the blaze, I watched my own hand reach out and drench the fire with a hard stream of water.

When the flames were out and the table steamed before us, mahogany wood now charred and black, Aydan finally turned his eyes toward me. I stared at my hands, then covered my face, shaking.

"Shaye . . ." he said softly.

"I'm sorry," I choked, wiping at my eyes. "I don't know what to . . . I'm so sorry." The room spun, and I felt like I might be sick.

"Is this the first time with water?" He took my hand. I did not pull away this time.

"Yes. Well, no," I said, looking down at the floor. I told him about the ice in the dress shop that day.

With his free hand, Aydan tilted my chin up and looked into my eyes. "It's going to be okay. We'll get this under control, I promise." His thumb brushed my cheek, wiping away a tear. I suddenly realized how close we were standing. Our breath mingled. I stepped back and wiped my eyes again before turning to leave—too quickly. I swayed and grabbed the back of the sofa to steady myself. Aydan reached out to help, but I raised a hand to stop him.

"I'm fine. I just need—I need to go. I'm so sorry, Aydan," I stammered again. "I'll see you tomorrow."

He called after me as I shoved my way through the door to the main hall. I didn't stop, and instead all but ran the length of the corridor to my suite.

Once inside, I shut the door, leaned against it, and let myself slide to the ground. I couldn't stand any longer if I tried. Sobs tore through my chest so hard it hurt, and Catchfly rubbed against my legs, nudging her head into my lap. I gathered her into my arms and held her tight.

Pressing my face into her warm fur, I whispered, "I just want it to stop." Catchfly purred against me until I drifted into darkness.

Chapter Twenty-Three

The next evening, the Cabinet members and I stood in Aydan's foyer, waiting to escort him to the temple, where the coronation ceremony would take place. I had been roused from sleep by Elise early that morning, with her shaking me and calling out my name.

"My lady, are you quite all right?" I blinked, peeling my head away from my arm and sitting up. Realizing I had slept on the floor the whole night.

"I'm fine. Thank you, Elise," I mumbled and rubbed the sleep out of my eyes. "Rough night."

"I see," she said, then held out a hand to help me to my feet. "Well, I hope it wasn't *too* rough. Today is a big day."

"I'll get in the bath," I said. "That'll help."

Elise had outdone herself. It was my first real event as a lady of the Cabinet, and did I ever look the part: Elise managed my hair into shiny waves and then into an intricate braided style that took hours to complete, even with magic to assist her. She'd kept my face nearly bare, save for some rouge on my cheeks, before curling my eyelashes and leaving me to dress.

Now we stood, counting down the minutes while Kenna tapped her foot impatiently. She and Hannele were stunning. When they'd entered the room, Gerridan's breath had hitched before he swallowed and quickly wiped the emotion from his face. He greeted them each with a kiss on the cheek, flirting as usual. Hannele's mauve dress had turned out exactly like her sketch, with full, flowing satin skirts and a neckline so low I nearly blushed—until I saw Kenna.

Kenna wore a lagoon blue gown with no bodice at all. The seer's breasts were covered only by panels of gauzy fabric, crisscrossed over the tops of her shoulders, and her skirt was made of the same bright cobweb material, with a slit to reveal her leg all the way up to her hip. Like Hannele's, it looked like it had been made especially for her. She clearly hoped to scandalize tonight.

The door opened, and Stefan entered with three other guardsmen. I recognized one—an older, graying mortal named Gregory who had accompanied me often when I was a servant. Stefan and his men all wore their ceremonial armor, plated in gold, embellished with the winged lion crest of House Aevitarus.

"You look so different." He leaned down to kiss my cheek. I flushed, glancing around to see if any of the Cabinet had seen or cared. Gerridan made brief eye contact with me and raised his eyebrows.

"Thank you, I think," I replied.

"You know what I mean." Stefan chuckled. I smiled tightly back at him. He was probably just nervous, I told myself. And I did look different; the gown Hannele had selected for me was a deep wine color, with a lace bodice and sleeves reaching down to my wrists. The gossamer skirts were light and easy to move in, and quite like Kenna's without the leg slit.

A door shut somewhere in the suite, and a minute later, Aydan appeared in the doorway. He paused, looking around at us all. His plain white shirt was untucked from black pants. He wore no shoes, no adornments, and no jewels of any kind. He was meant to be humbled when entering the temple for anointment. I thought he looked terrified.

We all began to kneel in unison, but Aydan bid us to stand.

"Thank you all, for your commitment to the Crown, and for your trust in me," he said. "I am not the king any of you expected, but I intend to make it my life's mission to be the king you deserve." He inclined his head toward us, and we remained hushed. Eventually, he cleared his throat and stepped past us into the corridor.

The temple, once a wing of its own in the Grand Palace, was now in a space hardly larger than a dance hall on the southeast end of the castle. Gerridan had told me weeks ago that King Zathryan's coronation had nearly a thousand guests in attendance. Aydan's would have perhaps fifty; the rest would be present at the feast and the ball following the ceremony.

"It's probably for the best," he said. "Lovely Aydan will be nervous enough as it is."

Walking behind Aydan now, slightly to his right, I could see him opening and closing his fist, occasionally wiping his palm on his thigh. I wished I could comfort him somehow. To my left, Stefan strode in step with me. He glanced in my direction and winked, smiling slightly. Uneasy, I returned the smile. It felt strange to have Aydan and Stefan so near one another. Wrong, somehow. I shook the thought from my mind as we reached the temple doors, which opened upon Aydan's arrival.

The High Priest stood before us, holding a chalice in his hands. The temple was dark behind him.

"The Tears of Ehnara," the High Priest murmured. With a wave of his hand, Aydan's shirt disappeared. He dipped his fingers into the chalice and brought them to Aydan's forehead, drew a moon shape there, and let droplets of the blessed water fall on his chest, over top of his heart. The High Priest then made his way to each member of the Cabinet, and the guardsmen accompanying us, tracing the moon on our faces as well. He stepped aside and bid us to enter.

Slowly, we walked down the darkened aisle toward a small stage, marked only by candlelight. I could barely make out the shapes around me but could sense that the temple was filled with people, watching and waiting. Stefan's guards took their places at the back of the room, but he followed beside me. When we had delivered Aydan to the temple alter, my new friends and I found our seats on a long bench in the front row. Stefan sat closely beside me, our legs touching. I felt him staring at me out of the corner of his eye but ignored him as I watched the ceremony unfold.

Aydan was on his knees at the altar.

"Father Lehrun and Mother Ehnara bless us this night," the High Priestess began in a low tone that reached the far corners of the room. "As we honor generations of tradition, we also look to the future."

Over the next hour, Aydan sat perfectly still on his knees while the High Priest and Priestess took turns reciting prayers and giving sermons about the grace of the Mother and protection of the Father, the significance of the crown Aydan would soon wear, and the unrelenting, holy power of anointed kings. Aydan's face was somber, and his eyes were glazed. It was time for the anointing.

The High Priest approached a pedestal on the dais where he stood and presented a glass vessel. The room shifted as the coronation witnesses realized what it was—the Dyadic Oil.

Hannele had explained in whispers, while supervising the planning of the feast, that the Dyadic Oil was said to be held in a secret location by the High Priest and Priestess. The oil, preserved by magic for seven thousand years, was the same oil that was used during the first coronation, when Ehnara and Lehrun themselves named the first King of Medeisia. Each anointed king—and the one anointed queen, Euna—were the only Medeisians to ever be touched by the blessed oil, which was as good as being touched by the gods themselves.

The High Priest dipped a gold-handled brush into the oil before drawing a shape on Aydan's forehead, where he had drawn the moon in holy water an hour before. He dipped the brush again and began drawing more symbols on Aydan's neck, arms, and chest. His tattoos shone beneath the oil in the candlelit temple hall.

The High Priestess opened a large box and lifted the coronation crown. I felt my palms grow hot as she raised it above her head and presented it to the witnesses. I wiped my hands on my skirt. *Gods, not now,* I thought. The crown, which was solid gold and encrusted with diamonds and sapphires, formed into tall points representing the rays of the sun. My breath shallowed as I watched the High Priestess lower the crown onto Aydan's head. She bid him to rise, and he faced us, expressionless. The magic in the room shifted, bearing down upon all of us who watched as the freshly anointed king gazed out into the audience. Every head in the temple lowered, and unexpected tears pricked in my eyes. I blinked them away. When we lifted our heads again, I glanced past Stefan to Gerridan, whose eyes were wet as well.

Aydan stood before us for a full minute before it was time for the prominent witnesses to make their oaths of fealty. Nobles from Xarynn went first, kneeling before Aydan, some kissing his hand before quietly reciting their prepared oaths. Next came the pair of representatives from Sylvanna, sent by Solandis and Priamos to observe the coronation by proxy. They swore no oath but knelt before the king and pressed his hand to their foreheads. Solandis and Priamos would swear fealty in person once the new treaties were signed.

Lord Declan was next, accompanied by Lord Dracus and half of the Ayzellen Council. He did not let it show, but I could feel the resentment radiating from Declan as he too knelt before his king and said the words. When the other council members were finished, it was time for the Cabinet to approach.

We stood from our seats and filed forward to the stage. Aydan's face had remained the same throughout the whole ceremony, and it did not change for us. I watched as Hannele, then Kenna, Alastair, and Gerridan each knelt before their friend and brother, pressed a kiss to his hand and brought it to their brow, as the other Sylvannians had done. Our words would be different, we'd decided. It was my turn to kneel. Like the others, I kissed my king's hand and touched it to my brow.

"Your Majesty, I swear to you now, before gods and men, that I will serve the Crown faithfully. That I will protect your throne with honor, do your bidding, and guard your realm, all the days of my life."

Aydan's solemn gaze shifted to mine for the briefest moment, then snapped forward once more. The enormity of my vow fluttered in my chest, and I did my best to push it down as I joined the rest of the Cabinet to the side of the stage, now facing the other witnesses. They stared intently at Aydan while the Guard, led by Stefan, took their turns kneeling. When they finished, the room fell fully silent.

The blue glow of the royal line began to encase Aydan's hands, and then his arms. Static like tiny lightning bolts sparked from his fingertips as the glow became a bright, nearly blinding light. I wanted to shield my eyes, but it was impossible to turn away. The light shrunk again and became small pools in his palms, which Aydan held upright toward the heavens. He stepped forward and began to walk back down the aisle of the temple. The Priestess called out from the stage as he reached the doors, "Long live the Anointed King—Aydan, the Lion of Medeisia!"

"Long live the King!"

Chapter Twenty-Four

Aydan would not be joining us at the feast. It was tradition for the newly anointed king to spend the feast secluded in silent prayer until the start of the start of the ball.

Stefan offered me his arm, which I accepted, while we walked to the great hall. The rest of the Cabinet trailed behind us, and a small knot formed in my chest. I wished they would walk beside me, if only for Gerridan to quickly refresh me on all the people I would be meeting in a few moments.

"Thank gods that's over." Stefan sighed. "You immortals and your ceremonies—I swear, you forget that not all of us have unlimited time."

"I thought it was beautiful," I said.

"Oh . . . yes, of course. It was just *long* . . ." he corrected. "Sorry. A bad joke." I forced a small smile and changed the subject.

"What will you do during the feast?" He knew that I would be with the Cabinet, greeting the guests.

"I'll go change out of my armor. Hopefully by the time I get back, you'll be nearly done." When we reached the great hall, Stefan bent and kissed my cheek before walking away swiftly toward his suite. I flushed.

As soon as he was gone, Gerridan swooped into the vacant spot, taking my arm and looping it through his own. He winked at me.

"Well, Lady Advisor." He smirked. "Are you ready to represent the Crown?" I swallowed.

"Am I allowed to say no?"

"Absolutely not," he declared, patting my hand. Hannele appeared on my other side, falling into place to flank me.

"You'll be great," she said kindly. I nodded, then took a breath and squared my shoulders.

"Let's do it, then," I said, stepping forward into the great hall.

The start of the feast went smoothly enough.

Gerridan stayed by my side for most of it, standing back and allowing me to take the lead once he'd introduced me as Aydan's new Chief Advisor. Alastair joined some of the lower generals for a drink, while Hannele and Kenna were roped into a conversation with one of the visiting Sylvannian representatives. Gerridan had found no need to correct me thus far. He only stepped in when we saw the broad-chested, heavily mustached Duke of Xarynn making his way toward us with a wide smile on his face.

"It looks like the captain has returned," Gerridan told me. "Perhaps you should greet him and let me take this one."

"I thought I was doing well."

"You are," he said, turning us away so the duke would not hear, "but the Duke of Xarynn is incapable of speaking to an unmarried woman without attempting to seduce her. So unless you want a man who eats nothing but clams and fish heads to spend the rest of the night breathing down your neck, I suggest you go greet your lover."

"He's not—"

"Go." He pushed me toward where Stefan indeed now stood. As I walked away, I heard the emissary loudly greet the duke, "Your Grace, how *lovely* to see you again . . ."

Stefan was waiting, holding two goblets and looking quite dashing. He'd changed into a pair of brown tailored pants, with black boots and a blue waistcoat embroidered in gold. It was more luxurious and expensive than anything I'd ever seen him wear before.

"You look handsome."

"Thank you." He handed me a drink. "The woman in the shop said it was fashionable, but I never know with these sorts of things."

"It suits you," I confirmed. One of the waitstaff walked by with a large tray of hors d'oeuvres. I stopped him and took two of the small plates offered with a variety of food. Lord Declan had insisted on this rather than a traditional, sit-down feast. Platters of food would be set up throughout the room for the night—preserved at its proper temperature by magic—for people to graze from as they pleased. Hannele and I had not objected to the idea, but the princess rolled her eyes later over Declan's eagerness for Ayzelle to appear modern and exciting.

Stefan and I stood making small talk for the next half hour as we watched the nobles interact, joking about their clothes and their obvious desperation to appear closer to the king than they were. After more than a century of gossiping about the Wayward Prince, many were now scrambling to save face.

"Well, it might not *all* be gossip," Stefan commented around a bite of finger sandwich.

"What do you mean?" I asked.

"The rumors about him," he said after swallowing. "Some of them come from very reliable sources in Sylvanna, across the sea . . ." I stared at him.

"What are you talking about?"

"What, you really don't know?"

He lowered his voice. "They didn't call him *wayward* just because he disobeyed his father. There are plenty of rumors about Aydan Aevitarus beyond family dramatics." Stefan took a drink. Was this his fourth? "Apparently, he has broken several courtships *and* engagements with members of noble families in Sylvanna—according to some sources, he has a bastard or two back home." I swallowed. "He *was* a decorated soldier in his grandmother's army, but that all fell apart after he executed a pair of civilians in Auperene—"

"Why would Sylvannian soldiers be in the faelands?" I asked.

"Sylvanna has been rogue for decades. Who knows what they've been getting up to? Apparently, the fae king was so furious that he threatened war with Solandis and she forced King Aydan to step down from his service."

"That doesn't sound like him. He told me he retired," I said, my brow furrowing.

"I'm sure that's what it says on paper." He shrugged again. I drank deeply from my goblet, emptying the last of it.

"What else?"

"Not much that I can think of," Stefan said as he beckoned for one of the waitstaff to come to us. He gave the man our empty goblets and took a pair of fresh ones from his tray. "Oh," he said after sipping from his new drink, "there was the supposed incident with Lord Vesper, but the details on that have been so muddled that no one I've heard repeat it can tell the same story."

"Lord Vesper… . . . as in Lady Kenna?" The seer was standing on the other side of the hall with Hannele, talking with the Floinn sisters, who I could only imagine would have plenty to say about my colleague's attire when they left. Stefan nodded. "What happened to him?"

"He was found slaughtered inside the Vesper family home some fifteen years ago," Stefan replied. "There was never any real proof that His Majesty was involved, but the circumstances—"

"If there's no real proof, then why tell me?" I asked, growing nauseated. "You shouldn't be speaking of such things." The time I'd spent with Aydan before the attack, everything he ever told me about himself . . . Did I even know him?

Stefan returned to chatting happily about the evening and about upcoming training for new recruits for the Guard, as if he had not just delivered to me a list of unsettling stories about our king, the man I had just sworn to serve without question. There had to be more to it than what Stefan was telling me. I made a mental note to speak discreetly with Hannele, and started tuning out Stefan in favor of looking around the hall again. It was not much longer until the herald cried out:

"His Majesty, King Aydan!"

Aydan entered alone, now in black pants and a deep plum tunic, with a gold crown formed into roses atop his head. He strode to the center of the hall to a round of applause. With his hands behind his back, he gave the room a tight-lipped smile. "Thank you," he said, raising a hand for silence. "I'd like to also acknowledge Lord Declan, for his careful planning of tonight's festivities." He gestured to the lord, who bowed deeply. I smirked, knowing how badly Declan would have wanted to complain about his lack of recognition. "Now please, enjoy yourselves. The night is still young." Applause erupted once again as Aydan made his way to greet the Duke of Xarynn, who had joined the Sylvannian representatives, and music began to play from an unseen orchestra.

"Why'd he change crowns?" I wondered aloud. "The other was magnificent."

"It would probably break his neck before the night was through. That much gold and jewels, I'd be shocked if it was lighter than fifteen pounds." I winced at the thought of that much weight balanced on one's head. "Though," Stefan continued, "*that* crown in particular is likely a message regarding the king's intentions with Sylvanna." The rose was the sigil of Sylvanna. I pursed my lips; more rumors, it seemed.

"You don't think the new trade agreements are a good idea?" I asked. The upcoming treaties were no secret throughout court.

"King Aydan has now spent nearly two mortal lifetimes under the influence of his grandparents. Reuniting the Crown with Sylvanna likely means handing the throne to Solandis."

"I don't know where you're getting your information, but I have seen no indication of such a thing," I said, glancing in Aydan's direction. He was still talking to the duke, whose boisterous laugh could be heard over the orchestra.

"Well, he wouldn't have told *you* yet, would he?"

"I'm his Chief Advisor, Stef. I'm at his side every day—"

"But you're not his Sylvannian inner circle, are you?" he argued. "You didn't know about his reputation, and you certainly haven't been active in court long enough to understand how the Lord and Lady of Sylvanna feel about the Crown. Mark my words, the Wayward Prince has no desire to govern. This unification pipe dream is a scheme laid out by his grandparents—"

"*Stefan,*" I hissed. "You are *completely* out of line."

"Out of line?"

"Yes. You've been spouting rumors all night, which I tolerated if only to know what's been said. But I will not sit here and listen to the Captain of the King's Guard spout *conspiracy theories* about the king's loyalties to his own throne, no matter how close we are—"

"My lady, might I ask that you join me for a dance?" I turned and saw Gerridan standing behind me patiently. I blinked a few times, and he glanced pointedly at my hands. A small stream of smoke was coming from my fingertips. I clenched and released my fists, which seemed to make the smoke subside.

"That sounds lovely." I took Gerridan's offered hand and allowed him to lead me to the dance floor, leaving Stefan alone and fuming.

"Careful," Gerridan murmured, his lips nearly grazing my ear as he leaned in. "You'll send this place up like a tinderbox if you keep getting into lovers' quarrels in public."

"Stefan is not my lover," I replied coolly. We stood at the edge of the dance floor, waiting for a new song to begin before joining in. Gerridan led me onto the floor when it was our turn.

"That's not what he thinks." He guided me through the first few steps with ease. I shook my head.

"Lord Stefan is my friend, that's it—" I cut myself off to concentrate on my footing. "Gods, I'm sorry, I don't know why I said yes to this. I can barely keep up."

"I've got it covered," he assured me, chuckling a little. He shifted his hand to grip my waist and pulled me closer. He held me off the floor, with my shoes just resting on the tops of his. I flushed, thankful that my dress covered my feet so no one could see.

"Now I feel like a child." I huffed an embarrassed laugh. Gerridan laughed too, then leaned to speak softly in my ear, his cheek pressed against mine.

"Your *friend* doesn't look so happy with us," he said. At the next turn in our steps, I was able to nonchalantly look in Stefan's direction. Most of the guests either watched the dance floor as a whole or mingled amongst themselves. Stefan stood alone, glaring directly at us as he drank from his goblet. Gods, how much wine had he drank tonight? Kenna, Hannele, and Alastair remained mingling throughout the hall.

"Why aren't our friends dancing?" I asked.

"They don't like Ayzellen dances," Gerridan replied. "Kenna says it doesn't feel natural, the rehearsed steps."

"And you do?" I inquired. If anyone seemed the type to dislike structure, it was Gerridan.

"I used to travel to negotiate with Ayzelle, Xarynn, Nautia before the rebellion—even some of the smaller territories. Feasting, dancing, and wooing the nobility are a bigger part of my job than you might think."

"So that's why you're such an insufferable flirt," I said. His eyes sparkled with mischief.

"Careful, my lady, or I might just drop you."

"Don't you dare."

We talked and joked, both of us admitting our excitement to be done with coronation planning so we could sink into a bit of normalcy. Truthfully, I did not know what normal would look like for me here. A routine, of course, as there was both a court and a kingdom to run. There was still the Sylvannian treaty and Aydan's goals with Nautia. But life without fear, life with freedom, was something I looked forward to a great deal. When I asked what Gerridan considered normalcy, he said, "Getting back into the sparring ring, for one. You can join me if you like."

"Sparring?" I repeated. "What, like fighting? Why would I need to do that?"

"Plenty of ladies train. Even if you never use it, it couldn't hurt to know how to defend yourself. It can be useful for developing magic as well—to know your body's limitations. As your powers grow, you might find that you need more strength than you currently hold."

I considered for a second but shook my head. "Thank you, but I think I'll just focus on magic for now."

"The offer remains."

The song ended. Those of us on the dance floor applauded the hidden orchestra, and almost immediately the music started again, this time with a slower tempo. The emissary raised an eyebrow and offered his hand once again. I smiled and allowed him to pull me in closely and led me in the dance, despite feeling Stefan's stare pounding into us.

After some time to adjust to the new steps, I decided what Stefan had told me couldn't wait for me to speak to Hannele. "Speaking of fighting . . ." Gerridan's eyebrows rose. "I heard a rumor, about Aydan's time in the army."

"And what might that be?" he asked, though his tone indicated that he knew exactly what rumor I was talking about.

"Something about executing civilians in Auperene." Gerridan led me through a turn and brought me back close before replying.

"Who could be whispering such treasonous tales in earshot of the Chief Advisor?" he asked sarcastically, glancing in Stefan's direction. I shot Gerridan a look and he sighed. "It's really not my story to tell. But it *is* public knowledge back home, so I suppose there's no harm." Another turn. "The fae king asked Solandis for soldiers to spare in a search and rescue that one of his sons—Alec, I think—was conducting. A string of kidnappings in their capital, girls being taken in the night. Aydan volunteered, and a week or so into the mission, they found the girls and the men who had taken them, preparing them for sale to the highest bidder." My stomach churned.

"The girls were rescued, and after Aydan treated their injuries, they were taken home to their families. It turned out the men were from the outskirts of Sylvanna. Normally, it would be left to Solandis and the fae king to determine who would imprison and sentence them, but Alec and Aydan decided they had as much authority as was necessary to handle it. They agreed, and given that the men were from our territory, Aydan had the pleasure of beheading the scum himself, right then and there. He retired when he came home, joined the council shortly after."

"Thank you," I said quietly, feeling quite guilty for believing Stefan. I was sure he would feel the same once I told him the truth.

"Anything else?" he asked as the final notes of the song played. "More rumors?"

"Only about supposed bastards and broken engagements," I joked.

"None of the former, just one of the latter," he quipped.

"What?"

"That one is *really* not my story to tell. Just ask Aydan about it. If you're lucky, maybe he'll tell you about how he ended *our* courtship." He smirked at the surprised look on my face, then added, "Don't worry yourself, Lady Advisor. It was almost a century ago."

The dance ended, and this time the men bowed to their partners. While Gerridan was bent, Stefan appeared at my side and gripped my arm.

"I'll take the next dance," he announced. Gerridan rose quickly, his face devoid of all its usual warmth.

"Proper etiquette dictates that a gentleman *asks* a lady to dance, my lord." His gaze darted to Stefan's hand on my elbow.

"I don't believe I asked for an etiquette lesson," Stefan replied. Gerridan's brows shot up and he took a step toward the captain.

"It's fine," I assured him, now thoroughly embarrassed. I gave the emissary a tight-lipped smile as the music started around us. He bowed again and stepped off the dance floor, where Stefan now dug his hand roughly into my waist and attempted to lead me in the steps. He reeked of alcohol.

"You're drunk," I said. "You're speaking badly about the king, and now you just completely humiliated me in front of a fellow Cabinet member. I don't know what's gotten into you Stef, but you need to get over it. Now."

"What's gotten into *me*?" he hissed, stopping and letting go of me completely. "Isn't it obvious?"

"No, Stef, nothing about your behavior in the past weeks has been *obvious*. I thought maybe you just needed time to adjust, so I gave you a second chance tonight and here you are, making a complete fool of me." I took his hand and led him off the dance floor, beyond where most of the courtiers were congregated. I crossed my arms over my chest. "So what is it? You don't like the king, yet you serve as the Captain of his Guard and accepted a lordship? You claim to want what is best for me, but now that I've been given back my title and awarded a position of power, you ignore me for weeks on end? None of it makes sense—"

"I'm in love with you," he blurted. "I have been for months, I just never—I never knew how to say it. I don't know what's wrong with me, why I'm acting this way. I just needed to tell you." I gaped at him He shifted impatiently. "Please say something."

"Stef . . ." I sighed. "I don't think this is the place to discuss it."

"No, this is the perfect place to discuss it," he said. "We've spent a year together, Shaye. Are you telling me that you feel nothing for me?"

"No," I said, "of course not *nothing*, but this is very sudden." Stefan stared, waiting for me to elaborate. "The past month—it's the first time in a year that I've been able to think of anything but *surviving*, Stef. You've been such a good friend to me—"

Stefan scoffed. "A friend. That's it, then." He turned to leave. I grabbed his hand.

"No, that's not it—or . . . it's that I don't *know*. This is the first you've told me of your feelings. You just spoke to me for the first time in weeks *yesterday*, and then you spend all night acting strangely and now I'm supposed to, what, throw myself into your arms or walk away forever? I need time. Give me time," I pleaded. "Let me be your friend, as a free woman."

"All right," he nearly whispered. "If time is what you need, it's yours."

"Thank you," I said, squeezing his hand. "Should we have that dance?" He shook his head.

"No, you were right. I've had too much to drink. I should go lie down."

"Okay." He kissed my hand and left me standing alone and baffled. I saw that I was near a table of desserts and quickly shoved a small pastry drizzled with honey and blackberry sauce into my mouth. When I turned back, Gerridan had reappeared.

"Are you all right?" he asked, looking me over.

"I'm fine," I said, blushing. "A misunderstanding, that's all."

"There was quite a grip on that misunderstanding," he replied before grabbing one of the pastries for himself and placing it on a plate.

"It was nothing," I said.

After a moment of silence, he set the plate down. "Shaye, we're friends, are we not?"

"I would like to think so," I said. The corners of his mouth were turned downward.

"Then let me make something abundantly clear, as a friend. If I ever see the captain put his hand on you like that again, it will be the last time he has use of it."

"It wasn't like that—"

"I don't particularly care what the reason was, or what your relationship is with that man," he continued. "But I've met enough men in my life to know that these types of misunderstandings tend to escalate." I could not think to do anything but nod. My hands coated themselves in frost as they hung at my sides. "Good night, Shaye. Please let me know if you need anything."

"Good night," I said softly. He bowed his head before turning and leaving me alone again. The music and laughter continued while I watched, my back to the wall.

Across the room, Gerridan joined Hannele, handing her a drink. I wondered if he was telling her now what he'd seen between me and Stefan. A couple of tables away, Kenna stood alone as well, drinking and staring at a blonde woman who seemed to be trying her hardest not to look at the seer, but would occasionally glance away from her friends, toward her, and blush. Kenna set her drink down and walked away, out of one of the servant's entrances. A moment later, the blonde excused herself from her group and followed through the same door.

Alastair was nowhere to be seen. He must have turned in early for the night. I could not picture the stoic general enjoying himself at parties.

I was debating if it was time for me to retire as well when a shrill laugh cut through the music. The Floinn sisters had finally found their moment and now held Aydan's attention, all smiles and batted eyelashes as they spoke to him. Aydan looked quite interested in whatever they had to say, and when he replied with a nod and polite smile the sisters erupted into laughter once again.

I thought of what Stefan had told me about Aydan's courting history and brought another small dessert, this time some sort of chocolate concoction, to my lips. When the cake touched my skin I nearly cried out. I dropped it to the floor, and realized it was smoldering, having burned to a crisp in my hand. I knelt and banished the chocolate to a waste bin in the kitchens, then swiftly left the hall before anyone could see what I had done.

Chapter Twenty-Five

Even with my tincture, it took nearly two hours to fall asleep. I tossed and turned, playing the evening back over in my head. The coronation, the ball—and Stefan. I wasn't sure which was the cause of the knot buried in my gut: his confession, or the stories he told me. Gerridan had an explanation for one, but what about the others? I shook my head, feeling silly. Stefan himself had told me that there was no proof Aydan had been involved with Lord Vesper's death. And why should I care if the king had broken courtships? He'd lived for more than a century, of course he would have had courtships over the decades. I'd had my own fair share of lovers long before I ever knew I was a sorceress— I was a hypocrite for even having an opinion on the topic. *Aydan's love life isn't for me to worry about,* I told myself as I drifted to sleep. The knot in my gut did not go away.

A couple hours later, I woke with a start and sat up straight in my bed, surrounded by darkness. I cast a ball of light to the ceiling and saw that the room was empty, save for Catchfly, who snoozed quietly at the foot of the bed. My nightdress stuck to my skin and I shivered, my breathing ragged, though I could not understand why. Perhaps my tincture had gone rancid.

Now thoroughly awake, I realized I was hungry. I looked up at the clock—half past two in the morning. Too long to wait for breakfast, so I hauled myself from bed and stepped over my discarded ballgown to look for a shawl. Not wanting to bother any servants for food at this hour, I wrapped it around my shoulders and headed into the corridor. I was nearly at the arched entrance to the north wing when I heard footsteps behind me.

"Shaye?" It was Aydan, still fully dressed from the ball, the rose crown on his head. He looked concerned as he stepped toward me. "What's wrong?"

"Nothing—I just woke up. I thought I'd find something to eat in the kitchens and go back to bed." Relief washed over the king's face.

"For a moment, I thought you were sleepwalking," he said. After a pause, he added, "I wasn't ready to sleep. I took a walk to clear my mind, and then before I knew it, it was the middle of the night and I was starved. Would you like to join me?" He gestured toward the door to his chambers.

I tightened my shawl around myself, remembering that I wore only a nightdress, but it wasn't the first time he'd seen me fresh from sleep.

I followed him into the chambers and down the now familiar corridor to the private council room the Cabinet met in nearly every day. He waved a hand over the table and produced plates of cheeses and fruits, as well as some leftover chicken and bread, a bottle of liquor, and two short glasses. I poured a drink for each of us and tried not to make a face when it burned my throat. We filled our plates and ate in silence, and when we'd had enough, Aydan banished the dishes and platters from the table surface, leaving only our drinks.

"How are you?" I asked after a moment. Aydan traced the rim of his glass with a finger.

"Me? I'm fine, all things considered," he said. "Though, I suppose if I'm honest, tonight was difficult to get through."

"I could imagine," I said. "It looked like it would take a toll."

After a few seconds of silence, he said, "After the Heirs' Duel, I never thought I'd have this life. I was, well, not *content* being the Wayward Prince, but I was settled enough. I had my family in Sylvanna and my position on the council. I had a life. Even with the past year to mentally prepare, I couldn't help but feel inadequate in that temple today." Aydan drummed his fingers on the surface of the table. "I found myself wishing for Irsa to burst through the door and tell us it was all a mistake."

"And now?"

"And now, I am the anointed King of Medeisia." He shrugged. "The scholars will document my reign. I can only hope that it is not used as the example of how *not* to govern, when some unfortunate future descendant of mine is forced to study it." Aydan drained his glass then poured another drink before asking, "And how are you? After last night, I mean." I blushed.

"Fine," I said. "I'm sorry that I ran out like that. I just—I was overwhelmed. The fire is hard enough to control on its own. I worry what other gifts Lord Ronan has passed on to me."

"There's nothing to apologize for. As I said, we'll figure it all out as it comes. We leave for Sylvanna in a few weeks. They have one of the largest libraries in the world. Perhaps we can make some inquiries with the scholars there." I nodded in silent agreement. "And all else is well? You're enjoying your work?"

"Oh yes, very much so." It was true. Even though so far all we'd done is plan the coronation and attempt to reverse some of Zathryan's end-of-life decrees. Even with Stefan's stories on my mind. "I feel like I finally have a purpose in Ayzelle—beyond scrubbing floors and linens, that is. It's only been a few weeks, but I feel like I could make a difference for the people here."

"Was it . . ." Aydan started, then paused, looking ashamed. "I never asked what it was like for you here with my father." I swallowed. "I know that the chambers were breeched. Elise and the others told me that you sent them away, and I know my father made you a servant." I couldn't bring myself to look up from the table. "But I also know that couldn't have been all that happened." Ice began forming at my fingertips and I quickly buried my hands in my lap before Aydan could see.

"I was interrogated," I admitted. "They moved me to that tiny room, and every few mornings for months, I was taken to the dungeons and interrogated about my supposed connections to Sylvanna." *Mostly true,* I thought. Aydan's hand clenched into a fist on the table and I pretended not to notice.

"The blood shield," he said. "Did it hold? Were you hurt?"

"The blood shield held." *Only a half lie.* I tried to blink away the memory of anguished screams filling my ears in the dungeon. Relief settled in Aydan's expression.

"I cannot tell you how sorry I am, Shaye."

"I was lucky that Stefan was around to help me," I managed to say. I could taste the metallic tang of blood dripping on my lips. The heavy air of the dungeons bore down on me and then—

I was being dragged by my wrists down a servants' passage by a pair of guards. The dirty shift I'd been dressed in by my captors was hitched up around my thighs, and a silver cuff was locked on my ankle—as if I could muster the strength for magic. I could barely hold my eyes open.

I heard a door open and was all but thrown through it. I remained there, unable to haul myself up and into the bed. Catchfly was growling from her perch on the edge of a bookshelf. I heard a guard swear, the sounds of a scuffle, Catchfly yowling. I looked up just as one of the men yanked her off the other by her tail.

"Don't hurt her," I moaned. "Please—"

"What the hell is going on here?" Standing in the doorway was Captain Whittaker, wide-eyed at the scene in front of him. The guard threw Catchfly onto the bed. "What have you done to this woman?"

"Nothing, captain," said the shorter of the two guards. "We were told to transport the prisoner back to her quarters. King's orders." The captain stepped forward.

"Did those orders include brutalizing her cat while she was left on the floor in nothing but—" He looked down at me, then barked to the guards. "Leave. Now." The order rang in my ears. I closed my eyes as the door shut behind them.

Then I heard movement as the captain rummaged around my room. A low, constant growl came from Catchfly while she watched him. Suddenly, rough hands slid under me. My body screamed at the touch, but I couldn't produce the sound from my raw throat.

"Please . . . no more," I whispered instead, too exhausted to even cry. The captain lay me on my bed. He covered me with a blanket.

"I'll be back, Miss Eastly," he said quietly, and left. Catchfly curled herself near my head, and everything else disappeared.

I didn't know if it was hours or minutes later when my door opened again. I forced my eyes open and saw the captain carrying a pair of buckets and a bundle of torn linens. His armor was gone. He set the supplies on the floor before peeling the blanket from me. He inhaled sharply. "I need to clean you up," he said. I nodded once, then watched as he reached for the knife strapped to his leg. "I'm going to cut the back of your shift." Another nod, and he carefully began cutting strips of the once white fabric, now mottled red and brown with my half-dried blood. I winced when his fingers grazed my skin. "I'm sorry," he murmured. When the whole of my back was exposed, the captain dipped a rag in one of the buckets. "I'm sorry," he said again as he brought the wet cloth to my skin and I cried out. "I'm sorry—"

"Shaye?"

My attention snapped back to the present. Aydan sat across the table, looking at me expectantly. "I'm sorry," I said. "I must be more tired than I thought."

"I should get some sleep too. Gerridan will never let me hear the end of it if I fall asleep during the meeting tomorrow."

He walked me to the foyer. "About tomorrow's meeting," I said when we reached the door. "Would it be possible to postpone until after midday?"

"Technically, you're in charge of the meetings."

"Technically, you're in charge of everything," I countered. He chuckled.

"I'll leave a note for Gerridan," he said. "Would you like me to walk you to your suite?" I shook my head and reached for the door handle.

"No, thank you." I opened it. "I'll see you tomorrow." Aydan placed a hand gently on my arm.

"Shaye." I looked up at him. "I really am very sorry. For leaving you here." I forced a smile to my lips. "More than you know. I can't even begin to explain how—"

"It's okay, Aydan. Really." The sad sort of smile he gave made me wonder if he knew I was lying.

We bid each other good night, and I returned to my suite, where I climbed into bed and lay awake until the sun rose.

Chapter Twenty-Six

I sent a note with Elise the next morning to invite Stefan to my suite for a late breakfast. He arrived quickly and greeted me with a kiss to the cheek before telling me I looked lovely. Elise had delivered a tray of pastries and a tea service, which we enjoyed at a small table in the center of my suite while I did my best to pretend like nothing happened the night before. *A clean slate,* I thought. He was talking about changes he wanted to implement in the Guard once given permission from Aydan.

"Do you need me to arrange a meeting for you?" I asked.

"No need." He waved off the suggestion. "I sent a request yesterday, and His Majesty replied this morning. I'll be sitting in on a Cabinet meeting sometime next month."

"Oh." I forced a smile. I found myself struggling to come up with things to speak about, and instead let Stefan do most of the talking, which he seemed happy to do. When I told him that I'd inquired about Aydan's supposed scandals and learned the truth surrounding the events in Auperene, he shrugged, unfazed.

"I was just repeating what I'd been told. It's good that you and your Cabinet friends feel you can trust him." He drained his tea, and I couldn't help but feel wary of that response. Why, I did not know. I knew Stefan, trusted Stefan. So why did every word he said to me in the past two days make me feel defensive? I shook off the feeling and turned my attention back to my friend.

"Speaking of the Cabinet, I should start preparing for my meeting."

He wiped his mouth on a napkin and stood. "Thank you for inviting me," he said. "Could I . . . could I escort you on a walk around the grounds this evening?"

I couldn't think of a reason to say no. "Of course, Stef. I'd like that very much."

"I'll see you then," he said with a grin before kissing my hand in farewell. I followed him to the door, and when it clicked shut behind him, I put a hand over my face and leaned against it. Catchfly rubbed against my legs.

"He's so eager," I said, looking down at the fat gray cat. I had spent the last year as his friend. He defended me, kept me safe at great risk to himself. He had defied the orders of the king he so dearly loved. For me. Catchfly meowed, staring up at me. Maybe I just needed to let him try. I at least owed him that, didn't I?

The rest of the day went by quickly.

Our meeting was short, as there wasn't much to discuss. Aydan informed the others of their upcoming audience with Stefan and then changed the subject, asking Kenna to focus her time on locating any unread documents of Zathryan's.

That evening, I met Stefan at the garden gates. He offered his arm and I took it, allowing myself to walk closely in step with him. I listened as he pointed out spots where he'd liked to play as a child, when his father had served as captain, and told me stories of his parents and the house he had lived in in the nearby village. It was fully dark by the time we'd walked the perimeter, so I summoned a ball of light to hover above our heads as he escorted me back inside, all the way to the north wing and to the door of my suite. He kissed my cheek and said good night.

We continued this routine for the next month. Each morning, Stefan would greet me at my door and eat breakfast in my suite. Once my duties were finished for the day, we would walk the grounds until we tired. After a couple of days, I found myself laughing with him and allowing him to wrap an arm around me while we walked. I remembered how easy things could be with Stefan. It was like before Aydan's return. We were friends again. He was mortal, yes, which would raise its own set of complications, but with the increasing stresses of life within the Cabinet, it felt good to have something totally separate to look forward to. So, after a month, when he said good night at my door and leaned in to kiss me on the mouth, I didn't stop him. We parted and he whispered, "Good night," once more before turning to walk away. I blinked after him, wondering if it had simply been so long since I'd been kissed that I had forgotten what it was supposed to feel like, or if the lack of feeling whatsoever was to be expected. When I looked toward the other end of the corridor, Aydan was there with Alastair, both staring at me. My face and hands grew hot.

"I am so sorry, Your Majesty, please excuse—"

Aydan resumed walking, with Alastair following close behind. "My apologies, Lady Advisor. We didn't intend to interrupt," the king said curtly. They passed me and, embarrassed, I shut my door.

Chapter Twenty-Seven

Over the next week, Stefan would send servants to deliver large bouquets of flowers wherever I might be. They mostly arrived at the door of my suite, but on one humiliating occasion, they were delivered to the king's chambers during a Cabinet meeting. I quickly reprimanded the poor boy who delivered them for interrupting Cabinet business and asked that any deliveries from the captain be taken to my suite no matter my location, then banished the bouquet back to my suite before Aydan could see it.

Since our last encounter, I could not bring myself to make eye contact with Aydan if it could be avoided. It seemed that he was avoiding me as well, never quite addressing me directly unless necessary. I wondered if it was mutual embarrassment or if he was angry with me, but he remained polite—cordial, even—so I let the question linger and hoped things would return to normal soon.

One morning, I woke to an urgent knock. Elise stood with a note holding Aydan's seal. I broke the wax and read the message quickly; all meetings with both the Cabinet and extended council would be suspended for the day. He and Kenna had found a new stash of Zathryan's papers, and Aydan would be spending the day sorting through them to look for the decrees. He wanted some time alone with the documents before dissecting them with the Cabinet. The rest of us were to enjoy a rare day off. "Well," I said, folding the note and placing it on my vanity, "I'm glad he sent word before I dressed.

Perhaps I'll get a little extra sleep—" I was interrupted by another knock on the door. "I spoke too soon." Elise laughed and opened my wardrobe to help me choose a gown for the day.

I wrapped a shawl around myself before opening the door. Stefan stepped inside without invitation, took my face in his hands, and kissed me deeply. I pulled away.

"Stef, I'm not dressed," I said, pulling the shawl tighter around me and glancing at Elise, who, bless her, had angled the wardrobe door to provide a bit of privacy from where she stood. "And I'm not alone in here."

"I need to talk to you," he said urgently. "Do you have some time?"

"I'll come back later." Elise laid my dress on the bed and shuffled out of the room, the door clicking shut behind her.

"Sit down." I pointed to the bed and took the dress into the bathroom to change. A few minutes later, I returned in a blush pink gown and sat at my vanity to run a brush through my hair. I could see Stefan behind me in the mirror; his leg bounced as he grew more impatient. "Okay." I set the brush back down and turned in my chair. "What's going on?"

He loosed a breath. "Shaye, I told you at the coronation how I feel about you. And you've been enjoying yourself, I think, spending time with me these past weeks?"

"I have," I said carefully. It was true. I was glad to have his friendship, even if Stefan's fonder feelings for me weren't mutual.

"I want to do this correctly," he said. "I want to be with you for as long as I can." He held up a folded piece of paper. "This is a resignation letter. For both of us. Come away with me. We can go to Xarynn. Or across the sea, to Auperene, or Keotis—"

"Stef." My brow furrowed. "What are you—you're asking me to abandon my position? To run away and—and do *what*, exactly?" Stefan stood and cupped my face in his hands, eyes intense.

"Be together. We can marry, if you want. Or not. I don't care either way. We can decide as we go, but what's important is that we'll be *together*—" He stopped when I shook my head. I pushed up from my seat to put distance between us.

"Stefan, I can't—" I stammered. "I'm the Chief Advisor, I can't just resign. I have a duty to the Crown, I swore an oath to—"

"To *him*."

"To honor the throne and serve the king, yes."

"You weren't so sure about that oath after the coronation," Stefan replied snidely.

"Because you repeated false claims against his character, which have been explained by trustworthy sources," I said. He rolled his eyes. "Stefan, this is insane," I pleaded. "It hasn't even been two months since the coronation, and you want me to *run away* with you? We're still—still getting used to each other, I mean we've barely just *kissed*—" He grabbed me and kissed me roughly. I shoved him away. "*Stop it.*"

"What do you want from me?" he asked, throwing his arms up with exasperation. "You say you're willing to try with me at the coronation. You're seen leaving *his* chambers in your nightdress the same night. And then you spend all this time stringing me along—"

"What—how did you know I was in the king's chambers on coronation night?"

"Does it matter?" I stared. In an instant he had gone from pouring his heart out to me to sneering at me as he spoke.

"Are you having me followed?" I asked.

"What were you doing?"

"Are you having me followed, Stefan?"

"The guards saw you and reported it to me the next morning," he said. "They were doing their jobs, and you weren't exactly stealthy."

"Yes, and shouldn't that tell you I have nothing to hide?"

"Maybe," Stefan replied. "Or maybe you think so highly of yourself as *Chief Advisor* that you don't care what's said about you."

"What's said about me?" I repeated. "By the courtiers? No, I don't particularly care what they think of me. Especially when I've done nothing wrong."

"What *were* you doing?"

"We were talking."

"About what?" he pressed. I knew I couldn't win this argument, no matter how I answered.

"That's between the king and his advisor." Stefan laughed humorlessly.

"I'm sure he needs plenty of advice from *you* in the dead of night."

"I think you should go." I stepped away and opened the door.

"What?"

"I know what you're implying, and I won't listen to you degrade me or insult the king any longer." I pointed into the corridor. "Get out." Stefan's jaw clenched as he glared at me before storming from my suite. I waited until he turned the corner at the end of the corridor before I stepped out and slammed the door behind me.

Fuming, I walked to the king's chambers to find Hannele. She was the only person I could think of who could make sense of whatever the hell just happened.

No one was in the foyer, or in the front parlor. I had never seen any of the bedrooms in the royal household, but I knew they were all down a long corridor immediately to the left of the entrance. It didn't take long for me to find a door cracked open. I knocked and pushed on it to find Gerridan lounging on his bed, surrounded by letters, documents, and gift boxes. He looked up.

"Shaye," he said, surprise in his voice. "What are you doing here?"

"I'm looking for Hannele," I said. "Where is everyone? And what is all this?"

"These are some of the letters sent from leaders around Medeisia." He pointed at the stacks of papers on his bed, then to the gift boxes. "And those are gifts from some of our correspondences across the sea, congratulating Aydan on his coronation. I told Aydan I'd write to each sender, extending his thanks, but I've been avoiding it. It all piled up and, well . . ." He gestured broadly to the piles surrounding him. "This is my life now. Oh, and Hannele joined Aydan in his study a half hour or so ago. Kenna's in there too, I think. Alastair had some meeting with the generals or something, I can't remember—"

"Thanks." I turned to leave.

"Wait," Gerridan called out. "Is everything okay?"

"I just need to talk to Hannele." I sighed.

"Anything I can assist with?"

I shook my head. "I think I've had enough of men for the day. Thanks, though." Gerridan feigned offense as I left the doorway.

I had only been in Aydan's study once but knew well enough where it was. As I approached, I heard abrupt voices coming from inside.

"You have to show her." It was Hannele's voice. "This isn't something to wait on."

"I know," said Aydan, "I know, but *how*—"

"She deserves to see it."

"I know she does."

"Then write a note and send it," Kenna said. "Better to do it now."

I pushed the door open, and all of them looked up at once. Aydan sat behind his desk, stacks of paper and an ancient leather-bound book spread before him. Hannele stood in front of the desk while Kenna sat perched on the arm of an overstuffed chair, her arms crossed over her chest.

"Hello, Shaye," Aydan croaked.

"What's going on?" I asked. "I heard you from the hall. It sounded urgent." My eyes darted to the papers in front of Aydan. I stepped into the room, walked past Hannele, and picked them up, along with the book. Aydan made a noise of protest as I flipped through the pages. "Letters from Zathryan?"

"His journal," Hannele corrected. "The book is the last ten years or so. The loose pages appear to start when you and Aydan were first captured."

"They were mixed in with the other documents I was looking for," said Aydan while I skimmed the writings. "Those make little sense on their own. But with the madness written in his diary, it's clear that my father's mind was slipping in his final months." I found a crumpled page in the middle of the stack, creased as if it had been read and passed around, folded and unfolded.

Advanced interrogation methods have proven ineffective, it read. *I have recruited Captain Whittaker in my pursuit of truth from the Redfern girl. She will be broken yet.*

I sat on the sofa opposite Kenna as I shuffled through the papers, more slowly. Another entry, from a later date, read: *The captain has been unable to make headway with the Redfern girl. She does not trust him. I have ordered him to convince the girl that he is deceiving me, that it is by his suggestion that the girl will be moved to the housekeeping staff.*

Another: *The Redfern girl remains frigid. No new information. Considering a return to previous methods.*

After what seemed like an eternity of reading King Zathryan's account, I realized that fat tears were landing on the pages in my hands, which shook. I looked up at the others. Kenna's expression was concerned. Hannele watched me closely. Aydan leaned back in his chair, his hand on his mouth. He looked like he might be sick.

"This is not madness," I whispered. Aydan straightened in his seat.

"What?"

"It isn't madness. It's an exact account of the last year of my life." I felt my face and hands growing cold. I gasped for air, pulling at the bodice of my dress. I couldn't *breathe*. "Stefan . . . he—he deceived me. He's been acting on Zathryan's orders."

"It would seem that way, yes," Hannele said. I blinked up at her and saw that her eyes welled as she stared at me.

"He just asked—" I stopped myself, closed my eyes and letting more tears slip onto my cheeks. "I need to go." I stood, slipped, and caught myself. Ice covered my shoes and the floor around my feet.

"Shaye, you shouldn't—" Hannele started. Without a thought, I cast fire down by my feet, melting the ice before rushing out of the room, leaving a small blaze still burning on the rug. Kenna swore.

"Shaye, wait!" Aydan called. I walked faster, gasping for air. Down the corridor and out the chamber doors, nearly crashing into Alastair, who was entering. I shoved past him and all but ran back to my suite, where I slammed the door and crumpled forward with a sob. I didn't realize Elise was in the room until she crouched in front of me and tilted my chin up, examining me as I shuddered, sobs ripping from me. Satisfied that I was in no immediate harm, she said, "I'll go fetch some tea." I heard myself thank her as she left the room.

A lie. All of it was a lie. The past year, everything I knew of Stefan, had been a lie. Allowing him to court me these last weeks, a lie.

I entered the bathroom and undressed. I was about to start filling the tub when I heard the bedroom door fly open. I grabbed a bath robe and tied the sash hastily as I stepped out to see Stefan. He shut the door behind him and locked it.

"Before you say anything, I'm sorry," he said. "I was completely out of line, and my behavior was unacceptable." I gaped at him. "What's wrong?"

"You need to leave," I said shakily.

"Shaye—"

"No. Get out." I pointed at the door. "Gather your belongings and leave this castle. You've been relieved of your position." Stefan's face twisted in confusion.

"What are you talking about? You can't—"

"I am perfectly within my rights," I snapped, cutting him off. The cold tears turned hot. I felt them sizzle and disappear from my cheeks. "As Chief Advisor to King Aydan, I have the final say on residency—and I say get the hell out."

"I apologized."

I glared at him. "Did you know that Zathryan kept a diary?" Stefan's face went blank. "The king found it hidden in his study this morning. In it was an exact account of every interaction you and I have ever had."

"I don't know what you're talking about."

"Zathryan used you to get to me. When his *advanced methods* didn't work, he told you to befriend me. To pursue me, *seduce me.* Your game is over, Stefan. You lost." The color drained from his face. He reached for my hand but I snatched it away.

"Shaye, I need you to listen to me—"

"You've done nothing but lie to me for *months*. You tried to convince me to break my oath to the king!"

"Look, you—you don't know what you're talking about," he said. I scoffed, shaking my head.

"Stop lying. I saw it in Zathryan's own hand. It was all planned, down to the steel cuff on my fucking ankle." Rage and embarrassment flowed through me. My fingertips sparked. I watched Stefan's eyes dart to my hands. I didn't care anymore if he saw. I didn't care anymore if *anyone* knew.

"It's more complicated than that," he blurted. "Yes, it started out as Zathryan's scheme, but then—Shaye, I do love you. But I had to keep reporting to Zathryan, I had to keep up the act or he would've taken you back to the dungeons, or sent me away, and I wouldn't have been able to protect you."

"Then why didn't you tell me once he was dead?" I cried. "Why didn't you tell me about your feelings? We both have been granted every privilege by Aydan, and yet you didn't tell me about your *feelings* until a few weeks ago. You waited until I was happy, you waited until I was settled—for what? To toy with me? Was it fun for you to watch me suffer?" Stefan's mouth was a hard line. He was silent, no longer scrambling for an explanation. "Well?"

"You're right, I should just go."

"This was my *life*, Stefan, and you've been fucking with me for months. What did you get out of it?" More sparks flew from my hands.

"I'm not going to stand here and be interrogated." He turned his back and I lunged for his arm, enraged. When I touched him, he whipped back around with a slap that sent me staggering. It felt as if a hot knife sliced my cheek.

I screamed, clutching at my face. I lost my footing and fell backward. My head collided with the wardrobe, and I pawed desperately to remove what was burning me. When I pulled my hand away, it was coated in blood. A stream of water gushed from my palm then, while a wall of flame burst from the other. I looked down to where thick gray smoke had started billowing from my chest and stomach, filling the room and blocking my vision. I was still screaming when I heard what sounded like an explosion and the door to my suite was blown off the hinges; men's voices cried out, followed by a clang of metal on metal that rang in my ears before everything stopped, and the world went black.

Chapter Twenty-Eight

I was in darkness, my feet bare and cold.

In the distance, a light. A doorway. I walked forward and looked in on a room filled with desks and tables covered in papers and books. A man with long auburn hair in a low ponytail was sitting at one of the desks, his head propped on his fist while he read from one of the open books before him. After a moment, he shoved the book away and put his head in his hands. He sat up and took a deep breath. His lips moved but I could not hear him, and he held his hand out before him.

A white cloud started to form, floating inches above his palm.

Fascinated, I stepped forward and slowly the cloud turned gray, then black. Lightning flashed within it, and then, though I couldn't hear it, I felt the vibration of thunder shake the room, shake the blackness beneath my feet. Was there even a floor beneath me? When I glanced down to check, I couldn't tell. I looked back up.

The man stared directly into my eyes. I gasped, and felt my body begin to fall.

When I landed, my eyes opened. I was in a bed, in a room I didn't recognize, sitting up straight. I began to cry. In the corner, a strange woman stood from her chair and approached me. "My lady, I'm a healer. My name is Jemma—"

"No," I cried, scrambling away and tearing the blankets from my lap. I stood and immediately my legs gave out, sending me crashing to the floor. The woman reached for me but I slapped her hand away. "*No!*" I crawled backward until I hit the bedside table and I hurled the first thing my fingers grasped—a book—at the woman's face. "Get *away*—"

The door opened and Kenna swept into the room. I panted as she helped the healer stand and then looked at me, searching for something. Her brow furrowed, and she didn't take her eyes off me as she called out, "Gerridan!" My body ached and didn't feel wholly mine. I struggled to breathe and could feel that my heart was beating much too quickly. The nightdress I wore was so soaked with sweat that I could nearly see through it.

Gerridan appeared and crouched in front of me before taking my face in his hands and looking into my eyes. His fingers made small circles at my temples. He held my gaze, taking deep, slow breaths, then released my face to take my hands, without breaking eye contact.

My breathing slowed. I blinked a few times, adjusting my eyes. The room became clearer, and my heart settled into a normal rhythm. Kenna murmured something to the healer, Jemma, who then left the room. Gerridan scooped me into his arms and laid me back down onto the bed.

"Thank you," I rasped as he pulled the blanket over me. My throat felt like I had swallowed glass. "What did you do?"

"You aren't the only one with extra gifts." He half smiled, sitting on the edge of the bed. "I can calm people down, remove fear, that sort of thing."

"What happened to me?" My voice was almost a whisper. "Why aren't I in my room?"

"We were hoping you could tell us," Kenna replied. "I can't see anything that happened in that room. All we know is that Elise came running, saying there was something wrong. Your door was locked, and she could hear a man's voice, and you yelling for him to leave."

"Alastair and Aydan broke the door down," Gerridan continued. "The captain pulled a knife on Al. They fought. The captain was injured, but he'll heal. Aydan said the room was filled with smoke and you looked dead. Your face was covered in blood, and you were unconscious. He carried you back here and brought in the healers to stabilize you." I touched my face, then hissed at the sharp pain.

"How long have I been here?"

"It's been three days," Kenna said. "Whatever you did, it was an enormous drain on your power. We thought we lost you a couple of times—"

"You're awake," said a soft voice from the doorway. I looked and saw Aydan, who appeared fatigued. He looked me over. "How do you feel?"

"Awful," I replied honestly, and winced as I shifted to sit up straight. "My face burns."

"Jemma is working on some sort of salve that may help," Aydan said. "None of the normal remedies are working."

"Why?"

"The cut was made with silver." Gerridan reached into his jacket pocket and pulled out a bundled handkerchief. He unfolded it, revealing a ring I recognized as Stefan's. He held the ring closer to me, careful to keep his fingers covered by the cloth. I peered closely at the loop and saw a metal spike, like a small thorn, protruding from it. "This type of weapon is banned in Medeisia. They're circulated among the mortal rebels. They put a gold coating on them so sorcerers don't notice, but the spike is exposed silver." He folded the ring back into the cloth and returned it to his pocket.

I stared at my lap. "Has a . . . sentence been carried out?"

"I haven't decided yet what that will be," said Aydan. "Until we knew you would survive, we didn't know yet what his crimes were limited to. I also wanted to offer you final say on his sentence, as is your right."

"What were you thinking?" Weighing in on sentencing criminals was not a task that I had prepared for.

"When he is well enough to travel, banishment seems appropriate."

"Is he so badly injured that he cannot travel?" I asked. Aydan appeared hesitant to answer. I looked to Kenna, who was giving Gerridan a sidelong glance. "*Stop that,*" I hissed. "Stop coddling me. *No more secrets.*" I met Aydan's gaze. "If I'm to be your advisor—if I'm to be of any use to this court—then I need honesty. Complete honesty."

To my surprise, Aydan did not object. "I'm afraid the captain's condition is best understood when seen," he said. "You have my word that as soon as you're feeling stronger, I will take you to see him myself if you wish."

I folded the blankets back and moved to stand, but Gerridan placed a hand on mine. "You need rest, Shaye." Kenna shooed him away and offered me a hand to help me out of bed.

"Let the lady decide how she feels."

"I'll need help dressing," I murmured. My muscles were screaming. Without a word, Kenna motioned for Aydan and Gerridan to leave the room. They obliged, and she shut the door behind them before walking to the wardrobe and pulling out one of my dresses. Confused, I said, "That's mine."

"This is your new room," she said. "Your suite isn't usable anymore. The servants moved your things here yesterday." Flashes of memory played in my mind—the utter destruction pouring from my body, demolishing everything in the room. I stood gripping the post at the foot of the bed for balance while Kenna helped me out of the nightdress. She did not gasp or otherwise indicate that she saw what was impossible not to notice covering the entirety of my back. She merely pulled the new dress over my head and began lacing up the back, leaving it loose. I was grateful that she did not ask questions.

I held Kenna's arm as we entered the foyer, where Aydan waited with Gerridan and Hannele. She hugged me briefly.

"It's good to see you on two feet," she said in my ear. I smiled even as I winced at the touch. When she pulled away, I looked over her shoulder at Aydan.

"I'm ready." He nodded and offered an arm. I took it, grateful for the stability, and he led me to a spot on the wall in the foyer where he pressed, opening a hidden door that revealed a tunnel lit by orbs of light.

"This might be less taxing than effuging for now," he explained, guiding us forward. We walked in silence until we reached a dead end, where Aydan once again pressed into the wall. We stepped into a corridor; on one end was a group of four guards blocking off the passage to anyone who might try to enter, and on the other was a door with two guards in front of it, listening as Alastair gave them instructions. The Lord General looked up at the sound of the secret door and frowned. He excused himself and approached us.

"Are you serious?"

"Lady Shaye would like to observe our prisoner."

"I really don't think—"

"Open the door, general." Alastair stiffened, but he obeyed the command anyway, leading us to the door and pulling a key from his belt. I let go of Aydan's arm.

"I'd like to go in alone," I said. The king's hand clenched, then opened again.

"Alastair will wait in the doorway," he said, "and I'll wait for you here." I nodded. Alastair pushed the door open and stepped aside to let me through.

The room was a disaster.

It was a generous choice for a holding cell, the other option being a dungeon. But being a lord of the king's court had perks, even when one stood accused of attacking the Chief Advisor and Lord General. However, though the room had once held a plush bed, a desk, even a wardrobe, it was all demolished now. The linens were shredded, clothes strewn about, and the wooden frame of the bed was cracked, with an entire leg splintered in half that sent the whole thing off-kilter.

There was only one clear path in the whole room, where Stefan now paced, disheveled and muttering to himself. "Stefan?" I called out softly. He kept pacing, chewing on his fingers. "*Stef,*" I said, louder this time. He looked up.

"Oh, Shaye, there you are. Hello. Have you been waiting long? I didn't hear you over all the noise." The room was silent. I took a step forward.

"Are you all right? Do you remember what happened?"

"I think so." He frowned. "I'm not sure. We were talking, and then . . . and then I woke up here. You got hurt—did you get hurt? I don't . . ."

"I'll be fine," I said. "Do you remember what we were talking about?" Stefan ran a hand through his hair, which was stringy and greasy, and he frowned deeper, thinking. He looked like he hadn't slept or bathed or even eaten in the time that he'd been here. The discarded trays of untouched food on the desk confirmed as much.

"The king," Stefan said finally. "And the prince. And her—we were talking about her. Or—*to* her. She—she told me. When the king was dead, he told me—she said . . . yes, it was her. I can see her, but—but *I can't see her.* She's right there and I can see her and she's right next to me and I can see . . ." He started muttering again, restless.

"Stefan, what are you talking about? Me? Who is *she*?"

His attention snapped to me again.

"It's *her*, Shaye. She's right there and I can't see her but she's right next to me and her face is right there but I can't see her and she—she's RIGHT THERE SHE'S RIGHT THERE BUT I CAN'T SEE HER—" I watched in horror as Stefan crumpled to the ground, curled himself around his legs, and began to weep. "*I can't see her I can't see her I can't see her . . .*" A hand rested on my shoulder and I jumped. Alastair was behind me.

"We should go now, Shaye." He guided me out to where Aydan waited with a grim expression. My vision blurred.

"Shaye . . ." I swayed, my knees buckling underneath me, and I would have hit the floor if Aydan had not caught my arm.

"I'd like to go back to my room now," I said softly. I took a step and lost my balance again.

"May I help?" Aydan asked. I was too tired to do anything but nod, so he scooped me into his arms and walked back through the hidden tunnel. He carried me in silence while I lay my head against his chest and drifted in and out of sleep, and when we reached the bedroom, he laid me down and covered me with a blanket. I was drifting again when I felt his hand press gently against my hair. Maybe it was a dream.

Chapter Twenty-Nine

I spent the next two days in and out of sleep, only waking to sip on the herbed broth Jemma had prescribed. On the third day, I woke from a nap to find a leather-bound book on my bedside table, wrapped with a green ribbon, and a note attached that read:

> *Something to help pass the time. Get well soon.*
> *Fondly,*
> *–A*

It was a new copy of *Enchanted, Enchanting*. My books had all been destroyed along with the furniture. My only belongings that had survived were my clothing shut in the wardrobe and Catchfly, who remained completely unscathed. She'd quickly grown bored of watching me sleep all day in our new room, demanded to be let out, and was now making herself at home elsewhere in the king's chambers. I ran my fingers over the fine leather cover before cracking the book open and smiling to myself as I began to read the first chapter.

Two more days passed by in this way before I decided that I had to get up.

I dressed myself easily, to my own surprise, and walked without difficulty across the empty dwelling to the other end of the king's chambers, where I found my friends eating lunch and talking amongst themselves. Aydan was slouched in his seat, picking at his food. It was Hannele who saw me first.

"Shaye, you're up," she said. Aydan straightened.

"I am. I thought I might join you, if that's all right."

"Of course it is," Aydan said quickly. He gestured to the empty chair next to Alastair. A plate piled with steaming chicken, buttery potatoes, and roasted vegetables appeared in front of it.

"Thank you," I said as I sat. Their plates were nearly empty, but no one moved to excuse themselves. I felt Aydan and Alastair watching me. Gerridan's eyes were on Hannele as she bickered with Kenna about a dress Kenna wanted to borrow. After a few minutes, I turned to Gerridan and asked, "Does your offer still stand?"

"I've made you many offers, my lady. To which do you refer?" He winked.

"I'm already regretting getting out of bed." I sighed. He laughed. "You offered to train me. To fight. I want to start as soon as possible. Today, if we can."

Interested, Gerridan leaned back in his chair. "Do you feel up for it?"

I nodded. "I never want to feel this weak again. If I can, like you said, help understand my body's limitations, protect myself, protect others—I want to do that. Even train for combat if you're willing to teach me."

"Well, I can certainly teach you self-defense. But as far as combat training . . ." He jerked his chin toward Alastair. "He's the one you'll want." The Lord General and I locked eyes.

"Can you teach me?"

He looked thoughtful. "Start with Gerridan this afternoon. I have meetings today. Tomorrow, you can join me. I train at sunrise."

"Thank you." I inclined my head before turning my attention to Aydan. "I suppose if I'm training with them, I should return to my studies with you as well," I said. "If you're willing."

"I am," he replied with a contented look on his face.

"I'm afraid I've been in that room so long that I'm unsure of your schedule."

"We'll make time after dinner, if you feel up to it after handing Gerridan his ass." Aydan smiled and reached for a glass of water. The man in question looked offended, while Kenna and Hannele broke into fits of laughter. I nodded, silently thanking Aydan, before returning to my food.

"If you stand like that your opponent is going to knock you on your ass." I glared at Gerridan and adjusted my feet for the fifth time.

We'd been out here for two hours. After lunch, Hannele had offered to loan me a set of training leathers and boots, which she then had to show me how to get into. The jacket was laced over the top of a padded shirt designed to absorb any blows I might fail to block, and was easy enough to figure out myself once I'd managed to stop fumbling with the laces. The trousers, with all their buckles and straps to fit the wearer and provide storage for extra weapons, were not like the simple linen things I had worn while gardening with Uncle Gideon as a child. They were snug. Hannele explained that this was so they wouldn't catch on anything and an opponent couldn't grab onto any loose fabric. This made sense, though I couldn't help but feel exposed as I stood in the sparring ring, listening to Gerridan's instruction.

When I'd entered the parlor room earlier to find him, Alastair and Aydan were there, looking over some documents spread out on a table while Kenna lounged on a sofa, reading. She glanced over from her book and looked me up and down with a low whistle.

"You look good in leather." She smirked.

"Thanks," I replied, resisting the urge to cross my arms. Gerridan straightened from where he'd been leaning against the arm of a chair and squatted in front of me to tug a strap on one of my boots.

"Good. Ready?" he asked.

"Yes, just . . ." I looked at Aydan, who was watching us. "I need you to remove my blood shield. I don't want Gerridan getting hurt if I fail to block him or something." For a second, I thought he might argue or reveal some reason that he couldn't do so, but instead, he stood and straightened his jacket before approaching me. Without a word, he placed his hands on either side of my face and pressed his lips to my forehead. Warmth shot from my toes, through my body, and out of the top of my head. I told myself that the fluttering in my chest was just part of the process.

In the sparring ring, Gerridan had been showing me how to escape from various holds, and the best spots to strike a person to weaken their grasp. He'd get me in position before grabbing me from behind, and it was my job to try and free myself. I had not succeeded yet.

"Can I just hit something, please?" I asked angrily as he threw me a canteen.

"No," he replied once he'd swallowed. "You need this lesson first. Then blocking. *Then* sparring." I started to protest, but he continued, "If you know how to escape but not how to fight, you can still survive an attack. If all you know is how to hit but not how to keep yourself from being injured—"

"Yeah, I get it," I snapped. His eyebrows rose.

"No one's forcing you to be here, *Lady Advisor.* You asked *me* for this lesson."

"I know." I huffed. "I'm just sick of everyone treating me like some delicate flower." I tightened a buckle on my jacket.

"I'm not treating you like a delicate flower. I'm treating you like every other student I've instructed." He pointed to the center of the ring. "Now, you can get back in and allow me to teach you the right way, or you can go back to the king's chambers and read some silly book while you pretend like you aren't staring at Aydan."

"Fuck you," I spat, blushing.

"You're not my type."

I shoved him in the chest and began to walk past him and out of the ring, when he grabbed me. I cried out as he twisted one arm behind my back and locked his own across my neck.

"Let—me—*go*!" I choked out angrily.

"No," he grunted as I struggled. "Escape. Get out of the hold." I thrashed and the arm around my neck tightened. My mind raced. *What do I do? What's available?* Feet—my feet were not restrained. I slammed my heel into Gerridan's instep. He jerked, and then, without thinking, I threw my head backward, into his nose. Twice. He let go when the second hit resulted in an unsettling crunch. I gasped and hit my knees, hand at my throat. When I looked up, Gerridan was rustling around in a satchel for a handkerchief as blood poured freely from his nose. He gave up and stripped off his shirt to press to his face.

"I'm sorry," I said, still catching my breath. "I shouldn't have questioned your lesson."

"Gods, Shaye," he said, voice nasal and muffled through the fabric. "Question me all you want. I'm not above being questioned. Just don't think I'd ever treat you any differently than anyone else who sits beside me in the Cabinet, or who joins me in this ring."

"I don't want to be weak."

"You're not," he assured me. "You have an enormous amount of power within you right now, and I'm not just talking about the magic. You're good for the Cabinet, you're good for Ayzelle. You're going to do great things for Medeisia, but first you're going to have to learn that not everyone who's trying to teach you something thinks they're better than you, or that you're weak." He pulled the shirt away from his nose, which was clearly broken.

"Good gods, Shaye, what'd you do to him?" called Hannele's voice from a few yards away.

"A new maneuver," Gerridan joked. "I'll be fine."

"Here." I waved my hand in front of his face. The blood disappeared, but his nose was nearly black with bruising and swollen twice its size. "*Fuck,*" I whispered.

"I came to tell you both that the final draft of the Sylvannian trade agreement is complete. The extended council wants you to look it over when you're finished. They'll need signatures," Hannele said, now standing just on the other side of the short wall.

"Thanks," the emissary replied. "We'll be there shortly." She shrugged and walked back toward the castle. As I packed my things, I saw that Gerridan's gaze followed her until she was out of sight.

"You're one to talk about pretending you're not staring," I teased as I picked up his satchel and threw it over my shoulder.

"I've never pretended I wasn't staring at Hannele," he said. "It's one of my favorite pastimes." The joke didn't cover the longing in his voice, and I knew better than to pry further.

Not much later, Gerridan and I arrived back at the king's chambers and found our friends in the dining room.

"I told you," Hannele said with a smirk. She held out a hand to Alastair, who grumbled and gave her a few coins.

"Nice work," Aydan said as he examined his friend's nose. Then to Gerridan, he added, "Jemma should be able to fix that right up."

"I'm not too worried about it," Gerridan replied. "I'm just glad she didn't freeze my eyes or burn off my hair."

"The night is still young," I quipped, striding to the drink table and pouring a glass of brandy each for myself and the emissary. Aydan barked a laugh while Gerridan grumbled, downed his drink, and set off to see the healer.

My lesson with Aydan that night was uneventful, except for Alastair's interruption to tell me he couldn't keep our meeting the following morning. There had been some sort of scuffle between officers back in Sylvanna, and he would need to effuge there to sit in on the reprimands.

Instead, the rest of us joined the Ayzellen Council to discuss our upcoming visit to Sylvanna. It was my first council meeting since the accident, and I couldn't help but notice that Lord Declan looked rather put out that I was back on my feet. After thirty minutes of what felt like an interrogation from the lord regarding what should be expected of our visit to Sylvanna, Gerridan and I signed the document the council had drafted, making it now ready to be presented to Solandis and Priamos. Afterward, we found ourselves in the great hall. Several families of the nobility had descended on the castle today. I was beside Aydan, observing while he chatted politely with a woman who wore both an ancient dusty gray wig and a face caked with makeup two shades too light for her skin. Aydan shot me a sidelong glance that screamed for a rescue, and I was about to open my mouth when the hall doors flew open.

A gaunt, ghost-like man stormed in, covered in ragged clothing and yet dripping in gold and jewels. He headed straight for me. A guard stepped out but did not stop him as he took my hand and fell to his knees before me in the center of the great hall.

"Ehnara has truly blessed us!" the man cried out to the now silent hall. "The lost princess, daughter of the Martyr King Ronan, has come home to us!" I tried to take my hand away, but he held fast. He kissed my hand and gazed up at me, eyes welled over with tears. "Blessed Lady of House Redfern, the one true Queen of Medeisia—Queen Shaye, I am your humble servant. My forces stand by on the grounds to await your command."

I thought my heart would fall out of my chest. "I am not your queen. Lord Ronan was no king. I hold no claim to House Redfern."

"Good and gentle queen, I have received your letters! I declare you now and forever our gracious ruler—the *true, goddess-blessed queen*. Your throne awaits." I finally extricated my hand from his clutches.

"I have sent no letters. This is a cruel joke, and you have spoken the words of traitors." I turned to the guard beside me. "Take this man outside to be flogged." The man drew letters from his pocket, folded parchment bearing the wax seal of the Chief Advisor. Letters from my desk. .

"You told me to present this to you upon my arrival." He pressed one into my hand. I dropped it as though burned.

"*I have sent no letters,*" I insisted. "Guards, take him away." I looked to Aydan, who said nothing, but now held the parchment open, reading in silence. He looked up at me, rage behind his eyes.

"This is a command to the remaining lords of House Redfern to gather their forces and lead an attack on this castle, written in your hand. You instruct them to show no mercy if I do not stand aside."

Wide-eyed, I opened my mouth to deny it, but before I could, the guard standing beside the king shoved his blade through the side of Aydan's neck. I screamed.

"*No! NO! STAND DOWN!*" I was on my knees beside Aydan, holding my hand to his throat as he choked on blood, clawing at my hands and his own neck. Shock and betrayal replaced the rage in his face as he stared at me. Hot tears streamed down my cheeks and I heard screams, swords crashing against each other, and the doors to the great hall breaking down as the Redfern forces filled the room, slaughtering all who stood around me. My own screams filled my ears, and my head bowed under the weight of the bloodstained crown the ghostly man placed there. I held Aydan, still crying out for him to hold on—"Don't go, *don't go, please—stay with me*!"—until the stars behind his eyes went out. I screamed his name again and again, shaking Aydan's body. "Please, *don't go, don't leave me—*"

Rough hands grabbed my arms and hauled me to my feet even as I fought against them, thrashing, fighting—

"*Shaye!*"

My eyes snapped open, and I was standing in my room. Aydan stood in the dark, gripping my shoulders as a violent wind whipped around us. I gasped, choking on tears, and the air stopped immediately. A cry ripped itself from my throat, and I threw my arms around Aydan's neck, burying my face in his bare chest as I sobbed. He held me, one hand rubbing lines up and down my spine while the other gently smoothed my hair and I gasped for breath. Minutes passed, and I finally pulled away, my face still hot and blotchy. This was real. Aydan was alive. I ran my hand lightly over his throat.

"You're okay," I croaked.

"So are you," he replied. His thumb brushed over the cut that remained on my cheek. "It's been a long time since we've met in the night like this." New tears spilled over onto my cheeks.

"I must have forgotten to take my tincture," I said. I realized he still held me against his bare skin. I took a step back and searched my bedside table for the bottle of lavender liquid. It had dropped into the drawer where I kept my new copy of *Enchanted, Enchanting.* "Oh." I sniffed as I held it up to show him. It was empty.

"Go see Jemma in the morning. She keeps that sort of thing on hand." I nodded.

After a pause, I looked around at my disheveled room and said, "So, the wind?"

"It seems you've been gifted with control of yet another element. Air."

My voice shook as I said, "It never ends." Aydan's hands reached for mine. I didn't step away.

"There's an answer somewhere. We just have to find it. It won't be like this forever." I wanted to believe him. "You should get some rest." Aydan waved his hand, and my room returned to order. Catchfly poked her head out from beneath the bed, where she had hidden from the storm.

"Sorry, girl," I said, patting her head lightly. She meowed grumpily and found her place on a pillow while Aydan helped me into bed. He placed the covers back over me, tucking me in for the night. His hand rested on my hair again.

"I can pull up a chair if you want me to stay," he said, and I remembered the night he watched over me while I slept. It felt like a century ago.

"I'll be okay. It's only a few hours 'til light anyway."

"If you need anything . . . well, you know where to find me if you need anything."

"Isn't it my job to take care of you?" I tried to joke as he turned to leave. He smiled sadly.

"We can take turns," he said. "Good night, Shaye."

"Good night."

Chapter Thirty

Aydan made no mention of our encounter the next day, and based on the rest of the Cabinet's silence on my most recently discovered ability, I assumed he didn't tell them. For the next three days, Alastair remained in Sylvanna. I continued my training with Gerridan in the mornings, followed by meetings and reports throughout the day before my lessons with Aydan in the evening. He tried his best to instruct me and gain a better grasp on the elemental magic within me, but most of his efforts were futile. The sorcery we practiced had been nearly mastered, aside from effuging, which still eluded me, but short of cuffing me in silver, there was no way we could find to gain a definite hold over the less savory abilities at my disposal.

On the fourth morning after my nightmare, I stood in the foyer, waiting for Alastair. He'd returned the night before and sent a message with Elise to tell me to be ready at sunrise. The sun had risen half an hour ago, and now I tapped my foot, impatiently waiting for the usually punctual general.

Gerridan emerged from his bedroom. "Shouldn't you be in the ring by now?"

"Alastair hasn't come out yet."

"That's strange," he said, looking back down the corridor. "Have you knocked for him?"

"No," I said.

"Well." He shrugged. "Go knock, then. He's probably just having a lie-in. The Sylvannian Council takes a lot out of you." I sighed and left Gerridan in the foyer while I approached the Lord General's door.

The truth was, I didn't feel I knew Alastair well enough to be banging down his door for combat training. He was quieter, more withdrawn, than the others. He was of course always friendly enough, and perfectly polite, but standoffish. When I raised my fist to his door, it felt like an intrusion. I knocked twice, and the door pushed open. It must not have been latched completely.

I stepped in carefully, not wanting to wake him if he was in fact still asleep, but the room was empty. I was turning to leave when a glimmer caught my eye.

On the bedside table stood a small gold frame containing a sketched portrait. I picked it up, blinking several times at the drawing as I tried to understand what I was looking at. It was my face. Or nearly so. A sketch of a woman with curly hair and large eyes, a hint of a smile on her lips . . .

"What are you doing?"

I nearly dropped the frame as I whipped my head toward the doorway where Alastair now stood, his face ashen.

"I-I was looking for you—"

"Put that down. Now."

"What is this?" I demanded.

"You have no right to barge into my room and rifle through my belongings."

"Why do you have a portrait of me?" I pressed.

"It's not you," he snapped. "Start walking to the ring." I set the frame down and walked out, not even looking at Gerridan as I passed him again on my way to the front door. I'd just crossed the drawbridge when I heard my name being called. Alastair was walking quickly, trying to catch up. I stopped and waited for him. When he reached me, we both said at once: "I'm sorry."

"I shouldn't have gone into your room—"

"I didn't mean to snap at you, I was caught off guard—"

We realized we were talking over one another, and both shut our mouths quickly. I chuckled nervously at the awkwardness.

"Can we start over?" I asked.

"Sure," he said, then gestured for me to lead the way. We walked in silence for a few moments before he said, "The portrait isn't you."

"You said that already."

"I know. I just—you should know that—" The general struggled for words. Finally, he stopped, took a deep breath, and said, "The portrait is of your mother. Brina." My mouth went dry.

He continued, "I drew it years ago, and I never had the chance to give it to her before she passed. I've kept it in sight ever since."

"You . . . you *knew* her?" I asked. Alastair nodded. "I don't understand. You're from Sylvanna."

"Thirty-two years ago, Ayzelle was attacked by mortal forces from Nautia. King Zathryan called for aid, and Sylvanna answered. I was just a foot soldier then, placed with the troops answering to Commanding Officer Brina Eastly." I remembered Aydan telling me about the attack on our first night in Ayzelle.

"And you were . . . in love with her?" I asked. It was the only reason I could think that he would be drawing my mother. Alastair laughed.

"No, I wasn't in love with her. Though half the men in our battalion were by the time we were through here. I only like men," he explained. That surprised me; most people I had met in Medeisia enjoyed lovers of any gender. "Your mother was my dearest friend. I never had siblings, and she was the closest I came to having a beloved sister."

"Why didn't you tell me when we first met?"

"Truthfully, I was shocked when I first saw you," he said. I remembered the shattered glass. "When I learned of your location in Nautia and sent Aydan to retrieve you—"

"*You* sent Aydan?"

"I did. I asked Lady Solandis's permission to fetch you myself, but she declined, and gave me duties that I could not abandon. I asked Aydan to go in my place." Understanding washed over me. "I knew I would see you eventually. I had been . . . preparing myself, mentally, for you to resemble your father. I feared I might unintentionally hold some disdain for you if I saw his face in yours, but when you appeared in the Cabinet lounge that night, it was like seeing a ghost. I'm afraid I've been cold to you these past months, and I want to apologize. It was not my intention to be rude to you, Shaye."

"I understand. Thank you for telling me."

"I'm sorry it took me so long to find the words. I hope, going forward, that we can be friendly with one another."

"I'd be pretty foolish to not be friendly with the man who's going to teach me how to wield a sword," I replied.

"Let's go." He chuckled, continuing toward the ring.

Hours later, I was bruised and sore, with bleeding knuckles. Each wound was a reminder of my failure to block the waster Alastair used against me. A reminder of my need to improve. The Lord General kept his pace slow as I limped back toward the castle.

"You're a lot like her," he said. "Brina, I mean. You favor her looks, but your personality, your drive. It's the same as well. Perhaps you'll be a warrior too."

"Not likely," I scoffed. "I don't think I have it in me to fight in battles. But who knows? I'm Medeisian. I have all the time in the world." I kicked at a pebble in our path. "I wish I'd had the chance to meet her. My father was a bad person. But my mother . . . I just wish I could have known her myself."

"Would you like to see her?"

"What?"

"It's a . . . a gift of mine. Can I show you?" He offered his hand. I hesitated, but took it anyway—

And then I was at the gate, walking swiftly to the great hall, where I knew she would be. My heart raced with anticipation. It had been more than a year since I last saw my friend. In the great hall of Castle Ayzelle, I heard her before I saw her. I'd recognize that laugh anywhere. The crowd parted and there she was—Brina, standing with the wives of some lords, talking and laughing. I stopped, not believing what I saw:

Rather than training fatigues or battle armor, she wore an elegant lavender gown. Her brown hair draped down her back in soft curls, the front pulled away from her face with combs that glittered with deep purple and blue gemstones. Then she saw me. A welcoming, familiar grin split her face.

"Alastair," she called, and excused herself from the courtiers. She crossed the hall to greet me, taking my hand in her own. "It is so good to see you . . . How are you?"

"I'm . . ." I took in her appearance. A lady of the court. Subdued, malleable. Beautiful. A pleasure to the eyes of men around her. Not the feared warrior who had led me and our comrades into battle. Not the sword master bellowing orders to her soldiers from the back of her horse. Not the commander dismounting and running into the mud and blood and gore to strike with her blade, cutting down soldiers who fell like stalks of wheat.

"What's wrong?" she asked, concern in her eyes. A soft voice, a soft gaze I didn't recognize.

"What happened to you, Brina?" I blurted. "I thought you'd be training new recruits."

A brief, tight-lipped smile. "I don't do that anymore."

"Why not?"

"Because it's not appropriate for a lord's wife," she said. I looked at her left hand wearing a gold ring adorned with small diamonds surrounding a blush pink pearl. I took my hands back.

"Wife." She nodded. "Who . . ."

"Lord Redfern, the king's Chief Advisor," said Brina, her chin held high. "Seven months ago."

I shook my head in disbelief. "Seven months and you didn't . . . you didn't write*—"*

"I wanted to tell you in person," she said, now lowering her eyes. "Ronan said we would be visiting Sylvanna sometime this year to meet with the prince, and then the trip was postponed so many times . . . Things have been busy . . . and complicated. There's so much that I need to tell you. I never wanted . . . Alastair, you're my dearest friend. I didn't want to hurt you by telling you in a note."

"Instead, you'd hurt me by waiting more than half a year to tell me you've given yourself over to a power-hungry monster like Lord Ronan," I said harshly. Brina's eyes snapped up, filled with anger I'd only seen on the battlefield.

*"You will not speak of my husband in that way," she spat. "You know nothing—*nothing*—about Ronan."*

"I know what is whispered about him across the territories," I hissed. "That he seeks power from forbidden sources. They say he's consulting witches *now, Brina."*

"And you believe everything you hear?" she replied coolly. "Should I have believed every rumor about the men you've taken as lovers? Doesn't my loving Ronan tell you everything you need to know? Am I not a good enough credential?"

"You claim a love match." It wasn't a question.

"I do." My eyes followed her hand as it drifted to rest on top of her stomach, which I now saw was swollen under the flowing skirts of her dress. I swallowed. My eyes traveled back up to meet hers. She held my gaze.

Silence.

"Brina—"

"I think you should go," she interrupted. "Replenish your supplies—take anything you need. But be gone by morning." My friend, my commander, turned to leave.

"Brina, please.*" I grabbed her hand. "Tell me what's really going on. I can help you."*

"My name is Lady Redfern," she snapped, taking her hand away. "There is nothing going on, except that my dearest friend cannot bring himself to celebrate my happiness with me. Goodbye, Alastair."

She strode back across the hall, the other courtiers now staring at me, at her. She marched with her chin high, straight to her husband, who now stood where she'd been mingling only moments before. Her face was filled with adoration as Ronan kissed the back of her hand. He placed his own on her cheek and murmured something, brushing his thumb as if to wipe away a tear. Brina nodded, then left the hall and didn't turn back. I watched until she disappeared around a corner, then glanced back at Ronan, who was staring at me. I turned on my heel, then—

I felt a strong *push*, and suddenly I was back on the grounds of Ayzelle. Alastair was hunched over, breathing heavily with beads of sweat forming on his brow. "What the *hell*—" He turned and vomited into the grass. I placed my hand on his shoulder, but he shrugged me off. "You were only supposed to see an image of her face."

"What was that, then?"

"That was the last time I saw Brina alive and well." Alastair gripped my wrist and pulled me with him as he began to storm his way to the castle. "We need to see Kenna."

Chapter Thirty-One

Half an hour later, we were in the Cabinet lounge. Kenna held either side of my head with a light pink glow pouring from her palms while she searched my mind, her eyes glazed over with the faraway gaze of sight. Aydan watched from the edge of the room, arms crossed, while I did my best to not make eye contact with him. Kenna abruptly stopped and placed her hands on her hips.

"Nothing," she said to Alastair. "No one's using her as a conduit. Her mind is her own." She looked back at me. "You're a mindwalker."

"Excuse me?"

"I intended to show you an image," Alastair said from his seat where he'd been watching intently since he burst into the king's chambers, demanding that Kenna look at me. "You experienced the full memory. A mindwalker who hones their abilities could manipulate a memory, make one believe that events happened differently than they did—or completely erase it. A skilled mindwalker could make you forget years of your own life."

"Mindwalking . . . is not an ability found in sorcerers, is it?" I asked, feeling a knot form in my stomach.

"No," Aydan replied. I rested my elbows on my knees and let my head fall in my hands.

"*Shit!*" Alastair stood and stormed from the lounge, passing Gerridan and Hannele on his way through the door. Hannele looked to each of us.

"What's wrong?"

"Shaye is a mindwalker." Kenna pressed a glass of brandy into my hand. I mumbled my thanks before knocking back the whole thing. She refilled it with a wave of her hand. Gerridan's eyebrows flicked upward and he looked to Aydan, who nodded, confirming they'd heard her correctly.

"Let's see." I tapped the edge of my glass and stared at the floor as I said the words. "I'm a mindwalker, with no explanation of how I did it. I can conjure three different elements, with no clue how to control them—"

"*Three?*" Hannele whispered.

"I conjured a windstorm in my bedroom a few nights ago." I looked at Aydan, who still hadn't reacted. "I resign." He straightened.

"No you don't," he said. "I know you're overwhelmed, Shaye, but we'll figure—"

"We won't figure it out," I snapped, standing up. "We *haven't* figured it out. It's been months and all we've figured out is that every day, I have less and less control over myself. Every day, I become more and more of a fucking monster." I drained my glass again before walking to the drink cart and refilling it. My hands shook, getting hotter.

"You're not a monster," Aydan insisted. "You did not choose this. You haven't done anything wrong here."

"Just stop, Aydan," I replied, refusing to turn and face him. "You should have just let Zathryan kill me." Before I could drink, Aydan was there, taking it from my hand. A stillness fell over the room.

"Kenna, take Gerridan and Hannele and find somewhere else to be," he said without taking his eyes off of me. The three of them left the room without another word. The door clicked shut and we were alone. "Are you thinking of hurting yourself, Shaye?"

"No."

"Then don't ever say such a thing in my presence again."

I should have been intimidated, but instead I said, "It's the truth." I stepped away and, with a flick of my wrist, took my drink back from Aydan's hand. I downed it before he could stop me. "It would have saved everyone some trouble. You'd still be king, only ruling from Sylvanna instead of dragging your Cabinet here to pick up the pieces of a broken woman—gods know *why*—"

"*Why?*" Aydan interrupted. "Do you really have to ask why I'm here? Gods, Shaye, sometimes when we talk, I feel like I'm going *insane.*" He stepped closer to me. "You're right, I could have stayed in Sylvanna. I could have ruled from there, declared Sylvanna the new capital, and let Declan and the council run Ayzelle. But I made you a promise, so I came back here for *you*. And I thought things would be different. I didn't think . . ." Aydan shook his head and fell silent.

"Look—I was fine. Really, I was. But then *you came back*. Then you asked me to be your advisor, and I *stupidly* agreed—"

"Why? Why did you agree? Why make an oath to serve the Crown if it's such a ridiculous notion?"

"I don't care about the *Crown*," I spat. The alcohol was doing its job. Aydan's jaw stiffened. "I care about the citizens of this country. You think that this—this *institution* means a damned thing to me? You think that if *Zathryan* had offered me this position, I would have taken it? The Crown doesn't mean a fucking thing to me if you're not the one wearing it, Aydan." He blinked, and the words continued to pour from my mouth, softer now. "When you came back, every time I saw you, I was reminded of how much I shattered when you left, and I think—I don't know—I think part of me was scared that if I said no, you'd disappear again." I clenched and unclenched my hands. My face was hot.

"Shaye," Aydan nearly whispered. "It wasn't my choice to leave."

"I know."

"I can't tell you how sorry I am. I can't imagine how scared you must have been. I wish I could have done more, but I knew you were safe here, blood-shielded—"

My hands heated so quickly, my drink exploded. I moved away, shaking bits of glass out of my palms, scoffing as I bit back the angry tears welling in my eyes. "Yes, the *blood shield*. A lot of good that did me." Aydan looked at me, baffled.

"What are you talking about?" The tears spilled over and evaporated into tiny clouds of steam from my face.

"Didn't you wonder what *heightened interrogation methods* your father was talking about in his diary?"

"You said they questioned you."

"No, I said they interrogated me," I corrected. "Even on his deathbed, Zathryan was clever and cruel."

"You were blood-shielded—"

"Do you want to see what good your precious *fucking* blood shield did me?" My voice grew louder. Aydan stared as I began undoing the laces of my jacket, tearing at them as they sizzled beneath my fingertips. I threw it to the floor, then brought the padded white shirt I wore beneath it over my head until I was in nothing but sparring pants and a camisole, my shoulders and midriff exposed. I turned my back to him, and though I couldn't see his face, the air in the room shifted to a feeling of horror.

From the tops of my shoulders, down my entire back were gnarled, thick raised scars that continued beneath my clothes, past the waist of my pants and over the backs of my legs, still angry and pink all these months later. Looking at them, you couldn't tell where one wound had ended and the another began. I turned around slowly.

"Shaye." Aydan's eyes were rimmed in red. "I don't . . ."

"The mortals that were captured the night of the attack were given a deal. Whichever one could make me confess to my involvement would be spared from execution," I said matter-of-factly, attempting to block out the memory. "They put a silver cuff on my ankle and left it there until Stefan was able to switch it out for the steel one, but the damage was already done. The mortals knew I had nothing to do with their plans, but they did it anyway. They were desperate. Most of them just whipped me. A couple tried using knives. None of them could survive their own torture, but I did. It didn't stop until Stefan stepped in, but we now know that was Zathryan's doing too."

Aydan opened his mouth, "Shaye, I—"

"I know you couldn't do anything. You couldn't have known. But I'm not the same woman you left in those chambers. I can't pretend that I didn't spend every day those first few months praying that *this* would be the day you returned, but you never did. So now I spend every second torn between being scared of getting too close to you and terrified of being away from you, because I know one day, you could decide your debt is paid and I will be left alone all over again." I snapped my mouth shut and closed my eyes, realizing I had said far too much. "Excuse me—"

Aydan didn't stop me as I walked out of the room and crossed the king's chambers, passed the rest of the Cabinet where they waited in the parlor. None of them said a word as I walked by. I locked my door behind me and curled atop my bed to cry.

Chapter Thirty-Two

I woke shivering the next morning. Sun poured through my window and into my eyes, and when I moved to get out of bed and draw the curtains shut, I realized my pillow was frozen to my face.

I didn't trust myself to use fire without burning my flesh, so I spent the next few minutes gently peeling the frozen satin from my face, which was left red and raw. When I sat up and looked around, now thoroughly awake, Catchfly was not in her normal spot next to me.

"Catchfly?" I called. I moved the blanket on her side of the bed and my hand sank into ice cold water. The bedding was soaked through. A low disgruntled sound came from atop my wardrobe. The fat gray cat was sat there, staring at me with disapproval. "Well I didn't do it on purpose," I said, reaching up to take her down from her perch. She swatted at my hand. "Suit yourself."

Still in my clothes from last night, I found a shirt and pulled it over myself. A pair of covered trays sat by the door when I stepped out, and I lifted the top of the first one. Dinner from last night. The second was breakfast from this morning.

The king's chambers were a flurry of activity. Elise, Alice, and a handful of servants I didn't know were darting in and out of rooms, carrying gowns and boxes in their arms. Beyond the bedroom wing, I could see trunks piling into the foyer. I took a few steps and leaned my head into Hannele's room, where I found her speaking with a servant girl about her belongings. "Yes, just leave all of the gowns," she said. "I'll need to keep them on hand for visits here." She saw me in the doorway. "You're awake. Good afternoon."

"What time is it?" I asked, searching for a clock. "What's going on, why did no one wake me?"

"Things were hectic this morning. When you didn't wake on your own, we figured we'd handle the details and fill you in when you decided to join us." She looked me up and down. "Rough night?"

"Something like that. What's going on?"

"We're leaving for Sylvanna in an hour," she replied, continuing to sort her things into various trunks and boxes around her. My heart sank.

Gerridan appeared next to me.

"Look who woke up." He smirked, looking at me the same way Hannele had done before adding, "Yikes."

"You really know how to compliment a woman, Gerridan darling," Hannele said.

"I do my best." He grinned, then asked her, "Do you have my book?"

"What book?"

"The . . . oh, what's it called? The one about the trees in the elf kingdoms—"

"What is the *title* of the book, Gerridan?"

"I don't *know*," he said. "I just know one is *missing*."

"If you loaned me a book, it's in my trunk now. You can look for it when we get home." Gerridan let out an exaggerated sigh before turning his attention back to me.

"What are you doing?" he asked.

"Oh," I said, my chest feeling heavy. "Sorry, I'll get out of your way and let you pack. If I don't see you—"

"Why wouldn't you see us?" Hannele asked. "I told you we're leaving in an hour. Do you need help packing? One of the servants can bring you an extra trunk if you don't have one ready." I blinked, trying to understand.

"I'm coming with you?"

"Why wouldn't you be?" Gerridan asked. "You're the Chief Advisor."

"I didn't realize I still had the job . . . after yesterday."

Hannele scoffed. "Please. You think *that* was enough to be set aside?"

"Technically, I resigned."

"No you didn't. Not really."

"I don't know if he wants me around anymore."

"Look, short of trying to kill him, Aydan isn't going to set you aside. And even then"—she gestured to Gerridan—"he'll probably still keep you around." He rolled his eyes.

"It was *one time*, and an *accident*—"

"Semantics." Hannele winked at me.

"Thanks," I said. "And I'm sorry. To both of you—all of you—"

Gerridan waved his hand dismissively. "It's nothing."

"Go pack." Hannele smiled. "We're going home."

Not quite an hour later, our trunks and suitcases—and a very unimpressed Catchfly—had been hauled into the parlor, where, with a wave of his hand, Gerridan made them disappear before my eyes. He explained that they now sat in Aydan's private residence, where they would be waiting for us until our arrival.

"Impressive," I remarked.

"Not really," Kenna replied, leaning against a doorframe and examining her fingernails. "It's pretty low-level magic." Gerridan held a hand to his chest, offended.

"I couldn't do it," I said.

"You could learn," Kenna assured me. "But, knowing you, you'd burn the place down or drown somebody in the process."

"Thanks."

She shrugged. "I'm not wrong."

"No, I guess you're not." I snorted.

"Everyone ready?" Aydan asked, strolling into the room. I couldn't help but notice he didn't look my way. "Where's Al?"

"Still packing up," Gerridan said. "He was doing perimeter checks while you bid the council farewell."

"I'm here." Alastair appeared next to Aydan, with a knapsack slung over his shoulder. He made it a point to catch my eye and give me a nod. I returned the gesture.

"All right. Let's do this, then." Aydan reached out and took Alastair's hand. Alastair took Gerridan's, and so on until Kenna grabbed mine. I waited for a moment and then realized the rest of them were waiting for me to complete the circle. I didn't look at him as I grasped Aydan's other hand. A heartbeat later, my stomach dropped and stone floors appeared beneath my feet where the rug had been. I blinked and quickly let go of Aydan, gasping softly at the room surrounding me.

The floors and walls were made of light gray stone, brightened by sunlight pouring in through the enormous windows that lined the room, three on each side, reaching from floor to ceiling. Brightly colored tapestries hung along the walls: one painstakingly woven into detailed pictures of wildflower fields, and another a perfect depiction of the night sky. Beautiful tables lined the room but lay empty, awaiting guests and food to fill them. At the far end of the hall stood a small group of people, hands folded, waiting for us.

The man at the front of the group wore a teal tunic with gold embroidery at the wrists and neck. The color was bright, and complemented well by the man's dark skin. His braided black hair was pulled back from his face, which was as smooth and youthful as any Medeisian. The woman beside him wore matching colors, her dress similar in style to the daring, low-cut ensemble Hannele had worn to the coronation. Her gown bore no embroidery or embellishment of any kind. Instead, she wore a simple golden circlet atop her head and a large necklace made of gold that extended down over her shoulders, forming into roses and thorns, something between jewelry and armor. The tattoos that covered Aydan's arm, and that I'd seen glimpses of on Gerridan and Alastair's bodies, covered every visible inch of the lady's skin, up the sides of her face, which was stoic but not unkind as they took in our arrival.

Aydan walked toward them, the rest of us falling into rank behind him. He stopped a few feet away and the couple, along with a group of people standing behind them, bowed in unison.

"Your Majesty," the woman said, "welcome home." Aydan took a step closer and kissed each of her cheeks.

"Grandmother," he said with a nod. Another nod to the man. "Grandfather."

Priamos and Solandis, the Lord and Lady of Sylvanna.

I tried not to gape as Aydan exchanged greetings with his grandparents, who were now hugging him and speaking casually. Solandis smiled broadly at Aydan. Her eyes fixed on me. "This must be the new one," she said. I swallowed.

"Yes, my Chief Advisor." Aydan gestured for me to come nearer. I took a few steps forward. "Lady Shaye Eastly."

I curtsied, then faced the pair, waiting for them to speak first as Hannele had instructed me. Lady Solandis looked me up and down once before saying, "Well, you must favor your mother's looks. You look nothing like Lord Redfern."

"Thank you, my lady," I replied, unsure if the comment was a compliment.

"It is my understanding that Lady Brina commanded our troops as well as any Sylvannian-born soldier," Priamos added. "Are you skilled in battle, Lady Shaye?"

"I'm afraid not, my lord," I said.

Aydan said, "Lady Shaye is recently under the instruction of both Lord Gerridan and General Alastair. They tell me she has improved greatly."

"Good. You may need it," Solandis said. A dismissal.

I fell back into place beside Gerridan, who gave the briefest nod of approval. Quietly, I let out the breath I'd been holding in. Aydan didn't care much for formalities, but from what my friends had told me, these ancient nobles certainly did.

"Your Majesty, will you be joining your grandfather and me for dinner tonight?" Solandis asked.

"Tonight, I have much to do," Aydan replied. "I've been away for a long time. I'll be getting my household in order. But perhaps tomorrow, after our agreements have been signed."

Solandis inclined her head. "Indeed, there is still much to plan for the eclipse as well. We look forward to our audience with you tomorrow night."

"Lady Grandmother." Aydan kissed her hand before turning on his heel and taking our hands once again to effuge out of the castle. As always, the falling sensation unsettled my stomach. Once I steadied myself, I looked around the sitting room where we now stood, in Aydan's private residence.

It was a house. Not a castle. Not a manor, or mansion. But a house, albeit a large one, large enough for the entire Cabinet to live with him, as well as his servants—

Behind me, I heard a gasp.

"My lady?" Isolde was standing in a doorway, staring at me as if I were a ghost.

"*Isolde.*" Her name caught in my throat as I stepped toward her. She moved to curtsy, but I wrapped her in a hug before she could.

"His Majesty sent word that you were safe once he returned to Ayzelle, but—" She cut herself off, pulling out of the embrace. "It is good to see you, my lady."

"And you, Isolde. Is Tory here? And Zale?"

"Yes, they're down in the kitchens, I—" She looked over my shoulder, and I realized that my friends were all watching us. Isolde curtsied. "Your Majesty, princess, my lords and ladies. Welcome home."

"Hello, Isolde," Gerridan said warmly before walking up a flight of stairs beside us. Hannele, Kenna, and Alastair all greeted her briefly and went their separate ways.

"I asked Elise to send a note ahead of us. Was it received?" Aydan asked.

"Yes, Your Majesty. The items you requested are in your study."

"Thank you." He turned to me. "Will you join me?" I nodded and followed as Aydan led the way through the house and into a back room. The walls were lined with bookshelves that reached from the floor to the ceiling and were filled to the brim. In the center of the room, there was a desk. He sat behind it and gestured for me to sit in the chair in front, where I watched and waited as he shuffled through a stack of papers nearly an inch thick. Over each one, he waved his hand and left his blue seal upon it. Once he'd made his way through the pile, he slid them across the desk. I picked them up and flipped through them.

"What is this?" I asked.

"Those are the deeds to the remaining properties once owned by Lord Ronan Redfern," he said. "Upon his execution, all properties in Ayzelle belonging to House Redfern were seized by the Crown and destroyed. As you can see, there is a considerable amount remaining here in Sylvanna. They are yours by right." I quickly slid the papers back to Aydan.

"I don't want them," I said. "I don't want anything to do with House Redfern. I don't want his properties. The Crown can have them."

"You can sell them if you wish." Aydan shrugged. "Or burn them to the ground if you so desire. But you are by right the head of House Redfern, and the owner of"—he quickly counted the deeds—"thirteen estates. None of them are operational, of course, but you are now a very wealthy woman. The Crown can offer you help in making any of them livable, so you have plenty of choices for the location of your new home. You could be settled in within a couple of weeks."

"My new home?"

"You seemed adamant to resign last we spoke," Aydan replied stiffly. A lump formed in my throat.

"I don't want to resign," I said softly. "I'm sorry for my behavior—"

"I'm not looking for an apology," he said. "I'm simply delivering to you what is yours by right." He slid the deeds back to me and added, "Your position was not offered to you as a debt to be repaid, but as it seems it has been perceived that way, I wanted you to know that you are not stuck with me, or this Cabinet, my lady. The choice is yours, and always will be." I took the stack of papers from him and placed them in my lap. *My lady,* he called me.

"If it's not any trouble," I said, "I would like to stay near the rest of the Cabinet. I will make a decision regarding these properties at a later date." He nodded.

"A room has been prepared for you, next to Hannele and Kenna. Your belongings have been placed there already. The servants will call you for dinner. Until then, the day is yours." He began shuffling through another stack of papers littering the desk.

"And after dinner?"

"What about it?"

"Will we be continuing our lessons together?" Aydan looked up.

"I believe you were correct in saying that our lessons weren't going anywhere," he said. "We'll have to rethink how to approach your extra abilities. Let's set it aside for now. Tomorrow we'll sign the new trade agreement between Sylvanna and the Crown, and the eclipse is the following night. Consider this a day off." His tone indicated that he didn't want to talk any longer, so I stood and matched his formality with a curtsy.

"Your Majesty," I said before turning to leave. I could have sworn I saw him wince.

Chapter Thirty-Three

Hours later, I was in the front sitting room, letting my stomach settle after an enormous roast venison dinner prepared by Zale and Tory to welcome the Cabinet home. Hannele and Gerridan sat on the sofa opposite me, her head resting on his shoulder, the both of them nearly asleep. Alastair had returned to his bedroom, saying something about training in the morning. Kenna sat in an armchair, her legs draped over the arm while she flipped through some book she'd been wanting to read.

"No lessons with Aydan, then?" she asked after a while.

"No, we're going to reassess after the eclipse," I said, plucking at a thread in the sofa. "When and what is that, anyway?"

"It's a festival," she said. "A feast and a ball honoring the union of Ehnara and Lehrun. The day after tomorrow. You'll have fun."

"Yeah, fun." I thought of the last ball I had attended. And with whom. "Is there any word on Stefan?"

"The captain's condition is the same, last I heard," she replied, putting her book down. "Still rambling. The healers in Ayzelle don't know what to do for him."

"Isn't there somewhere else he can go?" I asked. "Can the Crown fairly sentence someone who doesn't even remember committing the crime?" Kenna looked thoughtful for a moment, staring up at the ceiling.

"There may be some healers in Xarynn who could take a look at him. I've heard of a place where they help people whose minds have been affected by magic—particularly witchcraft. I wonder if . . ." She fell silent, then stood from her seat. "I'm going to write a letter."

I sighed. "I think I might go for a walk."

"I'll see you later, then," she said as she headed for the stairs. Before she reached the top, she called over her shoulder, chuckling. "This would be a lot easier if we had an actual witch around. They could reverse his condition—maybe teach you a thing or two while they're at it." I huffed a laugh as Kenna continued her ascent, then glanced over at Gerridan and Hannele, who were now fully asleep. Gerridan's arm was wrapped around the princess, both of them slumped over but looking peaceful. I waved my hand and spread a blanket over top of them before walking out the front door.

I made my way down a path leading from the house. It was completely dark out, but the ground was illuminated by the full moon and the beautiful glowing white flowers that lined the path. With their light I could see scores of trees and shrubs surrounding the area, and other houses in the distance. The whole of the village looked as if a gardener had designed it, but something within me said that it was the magic of this land that had perfected its own design.

The moon was so bright that I stopped to admire it, and I wondered if Ehnara watched over this place. If she was even real. I didn't know much about the goddess, nor her male counterpart, Lehrun. They were not to be discussed in Nautia. No gods were worshiped there, though most mortals celebrated Yule out of tradition. I wasn't sure how long I had been standing there when I heard footsteps behind me. "The moon is beautiful tonight," I said.

"It is," Aydan agreed from my side.

"I've waited a long time to see Sylvanna. For a while, I wasn't sure if I ever would. I couldn't wait until morning to step outside." He didn't reply; instead, he too looked up at the sky, watching the moon as the chill night air surrounded us both. "Kenna said the eclipse celebrates Ehnara and Lehrun," I said after a few moments. "I don't know much about them."

"The story goes that Ehnara embodies the moon: the mother, watching over her children as they sleep. A guiding light in the darkness. Lehrun embodies the sun: the father, life-giving, allowing all things to grow. Their love for one another is deep and all-encompassing, but for them to truly be together would mean destruction for the world—us, their children, whom they love dearly and protect fiercely. To allow us to thrive, they must remain apart.

An eclipse is a rare stolen moment between lovers. We celebrate their love, and their sacrifice."

"That's beautiful," I said. "Do you believe? In them, I mean."

"I never used to," Aydan sighed. "As a child I would get dragged to the temples for rituals at the solstices and equinoxes, but I never took it too seriously. After the duel, I abandoned what little belief I did hold. But during the coronation, when that oil touched me— I can't quite explain it, but it was like they were there. They seemed to approve, for what it's worth."

After another moment's silence, I said, "Kenna said something else interesting. It was just in passing, as a joke, but I'm curious what you think about it."

"Oh?"

I hadn't been able to get the words out of my head since she said them. "We were talking about Stefan's condition. She said that it's too bad we don't have access to a real witch to reverse whatever it was I did to him—and someone who could teach me a thing or two."

Aydan stiffened. "And?"

"What if . . . well, would such a thing even be possible? The Nautians employ witches in their palace. Could we . . . could we maybe locate—?"

"You want to learn from a coven?" he asked harshly.

"No, but—what we've been doing so far hasn't worked. We know what coven Lord Ronan sought out. Maybe the Children will be sympathetic. Maybe they'd be willing to make a deal." I turned to face Aydan, who was gaping at me. "I know it sounds crazy."

"You're right, it does," he said. I bit the inside of my cheek and turned back to pretend I was looking at the moon again.

"You said you wanted a different world. A united Medeisia. Extending an olive branch to a major coven could—"

"I meant quelling mortal uprisings. Opening trade with Nautia. Not cozying up to the very people who helped your father try to destroy this kingdom," he spat.

"You can't teach me how to control these powers." My fingers sparked. "Nor can any other Medeisian. The accident with Stefan made it very clear that I'm constantly just a step away from killing myself or someone else. You saw what I did to him. I shattered his mind. My motivations are nothing like Ronan's—how *dare* you compare me to him—"

"That's not what I—look, I know everything that happened with Captain Whittaker has been difficult, and that your recovery was brutal, but this isn't the answer."

"Then what is? It only gets worse, Aydan. I have to take that damned tincture every night, I now have three elements bursting from me without warning, and yesterday we learned that I'm a fucking *mindwalker*—" I threw my hands up in frustration, and along with the motion, a nearby sapling began to grow taller.

Taller.

Aydan and I stared as the tree grew so large before our eyes that its roots sprung up from the earth, loosening the dirt around it. Creaking out an ominous groan, the weakened roots gave out and the tree began crashing down toward us. Aydan swore and grabbed my hand to run, but we were too slow, and within seconds, the branches were just over our heads. Aydan threw his body over mine, tackling me to the ground.

We both coughed as the dust settled around us. Aydan was on top of me, with a branch laying over his back, pinning him to me, and me to the ground. I raised my arm and focused, willing the branch to break, or the tree to lift itself back into the air. Dark flecks floated in my vision and my breathing became labored as I clenched my teeth and pushed my will further into my palms and—

Everything went black.

"*Shaye*, come on, wake up—" Aydan's voice was frantic and I felt myself being shaken. My eyes fluttered open, and his hands held my face as he looked me over for injury. "Are you all right? Can you hear me?"

"I'm fine." I pushed myself up. Everything was spinning. I leaned to the side and vomited. "Make that four elements," I said before vomiting again. Aydan's hand rested on my back, but I shook him off as I moved to stand.

"Take it easy."

"I'm fine," I snapped, brushing leaves and twigs off my dress and plucking them from my hair.

"You just lost consciousness," he said.

"Yes, and I would love to learn how *not* to do that. But the one person who can help me find a teacher refuses to do so."

"It's not that simple. We're talking about millennia of animosity. The Children would sooner kill me on sight than make a deal. We don't even know where they *are*, other than somewhere in the Creg'tam Mountains." Aydan's voice was dripping in frustration. I fumed and tried not to stumble.

"I suppose you'd better start looking for a new advisor, then," I said, swaying. "I won't survive this much longer."

"Shaye—"

I felt myself hit the ground before passing out once again.

Chapter Thirty-Four

I woke with a pounding headache and clutched my head as I sat up and tried to determine where I was. It was a large bedroom suite, with a wardrobe and vanity similar to the ones in my room in Aydan's chambers back in Ayzelle. Even the embroidered white quilt matched, which had me half wondering if the contents of that room had simply been transported here, like my luggage.

"Easy there," said a deep voice. Alastair was sitting in an armchair in the opposite corner of the bedroom. He waved his hand and a glass of water appeared on the bedside table. I took it and drank deeply.

"What time is it?" I asked hoarsely. "What happened?"

"Aydan said you had another incident. He carried you back here. The healers looked you over and said you seemed to be all right, just drained. You slept through the night and all day yesterday. The others went to look at preparations for the eclipse tonight. I stayed to keep an eye on you—"

"I missed the signing?" I interrupted, moving to stand from the bed. Alastair put his hand out to stop me.

"No," he said. "Aydan wouldn't leave your side yesterday. He postponed the signing. The only reason he went anywhere this morning was because Kenna and Hannele dragged him out of the house."

"He's furious with me, I'm sure." Catchfly jumped up onto the bed and rubbed herself against my legs, demanding that I scratch her ears. I obliged.

"He's worried sick about you," Alastair said, raising his eyebrows.

"He won't listen. I had an idea—a way to address my 'incidents'—and he was furious." I focused my attention on Catchfly. Al seemed to study me as I did so.

"The last Chief Advisor—"

"Lord Ronan was trying to usurp Zathryan. I'm trying to not die, but that doesn't seem to matter to Aydan. Nothing I do seems to matter to him." Alastair's jaw clenched.

"You're an idiot," he said.

"Excuse me?"

"You're an idiot. You are so . . ." He stood and quickly paced the room, running a hand through his hair. "When you mindwalked, was there any drain to your power?"

"I don't think so." I scowled. "You vomited. So it must just be a drain on yours—"

"Good." He sat on the edge of my bed and held his hand out toward me. "Do it again."

"What?"

"Mindwalk again with me. I want to show you how wrong you are." I hesitated. "Look," he said with a sigh, "I'm not . . . I'm not usually one to meddle. I try to let people work these things out on their own. But you and Aydan are so hell-bent on ignoring what's right in front of you that I'm afraid you both are going to lose it before you figure this out. So, please. Let me show this to you."

"I don't know if I can do it on purpose."

"Try. I'll push the images forward, and we'll see if it works." I nodded and took his extended hand—

I was reading in my bedroom in Sylvanna when I heard a crash and a scream of anguish from downstairs. Gerridan and I burst from our rooms at the same time. We made eye contact, then effuged to the sitting room, where we found Hannele crouched before Aydan, who was trying to get up from the floor. He was disheveled and covered in dried blood—eyes wild as he sobbed. His breathing was labored, and he looked like he was going to be sick.

"NO!" he screamed while his blue glow crackled and turned to lightning around his fists. His power surged, then flickered—he was trying to effuge, but he was fizzling out. Something was blocking his attempts.

"Aydan—AYDAN, STOP," Hannele said, taking his face in her hands.

"I have to go back, Hannele, I can't leave her there, I can't—"

"Where is the girl?" I asked while Hannele hissed at Gerridan to send for Lady Solandis.

"She's still there—my father has her, it's—gods . . ." he tried to catch his breath. "There was an attack on the castle—mortals—Irsa is dead. My father is wounded. Dying. He named me Crown Prince and sent me away—" He choked, looking up at me from the floor. "He kept Shaye, Al. He ordered me to leave her, but I couldn't leave without saying goodbye, I—" Aydan tried to lift himself up but nearly collapsed from weakness. "If anything happens to her, I'll kill them all. I'll kill them."

It was almost two weeks later, and Aydan had barely come out of his room. He'd given us the full story about the attack on Ayzelle, and about his imprisonment with Brina's daughter, Shaye. The healers watching over his father had told him the king might last two weeks. Aydan was holding on to that number, spending his time in his room, pacing the floor, waiting for letters to arrive.

I was having tea in the sitting room when Zale and Tory, then Isolde followed shortly by Elise, all appeared in the room before me.

"My lord—quickly, where is the Crown Prince?" Elise asked me with terror in her eyes. Isolde wept silently behind her, while Zale and Tory were ashen, trying to comfort her.

"Elise, what are you—?" Aydan called from the top of the stairs. He rushed to her and gripped the servant's shoulders. "Why are you here? Where is Shaye?"

"Lady Shaye ordered us back here, Your Highness," Elise told him. "The guards were breaking down the wards, the doors were crashing down—she ordered us away, sir. She asked me to alert you. She says she'll be fine and not to worry, but . . ." Elise couldn't finish the sentence. Aydan ran his hands through his hair, then turned without a word and sat at the writing desk. He scribbled a letter before adding his seal and making it disappear.

"You are dismissed for the evening. Get some rest and resume your normal duties in the morning. Thank you."

"Your Highness," they each murmured before shuffling off to their respective rooms.

"Aydan," I started.

"I've just begged him to release her. Again. What if the blood shield doesn't hold? Or worse." He drank. "What if he doesn't care anymore? He's dying, Al. What if he takes her with him?"

"If he thinks she has information, he won't," I tried to assure him. "If she's anything like you described. If she's anything like her mother, she'll be fine."

It had been nearly a year. Aydan had thrown himself into preparations for his return to Ayzelle, to rescue Shaye Eastly. I took to opening his letters and reading them for him in case a direct order from Zathryan was included. In nearly every letter received from the dying king, he demanded that Aydan remove the blood shield on the girl. Aydan resigned from his position on Solandis's council, unable to focus on his duties. Instead, he spent each morning writing letters, begging for Shaye's release, each afternoon sparring with Hannele or Gerridan, and by the evening he'd received a response from the king declining the request.

More days had passed, and a letter arrived from Ayzelle, requesting Aydan's presence at his father's bedside. Zathryan had taken a turn for the worse. Aydan was jittery. Elise straightened his cape as we all prepared to accompany him to the castle.

"Do you think she'll still . . ." He didn't finish the question and hadn't directed it to anyone in particular. "We never. I never told her—"

"It will be fine," Gerridan said, clapping our brother on the shoulder. "We'll take care of business and then you can have her to yourself. As much as I'd like to finally take a look at that fire of hers, I'll wait until breakfast tomorrow." He winked. Aydan flushed.

"I don't think she would want . . . There will be a lot to discuss before anything even close to that. If she even feels the same way."

I walked from the kitchens back to the lounge in the king's chambers, holding a stiff drink. Watching that horrible man take his last ragged breaths had been draining. Watching Aydan take on the title of king in a matter of seconds . . . my best friend, practically my brother . . . King of Medeisia. I stepped through the door into the lounge and when I looked up, I saw Aydan and, to his left, the ghost of Brina Eastly. I dropped my drink, which shattered. Hannele cleaned up the mess, and I looked back up. Not Brina. Shaye. Why are they here? They should be busy reuniting.

Lady Shaye left the lounge after an uncomfortable hour of watching her try not to make eye contact with Aydan. When the door clicked shut, he ran a hand through his hair, disappointment and concern painted on his face.

"Aydan . . ." Kenna said carefully. He stood and started toward his bedroom.

"She's not ready," I heard him mumble to himself.

The morning after the coronation, Gerridan told us what he saw between Shaye and the captain the night before. Icy rage flashed in Aydan's eyes, but he only said, "If she says all is well, then believe her. But keep an eye out."

I entered the king's chambers and found Aydan pacing the parlor. Shaye had rushed past me as I came in the door.

"What's going on?"

"The captain's been deceiving Shaye. He befriended her on Zathryan's command," Hannele told me. Gods.

"And she knows this?" I asked. Hannele and Kenna nodded. Aydan didn't speak. The front door swung open and in ran Elise.

"Your Majesty!" she cried out. "Lady Shaye's door is locked. There's a man's voice. She's yelling for him to leave, but—the wards, I can't—"

Aydan and I were already sprinting past her, down the corridor. We could hear her through the door. Yelling, and then a scream, and a thud. Aydan's power surged through his arms, his hands engulfed in blue light. He broke through the wards at the exact same time the door shattered. I entered first, ordering the captain to stand down. He pulled a short sword, and I saw his face was sliced open and bleeding. He raised his blade and I struck. He got in a few good swings before I knocked the blade out of his hand and pinned him to the ground. Aydan finally made his way through the thick black smoke and emerged, carrying Shaye in his arms. Her face and hair were soaked in blood, and she was a terrifying shade of white. Aydan was stoic as he carried her motionless body back to the chambers.

"You couldn't have known," Gerridan said, pressing a drink into Aydan's hand while the three of us sat before the fireplace. "The blood shield worked. We just didn't know the extent of Zathryan's cruelty." Aydan slumped low in an armchair, defeated. He drank.

"You need to tell her the truth. All of it. Say the words. We can all see how she looks at you—"

"No . . . I can't do this to her anymore."

"What are you talking about?" I asked.

"She thinks if she leaves the Cabinet, she'll be left with nothing. She should be free to do as she wishes, otherwise she's just as much my prisoner as she was my father's. I'm accepting her resignation tomorrow."

"You can't give up," Gerridan said.

"I've damaged her life enough. The least I can do is let her go."

My eyes fluttered, and it took me a second to realize that the sound I heard was Alastair vomiting into a bucket. It took a second longer to realize that my eyes were wet.

"Does he know you're showing me these things?" I asked with my head in my hands.

"No."

"I'm so stupid," I whispered. "Al, I thought . . ." He sat on the edge of my bed, looking sympathetic and a bit queasy still. "I'm too late, aren't I?"

"I have no doubt that Aydan's feelings have remained the same since the night he left you. If you wanted to leave, he would let you go. But he would always hold out hope." I chewed on my lip.

"I said horrible things to him."

"He's said worse to himself, I'm sure."

"How long until the start of the festival?"

He looked at the clock standing in the far corner of the bedroom. "About two hours. The priestesses have estimated the start of the eclipse to be late afternoon." I swore and threw the blankets aside.

"I don't have anything to wear," I said, pushing away Alastair's hand as he tried to usher me back down. "I'm fine. I swear, I am. I just—can you call Elise for me? I need help dressing."

Within a minute, Elise was knocking at my door. I called for her to enter while I tore through my wardrobe. "My lady?"

"Hannele and Kenna insisted I buy all these damned gowns and none of them are good enough," I complained, rummaging around. "Help me. Please." She looked me up and down, possibly assessing my sanity. I had never been concerned about what I wore before. "I want to look pretty," I said finally. "I don't have anything to wear to the festival." Her face softened.

"Lucky for you," she said, crossing the room, "the king thinks ahead." She pressed a brick in the wall, and much like the passage in the king's chambers in Ayzelle, it opened. Instead of a lit tunnel, it was a small room, a bit larger than a closet. It was empty except for a large white box. Elise brought it to the bed and set it down. "Every eclipse festival, His Majesty commissions a pair of gowns as a gift to Princess Hannele and Lady Kenna. This time, he asked for a third."

With perhaps ten minutes to spare, I stood before Elise while she made her final adjustments. My hair she'd insisted remain in loose curls, free to hang down my back, with no embellishments save for a thin braid pinned over the crown of my head. She'd curled my eyelashes and brushed a hint of rouge on my cheeks, assuring me that I wouldn't need anything else. Now she crouched before me, adjusting my skirts and helping me step into the gold slippers that matched it.

The dress was the palest pink of a sunset. Thin golden threads, which Elise explained were not dyed but made of pure spun gold, were woven throughout, making the gauzy fabric shimmer in the sunlight that poured through the window. The golden threads met at my waist, and again at the edge of the neckline, to form solid gold embroidered roses. Panels of sheer fabric in the same pink color were attached just behind the tops of my shoulders, giving the illusion of a cape without the bulk and heat, perfect for the premature spring of the garden city. The low-cut neckline rivaled any that I had seen Hannele wear. I'd thought I would be nervous to wear such a thing, but today, as I examined myself in the mirror, I thought I looked powerful.

"This was in the box as well, my lady," Elise said from behind me. I turned, and she held a deep blue velvet box in her hands. She opened it, revealing a thin tiara made of golden leaves dotted with blush pink pearls, and let out the smallest gasp. She motioned for me to sit in front of the vanity, where she placed the tiara just behind the braided band of hair, then waved her hands, commanding my hair to subtly weave around it, fastening the tiara in place.

As we finished, there was a knock. "Shaye?" It was Alastair.

"Just a moment," I called, glancing once more in the mirror. I mouthed a thank you to Elise, who smiled warmly. I opened the door. The general let out a breath, looking me over.

"You look . . . wow," he said.

"That's good, I hope?" I tried to joke. My hands were slowly coating themselves with a thin layer of frost. I opened and closed them, trying to shake it off.

"You look lovely." He offered his arm. "Shall we?" I nodded, terrified. Alastair, rather than trying to help me down the stairs without tripping over my skirts, effuged us to the sitting room, where Gerridan, Hannele, and Kenna all stood waiting, the latter sipping on a glass of brandy. "Look who I found," he said by way of greeting. The trio looked shocked to see me out of bed.

"I didn't even know you were awake," Hannele said, crossing the room to hug me tightly. Her gown was a similar gauzy material in white, with golden caps on her shoulders resembling battle armor that connected to one another on the back with gold chains made of the tiniest roses. Her tight black curls hung freely around her shoulders, bouncing with each motion. Kenna, who wore midnight blue in the exact same cut as her coronation gown, approached as well to peck me on the cheek.

"Stunning," she said before returning to her spot near the drink cart.

"Do you think he'll like it?" I whispered to Hannele. She gave a knowing smile and squeezed my hand.

"Dearest Shaye," Gerridan said. "I'll have you know that finding soldiers willing to scout the Creg'tam Mountains is proving *quite* the chore."

"Scouting the Creg'tam Mountains?" I repeated. Then my eyes widened. "You're searching for the Children."

"Sweet Aydan asked me to do so—discreetly. You made quite a convincing argument it seems."

"Well, dropping a tree on us was certainly effective," I replied dryly. Gerridan snorted, nearly dribbling wine on his forest green jacket. Hannele conjured a handkerchief and dabbed the corner of the emissary's mouth while Alastair and I chuckled at the pair. The door opened.

"All right, let's go get this over wi—" I turned, and Aydan stopped short. "You're here."

"I am," I said. "I thought I might join you at the festival, if that's all right." He stared for another second.

"I'd be honored, my lady." The king inclined his head. He wore the golden crown of roses once again, along with a finely made black ensemble. His jacket, perfectly tailored, was embroidered with gold thread at the breast to form a familiar lion within a wreath of bloomed roses, a marriage of the sigils of both his parents' houses.

"Well then, let's go. We're due outside the temple," Alastair said, looking at his watch again before shoving it back into his pocket.

The six of us joined hands, and suddenly we were in a lush green field outside of the Sylvannian temples to Lehrun and Ehnara. The houses of worship stood on opposite ends of the field, forever separated, like their patrons.

A crowd had already formed, and applause broke out when we appeared. Aydan marched forward, toward two figures in the distance that I quickly realized were Solandis and Priamos. The rest of us fell into rank behind him. As we passed through the crowd, people stopped to bow or curtsy to their king, and kept their heads lowered until the rest of us had gone by. I followed Hannele's lead, smiling warmly and nodding at those who did the same to me.

"Lady Grandmother." Aydan greeted Solandis with a kiss on the cheek. "Grandfather," he said, clasping Priamos's hand.

"Right on time," Solandis replied. Her eyes landed on me. "I heard you had an accident."

"Yes, my lady."

"Well, you seem to be in good health now." Her eyes flicked to the tiara on my head. She paused, looking to Aydan out of the corner of her eye as he spoke with Priamos and paid her no mind. "Enjoy the festival."

"Thank you, my lady," I said as she walked away. I shuddered slightly and realized my hands were now completely coated in ice. I tried to discreetly rub them on my skirts. Kenna handed me a handkerchief, which I accepted eagerly, nearly wringing my hands out on it.

"It's starting," she said. I started to look up, but she stopped me. "Wait. You'll fry your eyes out of your skull."

A moment passed, and I noticed everyone looking at each other with large grins, or at the ground watching the shadows form and the sky grow darker. "You can look now," Aydan's voice said from behind me. Though his lips nearly grazed my ear, I didn't turn, instead looking up toward the sun, only to see the dark moon sitting in front of it. "It's safe for a few moments. Ehnara and Lehrun's stolen kiss, and then they must part."

"It's beautiful," I breathed.

I thought I felt his hand brush mine lightly, but as soon as I looked, Aydan was walking away to join his grandparents. I turned back to the sky, but those around me were already averting their eyes. And then it was over. The moon passed over the sun and the gods would have to wait, apart, for the next opportunity for their moment alone. The crowd cheered, and Aydan stepped forward.

"My friends," he said once they had all quieted. "I am delighted to be here with you. At such a time of great change, it is a comfort to know that the traditions of home are waiting. There is much to look forward to, and much prosperity to come between Sylvanna and the Crown—" Aydan stopped abruptly and glanced down. My attention, and everyone else's, landed on a small girl, perhaps no older than four, tugging on Aydan's pant leg. A gasp, and a wide-eyed woman, who I assumed to be her mother, rushed forward. Aydan looked surprised, but smiled warmly and raised a hand, saying something quietly to the woman. He knelt before the little girl, who leaned in and whispered in his ear, then held up a crown of daisies from the field. Aydan removed his golden rose crown and bowed his head for her to place the daisies there. The girl's smile was infectious. A chuckle rippled through the crowd as Aydan led the girl by the hand back her mother, who curtsied. He smiled, then winked at the girl, who giggled and hid her face in her mother's skirt. He turned back to the crowd. "Let the feast begin." He grinned.

Solandis and Priamos effuged away, as did half of the crowd. The rest of us began a slow stroll away from the temples and toward an enormous wall made of shrubbery. Hannele held Alastair's arm, the two of them walking a few paces ahead, while Gerridan offered each of his arms to Kenna and me.

Behind us Aydan walked with the girl and her mother, smiling and chatting away merrily.

"Who is that woman talking with Aydan?" I asked Gerridan. He glanced back.

"That would be Lady Reyna Hazelwren," he said. "Haven't seen her in a while."

"You know her?"

"I know everyone, darling," Gerridan corrected.

Kenna sighed and offered, "Aydan was supposed to marry Lady Reyna years ago." My hands grew hot.

"Easy," Gerridan said, patting the top of one.

"Is she one of the, uh, broken courtships I've heard about?"

Kenna laughed. "The *Wayward Prince's* reputation still lingers, then? Fantastic. He'll love that." I didn't smile. "Solandis and Lord Hazelwren pushed for the match. They agreed to the engagement, accepted the arrangement for a while, but neither of them were interested. Lady Reyna eloped with a mortal soldier. He died while she was with child. Poor thing." I resisted the urge to glance back once again as we arrived at the shrubbery wall.

A portion of it now lay open, as if an invisible hand had pushed and created the perfect gate for the crowd to file through. Once we were in, I gasped at the sight of what was before me: the Grand Palace of Sylvanna.

The Grand Palace of Sylvanna was twin to the one in Nautia, and Gerridan once told me during one of our early lessons that it had been built by the same architect five thousand years ago, at the start of the Aevitarus Dynasty, to house a family of princes—Hannele's ancestors—who would rule over the western territory in the king's name. Apparently, they were built with such precision that one could walk in a straight line from the front gate of one and eventually reach the front gate of the other in two months' time.

The gardens surrounding the palace were magnificent, and as the sun set, white, luminescent flowers began to open, revealing a soft glow. They illuminated the other flowers surrounding them, most notably the striking deep red Sylvannian roses. The grounds were an endless sea of green, interrupted only by more shrubs forming paths throughout. Vines grew up the sides of the palace, the same glowing flowers scattered along them.

We followed the crowd inside to the great hall, which was lavishly decorated and lit with endless floating orbs of light. Tables of food were spread out, with people already eating and drinking around them. The three of us joined Hannele and Alastair at a table. They all filled their plates and began to eat, laughing and talking. I picked at my plate; my stomach was in knots. I wanted to find Aydan but felt terrified at the thought of doing so. Kenna pressed a goblet of wine into my hand.

"Drink," she said. "You look like you're going to jump out of your skin." I obliged.

"The dancing will start any minute," Alastair said softly, leaning over so I could hear him. "Then you'll have a better chance of talking to him. Right now he has to mingle." I looked over to the head table where Aydan sat beside his grandparents, and saw that he was still talking with Lady Reyna. Solandis seemed to be chiming in here and there, smiling as she did so. A spark flew from my fingertip and landed on the tablecloth, causing a small flame to appear. Alastair smothered in with his napkin before it became a spectacle. "That's one way to get his attention."

"Sorry," I mumbled. The roar of the crowd fell quiet, and everyone's attention turned to Lady Solandis, who was standing. Her gown of sea-foam green complemented her brown skin and hugged her figure nicely, and was embellished with the same armor-like jewelry she had worn days before. The dress was cut similarly to Kenna's, and nothing about the Lady's appearance or stature gave any clue of her age—only her tattoos were a reminder to all who laid eyes upon her of her might and power.

"My friends," Solandis greeted the hall. "In years past, my beloved husband has been kind enough to join me in the first dance of the evening. However, tonight marks a historic occasion. Our gracious King Aydan joins us for an eclipse, the first anointed king to celebrate with us." Aydan gave his grandmother a small smile and a nod as scattered applause rang out. "Tonight, our king will open the dance floor with Lady Reyna Hazelwren."

I forced myself to keep looking straight ahead, clapping as the rest of the hall did, though I could feel my friends' eyes upon me. I fought to banish the heat rising in my hands, and surely in my face as I felt myself blush, as I watched Aydan take Reyna's hand and lead her to the dance floor, leaving the child to sit patiently with Solandis and Priamos. They took position in the center of the great hall, his hand resting low on her waist, as the music started.

"It's quite hot, isn't it?" I said to no one in particular. "I think I'll get some air."

"I'll go with you," Alastair started.

"No need," I lied, smiling stiffly at him. "I'll be back in a moment. Just need to cool down . . . lots of excitement." I stood quickly and slipped out the same way we'd entered, walking swiftly toward one of the illuminated shrub-lined paths. Smoke was coming off my hands as I rushed deeper into the darkness, away from prying eyes.

I forced myself to take a deep breath. Another. Aydan was dancing with Lady Reyna. His former fiancée. *Neither of them wanted it,* I reminded myself of Kenna's words. A king dancing with a lady was hardly scandalous. Hardly a betrayal. *There's nothing to betray. He doesn't belong to you.*

More sparks, then my hands were completely engulfed in flames. My breath shuddered and, without thinking, I went to my knees and shoved my unruly hands into the soil, which softened at my touch. The cool earth felt safe on my hands, and slowly my breathing returned to normal. The fire settled back into my core, no longer fighting to reach the surface.

"Shaye."

I practically jumped to my feet, brushing the dirt from my hands and turning to see Aydan walking toward me in the darkness. "What are you doing?" he asked.

"Oh, er, nothing," I said unconvincingly. He raised an eyebrow. "My hands were sparking. I was putting them out," I admitted.

"Is everything all right?"

"Oh, yes. Just a lot of excitement," I lied again, peering behind him. "Is Lady Reyna with you?"

"No," he replied, shoving his hands in his pockets. "Reyna was a bit mortified by dancing in front of the hall, and Calliope was ready for bed anyway." I pressed my lips together, unsure of what to say next.

"She seems sweet," I said. "Your new crown is lovely." Aydan reached up to his head, realizing that he was indeed still wearing the crown of daisies. He chuckled a bit.

"She is," he agreed. "I haven't seen Calliope since she was a baby. Reyna took her to her family's home on the eastern border shortly after she was born. They're here visiting Charles's parents and attending the festival at my grandmothers' invitation."

"Charles?"

"Calliope's father," Aydan explained. "He died shortly before she was due. A terrible accident in the sparring ring. He fell backward and hit his head on the brick barrier. He was dead before anyone could draw the breath to call a healer."

"That's terrible," I said.

"It was. She always knew she'd have to face losing him one day, but she never considered it might be that soon. She was in a dark place the last time I saw her. It was good to see her in such high spirits tonight."

"Kenna said you were meant to marry Lady Reyna," I blurted before I could stop myself.

"We courted briefly, after succumbing to pressure from our families. We were technically engaged for a month before we both confessed that we had no romantic interest in one another." Aydan chuckled. "My grandmother and her father desperately wanted the match. Her father disapproved of her interest in Charles. He believed it would end in her heartbreak. She told him she was dining with me the night she and Charles ran off to elope. About ten years ago now." I nodded, looking at the ground, looking anywhere but his face, knowing I might completely unravel if I met his eyes.

"Well," I said. "I, um, I'd better get back inside. I owe Gerridan a dance." I curtsied and walked past him. I only made it a few paces before he spoke:

"Had I been allowed to court you," he started. I stopped in my tracks, then turned to find an emotion like regret written on his face. "Had I been able to bring you to Sylvanna that first night we met, bring you to my home, and court you, I would have brought you to these gardens every night." My heart was in my throat, and frost coated my hands once again. "You would have been able to spend your days reading and roaming, or training with Gerridan and Alastair if you wanted. You wouldn't have been trapped in Ayzelle . . ." He clenched and unclenched his hand. "Shaye, I failed you in every way. I thought I protected you—I thought that the wards were strong enough, but they weren't. You suffered because I couldn't—"

"Aydan, stop." I stepped forward. "You did everything that you possibly could have. And yes, I was still hurt. But that doesn't mean you failed me."

"I told you it would be two weeks," he croaked, swallowing.

"There was nothing you could do." I took another step toward him. "I'm not scared anymore, Aydan." He looked down at me, emotion flooding his face as he recalled my words from a few days before.

"You look beautiful, by the way," he said. "The dress suits you perfectly."

"Thank you," I replied, running my hand along the skirt. "It was a gift, from a dear friend with impeccable taste." Aydan huffed a laugh, then offered me his hand.

My stomach swooped, and suddenly we were back in the Great Hall of Sylvanna. Music swelled around us, but not the orchestra of Ayzellen balls that I had grown accustomed to. This music was a combination of strings and beating drums, percussion instruments of all kinds, moving fast. The occupants of the hall spun and twirled—no practiced choreography to be found. Gerridan and Hannele, who were dancing with one another, waved me and Aydan over to join them. I hesitated half a second too long, as I felt a small push and found Kenna with her hand on my back, directing me toward the dance floor. When I glanced back at Aydan, I laughed when saw he was receiving the same treatment from Alastair, who looked to be joyfully drunk.

I danced with my friends—carefree, with no expectations—until well into the night. I paired off with each of them at one point or another, though, when a slower tune did finally start to play, I found myself dancing with Alastair, Aydan, or Kenna, as Gerridan and Hannele clung to each other. We danced and laughed and drank, until Kenna was well beyond her limit and had to hold tightly to Alastair to keep from falling over. Aydan effuged us all back to his house after bidding farewell to our hosts.

Hannele and Alastair helped Kenna up the stairs to her bedroom, while Gerridan trailed behind, then entered his own room. I saw Hannele's attention turn at the sound of the door latching shut. Aydan and I remained downstairs.

"Join me for a nightcap?" he asked. I nodded, and he took my hand—frozen again—in his own, interlacing our fingers before leading me to a bedroom in the back of the house. He held the door for me and closed it behind him once we were inside. The room was large but simple. Mostly dark, with a small fire burning. There were some reading chairs with a small table holding glasses and a decanter on one end; the other end led to a bathroom. His enormous bed covered in bright white blankets and sheets sat upon a dark oak frame. Fit for a king.

Aydan poured me a glass of brandy, and I ignored the burn of it in my throat.

"You look beautiful," he said for the second time that night.

"Thank you," I replied. "You look quite handsome yourself." He bowed his head. He opened his mouth, then closed it again. He paused another minute, then asked, his voice tight:

"Did you have fun?"

"I did. Sylvanna knows how to throw a party," I said. Aydan smiled.

"That they do." His empty glass shook in his hand. He set it down and fiddled with his shirt sleeve. "Shaye, there's something . . . I've wanted to tell you. For a long time now."

"Oh?" was all I could think to say before I set my own glass down. I wasn't sure I could stomach drinking anything else.

He finally choked out, "Since we met, I've had this . . . this urge to be near you. To keep you safe if I could. To make you happy. I've failed at many things in my life, but my worst failure, my biggest regret, was learning that I didn't protect you, and worse—that I didn't give you what you needed to protect yourself. I left you in Ayzelle, alone—"

"You didn't have a choice," I said hoarsely. "You didn't fail me."

"Still."

"What is it you want to tell me?" I breathed. He stepped closer.

"I've wanted to tell you . . . since before." Aydan's breath mingled with mine. "Back when I was just the Wayward Prince. When I'm near you, I feel like my heart will burst. You are the most extraordinary person I've ever known, and I . . . I've been so afraid to tell you. I never wanted you to feel like . . . like you *had* to do or say anything because I'm the ki—" He choked. His eyes were brimmed with tears. "Gods. Shaye, I'm so in love with you," he said softly as they spilled over. "You don't have to say anything, I don't expect—"

I closed the space between us and pressed a kiss to his mouth.

When I pulled away, Aydan's eyes were wide with surprise. I brushed the tears from his cheek, even as I felt my own tears fall to my face. "I love you too, Aydan."

He took my face in his hands and kissed me softly. Once. Twice. Then I found myself kissing him more deeply, more urgently. Closer, I had to be closer to him, feel him, be held by him. He moaned quietly into my mouth, and I thought I might catch fire—

my palms burned with heat rising to the surface. I banished it, refusing to let the elements ruin this.

My hands explored his chest while his dug themselves into my hair. I pulled off his jacket, then tugged at the shirt beneath it, breaking the kiss to pull it up over his head. Aydan grabbed it and tossed it to the floor. I ran my hands over his chest, tracing the muscles from his neck to his stomach. He shivered when I traced a line below his navel, then put his hand on my chin, tilting my face toward him. "You're sure?"

"Yes," I breathed before I reached up, pulled his face down toward mine, and kissed him deeply once again.

Aydan began to tear at my clothes, reaching behind me to undo the laces of my gown until it fell to the floor. His breath hitched when he saw my naked body step out of the mass of fabric. Goosebumps pricked on my skin as he circled behind me and loosened the tiara from my hair. He leaned to press a line of kisses to my scarred back, and when he stood straight again, his hands warmed my arms, my shoulders, before making their way down my front, grazing my breasts with his fingertips. I heard myself whimper as he did so, eliciting a low moan from deep in his throat as he gripped them, dragging his thumbs lightly over the peaks. In an instant, Aydan slid an arm under my legs and scooped me up to carry me across the room. He shifted me and I felt the hardness of him press into my hip until he laid me down on the sea of blankets covering his bed. He took half a step back, staring at me. To my surprise, I didn't balk from his gaze.

"You are so beautiful," he said, kneeling on the ground at the foot of the bed. He pressed a kiss to each of my ankles, then made his way up one of my calves before starting on the other. Higher. He took his time, kissing slowly up my thighs, alternating as he came closer to his destination. Higher. My breath was ragged, and I felt him smile against the inside of my thigh upon hearing the small whimper escape from my throat. Higher. He made his way to the hollow of my hip before passing the throbbing destination I'd hoped he would arrive at. Another grin against my stomach, just below my navel.

"You're a fucking tease," I gasped as he began to make his way lower. Aydan laughed huskily against my skin.

Lower.

He had teased me so long that I nearly yelped in surprise when his mouth closed around the bundle of nerves between my legs. He moaned when my hands dug into his hair while he kissed and stroked and brought me just to the edge of starlight—the edge, that was, until he slipped his first two fingers inside me to join him in the motion, and I fell right over it, crying out as he continued pumping those fingers within me, letting me ride out the end on his hand.

Aydan rose from his position and climbed over me to press a deep kiss to my mouth, letting me taste myself there, on his lips, his tongue, while he touched my face, then my breasts, with one hand as he held himself over me with the other. He shifted, and once again I could feel him hard against me. I adjusted my legs, allowing his hips to rest on top of mine.

"Are you all right?" he whispered, kissing my face. I realized he was kissing away tears that had slipped free.

"Yes." I nodded. "I love you." He pressed his mouth to mine again, reaching down with his free hand and circling his fingers around the slick, sensitive mound there. Once he had me nearly panting again, he brought his hips up and inserted himself between my legs, moving slowly, allowing me to adjust. "Gods, Aydan," I mumbled in his ear, lost in an ocean of sensation. He groaned as he was fully seated and started to pump himself into me, keeping a hand on my breast, playing with my still peaked nipple, occasionally reaching down to take a breast into his mouth or simply kiss them before coming up to kiss my lips again. This time when I reached the stars, he joined me shortly after, crying out as he finished.

Chapter Thirty-Six

We lay there, facing one another with our limbs tangled together, for a while afterward. Saying nothing, Aydan would kiss me occasionally, as if confirming that I was indeed there with him.

"I love you," he reminded me, breaking the silence.

"I love you too." I smiled. He pressed a kiss to my forehead before pulling me in closer, wrapping his arms fully around me. I let my head rest on his chest and listened to his heartbeat. "What's on the agenda tomorrow?" I asked.

"As of right now, I'm supposed to meet my grandfather in the sparring ring after breakfast to fence, and then we meet for tea and to sign the new trade agreement. However," he added with a sigh, "I have half a mind to cancel everything and spend the rest of time laying here with you."

"As the woman in your bed, I have to say that sounds like a wonderful idea," I replied "but as your Chief Advisor, I must advise against throwing out the most important legislation the Crown has signed in centuries in favor of sex."

"I thought you didn't care about this *institution*?" he teased. My face heated.

"That's not funny," I said, hiding my face in his chest. "You know I didn't mean that."

"I know, my love, but I've missed teasing you. I have to make up for lost time." One of Aydan's hands began tracing lines up and down my spine, making me shiver even as heat rushed to my core. "Speaking of lost time."

He rolled to his back, pulling me on top, where I lay flat against him and began to kiss his chest, traveling upward to reach his mouth. All the while, Aydan's hands rubbed and massaged my back, gripped my backside, then kneaded their way back up again. The next time his hand moved down, just before reaching my bottom, he brought it around and shoved it between our bodies, sliding it down to slip his fingers into me. I gasped, and Aydan's expression glazed over, his eyes hooded and his mouth slightly open as he watched me. I pushed myself up to straddle him and lowered myself onto his hand, riding for a moment before he pulled it away. I let out a noise of protest that turned into a groan as he lifted my hips and brought them back down, inserting himself inside me. I adjusted and slowly rocked back and forth. Aydan swore, gripping my hips and thrusting into me. A wave of pleasure tore through me, and just as I thought another would, he lifted me off of him.

"Wha—oh *gods*—" In one movement, he'd slid his own body down before I lowered again—this time atop his face. His mouth finished the work his hands and body had started. More waves tore through me, and my body seized while I cried out. Aydan gripped harder into my hips, holding me in place while I finished. Once I regained my senses, I focused and banished the sparks yet again while climbing off of his face. He sat up straight, still erect, and I moved to his lap. My legs wrapped around his body as he slid back inside. I brought my arms around his neck, kissing him deeply and slowly, riding him at the same speed, until he tensed and shuddered, moaning with his mouth still open against mine and his hands gripping into my hair.

Once he'd settled back, letting me roll off of him while he scooted up behind and wrapped his arms around me, I said, "Okay, you win. Bed forever it is." He chuckled into my hair and pressed a sleepy kiss to my shoulder.

After only a few hours of sleep, I woke to the sun pouring through the window and directly into my eyes. Irritated, I tried to will the curtains shut, but exhausted as I was, my magic only made them flutter. Aydan's arms still held me. I moved his arm and slowly climbed out of bed so as not to wake him, then marched over and shut the curtain quickly.

"As much as I enjoy the view, it is absolutely freezing without you next to me," said Aydan from the bed. I turned to see him propped up on an elbow, staring at my naked form in front of the window. He lifted the blanket and I crawled back in to join him.

"I tried not to wake you," I said apologetically, curling up close and resting my head on his chest.

"Mmm," he replied, "I would have had to wake soon anyway. Perhaps—?" He ran his hand along my arm at a speed which suggested only one early morning activity. I was not opposed to the suggestion. I pressed a kiss to Aydan's chest, then his neck, moving to climb on top of him—

There was a sharp knock on the door.

"*Shit,*" I whispered, having forgotten that anyone outside of this bed existed. Aydan stifled a laugh.

"Aydan darling, join me in the ring this morning," Gerridan's voice called from the other side of the door.

"No," Aydan replied, face buried in my neck. I sank down into the pillows and blankets as another knock rang out.

"Come on, don't be an asshole, I'll go easy on you."

"Fuck off."

The knock was more persistent now. Aydan ignored it this time. A mistake, as Gerridan simply barged into the room.

"Come on, Al and Kenna are hung over, and Hannele won't—" Aydan stood up, holding a sheet around his waist, and chucked a pillow at Gerridan, which hit him squarely in the head.

"I said go away."

"I just—" His eyes landed on the bed in disarray, and then upon me as I held the blanket around my naked body. Gerridan's face was struck with realization, and then lit up like the orbs in the great hall the night before. "*Oh.*" He grinned, crossing his arms over his chest and leaning against the doorframe.

"*Out*, Ger," Aydan said, pointing to the door.

"I'm going, I'm going." He smirked at me. "Morning, Shaye." Aydan threw another pillow at the emissary, who ducked this time. He shoved his hands into his pockets and whistled, walking away and leaving the door open. Aydan crossed the room to shut it, and just before he did, Gerridan's voice rang down the corridor, "Al, get out your coin purse, you owe me a *lot* of gold—" He clicked the door shut and leaned against it.

"That's one way for them to find out," he said to himself. We locked eyes and burst out laughing. Aydan dropped his sheet and kissed me soundly on the mouth. He smiled against me. "Sorry about that."

"They had to know," I replied. "Although, I'm not sure I want to know how Gerridan is currently embellishing the story to the rest of your Cabinet." He chuckled. "I suppose we should join them." I sighed, looking around. "I don't have any fresh clothes. Gerridan would *love* to see me walk out there in a bedsheet . . ." Aydan snorted, then opened his wardrobe and found a pair of pants. He put them on before snapping his fingers once. Within seconds, there was a knock on the door.

"Enter," he called. The door opened and Elise stepped in. She saw me on the bed but had no reaction other than the faintest hint of a smile on her lips.

"Yes, Your Majesty?"

"Would you please select some clothing for Lady Shaye, and feed Catchfly?" he said. The cat was probably furious with me for not being in bed with her last night.

Elise left us, getting straight to work. Aydan made his way to the bathroom to wash his face and clean his teeth before he finished dressing. I shivered and covered myself with the blankets as I watched him select a blue tunic. He was sat at the foot of the bed, putting on socks, when Elise returned with my pewter gray dress and black slippers, Catchfly trailing behind her.

"She insisted, my lady," she said apologetically.

"That's all right," I told her. Catchfly jumped onto the bed and pawed at my hands. I scratched her ears. "See? I'm fine." She meowed.

"Will you need help dressing?" Elise asked.

"No," I said, "but thank you for bringing these to me."

"My lady," was all she said before leaving.

A toiletry case was on top of the folded dress now sitting upon one of the chairs on the other end of the room. I summoned it and walked to the bathroom to clean my own teeth and run a brush through my hair before braiding it.

When I was done, I stepped into the gown and pulled it up around me, but when I reached back to deal with the laces, Aydan was there. He weaved them in and out of the eyelets before tying it off, and with one last peck on the cheek, we made our way to breakfast.

This would be my first breakfast in Sylvanna, at Aydan's table. Alastair was reading from a stack of papers in front of him, handing Hannele each page as he finished with it. He looked a pale shade of green as he sipped slowly from a steaming cup of tea. Hungover, indeed.

Hannele seemed to be in good spirits, if a bit tired, as the rest of us were. She had a plate in front of her, filled with items from the platters lining the table—bacon, pastries, bowls of fruit, I saw at first glance—which was more than could be said for poor Alastair. I walked past him and squeezed his shoulder lightly. He patted my hand.

"You don't look so good," I told him sympathetically. "Maybe you should go lie back down."

"I just drank too much." He waved me off, then passed the next page to Hannele. "Tory made me some concoction of his. I'll be fine in an hour. Kenna on the other hand . . ." I looked around, furrowing my brow when I realized she wasn't there.

"Still sleeping," Gerridan said around a mouth full of pastry.

"Swallow your food," Hannele scolded without looking up. "No one wants to see that."

"Yes, mother." He rolled his eyes, then turned his attention to me. "She had a busy night as well." He winked. Aydan shot him a warning glance.

"She went to bed when the rest of us got home," I replied, sitting beside Alastair and filling a plate. "I watched her. You can stop fishing for details, I'm not biting." I winked back. Aydan kissed the top of my head before sitting beside me. I turned to Al and Hannele. "What are you reading?"

"The final verdict on the conflict with those officers a few days back," Alastair said, his voice dripping with boredom. "Some field reports from the generals and officers. Inventory from the armory." He looked at me, sighing. "Excitement all around."

"You're the Lord General. When your life is exciting, it means the rest of us are in grave danger," Aydan replied, piling his plate with food.

We continued eating, mostly in silence, for a short while before Kenna finally joined us. She wore sparring leather and held an open letter in her hand. "Fantastic news," she said to Aydan. He wiped his mouth with a napkin and accepted the folded parchment.

His eyes skimmed the page, and then he passed it to me and rested his hand on my thigh. "The healers at Ironridge have agreed to take on Captain Whittaker as a patient. He's too unstable to be effuged, but I can spare a few Ayzellen guardsmen to provide an escort to Xarynn." I scanned the letter, reading the healer's hopeful prognosis. "They'll leave in a week or so."

"Good," I said, setting it back down and returning to my food. "Maybe we can figure out what the hell he's been rambling about—"

"What is this." Kenna demanded suddenly. She was staring at Aydan and me sitting closely beside one another, his hand on my leg. Her eyes grew wide. "Did you—*last night*?" I started to smile, but it quickly faded when I realized the look on her face was absolute fury. Then Gerridan nearly burst with laughter from the other end of the table. I turned my head to see him shaking, attempting to stifle his outburst, while holding out his open hand.

"Pay up, Ken." The emissary grinned. Kenna scowled, summoned her coin purse, and began counting out gold pieces.

"I thought Kenna wasn't allowed to participate in your gambling anymore?" I asked Gerridan, who was now counting the twenty pieces she'd shoved in his hand.

"I wasn't," she grumbled, taking the spot opposite Aydan. "But as you've been developing your *extra* abilities so quickly, you've now completely disappeared from my sight. Not even a hint of you remains."

"If it helps you feel better," Alastair told Kenna, "I lost fifty pieces to Gerridan this morning." Kenna snorted, and it was obvious that, no, she did not feel better. "If they'd waited until summer solstice, I would've won two hundred." She and Gerridan groaned.

"If they'd waited until summer solstice, I would've effuged to Xarynn and walked into the sea," Gerridan said. I scowled at him. "Sorry, darling, watching the two of you dance around each other has been exhausting." Kenna nodded heartily, while Alastair and Hannele sheepishly avoided eye contact with me. Aydan laughed and kissed my temple.

"You've won them over, my love," he said. "Now they're going to stop being polite."

"You say that as if they ever were," I replied sweetly. Hannele laughed, and Kenna pretended to look outraged.

A few hours later, I stood outside the sparring ring, watching Aydan fence against Priamos. It was their third round, *and hopefully their last*, I thought as my stomach growled. We were supposed to have lunch with the Lord and Lady after the match was over.

Watching their sabers clash against one another made me want to pick up where I'd left off with Alastair. We'd never trained beyond my first lesson, and I hadn't gotten much farther with Gerridan. I made a mental note to tell them both that I wanted to continue.

"The last one standing, it seems," said a voice from beside me. Lady Solandis had appeared.

"My lady?"

"The king usually has his entourage nearby. I assume they've left you to remain as the final audience member."

"Oh, yes," I replied. "I believe Princess Hannele will be joining us for lunch. The rest of the Cabinet have other matters to attend to."

"I see." We remained in silence as the men chased each other through the ring, jumping over barrels and stepping over walls. It was a few moments before Solandis said, "You were a vision at the festival. Your ensemble was stunning."

"Thank you, my lady," I said. "As were you—"

"Yes, the king has wonderful taste." She talked over me. "I was surprised, though, to see that *particular* tiara on your head." I closed my mouth. "You see, it has been over a century since I have seen any of my daughter Astra's belongings in person, let alone the tiara I myself gave her the day she came of age." Her tone was cool, and polite enough that I almost didn't hear her disapproval.

"My lady, I didn't know. I never meant to offend—"

"No need." A cheer, and our attention turned back to the ring, where Priamos had knocked Aydan's saber from his hand. Solandis and I clapped politely. "My grandson has every right to give whatever he wants to whomever he wants. Although." Solandis gave me a sidelong glance. "Such a *sentimental* piece would generally be reserved for someone the king was courting." Aydan and Priamos were walking back toward us.

"Well, then the king has done well to stick to tradition," I said, smiling at Aydan and avoiding the urge to turn to Solandis.

"Are you telling me that the king is having an illicit affair with his Chief Advisor?"

"No, my lady. I'm telling you that the king's courtships are a private matter, which he will no doubt share with you when he deems it necessary." I didn't give her the chance to respond, as the men were now greeting us. Priamos kissed his wife's cheek and I congratulated him on his win. Aydan feigned disappointment, but laughed while greeting his grandmother, and then me. He offered me his arm and a swift kiss before leading the way back to the Grand Palace, ignoring the disapproving glare of Lady Solandis.

Part Three

The Children

A month had passed since the eclipse festival.

Each day spent in Sylvanna felt like something new sprinkled into a growing sense of familiarity and home. Every morning, I woke at dawn to join Gerridan or Alastair in the ring, alternating each day. Even in such a short time, I felt myself growing stronger, more precise in my actions. My magical outbursts occurred less often, though they always lingered beneath the surface. Gerridan had moved on from shielding and escaping, and was now teaching me how to strike. While Alastair still made me use a waster when practicing swordplay, he also introduced me to the bow and throwing daggers, as well as the importance of weapon cleanliness and care.

After training, we ate breakfast with the rest of the Cabinet in Aydan's home, followed by days filled with much of the same as we found in Ayzelle. There were many meetings with the Sylvannian Council, which was now made of almost entirely new members, thanks to Aydan recruiting the previous ones. They were certainly more productive than Ayzellen Council meetings. After the trade agreements and new treaty were signed, there was no practical reason for us to stay, beyond Aydan simply being happy to be home for the time being.

In the evenings we all crowded around a cozy dining table for a meal prepared by Zale and Tory. These were spirited affairs, filled with laughter, and we'd eventually make our way to the sitting room for drinks or tea. Sometimes we'd continue our discussions, or some of us would simply read or enjoy the silence. Then, when we'd all grown tired enough for bed, Aydan would take me to his room, now our room, where we talked, laughed, made love—and some nights just held each other in the dark until we fell asleep. I was happier than I could ever remember being.

One night, I woke to the sound of soft knocking.

Aydan shifted beside me, and I heard him quickly put pants on and cross the room to answer it. I was not particularly pleased. Gerridan would be in Xarynn today, so I had my first opportunity in weeks to sleep undisturbed until after sunrise, and this person was ruining it. Aydan opened the door a crack, drowsily greeting whoever had summoned him. But then I heard his voice shift into urgency, and the door clicked shut. I looked up and he was gone. Now thoroughly awake and irritated, I climbed out of bed and threw on my discarded nightdress from the armchair near the fireplace. I wrapped a shawl around myself and stepped into the hall.

". . . alerted the families?"

"Word has already been sent to the new captain . . . Adler, I think. He'll be notifying them himself." Aydan was shirtless beneath the orbs of light illuminating the corridor as he stood with Kenna also in her nightclothes.

"What's happened?" I asked, startling the pair. My eyes fell on a stack of papers in his hands, which he gripped tightly, wrinkling them. He pressed his lips into a thin line and glanced at Kenna, who looked like she'd seen a ghost.

"There's been an incident near Xarynn. An attack."

"Where is Gerridan?" I asked sharply. A blast of cold wind rushed around us, whipping mine and Kenna's hair around our faces.

"Gerridan is fine, he hasn't even left yet," Aydan assured me through the gusts. I let out a breath and it stopped.

"What, then?"

"There's been . . . " He paused, handing me the letter. "The wagon that was transporting Stefan Whittaker to Xarynn was attacked by something last night. An animal of sorts. They were about two days outside the border . . ." The writing described the scene covered in blood, scratch marks in the wood of the wagon. *No survivors,* it read. I gripped the pages so tightly that the corners curled into blackened ash that crumbled to my feet. I stared, wide-eyed at nothing in front of me, while the reality of what I'd read began to sink in. I didn't realize that tears had spilled over, or that I was crying aloud until Aydan held me, dismissing Kenna and ushering me back to bed.

I spent the rest of the day there.

The next morning, I forced myself to bathe and dress. We had a meeting scheduled with the Ayzellen Council, and now with the tragic death of Stefan and the guardsmen escorting him, it was only right that Aydan address the Guard.

"You don't have to come," Aydan said from across the room while I sat at the vanity, brushing out my hair. "I know this is painful for you."

It was. Even with his deception, even if none of it was real or true, even though he had attacked me in the end, Stefan was the only familiar face that I saw for nearly a year. Yes, it had all been a lie, and perhaps I was a fool for mourning him, but I couldn't shake the feeling of loss.

"I know I don't," I said, arranging the hair at my nape and shoving pins into it. "I want to. I want the Guard to see that the Cabinet is addressing this properly, that we're taking these deaths seriously. Besides," I gestured toward the bed. "Staying there isn't going to bring him back."

"Neither will throwing yourself back into work too early, my love." He was behind me now, leaning down to kiss the top of my head. "I'm not upset with you for mourning him if that's a concern to you. I know you loved him—"

"I wasn't in love with him."

"I know. But he was your friend, or pretended to be, and you never processed his betrayal." He met my gaze in the mirror, his hand on my shoulder, stroking up to my neck and back down in soothing lines. "It would be understandable if you missed him as much as you want to hate him, too." I put my hand on top of his, and mouthed *thank you* to his reflection. Another kiss to my head, and then it was time to go.

Aydan and I nearly collapsed into bed.

It was just after sundown, our second night back in Ayzelle, and we were dead on our feet, exhausted both physically and emotionally from nearly two days straight of speaking with Captain Adler, the Ayzellen Council, and the families of the deceased. The guards who'd escorted Stefan were young, new recruits, most just having reached maturity in the last couple of years, and so it was not mourning wives I comforted, but wailing mothers.

I remembered, years ago in the village with Gideon, a young girl of maybe fourteen had fallen ill and died. We heard her mother's cries for days, and Gideon told me that it was a fate worse than death to outlive your own child. In Nautia this happened commonly. The healers there could not do much more than bandage you and prescribe an herb, while hiring a witch cost so much money that saving one child from illness could mean all your other children would starve come winter. Here in Medeisia, sorcerer parents expected their children to grow and spend centuries with them. Mortal families could expect their children to watch them grow old before growing old themselves. This attack was an unthinkable loss for any Medeisian family.

Aydan instructed the council to select a group of skilled soldiers to scout the area and kill whatever beast had attacked these guardsmen. Lord Declan was somber during the council meeting, and despite his reputation for arguing, the lord didn't put up a fight. Later, when I asked why, Aydan explained that Declan's nephew was one of the lost guardsmen, a young man named Donn, who was only nineteen.

Now we lay in bed back in the king's chambers of Ayzelle. Alastair was the only one who had joined us, aside from Isolde, deeming it necessary to meet with the families of those lost. He elected to stay up reading in the Cabinet lounge, but the look on his face indicated that he wouldn't be awake much longer either.

I startled when a pair of hands ran themselves down my back. I had been nearly asleep, and the hands were now pulling at the laces of my gown.

"I'm sleeping," I mumbled.

"I know," Aydan said, continuing his work on the laces. "You'll be more comfortable in bedclothes."

"You're just trying to see me naked."

"Always, my lady." I could hear the grin in his voice through the dark. "But you need your rest and frankly I'm too exhausted to live up to your high expectations." I scoffed while Aydan chuckled.

"Careful," I warned playfully. "Keep up with that flirting and you'll earn as bad a reputation as Gerridan."

"Well, then I will be in good company. Like Gerridan, I've only ever truly had eyes for one woman." I blushed, then stood, stepped out of the gown, and brought the nightdress down over my head before crawling back into bed. Aydan undressed in the dark and wrapped me up in his arms beneath the covers.

"Why is it that they've never . . . ?" I said to the darkness, letting the question hang in the air. Aydan sighed.

"They've danced around one another longer than I've been alive," he said. "I suspect they're scared of what might happen if things don't work, and I know Gerridan doesn't think himself worthy of a princess, whether her title is just in name or not."

"Gerridan is . . ."

"The bastard son of a wealthy merchant's daughter," Aydan finished. "He's been a soldier, a diplomat, a lord of the Sylvannian Council, and now the emissary of my Cabinet—but he will always believe that the circumstances of his birth make him less than worthy."

"That's awful," I said sadly.

"It is," Aydan agreed, burying his face in my hair and pulling me closer. "He's waiting for Hannele to find someone else, but she loves him too much to give up. So they orbit one another, living on stolen glances and hoping that if they take enough meaningless lovers to their beds, the other will give up hope." Aydan's voice was strained with sadness for our friends. I didn't know what to say, so I took his hand and kissed it, and as he held me tighter, I knew we were both thanking whatever gods might be out there that we had each other now.

Chapter Thirty-Eight

It was two more days before we were home in Sylvanna, joining Solandis and Priamos for dinner in their private residence.

We sat in the parlor room, sipping on wine while we waited for the meal to be served. Priamos was telling an entertaining story about his time living in the faelands, but I couldn't pay attention. I was too busy pretending I didn't notice each time Solandis stared at me, her eyes fixated on my knee where Aydan's hand rested casually while he listened and laughed at his grandfather's story. It was hard to read her tattooed face, whether her disappointment lay in the intimacy of Aydan's touch, or simply in my being present at all.

Either way, I was trying to think of a way to feign illness and excuse myself when a servant entered the parlor and whispered in Solandis's ear.

"Oh good, send them in," she told him. The servant nodded and walked away swiftly.

"Is someone joining us?" Aydan asked. Priamos looked at his wife with raised brows.

The door opened, and the servant reappeared, this time followed by Lady Reyna and Calliope, who upon seeing Aydan rising from the sofa, broke into a run to hug his legs tightly. Her chocolate brown curls, twin to her mother's, flew back behind her as she ran. "Hello, Calliope." Aydan chuckled, patting the girl's head. When she let go, he turned to greet Reyna, who curtsied. "I thought you'd gone home already," he said, smiling broadly at the sight of her.

Reyna, whose face grew prettier each second I looked at her, said, "Charles's sister and her family came home to visit their parents unexpectedly, so we stayed a little longer to let the children spend time together." Calliope ran back to her mother and ducked behind her legs, hiding in her skirts. "Lady Solandis heard that I was still nearby and sent us an invitation for dinner tonight."

"We're glad to have you," Aydan said, still grinning. My hands grew hot, and I rubbed my palms together as I stood. Aydan turned and ushered me forward. "This is Lady Shaye, my Chief Advisor and—friend." Lady Reyna curtsied; I bowed my head. *Friend.*

"Lady Advisor," Reyna said, "I have heard so much about you. I was so disappointed that we didn't have the chance to meet at the eclipse festival."

"Just Shaye, please," I replied as sweat beaded on my forehead, and I focused all my attention on not bursting into flame. "I am delighted that we could finally meet. I've heard much about you as well." She beamed at me, and her bright blue-violet eyes sparkled. I hated myself for wanting so badly to dislike her.

I watched as pleasantries were exchanged for another moment before Priamos suggested giving Reyna and Calliope an updated tour of the gallery. He led the way, talking about the many renovations that had been done since the last time Reyna had been in the palace. Solandis walked behind them, smiling down at Calliope, who ran happily alongside us. Aydan offered me his arm, and we walked at the back.

"Isn't the king supposed to walk at the front?" I asked quietly. Aydan shrugged.

"It's their home." I barely heard him, but nodded anyway. The heat pounded its way through my veins. I could feel my body fighting it. "Are you all right, my love?" Aydan nearly whispered. "You're burning up."

"I just need a bit of air, I think," I lied. "I'm going to step outside for a moment."

I let go of Aydan's arm and walked away, out a side door and onto a balcony, where I gripped the railing and gasped for breath as I allowed a stream of sparks to pour from my fingertips. I groaned softly at the release of pressure. Footsteps approached from behind me. I cut off the stream and tried to compose myself.

"Lady Shaye, are you all right?" Solandis's voice asked from the doorway.

"I'm fine, my lady," I swallowed. "Though I don't think you particularly care if I'm all right."

"Oh? And why do you think that?"

"You've invited Lady Reyna here to get a rise out of me," I said. "It's very clear you don't like me, although I have no idea what I've done to you."

"On the contrary, Lady Shaye, I like you very much." I turned, stunned. "You're good at your job, you're honest. Frankly, you remind me a bit of myself at your age. Above all else, you clearly make my grandson very happy."

"Then why—"

"Look at them," Solandis directed my attention to the window next to the balcony, which I could see through if I leaned forward a bit. Reyna stood by smiling while Aydan held Calliope up for a better view of the paintings on the wall, pointing out various flowers and birds. Priamos must have made some comment because they all broke into a fit of laughter. Reyna looked beautiful at Aydan's side, with him holding the child on his hip. They looked like a family. "They're quite handsome together, aren't they?"

"Aydan said he's not interested in a match with Reyna. He never was."

"Things change," Solandis said.

"He loves me," I insisted. "And I love him too. Very much."

"Oh, I don't doubt that, my lady," she said. "I've seen the way you look at each other. There is a bond there that many do not get to have even once. You should consider yourself a very lucky woman."

"Then why are you doing this?" I asked. "Aydan is the king; certainly he can choose for himself who to court."

"He is, and he can." Solandis took a step toward me. "But he is unmoved by my words, and so I am asking you, Lady Shaye, to be the reasonable party here."

"You spoke to him?"

"Yes. And he said the same thing to me, that he can choose his own courtships, his own bride, his own queen." I swallowed again, refusing to dwell on that last word. "I come to you, because I need you to make him see that he cannot expect to marry you." My mouth went dry.

"Why would I do such a thing?"

"Aydan Aevitarus is no ordinary man. He is a king. He *cannot* choose a marriage based solely on his emotions. In all things, he must put his people first," Solandis insisted. "If my granddaughter Irsa had not perished that night in Ayzelle, I would have no objections to your match. You make him happy. But as king, personal happiness cannot be his goal. If it is the side effect of a well-arranged match, then so be it. But there is more to a royal marriage than love."

"Astra and Zathryan were in love," I reminded her. She stiffened at the mention of her daughter's name.

"Yes, and look where that got them," she snapped, then took a deep breath. "You must understand that no matter how much you insist your name is Eastly, you are the head of House Redfern. Your whole life, you will be followed by your father's legacy. The royal family will be the topic of constant gossip and conspiracy theories. Your children will be targeted, either by those wishing to wipe out the Redfern line, or those wishing to lift it back to glory. There would be no time to govern in between putting out the fires of scandal." I tried to hide the realization on my face. "No matter how virtuous and honest and kind you are, no matter how much the two of you love one another, you will not know peace." I remained silent and looked back to the window. Calliope was playing on the floor with Priamos, while Aydan offered Reyna a drink and a smile. I bit back the tears threatening to form, then flinched when Solandis placed her hand on my shoulder. "I'm sorry, I truly am. I do not wish to be cruel to you."

"My lady, I love him. More than you know. I do not plan to give him up so easily." My palms were icy. "You cannot expect me to simply step aside if this is what we both want."

"You don't have to. Not yet. You will know when it's time. Just consider what I said." I kept what I hoped was a cool mask of indifference, though I knew tears continued to well in my eyes.

"I think I'll go home now," I said. "I need to lie down."

"I'll have an escort take you."

"There's no need—" But Solandis snapped her fingers, and the manservant from before appeared at the Lady's side.

"Luca, will you please escort the Chief Advisor back to the king's residence?" Luca responded by taking my elbow.

My stomach dropped, and we were at the front door to Aydan's home. Luca bowed deeply before disappearing once again. I opened the door, expecting to have to fight off a dozen questions from my friends, but no one was inside when I walked through the sitting room. I made my way to the bedroom I shared with Aydan, and when I opened the door Elise and Isolde were changing the sheets. They looked up, and one concerned expression from Elise was enough to make my face crumple, and fat, hot tears spill over onto my face as I hid it in my hands. The women were there in an instant, Elise shutting the door behind me while Isolde wrapped her arm around my shoulders.

They ushered me to the bed, sat me down on fresh sheets and let me lie in Isolde's lap until there were no tears left in me. Neither of them asked what was wrong. Neither of them said anything. When I ran out of tears, they drew me a bath and helped me undress before leaving me to my thoughts. Elise left a few candles burning rather than casting the normal orbs of bright light to the ceiling. I was dozing off when Aydan walked into the bathroom.

He didn't say a word as he sat on the floor, leaned against the tub, and rolled up his sleeve. Beneath the water, he caressed my leg with a comforting touch. We sat like that for some time, gazing at one another. I lifted my hand from the bath and stroked his hair, noticing his furrowed brow. Then I realized that I was crying again.

"Solandis spoke to you, didn't she?" Aydan finally asked. I gave a single nod. He sighed. "I'm sorry. I told her to stay out of it. I'll be having a word with her in the morning—"

"She's right though, isn't she?" I whispered, trembling. "My name, my family . . . it will haunt you forever, if we continue on like this. If we . . ."

"I don't care about any of it," he insisted. "You are not your father. You are not his choices, or his betrayals."

"She said there would be no peace if we . . ." I stopped myself, not wanting to say the word. "If we continue on. Your reign would be tainted."

"Last I checked, Solandis is not a seer," Aydan said. "Kenna sees prosperity in my future."

"She can't see me," I reminded him.

"No, but she can see me." He drew circles around my knee. "I love you, Shaye."

"I love you too," I said tearfully.

"Good," he said. "Then we can figure out the rest as it comes. Don't let Solandis's fears ruin us. Not when we've just started." He leaned forward and kissed me deeply. I gasped in surprise when he reached down and scooped me into his arms, lifting me out of the tub.

"Aydan, you're soaked—"

"Doesn't matter," he kissed me again as he carried me to the bed and laid me down before snapping his fingers, rendering me dry and warm.

He spent the rest of the night kissing and touching me until I forgot my name. Until he was no longer the king and was just a man. Until nothing and no one beyond the walls of our room, our sanctuary, in that very moment mattered. When he finally did make love to me, tears soaked my face once again. We moved together, our bodies and hearts in rhythm, our limbs and souls equally intertwined. We reached the edge of ecstasy as one, and fell over together, breathing heavily, our foreheads pressed against each other, afraid to move, to disturb the magic that swelled in the air around us.

We slept that way, holding one another tightly, breath mingling, one of us occasionally waking just enough to softly kiss the other, until the sun rose and reality came pouring back into the room with the light.

Chapter Thirty-Nine

The weeks that followed were largely uneventful. Reyna went home to her family's estate with Calliope, which made attending events less stressful. Without the fear that Reyna would suddenly appear and Solandis would find reasons to shove her and Aydan together, I found myself easily avoiding the Lady of Sylvanna. The morning after our conversation, Aydan had announced at the breakfast table that he would be having a private meeting with his grandmother, then kissed me goodbye and disappeared for several hours. He didn't tell any of us what had been said, but Solandis now avoided eye contact with me, and I wasn't complaining. Aydan had done everything to protect and assure me that her words meant nothing, but even though I could allow myself to forget them each night as he held me in our bed, each day that I saw her stoic, tattooed face, I was reminded of her warning.

Alastair finally set the wasters aside and was allowing me to spar against him with a real sword. Every other morning, he and I met at sunrise, and with each lesson, I improved. Soon, rather than him simply instructing me, our time became practice for the both of us. Wielding a blade and drawing a bow made me strong. I noticed in the mirror one morning that my arms, stomach, and thighs were all defined with muscle I had never seen on myself before. Soon after, I had to ask Isolde to let out most of my dresses when I found myself rotating through the same few that still fit.

The stronger I got, the less severe my elemental outbursts became. Most days, I would still find myself with hands frosted over, setting loose a few sparks, or in one instance, touching a potted herb in the kitchen while popping in to say hello to Zale and Tory and accidentally producing a large shrub's worth of rosemary in the window, shattering the glass. I apologized profusely while Zale insisted on cleaning up the mess and Tory ushered me out of the kitchen. Gerridan's laughter was nearly uncontrollable when I told him what happened.

One morning, I was sitting in Aydan's study, pouring over documents laying out the new trade routes connecting Sylvanna to Ayzelle. It had been almost two months since the agreement was signed, stating the Crown's intent to open trade with the garden city, but the logistics were proving harder to wrangle than we'd expected. Granting certain routes to Sylvanna ran the risk of cutting off or delaying shipments for Xarynn, who had maintained an excellent trade relationship with all territories for centuries, given they were the only territory with access to imported goods. Disrupting their routes could prove disastrous for interterritorial relations, if the reasoning was perceived to be favoritism shown by Aydan to his grandparents.

The door to the study flew open, and without looking up, I declared, "We're going to have to build a new route entirely."

"Where's Aydan?" I looked up and Alastair was standing in the doorway, looking alarmed, holding a heavy letter in his hand.

"I think he and Kenna are with Priamos," I said. "Why?"

He didn't answer and instead effuged away. I stood and rushed into the sitting room, where I found Gerridan and Hannele looking as confused as I felt.

"What's up with Al?" I asked them. Hannele put her hands in the air.

It only took a moment for Alastair to return with Kenna and Aydan in tow, both ruffled and confused.

"Al, what the hell?" Kenna said, brushing off her skirt.

"I second that," Aydan said. "Why did you just kidnap me from the palace?"

"Because of this." Alastair held out the letter, which Aydan took from him.

"Is that . . . ?" he said softly to himself, turning the parchment over in his hand.

"What?" Gerridan asked, peering forward to see what it was that was so special.

"It's the royal seal of Nautia," Alastair declared. "We've received a response directly from the king's desk."

"You're kidding." I took the letter from Aydan's hands. I examined the seal and the Thandreil family's sigil, a pair of crossed battle-axes, stamped clear as day in red wax. The other side, in a neat scrawl, showed the letter addressed to *His Majesty, King Aydan of Medeisia.* I passed it to Gerridan's outreached hand, who showed Hannele as well.

"Shit," she said under her breath. "It worked."

"We don't know that yet," Aydan said, taking the letter back and breaking the seal. He paused, and then displayed it to Kenna, who placed a hand on it. "Anything I should know before I open this?"

"I can't see anything," she replied in a huff. "A witch has handled that letter. Be careful."

Aydan unfolded the paper and read aloud:

> *Greetings, Your Majesty,*
>
> *It was, as I am sure you can imagine, quite a shock to receive a letter containing the seal of House Aevitarus on my desk. My deepest apologies for such a delayed response. I have been unsure how to react to your proposal, and must admit that I write to you now without approval from my council.*
>
> *My late brother, King Mal, named me regent before his death, knowing that I would govern fairly and faithfully, with our people's well-being at the forefront of my thoughts until the time that my nephew, King Callum, comes of age and takes his place on the throne of his destiny. It is my sworn duty to prepare him and guide him to be a fierce, just leader for the people of Nautia.*
>
> *Our nations have a bloody history, there is no denying that fact. However, Your Majesty, with recent changes on the thrones of both our nations, I agree with your statement that there is room for hope in our futures.*
>
> *I am open to your suggestion of negotiations between Nautia and Medeisia, and look forward to your next correspondence.*
>
> *Sincerely,*
>
> *Prince Gram, Regent of Nautia*

I watched Aydan scan the letter over again in silence twice more before he looked up at us, wide-eyed.

"Holy shit," said Gerridan, finally breaking the silence. He clapped Aydan on the shoulder. "You did it."

"Not yet—but it's a start," Aydan said, still stunned. I planted a kiss on his cheek.

"It's a start," I said earnestly. He looked at all of us in disbelief.

"I have to go and draft a reply," he said, running a hand through his hair. He looked to Gerridan. "Can you assist me?" The emissary nodded. Then, to me, "I need to use my study . . ."

"Go." I shooed him toward the room. "I can work at the dining table."

He pecked my cheek before swiftly walking to the study, with Gerridan at his heels. Seconds later, when I walked into the dining room, there sat my paperwork, neatly stacked and ready for me to get back to work, as if I could think about anything but the letter from Prince Gram. I sat anyway and attempted to focus.

An hour or so later, I abandoned my work and found Alastair in his room, reading, of all things, a book about the Nautian Rebellion, while stretched out on his bed.

"Refreshing your memory?" I leaned against the doorframe.

"Not quite." He closed the book and set it on a desk. "The rebellion happened long before I was born."

"Really?" I had always been of the impression that Aydan was the youngest among his friends, aside from myself.

Alastair nodded. "My mother was living in the elf kingdoms at the time, so she heard about it after the fact, but I wasn't born for another sixty or so years."

"Where is your mother now?" I pried.

"Around. She doesn't stay in one place too long." His tone indicated that that was all he had to say on the matter.

I let the silence hang there for a moment before asking, "Do you want to take a walk with me?"

"A mindwalk?" he joked.

"No, you ass, a walk around the garden. I've been cooped up all day trying to figure out those damned trade routes. If I don't get some fresh air soon, I'm going to—" I was cut off by the sound of glass breaking and a chilling scream from downstairs.

"What the fuck?" Alastair and I bolted from his room. Before we hit the stairs, he grabbed my wrist and effuged us to the dining room where all the commotion was.

Isolde was shaking on the floor, surrounded by broken glass, while Tory crouched before her, holding her upright and murmuring gently in Xarynnea. Hannele squatted beside them, trying to calm her down enough to speak. Isolde's terrified eyes darted wildly around the room. Aydan and Gerridan rushed in then. Aydan met my eyes in silent question, and I shook my head helplessly.

Zale and Elise came next, and Zale immediately joined them on the floor around his sister. Isolde continued to sob and shake her head.

"What is wrong with her?" Elise asked, her hand resting on her throat.

"That."

Kenna, who had been silently watching this whole time, pointed to the dining room table, which held what looked like an oversized wooden jewelry box. I stepped toward it.

"Don't touch it," Kenna hissed. "It's cursed."

"Cursed?"

"It's witchcraft," she said. "Isolde must have touched it, but it wasn't meant for her." I peered at the box and saw what Kenna was talking about: carved into the lid in perfect calligraphy were the words, *Long Live the King.*

Magic pulsed from the box. The sensation was like the night Aydan brought me across the border into Medeisia. Something was awakening. I summoned the box to float in the air in front of me and stared at it from different angles, my mind filling with understanding and even more questions.

"Shaye," Aydan said carefully, his hand outstretched and face etched with worry, "give it to me, my love." I blinked, let go of my hold on the box, and watched it drop gently into Aydan's hands. He held it still for a moment, as if waiting for something to happen. Nothing. Kenna was right— the box was meant for him.

"Isolde, whatever you saw isn't real," I said, turning to her. Hannele's brow furrowed. I explained, "It's not cursed. It's psychic magic. Just a spell."

"How do you know?" Kenna asked.

"I'm not sure." My head tilted as I examined the box in Aydan's hands. I looked up at him. "It won't hurt you."

He still looked concerned but set it back down on the table. The rest of us, minus Tory and Zale, who carried Isolde from the room, gathered around, looking over his shoulder as he carefully lifted the lid.

Inside was a folded white handkerchief, which Aydan gingerly lifted the corner of, revealing what lay within. He inhaled sharply. Alastair swore and Gerridan looked like he might be sick. Kenna quickly turned Elise away, telling her not to look. Hannele just stared into the box, perhaps, like me, trying to make sense of what she was seeing:

Arranged in neat, clean rows on the bright white handkerchief were approximately forty fingers, cut off at the knuckle of whatever hands they had come from. Without breaking my stare, I asked Gerridan, "How many men did you send to Creg'tam?"

"Four." The word was spat from his lips.

Aydan snapped the lid shut. "We need to send out a search party for the sentries. Keep it quiet until we know for certain what has happened—"

"No need," said Kenna, cutting him off. She had the faraway look of sight behind her eyes. After a moment, she blinked and looked to Aydan and me. "You need to get to the border. The sentries just arrived there."

Chapter Forty

It didn't take long to locate Gerridan's men. The four of them were stumbling along the rocky Sylvannian border, their hands wrapped in white bandages with blood already starting to seep through. Aydan grabbed my hand each time we effuged, first when we arrived at the border, then again when we took the men to the healers in the palace.

The men were confused. I sat near one of them, a young man named Brenn, while a raven-haired healer knelt before him. Brenn seemed shocked at the appearance of his hands, having no recollection of the fingers being removed.

"Are the . . . erm, pieces, anywhere to be found?" the healer, Cian, asked.

"Yes, all of them, we believe," I told him. Cian glanced up at me.

"All?"

"Yes, we think so." I motioned for Aydan. He opened his hands and the box appeared. He lifted the lid for Cian to see the forty fingers laid out before him.

"Be careful not to touch the box," he warned. Cian reached in carefully and selected a finger that appeared to match Brenn's skin tone before holding his hand over the connecting flesh. A green glow came off Cian's palm, and I watched, fascinated as the flesh of Brenn's finger stitched itself back to his hand.

It was in observing Cian do the same thing with each of Brenn's fingers—then with the fingers of the other three men—that I realized how cleanly cut the wounds were. The fingers were removed with extreme precision and then preserved in their box, and not one of these men had memory of the encounter. None of them could say where they were, beyond being in the Creg'tam mountain range and seeing the Five-Peak Summit. None of them remembered seeing anyone, witch or otherwise, during the entirety of their journey.

Gerridan hovered anxiously, his arms crossed and eyes wide while Cian worked. The men were not employed by the Crown but by the Hollick estate, owned by his grandfather. It was Gerridan who had selected these men to carry out this mission, and their loyalty to him that made them agree to such secrecy. The guilt was etched deeply into his face. He would not soon recover from this. He watched the last finger stitch itself back onto its owner before he turned and swiftly left the room.

I followed into the corridor, where he paced its length, running a hand through his hair.

"Ger, settle down," I told him. "This isn't your fault."

"I sent them, Shaye." He halted in his tracks.

"It was a volunteer mission."

"They went because I asked them."

"And you asked because I asked first," I countered. "If you're going to blame someone, blame me." He clenched his jaw. "Do you want to get out of here?" I asked. He nodded and reached for my extended hand. We arrived back at Aydan's house.

The servants were nowhere to be seen. I left Gerridan in the sitting room and went to the kitchen to pour us each a drink. When I returned, Hannele sat beside him with her hand on his back while he held his head in his hands.

"They're going to be okay," the princess insisted. "Gods willing, their memories won't return, and the worst of it will be the procedure." I handed Gerridan his drink, which he took and downed silently in one motion.

"That's the strange thing, don't you think?" I mused. "You'd think if the Children were so bloodthirsty, they would have done something . . . I don't know, *more*."

"More than cutting off my mens' fingers and sending them to Aydan in a box?" Gerridan snapped. "What, was it not brutal enough for you?"

"That's not what I said. I just—I feel like if they were going to send a message living up to our expectations, they wouldn't have bothered letting Brenn and the others live."

"Wow." Gerridan huffed. "That's very nice, Shaye, *really.* They send a direct threat to your lover—your *king*—and you're sitting around disappointed that it wasn't more exciting?"

"That's not it." I glared. "I just . . ." Gerridan was livid. Hannele's worried eyes shifted back and forth between us. "Look, if they wanted to send a message to Aydan, why not dump the sentries' bodies at the border? Why just the fingers, easily reattached by our healer? Why erase their memories, and why did none of them experience any pain?"

"It's the *Children*, Shaye. They're witches—absolutely *insane*—"

"I think there's a lot more to learn here."

"You read the message on that box. Do you want to start a war with the covens? Because that's where this type of talk is headed."

"No, of course I don't want a war. But maybe . . ." I sighed. "Maybe if we sent someone who could speak on Aydan's behalf, speak to them directly—"

"You've got to be fucking kidding me." Gerridan was on his feet now, raising his voice. My blood boiled as he did so, and my hands started smoking. "My men were tortured, their minds played with by the Children, and you're talking about a follow up mission? With whom? Someone closer to Aydan so they can tear their mind open and loot it for information? *You*?"

"What's going on here?" Alastair had effuged into the room. He looked to Gerridan and me, who were inches apart and furious. "You left without saying anything."

"Shaye has lost her gods-damned mind," Gerridan said through gritted teeth.

"I'm only saying that there might be another solution besides tucking our tails between our legs and hiding away so the Children don't come for us." I flexed my hands and realized they were fully engulfed in flames.

"I'm sure Shaye only has everyone's best interest in mind, even if you're upset right now—"

"She wants someone close to Aydan, someone with more bargaining power, to seek out the Children in a follow up mission," Gerridan spat. Alastair's eyebrows rose so high that they nearly disappeared into his hairline. He gawked at me.

"Shaye . . . you can't be serious."

"It was just a *thought*, and then Gerridan . . ." I glared at him again. "Is it such an inconceivable thing, that the Children might be making themselves appear to be more dangerous than they are?" I then listed off the reasons for my theory to Alastair, who at least gave me the courtesy of listening before sighing and running his hand over his face.

"Look, maybe you're right, but the risk is too great. There's too much at stake. We cannot afford a war right now."

"Again, I'm not looking to start a war. I just think that it's a bit early to be calling it quits."

The front door opened and in walked Kenna and Aydan, who must have taken the long way home. Kenna read the room and a frown formed on her face.

"Is everything all right?" Aydan asked, slipping his hands into his pockets.

"No," said Kenna, answering for Gerridan and me.

The emissary looked to Aydan and said, "Talk to her." He waved an irritated hand in my direction.

"Don't talk about me like I'm not standing right in front of you," I snapped before turning to Aydan. "I made the mistake of voicing an idea aloud in front of Gerridan, and now he's acting like I'm crazy—"

"You want to seek out the Children!" Gerridan roared. "After everything you saw just now. Right when we're on the brink of peace with Nautia, you want to stir shit up with the covens."

Aydan blinked. "Is that true?"

"No. Well, yes—" I fumbled. "Gerridan is completely oversimplifying what I said."

"And what did you say?" His voice wasn't unkind, but it wasn't the voice I knew either. It was the voice of a diplomat solving a dispute between warring nations.

So I told him everything. "I think it's worth considering sending someone who can do more than deliver a message. Someone with real bargaining power, to negotiate terms." Aydan was quiet, looking at the floor with his hands still shoved into his pockets. It felt like an eternity, waiting for him to speak. When he finally did, I wished he hadn't.

"Shaye . . . this cannot happen." I clenched my jaw. "I know how much you'd hoped we would find someone to help you, but we will have to seek a teacher elsewhere."

"Oh, you mean in one of the hundreds of other covens lined up, waiting to teach me how not to kill myself?" I rolled my eyes, then held up my hands. The flames had extinguished but my palms still smoked. "Sparring with Al and Ger can only do so much. I don't know how many more outbursts I'll survive."

"I'm not saying we give up," Aydan said. "I just don't want you seeking out the Children. It's too dangerous."

"I'm capable of protecting myself."

"We don't know that," he replied. My eyebrows shot up and he added, "You've never used your training outside the sparring ring. You are the highest-ranking member of my Cabinet. War and unrest would follow if something happened to you."

"It doesn't have to. I'll go, knowing the risks. I'll negotiate a truce on your behalf. We could achieve the same peace with the Children as we will with Nautia. If it goes poorly, and they are what you claim, then there will be nothing left to do. No fights to engage them in. You're the king, you don't have to go to war over an advisor." It felt as if all the air had been sucked from the room as I met Aydan's eyes. Behind the anger lay something else. Hurt. Frost crept up my hands and smothered the smoke.

"Firstly," Aydan started after a silent minute. The rest of the Cabinet watched on. "Your plan assumes that the Children simply kill you and don't attack *us*, at which point I would have to engage, no matter your request. Next, if you think for a *second* that I wouldn't tear that coven apart with my bare hands if something happened to you, then you severely underestimate my feelings—"

"*You're not listening to me,*" I said. "Aydan, I know you love me. I do. I love you too. I'm begging you to try and understand where I'm coming from—"

"I understand where you're coming from perfectly fine. It's why we sent the sentries in the first place and *look what happened.* You're not going. It's not happening. You're not going to get yourself killed over this."

"Your grandmother would certainly be pleased," I mumbled. "Then I would be out of the way and you could marry Reyna and play happy family with her and Calliope."

"Don't be petty," he snapped. "Reyna is a friend, and she has been nothing but kind to you. I've told you my feelings on the matter, and I have addressed the issue with Solandis. Don't throw things I've already taken care of in my face because you're pissed and feeling insecure."

I clenched my jaw and blinked a few times. Aydan's mind was made up.

So was mine.

Silently, I turned and poured myself a drink from the cart. I felt everyone's eyes on me as I drained the glass and set it down. Without turning back to them, I said, "I think I'll go to bed." Aydan's warm hand rested on my shoulder.

"I'll be there in a minute," he said in a near whisper. I shrugged out of his touch.

"I think I'll go to my own bed tonight," I replied softly before walking toward the stairs.

"Shaye," Aydan croaked, and my heart shattered. I walked until I reached my old room, where I let the door click shut behind me.

Hours later, I lay on top of my bed, fully dressed, staring at the ceiling in the darkness.

An hour after our argument, Aydan knocked softly on the door, calling my name just once. I didn't answer, and after a couple of minutes, he left. I wanted so badly to open the door, to let him talk to me, to sleep next to him tonight. But I knew if I saw his face, I wouldn't be able to muster up the courage to do what I was about to.

I stood and cast two orbs of light. There was nothing in the wardrobe, save for a couple sets of sparring leathers folded and placed in the bottom.

I put one set on, fastened the buckles and laced my jacket, before pulling on a pair of boots. In a trunk, I found a Sylvannian army knapsack like the one Aydan had used during our first days together. The other set of leathers went inside, as well as some socks and other essentials, and I strapped a single dagger to my leg. I wrapped my hair into a tight braid and secured it before creeping my way silently down the stairs of the sleeping house and into the kitchens, where I filled the bag with food and a canteen. In a closet, I found an extra cloak and a bedroll, but no tent. I hoped I wouldn't encounter any storms while wandering the mountains.

I found a pen in the kitchen and, on a spare sheet of stationery, wrote just two sentences: *I'm sorry. I love you.* I crept back to set it on the dining room table and was about to make my way to the door when an orb of light appeared, floating dimly in the middle of the room. I turned and saw Hannele's face illuminated in the darkness.

"Where do you think you're going?" She looked me up and down.

"Hannele. Please, I have to—"

"You know this is treason? That you're breaking every oath you've made to Aydan and the Crown?"

"I do." I swallowed. "But this—I can't wait around for answers to fall into my lap, Hannele. If I'm successful, not only will I know how to manage my powers, but we could bring an era of peace that Medeisia has never seen."

"And if you fail, you'll be dead and Medeisia will be at war with the Children and their allies."

"I—"

"Better not fail, then," she finished. I gawked at her, finally taking in her outfit. She was in sparring gear too, and carried a bag.

"Han . . . what are you—"

"I'm coming with you." She gestured into the darkness. "She'll keep watch here." I peered behind her and watched in disbelief as Kenna stepped into the light.

"Ken," I choked.

"Don't start acting sentimental," she said, eyeing me. "You can thank me when you come home. *Alive*, please." I nodded with silent promise.

"So you're going to keep your sight on me?" I asked.

"Not on you. Her." She nodded to Hannele, who was checking her bow now slung over her shoulder. "I'll be able to see her while you're traveling, but I have a suspicion things might be spotty once you're in their encampment. As soon as she crosses the border back into Sylvanna, I'll feel her."

"Don't let him do anything stupid," I told her. "I'll be back."

"I can keep him steady for a couple weeks," Kenna said. "Try to be home before then."

"We need to go," said Hannele. She threw her arms around Kenna and squeezed tightly. I did the same, and the three of us held each other for a moment.

When we let go, I said, "Just one more thing," and grabbed the pen and note I'd left for Aydan. I'd barely finished scribbling one last line when Hannele snatched my hand and effuged us out of the dining room.

I'm sorry.

I love you.

Two weeks.

Chapter Forty-One

We landed at the base of a mountain where wind and snow whipped around us in the dark, making it almost impossible to see. Hannele grabbed my hand and shouted over the screaming winds, "Keep moving, we need to cover as much ground as possible."

In his research, Gerridan had determined that the most likely location of the Children's encampment would be somewhere near the Five-Peak Summit. Though I couldn't see far enough ahead to confirm for myself, I assumed that that was where Hannele had effuged us. The strategy expert knew we were on limited time, and the only thing more efficient than starting at the base of the five peaks would be effuging directly to the summit. Two Medeisians accidentally effuging directly into the encampment would likely be executed on sight. The base it was.

We stumbled through the snow for about an hour before Hannele grabbed my arm and pointed ahead to a cave in the side of the mountain. We made our way there, and I sighed when we entered, still freezing, but at least not in the direct path of the storm.

"Can you start a fire?" she asked, setting down her pack and conjuring an orb of light to the top of the cave. I held up my hand and willed a spark to come out.

"If we can find wood and kindling, maybe," I said. Hannele pointed to her pack.

"I have a few things in there that might help. I'm going to make sure we're alone in here," she said, gesturing to the back of the cave. Something I hadn't considered. I shuddered. "I won't be gone long." She started toward the back of the cave and I began digging through the bag.

When she returned, I had a fire crackling. There had indeed been a bag of kindling in her pack, and I'd managed to find enough dry wood to at least get us started. It wouldn't last us the whole night, but it would help us get warm for the time being. "All clear." Hannele sat next to me and held her hands out to the fire. We were quiet for a few minutes before she asked, "So what's your plan?"

"My plan?"

"What are you going to say to the Children if we find them?"

"I'm not completely sure," I admitted. "I'll have to pretend I can speak on Aydan's behalf. If they listen to me, I'll try and strike some sort of deal—"

"You can," Hannele said, rummaging through her bag for food. "You're the highest-ranking court official in Medeisia. If you can't speak for him, who can?"

"If we live through this, I doubt I'll be the Chief Advisor for much longer," I replied, reaching for my own bag and pulling out some dried meat and an apple. "I'll be lucky if I'm even allowed to keep the Redfern estates, let alone show my face at court."

"He'll forgive us. Well, he'll forgive you, at least. Me, I'm not so sure. Gerridan certainly won't." She stuffed some bread into her mouth.

"Gerridan loves you," I said.

"I know," Hannele replied. I started to press further but she cut me off. "We'd better get some sleep. Not too much, though. I don't want to get snowed in. We'll take shifts."

"You go ahead and rest," I told her. "I'll take the first watch." She pulled a thick bedroll from her pack and spread it out.

"Wake me in an hour."

A few hours later, we trekked through the snowy mountainside in silence. The sun was starting to rise, and as I watched it come up over the top of the five peaks, it was hard to believe that only yesterday I was plotting trade routes. I wondered if Aydan realized we were gone yet. I imagined his distraught face reading my note, Gerridan's hurt and Alastair's anguish. Alastair, who had finally found one last piece of Brina in me, would be sick with worry. *No*, I told myself, pushing the thoughts away. Better to focus on the task at hand.

As we climbed higher, the air became thinner and there was less walking on trails and over rocks and more scaling the sides of huge boulders. Our hands and knees rubbed themselves raw over the tops of the rough terrain, slick and slippery with ice and snow. By nightfall, we had reached the top of the lowest peak, with much more to cover come morning. It was a hell of a feat to not collapse onto my bedroll when we found another cave that night. Instead, I took the first watch again.

It was five days later that I began to worry that we weren't going to find anything. Wandering the mountains for nearly a week now, we had seen no life aside from each other and an occasional mouse—no sign of the Children anywhere. We finally stopped for the night, once again having hiked and climbed until it was too dark to see. I peered inside my pack and frowned, while Hannele massaged her swollen feet and dried her socks near the fire.

"That's the end of anything fresh," I said, pulling out the last portion of bread I'd saved for dinner. It had gone moldy. "Down to the dried meat."

"I still have a few apples and a lump of cheese," Hannele replied. "We can share." I handed her some of the meat and took an apple from the bag she shoved in my direction. "Tomorrow we should make it a point to find more food. Better to take the break and look now than wait until we're out of supplies."

"Good idea," I said with a sigh. Putting ourselves a day behind schedule wasn't ideal, but it was better to be prepared. I yawned. "Want me to take the first watch?"

"No, I'll do it." She pulled her warm, dry socks back on her feet. "Get some sleep."

I was too tired to argue. I smoothed out my bedroll and lay down, not bothering to remove my boots. "'Night," I said.

"See you in a few hours," said Hannele.

As soon as I felt myself slip into sleep, my eyes snapped open in darkness. I recognized the feeling of cold bare feet on the black floor—if you could call it that—and looked up to see a light once again in the distance. I followed it.

Sure enough, I soon found myself standing at the edge of a room, watching the same red-haired man pour over books and mutter what must have been spells to himself. This time, I could see his face more clearly, and I gasped when I realized who stood before me. I saw him the day I'd mindwalked with Alastair.

It was Lord Ronan.

I was watching my father practice witchcraft in what I could only guess was his secret study. His finger traced along the words on the page, then he reached for a nearby bottle containing some dried, black herb and examined it before tapping the page. The volume snapped itself shut as soon as he pulled his hand away, and Ronan walked away from the desk, toward a table holding a cauldron. He took a pinch of the substance and sprinkled it into the potion, which glowed a bright shade of purple. Ronan sighed. He seemed disappointed in his creation.

"You're back," he said without turning. I froze. "Tell me, are you a specter come to haunt me? Or a messenger from the gods to warn me of my misdeeds?" I remained silent. Ronan turned, facing me and gripping the table behind him. He glared at me. "Well? Speak, girl."

"You can see me?" I nearly whispered. He raised his eyebrows and nodded once. "I—I'm not a specter. Or a messenger," I told him. "I'm just a woman. Sorcerer, like you."

"And how did you come to find me?"

"I think I'm asleep. I think this . . . this place is in my head," I replied. Ronan crossed his arms over his chest and leaned back.

"That's new." His voice was full of curiosity. "If you're in your head, where is your body?"

"I'm in a cave, in the Creg'tam Mountains," I said. "I seek the Children." The lord's mouth became a flat line.

"That is a dangerous task, girl. You'd do best to return to your home when you wake."

"I can't, my lord—"

In the distance, a sudden scream rang out. I whipped around and felt myself dart back into my body, my eyes flying open in time to see a bag go over the top of Hannele's head, muffling her screams as a group of men pinned her to the floor of the cave. "No!" I screamed, raising my arm to retaliate, only to be met with the grip of another man who forced it behind my back so fast and hard that I thought it would snap. More men appeared, pinning me to the ground while they fastened what I could feel were a set of silver cuffs onto my wrists. One of them cast a purple glow around their hand and pressed it to Hannele's head. She went limp as I screamed again, "*No!*" before a bag was shoved over my own head, blocking my vision. A cold hand gripped the back of my neck, and my consciousness fled.

Chapter Forty-Two

I was shaken awake by slender hands gripping my shoulders.

"Shaye!" My eyes fluttered open and Hannele was bent over me, looking me over for signs of injury. "Can you hear me? Are you all right?"

"Yes," I said. "Yes, I'm fine." She moved off of me and I sat up, groggy as I rubbed my eyes and looked around.

We were in a bedroom. An enormous, luxurious bedroom, with a giant bed covered in plush blankets and expensive furs. Beautiful, hand-carved oak furniture filled the room, including a table filled with food: fresh fruit, cheese, bread, and a steaming roast chicken.

"What the fuck is going on?" I asked, looking around for our captors.

"I have no idea." Hannele looked scared. Her face was dirty and her hair disheveled, as if she had only awakened moments before I did. My own clothes and hair were a mess, and our packs were nowhere to be found. I scanned the room.

"There's no door," I said, heart sinking.

"No windows either," she replied. We both swung our legs over the sides of the bed and walked the perimeter with our hands grazing the wall, looking for a notch or a special brick, like the ones in Ayzelle and Sylvanna. Nothing.

We stopped before the spread of food. My stomach gurgled.

"Think it's safe?" I picked a strawberry from a platter and examined it. Hannele grabbed an apple.

"I don't think anything is safe anymore," she replied before taking a large bite. I did the same and nearly moaned. It was the sweetest strawberry I had ever tasted. I grabbed another. Then reached for the chicken. I tore off a leg, took a greedy bite, and let the juice run down my chin. I wiped at it with my arm and kept going. Hannele was eating with just as much vigor. I tore a chunk from a loaf of bread with my hands and ripped a bite out with my teeth before starting back in with the chicken.

"Well, well—you Medeisian nobles are *quite* the savages, aren't you?" a jeering voice rang out from behind us. We dropped the food and spun.

Standing in an opening in the wall was a man roughly my height, pale as moonlight with silvery hair and violet eyes. He wore a silk shirt of midnight blue, with black leather pants and boots made of what appeared to be snake skin, rather than common leather. He looked us over with an amused sneer.

"I request an audien—" The back of the man's hand collided with my face, sending me reeling. Hannele cried out and took a step forward, but guards filed into the room, swords drawn.

"You request nothing. You have already been granted another day of life after trespassing in our lands." He smoothed his hair back. "Did you really think we wouldn't be watching, after you sent soldiers looking for us? Though, I suppose I can't expect much from fools who would think we'd have strawberries to give them when we're encased in snow."

I furrowed my brow, turning back to the table of food, only to find, to my horror, the same table piled with the discarded carcasses of rats. Platters filled with cockroaches and moldy, decaying bread lined the tables, while maggots writhed over the top of nearly every surface. I vomited on the floor. When I looked up, I saw Hannele wiping her mouth, having just done the same. My stomach turned and I heaved again, and again, until there was nothing left to expel.

The guards and the man were all stone-faced, watching while we vomited up their disgusting trick.

"Are you finished?" he asked. I nodded, panting and shaking. "Good. The Mothers would like to decide your fates themselves. Come along." He turned on his heel and marched through the doorway. A guard's hand shoved into my back and I followed, trying not to stumble.

I had assumed we would be taken outdoors and led to the encampment rumored to be the home of the Children, but the further we walked through the empty corridors, the more it dawned on me that we weren't just inside a building. We were inside the mountain itself.

That was why they couldn't be found. Not because they were some roaming, nomadic tribe of witches organized into tents by their queens. But because their home—their palace—was built deep into the mountain itself. When we came to a stop, we stood before a pair of large carts. The man got inside one, with two guards joining him. Hannele and I crammed into the other, joined by three guards who squeezed in behind us. The man's lips moved, and he pointed at our cart, then his own. Both lurched forward, up a steep, spiraled slope and into the darkness. I clutched Hannele's hand.

We emerged into the light, opposite a pair of large doors that looked to be carved from onyx stone. The man spoke words I did not recognize, and the doors flew open. Hannele and I were ordered out of our cart and marched forward through the doors.

Much like the first day in Ayzelle with Aydan, people lined the huge, black room. The walls, floors, and ceiling were all onyx, down to the dais containing three empty thrones on the opposite end. My legs resisted and my mouth went dry as we approached, then were forced to our knees before the thrones. Though hundreds of witches lined the room, it was completely silent.

"Alert the Mothers that our guests are waiting at their pleasure," the man said to a guard, who swiftly exited through a hidden door. Minutes passed, and I began to wonder if this might be a trick, if there were any queens coming at all, or if we were on our knees awaiting an executioner—when the door opened and out walked a trio of crowned women.

I watched as they glided silently toward their thrones, where they sat in unison, and I trembled. None of their faces were showing. The queens—Mothers—on the left and right sides wore long red veils that draped over their entire bodies, held in place with golden crowns upon their heads. The left Mother's hands were pale, like the man's skin, while the right's were a deep brown. The middle queen wore a more elaborate crown: gold, and completely encrusted with rubies and emeralds, with a piece like a knight's visor covering her eyes but leaving her pale mouth and nose in view. Her face and hands, like the hands of the other Mothers, were covered in reddish tattoos—runes, by the look of them—that I didn't recognize.

The middle queen spoke. "Deimos, are our guests well rested?"

The man who had retrieved us from the room slapped me forward. "Yes, Your Majesty. However, they *were* quite displeased with the meal we provided them."

"How ungrateful of them," the middle Mother observed, bored. "Tell me, ladies, why has Zathryan Aevitarus sent more spies to lurk around our territory?"

"We don't work for Zathryan, Your Majesties," I said, keeping my eyes averted.

"Oh?"

"We are members of the Cabinet of King Aydan Aevitarus, son of Zathryan. Zathryan has been dead several months now." The Mothers did not seem interested in this information.

"What is it that you seek?"

"Peace, Your Majesties," I replied. "And a teacher, for myself." The left Mother straightened.

"A teacher?" she repeated.

"Yes," I said. "You see—"

"The last sorcerer who came searching for a teacher also promised peace between Medeisia and the Children. He sought the power to defeat his great enemy. What is it you seek?" the left Mother asked.

"I seek nothing more than someone who would teach me to control my powers," I replied. "The last sorcerer you spoke of, it was Lord Ronan Redfern?" No reply. "He was my father. Executed before my birth. My name is Lady Shaye, head of House Redfern. The powers my father acquired passed on to me, in addition to the magic that runs through my veins as a sorceress. I am a born witch."

I had their attention now. The middle Mother tightened her grip on the arms of her throne, and the right one sat straighter.

"Such a thing does not exist," said the middle Mother.

"Your Majesty, I have no reason to lie."

"You belong to the Cabinet of the Medeisian king, you need no more reason than that," she snapped. "The Children of the Onyx Temple have always remained neutral. We have never stepped into the affairs of the Medeisian Courts, or the grudges the other covens hold toward you. We've simply wanted privacy. And you cannot grant us even that. What is it you have to offer us? Peace? We would already have that, had you not come snooping."

I glanced at Hannele, who had sweat beading on her forehead. The strategy expert was playing out the plausible outcomes of this audience in her head, and by the look on her face, I could tell our odds were not good. "Your Majesties," I said, "I am the right hand of King Aydan—his Chief Advisor. I tell you now that I am acting as his voice, and any promises made to you now will be upheld by the Crown of Medeisia. You have my word." The Mothers said nothing, so I continued. "As you know, the mortal kingdom of Nautia broke from Medeisia over a century ago, and we have been at war or close to it ever since. Under King Aydan's leadership, we are now organizing peace talks with the Regent of Nautia. His Majesty has no desire for war, and in fact wants to build a new world, a new era of peace, friendship, and prosperity between former enemies. We would like to offer you a seat at the table. To be part of building this new world with us."

The room was silent, save for the gentle tapping of the middle Mother's tattooed fingers on her throne. "A lovely speech," she said finally, "though I cannot say that I find your pleas for a better, more peaceful world to be too convincing when they come with the attached strings of our court giving up a member to teach you." Her head moved as if she was looking me up and down, though I could not see her eyes. "You say you're a born witch. What powers do you claim?"

"I can conjure the four elements, Your Majesty," I said. "And I have displayed the abilities of a mindwalker."

The Mothers did not reply. Instead, the middle one spoke again, this time saying softly: "Lyra."

A young woman who looked no older than twenty stepped forward. Lyra's brown skin held the same tattooed runes as the Mothers', with snow white hair standing out in bright contrast against it. She wore layered black skirts with a brown sleeveless blouse that revealed more runes coating every visible inch of her skin, save for her face. Her eyes—one an icy shade of blue, the other nearly black—looked me up and down while the rest of her face remained expressionless. She approached, then stopped at the edge of the dais where the Mothers sat.

"Dearest Lyra is what we call the keeper," said the Mother seated to the right. I bowed my head. No response.

"Lyra, what do you think of this proposal offered by the Medeisians?" The left Mother asked.

"I think that I would be inclined to consider this offer," she said with a girlish, lilting voice, "if I felt that I could trust them."

"And how would you build trust with these women? With this supposed Voice of the King?" asked the center Mother.

"By inviting them to stay, of course," Lyra smiled sweetly.

"Yes, an extended stay may be the only way to determine their trustworthiness," the center Mother agreed. "Guards."

My body seized as invisible hands gripped my arms, legs, and neck, holding me in place where I knelt. My eyes darted around the room, and dotted throughout the crowd, I saw various men and women holding out their hands, using their minds to pin me in place. I looked to Hannele, who was pinned as well.

"The Medeisians will be our guests for the time being," the Mother announced to the room. Her focus landed on the man behind us. "Deimos, if you please."

Deimos's hand connected with the back of my head, and the world went black once again.

I woke to my arm being roughly lifted above my head. A large hand gripped my wrist tightly, attempting to lock me in another silver cuff. Instinctually, I tried to break free, but my resistance was met with a slap to the face. I blinked away the stinging and let my eyes focus on the room around me—a dark, dirty cell with water dripping from the walls. On the opposite wall, another guard was chaining Hannele, who was struggling even as they hit her.

"Get your filthy fucking hands off of me!" she growled. The man just chuckled and fastened the lock around her wrist. My attention turned toward the door as I heard the disapproving clicking of Deimos's tongue.

"*My lady*, is that any way to speak to your gracious host?" he asked Hannele. She spat at him, and he watched as the spittle landed a foot away from his boot.

"She's a princess of Sylvanna. Address her as such," I corrected him. "And most *gracious hosts* don't throw their guests in a filthy cell—"

"Are your accommodations not to your liking? They didn't seem to be a problem an hour ago, Lady Advisor." I scanned the room again and understood that we had in fact been in the same room before. The glamours were now removed.

"How do the Mothers—and that keeper woman, Lyra—expect us to prove ourselves, to earn their trust if we're locked away like this?" I asked.

"The Mothers will convene with Lyra and decide what they want done with you," said Deimos. "My wife is a creative woman. I'm sure she'll think of something. Prepare yourselves for . . . challenging days ahead."

"Wife." I leaned my head against the wall. With what we had seen of Deimos, I didn't have much faith in the compassion of anyone who would choose him as a husband. He crouched in front of me and lifted my chin, forcing me to look him in the eyes.

"Trust me, my lady, when I say the days ahead will not be restful for you," he murmured, barely an inch from me. His gaze lowered to my mouth, and he dragged his thumb over my bottom lip. I snapped my teeth but his hand narrowly escaped me, then slapped my cheek once again. "Manners, my lady," he chided, standing up again. "Someone will come for you when a decision has been made. Try to stay alive until then, I suppose." Deimos left the cell, and the guards followed closely behind him.

When the door to our cell slammed shut and the footsteps disappeared in the distance, I said to Hannele, "Are you hurt?"

"Not that I can tell." She pulled at her cuff. We each had one wrist in a silver cuff, which was attached to a chain and then to the wall, and our other arm free to move. The solid silver was no match for the free hand, and we were far enough away from each other that we could not touch. Not that we would be of any help to one another without access to our magic.

"I'm sorry," I said. "I tried—I tried to make them listen—"

"Your little speech likely bought us some time," Hannele replied. "They're intrigued by you—they want to see what you're capable of. Good work."

"Does that help you? Their interest in me, I mean?"

"Maybe, maybe not." She shrugged, giving up on the cuff and leaning against the wall. "If not for my power, they may still decide that a princess has information they'd like to hear. I'll likely be tortured if we don't escape, and"—she gestured around the cell—"*that* doesn't seem likely."

My mind drifted to memories of a whip cracking against my naked body, the sound of my own pleas and screams filling my ears—

"No, no they won't—they *can't*—"

"Shaye, calm down," Hannele said, her own voice steady. "I know how to do this. If it can be avoided, fine, but I am ready and willing. We need this mission to work." Ever the strategy expert, the military official. "If we go home empty-handed, then this was all for nothing." I breathed out shakily and nodded.

"So," I said. "What do we do now?"

"We wait."

Chapter Forty-Three

We waited.

And waited.

Days passed and we saw neither hide nor hair of Lyra, or even Deimos. Cold, barely edible meals were left nearby each of us while we slept, our days' rations within reach of our unchained hands so we could pick mold off of bread and shoo rats away from the scraps we wanted for ourselves. The only time we saw guards was when, twice per day, someone would come in and let us take turns using a disgusting chamber pot in the corner.

The cell itself was dark and wet, with no windows. Time seemed to press itself together. Keeping track of the days grew more and more difficult, and when I tried to make sense of the guard shifts, I realized they were switching guards out at random, with no measurable schedule to be seen. Hannele and I grew lethargic, sleeping often both from boredom and weakness. I wondered quietly if we would simply be left here to rot.

My question was answered when, one day, the door opened, and it was not a guard coming to let me use the chamber pot, but Deimos striding into the cell, sneering down at me. He glanced at Hannele. "Come with me, princess. I have a few questions for you." My mouth turned to ash as I watched Deimos unlock Hannele's cuff, and it fell from her wrist. She weakly pushed herself upright. Her expression was ice cold as she met his gaze.

"No," I said. "She knows nothing, she's just my traveling companion."

"Keep your mouth shut," he spat. "You'll have plenty of time to answer my questions for yourself."

"I'll be fine, Shaye," Hannele said, her voice unwavering. I met her eyes and they held no hint of fear. She turned back to Deimos. "Let's go." I watched as she was led from the cell and the door slammed shut behind her. A sob tore from my throat as soon as I was alone. I did not know if I would see my friend again.

I counted the minutes while Hannele was gone, and, to my surprise, it was less than an hour before the door opened once again and the princess stumbled back into the cell, followed by Deimos and the same guard he had come with before. Hannele clutched her arm, and it wasn't until the guard forced a wrist back into her cuff that I realized her other arm was limp. Blood trickled down beneath the leather sleeve of her jacket and onto her hand. She was trying to hold it close to her body. Her face was pained.

"*What did you do to her?*" I snarled as the guard approached me.

"I did nothing," Deimos replied. "We didn't even make it to the interrogation room. The princess tripped over her own boot and landed on her arm. Nasty break, by the sound of it." I twisted as I was dragged to my feet by the guard. If she was bleeding that freely, it meant bone had punctured the skin beneath her jacket.

"Heal her," I demanded.

"No." It was Hannele's voice this time. My head snapped toward her. "I don't want their help."

"Come along, Lady Advisor," said Deimos, turning again on his heel. He led me into the corridor, followed by the guard. I tried to look back, but the cell door slammed shut before I could catch a last glimpse. Palms clammy, I marched forward.

"So, Lady Redfern, we're finally alone."

I glared at Lyra, who sat opposite me in an interrogation chamber. Deimos had led me around, marching me up and down corridors for nearly half an hour before we arrived at the door to the room I now sat in. He'd remained outside while a guard chained me to an uncomfortable wooden chair. I waited alone, anticipation brewing in my stomach while sweat beaded on my forehead, sure that at any moment, Deimos himself or one of his men would enter, whip in hand, ready to reopen the scarred flesh on my back. Instead, the door opened and in strode Lyra, humming softly as she made herself comfortable, crossing her legs and tapping her fingers on the arm of her chair.

"What do you want from me?" I asked after several minutes' silence. "I've been locked away for I don't even know how long—"

"You've been our guest here for just under a month, Lady Advisor," the keeper replied. "The Mothers wanted to be sure that the Medeisian armies wouldn't come marching in to save you."

A month. I clenched my jaw.

"They won't. The Crown will honor its promises." *A month.* "All we ask is for someone to teach me to control my powers. We've tried with sorcerer teachers, it doesn't work. The magic I inherited from my father, the magic he learned from the Children—I believe only someone from your coven can teach me to manage it."

Lyra scanned me up and down, still tapping her fingers. "You say you can control the elements. How did you come to learn this?" I blinked.

"It was an accident, I suppose. First it was fire. I was scared, having a nightmare, and I woke with my hands engulfed in flames . . ." I continued to describe each instance in which a new element had appeared to me. Lyra's expression did not change.

"And the mindwalking?"

"Another accident," I said. "My friend, he has a peculiar gift. He was trying to show me an image from his memory, but when I took his hand, I was able to relive the whole thing from his perspective. I've only done it twice."

"I see."

"What is it that you're trying to learn from me? If you want to know my intent, just have another mindwalker come in here and look at my thoughts."

"That would be impossible, my lady," said Lyra. "We have not had a mindwalker among our ranks in years."

"I don't understand," I said. "Witchcraft is learned, is it not?"

"It is."

"So how can there be no mindwalkers? No one has bothered to learn—"

"Do you know much about our goddess, Lady Shaye?" Lyra asked, folding her hands in her lap.

"Your goddess?"

"Otana," she said with a single nod. "Much like the Medeisian goddess Ehnara, we consider her a mother figure. But her main passions lie in wisdom and learning. She gifts us with our markings to show the world what we have achieved in our studies, our practice of her craft. It is said that only when one's markings cover them from their head down to the bottoms of their feet are they worthy to learn the art of mindwalking," she said solemnly. "In my two hundred years of life, I have never met a mindwalker. No one still living has."

"But—but the elemental magic. Someone could still teach me *that*, couldn't they?"

"Of course they *could*, my lady," Lyra said. "The question is whether they will."

My palms were sweating. If I weren't in silver, I was sure I'd be aflame by now. "Will they? Have you learned anything new from this conversation that will help the Mothers make their decision?"

"We've barely had a discussion," she said. "It may take three or four more—"

"*I don't have that kind of time!*" I nearly yelled. "I have a *life*! I have a family—" I stopped myself, realizing it was the first time I had called them that. "My king awaits my safe return," I said softly, not caring if I sounded weak. "I am begging for a teacher, Lyra. If the answer is no, then . . . then wipe our minds and send us back, like the sentries. Let us think we failed. But don't live up to the cruelty my people think exists here."

Lyra stared at me blankly for a moment. "You said your flame appeared after having nightmares." I sighed.

"Yes."

"Do you often have nightmares?"

"I did," I told her. "Until I found myself sleepwalking so many times that Aydan sent for a tincture from a trusted healer. Keeps me from dreaming."

"You call your king by his first name," she observed. I pursed my lips. "You haven't had any of your belongings since arriving here. Have you been having nightmares these past few weeks?" she asked. I frowned.

"No," I said. "I didn't realize . . ."

"Have you had any dreams at all since leaving your home?"

"Just—" I stopped myself, not sure if I should continue. I lifted my gaze to meet hers and felt the words escape my lips. "I had a dream about my father, the night Hannele and I were captured by your guards." Lyra rested her chin on a fist.

"I think I have what I need for today," she said suddenly. She snapped her fingers once and the door opened; Deimos swept in and roughly hauled me to my feet.

"Wait—" I said, pulling away from his grip. "*Please*, Lyra, I want peace between our people. I want to learn—" Deimos clutched me tighter, dragging me from the room. I resisted, and one of the guards' fists collided with my jaw, filling my mouth with blood almost instantly. I heard Lyra's muffled voice scold the men while I blinked away stars. When the world came back into focus, I was being all but dragged away, back to the darkness.

Chapter Forty-Four

Time continued to pass.

When I had been tossed back into our cell and my chains fastened once again, Hannele questioned me about my so-called interrogation.

"It felt like she was trying to get to know me," I said. "She was just asking questions about how my witchcraft appeared, and then Deimos and the guards were there and I was getting punched."

"Strange," was all Hannele had to say. She looked ill, with her arm still kept close to her body.

"Won't you let them look at that?"

"No," the princess said. "If there's any chance of Kenna still knowing where we are and if we're alive, I can't let them perform spells on me."

"I highly doubt Kenna can see you right now."

"Maybe not, but when we get out of here she needs to know where we are. If I'm tainted by their magic, it won't matter," she snapped, then winced.

"Okay," I said, not wanting to get her any more worked up. "I'm sure we'll be out soon."

A few days passed, and Hannele was starting to scare me. A permanent sheen of sweat lay across her forehead, and her breathing had become labored as her limp arm lay across her lap. Any movement on Hannele's part made her cry out in pain. She couldn't eat. She couldn't reach for food, let alone bring it to her mouth if she tried. The princess's complexion was ashen, and bags had formed under her eyes, which were bloodshot from lack of sleep. Between the weakness from lack of sustenance and what was almost certainly an infection in her wound, I knew she wouldn't live much longer unless she got some help.

When a guard entered to allow me to relieve myself, I begged him to let me feed her.

"Please," I said, pulling against his grip on my arm. "Keep the cuff on me, chain me next to her, but let me give her some food—" The guard kicked my leg out from underneath me, knocking me to the floor, where I landed with all of my weight on my other knee. The unsettling cracking sound and sharp pain of my flesh against the stone floor brought bitter tears to my eyes. "*Please,*" I begged again as I was hauled to my feet and the guard again fastened the chain to my cuff. "She's dying, please—get her a healer, let me feed her—" He left, slamming the cell door behind him. A sob tore from my throat.

"It's no use, Shaye," came Hannele's weak voice. "They won't kill me outright, but I will die here. You're going to have to—"

"*Shut up,*" I snapped at her. "You will *not* die here. You will not give up. I *order* you—" I stammered through the tears. Staring at my lap, I whispered, "Don't leave me alone."

She didn't reply, and when I looked up, she was asleep.

Hannele didn't wake much the next day. Each time a guard entered to make their rounds, I begged for a healer. Each time, they ignored me.

Finally, after being ignored once again by the guard dragging me to the chamber pot, I bent toward his arm and bit down as hard as I could, and he roared in pain. He ripped his arm from my mouth, my teeth tearing a chunk of his flesh from the limb. Blood poured from the wound, and when he raised his arm to strike me, I dodged him, ducking out of the way and shoving my weight into him. He raised his other arm to block me and I bit that one too. He grabbed a fistful of my hair and I shoved my knee into his groin, sending him to his knees with a yelp. I got in a few punches before the cell door flew open and in poured another four guards who yanked me away and pinned me to the ground. I shielded my head as I received several blows to my face and body.

"Trying to escape, are we?" crooned Deimos's voice from the doorway. The guards moved and I saw the witch leaning against the frame, smirking at me. "I have to say, I expected better from you, Lady Redfern."

"I'm not trying to escape," I said, flecks of blood falling from my mouth to the floor. "I just need someone to listen to me."

"Oh?" said Deimos, now approaching me, bending so that his face was inches from mine. He spoke softly. "And here I thought we were such gracious hosts. The Mothers will be devastated to hear that you feel so ignored. We'll be sure that you receive the extra special attention you so crave—" I spat in his face.

Deimos jerked away, wiped the blood and spittle from his eye, and chuckled darkly. Then he moved so quickly that I didn't realize what was happening until the back of his hand collided with my cheek. Fingers wrapped themselves around my throat. I choked, clawing at him, but the guards caught my hands. That smirk remained on his lips as my vision grew fuzzy. It felt like hours, but only a few seconds later, I heard a muffled voice say, "What the hell are you doing?"

Deimos let go and I gasped for air, nearly crying as relief filled my lungs. Coughing, I looked up and saw Lyra standing in the doorway, gawking at the scene before her. "Are you fucking kidding me?" she asked as he turned to face her, smoothing his hair back.

"You have your role, darling, and I have mine." He reached to place his hand on her chin, but Lyra slapped it away.

"Your role is to do as the Mothers say: keep the prisoners safe."

"She was never in any real danger—"

"Because I happened to show up." She moved to clear the doorway, pointing to the corridor. "Get out." Deimos clenched his jaw but didn't say another word as he strode into the corridor and turned the corner. Lyra glared at the guards holding me. "Secure the prisoner and leave." They quickly followed her instructions, this time chaining me beside Hannele before they left. The three of us were quiet and alone, Hannele likely not even aware of what had just happened.

"Lyra, please," I said, my voice dripping in desperation. "You have to heal her. If she dies—"

"I can't," she said, squatting and examining Hannele's arm. Her finger grazed the princess's jacket, and Hannele cried out softly in her sleep. "The infection is too widespread. Nothing that I know how to do will help. But, here—" Her hand hovered over the broken arm as she murmured under her breath. "I can't stop the other effects, but she won't feel any pain from the injury now."

"Thank you," I whispered, tears slipping down my face. The keeper gave a small nod before turning and leaving, the cell door shutting behind her with a *thud.*

It was a struggle to stay awake.

I spent the next two days drifting in and out of sleep. My body was too exhausted to do much else, and for the first time since the night in the cave, I dreamt—mostly of Aydan. Of the future we would never have, of his face, so stoic and serious when we met, smiling and laughing for me. I dreamt of Kenna and Gerridan. Of Alastair—and even my mother. All the people I loved, and who loved me, all the people I had betrayed by being so selfish, so foolish as to think I could stride into the Onyx Temple and talk my way into an agreement with the Children.

Hannele was dying, and there was nothing I could do but watch her waste away. The infection, which if not for the silver cuff on her wrist would have healed itself by now, was ravaging her body. She drifted in and out of consciousness, trying to fight it, but she was weak. She couldn't chew any of the food I gave her, and when I was given broth to help her sip, I saw that it was barely more than water.

Hannele shivered with fever, and when she did open her eyes, they were glazed over. As I slipped into sleep once more, I doubted she would make it through another day.

I stood in blackness again, watching on as Lord Ronan paced his secret study. I didn't feel any of my injuries here, only the chill of the darkness surrounding me. I stepped into the room.

"Hello." I didn't wait for him to notice me this time.

"You again," he said with his back turned, rearranging some books on one of the many shelves lining the perimeter of the room. "Did you make it home safely?"

"No," I replied. "My friend and I were captured. We've been in a cell in the Onyx Temple for weeks. We're injured, and held in silver. She'll soon be dead." Ronan faced me.

"That is unfortunate," he said. "Weeks, you say? Interesting."

"Why?"

"It's been two days since you last appeared to me."

"That is interesting." After a pause, I continued, "I wonder if you could help us, my lord."

"How and why would I do that?"

"Because I am like you, sir, and I—I don't even know if this is *real*—" I halted. "I am a sorceress of Medeisia, but I can also wield witchcraft. Perhaps a spell—"

"If you are held in silver, young lady, no spell I know can help you."

"I thought as much," I sighed. "It was worth a try." I quieted, and Ronan went back to his work. He shifted items around while flashes of red and purple burst from his hands. Some were accompanied by words muttered under his breath, but nothing changed. "What are you doing?" I asked.

"Warding," Ronan replied.

"Against whom?"

"Anyone who might stumble across this place." He faced me again. "Tomorrow, my king wishes to honor the officers who fought for us last year. Some trouble with the Nautians. There will be visitors everywhere. Can't have anyone go exploring and find this place by accident." My heart was in my throat. Tomorrow was the officers' ball. Ronan would meet Brina tomorrow. I swallowed.

"You mustn't—" I started impulsively before pressing my lips shut.

"What?"

"Nothing—nothing of importance," I replied. If this was real, if I was really seeing Ronan, then I must tread carefully with what I might tell him. He opened his mouth to speak, but a loud noise startled me, and when my eyes snapped open, I was back in the cell.

Deimos towered over me, and a plate of what barely passed as food lay on the ground, most of its contents scattered on the stone floors. The witch stood with his legs on either side of mine, so when he squatted down, he straddled my lap.

"Wakey wakey, Lady Redfern," he crooned, brushing hair from my forehead. Dried blood flaked beneath his fingers as they dragged across my skin.

"Stop," I rasped. "You win—just, just stop."

"My lady, I've barely started," he murmured.

"My king will have your head," I said with all the venom I could muster. "Kill me, do what you want—but know that he will not rest until your head is on a spike at the palace gates." Deimos huffed a laugh.

"I'll take that into consideration after I've had my fun." He slammed his mouth against mine. I tried to turn my head away, but Deimos grabbed my jaw with one hand and held me still while the other pressed in between my legs. His slimy tongue forced itself between my lips, my teeth, and into my mouth—

I bit down, hard.

I wasn't sure which was worse, the feeling of a severed piece of tongue floating around in my mouth or Deimos's shriek as he pulled himself away. His hand clutched at his mouth as blood gushed past his fingers and his wide eyes stared into mine in disbelief. I spat his tongue out onto the floor, a mouthful of his blood sprayed out along with it. He looked like he might vomit or strike me. Instead, he snatched the piece of tongue and fled the room.

I heaved, dropping my head back against the wall and looking toward Hannele. She hadn't stirred during the scuffle. I stared, unsure if she was breathing, and finally relaxed a bit when I watched her chest rise and fall. I wondered how long it would be until her last breath. Until mine.

Chapter Forty-Five

My eyes grew heavy, and though I wanted to sleep, I forced myself to stay awake. I did not want to be surprised by Deimos again, and hours later when I heard swift footsteps coming down the corridor, I braced myself, pressing back tightly against the wall. But when the door burst open, it wasn't Deimos looking for revenge.

It was Lyra, wearing a hooded cloak. Wordlessly, she crouched before me and pulled a key from her pocket. My cuff and chains clattered to the floor.

"Lyra, what are you . . . ?" I rubbed at my raw skin and moved to stand. My knee screamed at the full weight of my body, slight as it now was.

"Were you truthful in your request?" she asked, looking over her shoulder. "A teacher, in exchange for peace? A place at the table for the covens?"

"Yes," I breathed.

"Even after all of this?"

I hesitated, but still said, "Yes."

"Then get ready to run." She knelt before Hannele. "Is she alive?"

"I think so," I said shakily, wondering if this might be a trap. "Last I checked, she was still breathing." Lyra felt for a pulse.

"She's there," the keeper said, "but just barely. We need to go." She unlocked the chains and the cuff on Hannele's wrist before scooping her up into her arms, then over her shoulders like a new lamb. "I can't—what is it your people call it? Effuge? I can't effuge in here. Too many wards. We have to make it down the corridor and through the door. Once we're on the other side, I can take the three of us out of the Temple." I nodded, limping to the side and allowing Lyra to open the door and peek out. "All clear," she muttered, turning right. I followed shakily. With the cuff gone, my mind was suddenly clearer than it had been in weeks, but my body would need more time, and a healer, to recover.

Lyra walked at a swift but unsuspicious pace. The corridor was empty, but seemingly endless in length. We'd only been walking a few seconds when a door opened and closed behind us. "Don't look. Keep walking." Lyra picked up the pace, which I attempted to match.

"Hey! Stop—" a voice called. Before another word could ring out, Lyra murmured something as she twisted, launching a wave of purple light from her hands. I didn't turn to see if he had dodged it, but a second later heard multiple pairs of feet chasing us.

"Go—*go*!" Lyra commanded. My battered knee was screaming for me to stop, but I kept running alongside the witch, finding myself just feet from the door when it swung open.

It was Deimos.

He stood before us as we came to a sudden stop, the guards still approaching. White-hot rage and disbelief flashed in his violet eyes as he looked us all up and down, and raised his hand—

But I was faster. With all the strength I could muster, I sent a wall of flame crashing toward him while Lyra shouted a spell and her purple light sent him flying. Down, down, down the corridor, where he collided with the wall on the opposite end. I stepped through the door while Lyra nearly fell through it, catching herself on my arm as she did. As soon as she touched me, my stomach dropped and we landed, shivering, on the top of the Five-Peak Summit.

The wind screamed in our ears while snow came down upon us, melting as it hit my skin. I gasped, almost laughing at the sensation. I had not felt fresh air in so long. Until now, I had not been sure I would ever feel it again.

"We don't have much time," said Lyra as she gently laid Hannele's sleeping body on the ground. She reached under her cloak and into a hip pack for a folded map, which she spread on the ground, showing the entirety of the Medeisian Realms. Though it was in nearly perfect condition, one glance told me that it was outdated. Nautia was still the capital. "I need you to show me where to go."

The Grand Palace was dead in the center of the Sylvannian territory. We'd never make it past their wards, and if we simply arrived at one of the entry points scattered along the border, Lyra would surely be taken prisoner, if she wasn't killed on sight. I scanned the map and noticed the rocky Sylvannian border nearest the sea—unlikely to have many patrols, with nature providing an adequate barrier. There was a symbol indicating a town just past the border. We could get help, get word to the palace. "Here," I said, pointing. "We'll have to walk a little way to get over the border, but—"

"Fine," she said, bending down and hoisting Hannele back over her shoulders. Before I could say another word, she gripped my wrist, said her words, and again my stomach dropped.

We landed, hard, on the rocks just outside the Sylvannian border. Lyra was out of breath and sweating.

"Are you okay?"

"Fine," she said, adjusting Hannele's body before straightening her posture and raising her hood. "That was just a long way to transport three people. I'll be okay in a minute."

"Let's get moving, then. We need to get to town before sundown." I led the way, limping.

We lurched and stumbled our way over rocks and rough terrain for an hour, Lyra carrying the still unconscious Hannele the whole time, never complaining or stopping to rest. It was at the end of that hour that I felt the air grow heavy, and realized we were approaching the warded border.

"Will I be able to cross through that?" Lyra asked, clearly feeling the same weight in the air.

"I guess we'll see," I replied.

A few more feet and there we were, stopped before the invisible border. I took a step forward and passed through without consequence. But when I motioned for Lyra to do the same, she halted abruptly, as if she had run into a brick wall.

"Ouch," she muttered.

Panicking, I wracked my brain, trying to remember anything I'd been told about the wards of Sylvanna . . . and could remember nothing. Nothing, that was, until I recalled my first trip to Sylvanna, when Aydan had clasped hands with all of us, allowing us to effuge directly into the palace. Once I had entered Sylvanna that first time, the wards were lifted for me as a member of Aydan's Cabinet. I crossed back over and clutched the witch's hand before nearly dragging her behind me. She passed through with no resistance.

"Keep going," I panted. My leg was throbbing, but in the distance I could see the edge of a town. We were nearly home.

Another hour of limping, with Lyra stopping twice to readjust the princess she still carried—now cradled in her arms rather than over her shoulders—and we were there. The streets were quiet, the villagers likely retreating into their homes for dinner. "Make sure that hood stays up," I muttered breathlessly. Lyra said nothing, but adjusted the hood to cover her face, keeping her tattooed hands hidden beneath Hannele. Up ahead, a shopkeeper was locking his storefront for the night, and I called out to him. His eyes widened at the sight of me—covered in blood and two months' worth of filth.

"Ma'am, are you all right?" he asked as I approached.

"My friend needs help," I said. "A healer. Please, is there someone—?"

"The only healers nearby live on the Hazelwren Estate, at the other end of town." He pointed down the road behind us. I thought I might cry.

"Please, can you tell us how to get there? Perhaps on a map?" Lyra's lilting voice asked from beneath her cloak. The man patted his pockets as if to search for one, then thought for another second before realization struck him. He waved his hand over the dirt road at our feet and a basic map appeared, guiding us from the shop where we stood, down the main road, and through some twists and turns to where the estate claimed to be.

"Thank you," I said. The man bent over in a bow, but before he came back up Lyra gripped me and we were gone.

The ride was rougher this time, and when we appeared on the other side, the three of us crashed to the ground, right at the doorstep of the Hazelwren Estate, bypassing the gates completely. Hannele moaned, but her eyes remained closed as I stood, panting. I steadied myself on the doorframe and knocked as hard as I could, over and over and over—until the door flew open and a bewildered servant stood before us, staring at me and then the injured women behind me.

"Please," I rasped, "please, we need a healer—we need to send word to the palace—the king . . . Lady Solandis . . ." I felt myself sway.

"What in Ehnara's name—" the servant started.

"My name is Lady Shaye Eastly. I am the Chief Advisor of King Aydan's Cabinet—"

"Lady Shaye?" a voice called from inside. Hurried footsteps approached and into the light came Lady Reyna, disbelief written on her face. "My gods." She turned to the servant. "Get the healers—and send word to the palace. Now."

Chapter Forty-Six

Within minutes, we were taken to a suite where Hannele was placed on a plush bed and a healer began to examine her wounds. Every few seconds, it seemed, another healer would come to join in her treatment, and every so often someone would ask me a question about her condition. I did my best to answer but struggled to give a clear statement. With the cuff gone, I felt my magic simmering beneath the surface once again, but it was working hard to heal my injuries now and could not be bothered with keeping me awake.

The healers banished Hannele's jacket from her body, revealing the putrid, festering wound on her arm. Through the blood and pus and every other awful substance there, I could see the white, jagged splinters of bone peeking from beneath the princess's dark skin. They got to work, a pair of them focused on stitching her arm back together, while three others held their glowing green lights over her head, heart, and stomach. Minutes that felt like eternities passed while I watched the healers put her back together. For the first time in my life, I sent a real prayer to the gods.

Reyna was kind enough to bring me a bowl of broth, which she insisted I sip, but after a couple of mouthfuls, I couldn't stomach any more and set the bowl aside. She watched on for a minute or so, saying nothing. It was nearly silent in the room while the healers worked, until loud voices rang out from elsewhere in the house. Reyna scowled and opened the door to see what was happening.

"What in the world—"

"Where is she? Reyna, please, let me through—"

The door pushed open fully and in flew Gerridan, followed closely by Kenna. Gerridan was pale, and when his eyes landed on me, I felt the color drain from my own face. Reyna slipped into the hallway, attempting to give us some level of privacy while Gerridan gaped.

"Ger, I . . ." I started, my voice shaking. He took a step toward me and wrapped me into a long, tight hug.

"I can't believe it's you," he said, voice tight. "Of all the stupid, *selfish* things—"

"Oh, don't start," said a weak voice from behind us. I whipped my head around to see Hannele's eyes were open, though still looking quite heavy. Gerridan's breath hitched, and a small smile formed on the princess's lips.

Without another word, Gerridan crossed the room and sat on the edge of the bed, where he took her hand in his and kissed her palm. Taking their cue, the healers bowed their heads to the princess and filed out of the room. I motioned for Lyra, who had been standing in the corner this whole time, to follow Kenna and me into the hallway. Once outside the door, Kenna threw her arms around my neck.

"I can't believe you're here," she said softly.

"Me either," I said as she pulled away. Kenna looked Lyra up and down. "This is Lyra," I explained. "She . . . she's my new teacher."

"I see," the seer replied, giving the witch another once-over before turning back to me. "He's on his way," she said. "He's been in Ayzelle the past few days. I sent word with Elise." I nodded.

"Thank you," I said. "Can you . . . will you please take Lyra home? Our home, I mean."

She sighed but offered her arm to Lyra, who looked between us with hesitation.

"You are safe here, Lyra," I told her. "No harm will come to you within these borders. Kenna will have the servants get you a bath and something hot to eat, and I'll come check on you later."

"There will be much to discuss," Lyra said. I nodded as she took Kenna's arm, and the pair of them disappeared.

I debated whether I should go back into the room, to climb in the other bed there and rest, but decided against interrupting Gerridan and Hannele's reunion and instead found an armchair in a nook at the end of the corridor. I rested my head against the plush back of it and let my eyes drift closed.

I was nearly asleep when commotion sounded from downstairs. Groggily, I stood from my chair and headed down the hall toward the noise. Reyna had been running in all different directions since our arrival, and I didn't want her to deal with yet another interruption to her life on my account. Heavy footsteps bounded up the stairs, and I was only a few steps away from the top of the stairwell when Aydan rounded the corner and came to a stunned halt. I inhaled sharply as he stared, wide-eyed, as if seeing a ghost.

My face crumpled. I threw my arms around his neck and cried into his chest while he squeezed me tightly, running a hand over my matted, dirty hair and pressing a kiss to the top of my head. I pulled away, still blubbering, and placed my hand on his cheek. His eyes were glossy.

"Do you—do the healers need to see you?" he asked.

"No, someone looked me over while the rest worked on Hannele. I should just need rest, but they'll check on me again later."

"Is Hannele . . . ?"

"She'll need time, but she'll be okay. Gerridan is with her." Aydan took my hand without another word.

We landed in Aydan's room—*our* room—back at home in Sylvanna. I swayed on my feet at the sudden effuging, but he caught me and carried me to bed. He crawled in beside me and held me close, refusing to let go. I didn't want him to.

"Aydan," I choked after a few moments of silence. "I'm so . . . I'm so sorry. I'm so fucking stupid, and selfish—"

"Stop," he murmured. "It doesn't matter."

"I betrayed you. I betrayed the Crown."

"It doesn't matter," Aydan insisted. "You're home."

"But I—"

"I didn't listen. I was resigned to saying no. You had an idea, and Gerridan and I . . ." He searched for the words. "I should have at least looked into the logistics. I set you up for failure."

"I didn't fail," I told him. The hand he had been rubbing up and down my arm stopped. "There's a witch. Lyra. She's here in the house. She saved Hannele's life, and mine. And she's agreed to be my teacher, provided that the Crown upholds its end of the bargain."

"The Crown has made a bargain with a witch?" A hint of amusement coated the words. "And what bargain would that be?"

"That in your quest toward a new, more peaceful world through a possible alliance with Nautia, witches will have their voices heard as well. A seat at the table for the covens." I stated. Silence, followed by Aydan's hand continuing its path up and down my arm.

"Not bad, Lady Advisor," he said softly before kissing my head again.

"Careful," I told him. "I'm filthy."

"Sorry—here, let's get you cleaned up." He scooped me into his arms again and brought me to the bathroom, where he sat me on a stool and set the tub to fill. I bent to peel off my boots and let out a small cry as I did so. They had remained on my feet for the entirety of my and Hannele's imprisonment, and though my feet had already begun to heal with the silver cuff removed, they were still painful and swollen. Some of the skin peeled back along with my socks as I pulled those off too, revealing the purplish flesh that remained. I gasped softly at the feeling of tiles beneath my feet before I stood and removed my shirt, and then the pants as well. The air felt foreign on my skin, and it wasn't until I reached up to untangle my hair that I realized how thin my arms were. All of my hard work with Alastair, wasted. I'd have to start building my strength up again as soon as he let me back in the ring.

"Where is Alastair?" I asked, trying and failing to unwrap the braid that had become a single, long knot on the back of my head. Aydan waved a hand and it unknotted itself, falling down my back in dirty waves. Though his expression didn't change, I could see that Aydan's eyes were dark at the sight of my weakened body.

"Al is in Nautia on my behalf," he said. My eyes widened.

"*Nautia?*" I repeated. He nodded. "What is he . . . ?"

"When you went on your . . . mission," he said, "I couldn't focus on the Nautian deal. Alastair stepped in and continued correspondence with the Prince Regent. They've been having some preliminary meetings this week, which will determine whether I sit down with the Nautians in a few months' time."

"I see." I crossed the room and stepped into the full, steaming tub scented with rosemary and mint bath oils. I thought I might cry at the sensation as I lowered myself in, and a deep moan escaped me as I lay my head back and let my eyes close. I kept them closed while Aydan brought over the stool, sat beside the tub, and began to wash my hair, gently clearing the grime and dried blood from my scalp. "Kenna said you were in Ayzelle."

Aydan paused. "I was."

"Tell me about your trip," I said. "How are things with the extended council?"

"I wasn't there for the council, although they thought they should have a say."

"In what?"

"Planning your funeral," he said in a low voice. I stiffened at the words. "Your note said two weeks. After one, Kenna couldn't see Hannele anymore. At the one-month mark, Lord Declan suggested you two might have been killed and I nearly had him flogged. A few days ago . . . I was convinced that if you weren't home by now, you must be dead."

"I'm so sorry—"

"I can't tell you how glad I was to be wrong." He pressed a kiss to the back of my neck. I remained silent while Aydan continued to wash me, running a cloth over my limbs and revealing that many spots I'd assumed were covered in filth were actually bruises. Aydan sighed, and the air grew heavy with his anger.

"Do you often bathe your advisors?" I joked, hoping to cut the tension.

A pause, and then Aydan replied, "Only the ones I intend on making my queen."

I swallowed and bit the inside of my cheek. "That's not funny."

"I'm not joking." He stood and found a towel before lifting me from the tub and wrapping me in it. Once I was balanced on my feet, he summoned a robe, which he helped me slip on and secure around my waist with the belt. He led me to bed by my hands and sat beside me there, angled so our knees brushed. "I'm sure there are a million more appropriate times for me to do this, but I love you—more than anything. I've known it since I was still called the Wayward Prince. All I've wanted for a long time now is to spend the rest of my life with you." My mind raced with echoes of Solandis's warnings, the unrest that would follow if I remained by Aydan's side. I thought of all the ways I'd failed him, all the mistakes I had made. And yet, I couldn't think of anything I wanted more.

"Aydan, I—I don't. I mean, of course I—I don't know what to say—" I stammered. Wrong. This was coming out wrong. Of course I wanted—

"There's no need to answer right this second. I shouldn't have brought it up, I'm sorry." He kissed me, and when I pulled away, I glanced at the clock on the wall, then swore under my breath.

"What's wrong?" Aydan chuckled as I sprung to my feet. When I swayed, his amusement turned to concern and he offered me a hand to steady myself.

"I need to go see Lyra," I said carefully. His expression didn't sour as I thought it might. "Where do you think Kenna took her?"

"If they came here, probably your old bedroom. Hannele's still has all her things in it," he explained. "Although, I'm interested to know how that's working out. Catchfly hasn't let anyone in that room since you left. Elise has been sending food and water in there blindly." My heart fluttered. Oh Catchfly, you bitch.

Aydan helped me dress. My movements were labored enough that even the simplest of dresses would have required assistance. It felt strange to be wearing something clean; the sparring leathers had become like a second skin in the last weeks, and now the simple cotton of my favorite gray dress felt like the height of luxury. He'd tied my hair back in a simple braid, saving me from the labor of reaching back and doing it myself, and I gripped his offered arm. He effuged us to the top of the stairs, where we found Kenna sitting on the floor of the corridor with her back to the wall.

"Standing guard, Ken?" Aydan asked. The seer grunted.

"Your *teacher* is in there," she said to me, pointing to the door to my old bedroom.

"Her name is Lyra," I reminded her. "She's put herself at great risk to come here with me."

"I know. And I know there was no other choice but finding one of *them*, but it doesn't mean I have to like it." Kenna rose to her feet, groaning as she did so. She looked me over and let out a low whistle. "Those bastards really did a number on you, didn't they?" I brought my hand to my face, where even the slightest touch felt like dragging glass over my skin.

"Just one of them, really," I replied, and Aydan tensed beside me. "He had his men do most of the dirty work, but it was on his orders." Kenna's face hardened, and the faraway look in her eyes told me she was attempting to see what had happened, though I knew she could not. After a moment, she gave up, bid us farewell, and bounded down the stairs to disappear elsewhere in the house.

I wasted no time and reached forward to knock.

"Yes?"

I pushed on the door and found Lyra sitting politely on the foot of what used to be my bed, with Catchfly perched next to her. The fat gray cat sprinted to my feet. I crouched to scoop her into my arms, and scratched her ears while she purred deeply. "I missed you so much," I whispered. "I'm sorry I had to go."

"Your abilities are more developed than I thought, Lady Redfern," Lyra said, now standing with her hands folded in front of her. I didn't bother correcting her on my name. "It is quite unusual that an untrained witch would have acquired a familiar."

"Excuse me?" I asked, cradling Catchfly like a baby.

"The cat has made itself known to me as your familiar. Her attachment to you is a deep soul-bond. She will remain with you in this form for the entirety of your natural life." I looked down at the cat, who had begun to drool.

"If you say so," I said, setting Catchfly on the floor.

"She will be of use to you," she assured me. I realized Aydan was still standing beside me.

"Lyra, this is my . . . betrothed. King Aydan of Medeisia." Aydan tensed for just a second upon hearing my answer to his proposal. He wrapped his arm around my waist, and by the way he held on to me I knew he was refraining from kissing me there in front of our guest. Instead, he nodded at the witch in greeting. Lyra curtsied before him.

"Your Majesty," she said.

"Lady Lyra, I thank you for your services thus far. You have saved Princess Hannele and Lady Shaye, and thus the future queen of this nation. The Crown is in your debt."

"No need," Lyra replied. "Simply uphold your end of our bargain."

"Of course," Aydan replied with a bow of his head. "If there is anything you require to begin your lessons with Shaye—"

"I will need access to an herb garden, as well as a library. Preferably one that will contain whatever knowledge Medeisians have on the art of witchcraft. My understanding is that such information is hard to come by in your kingdom, but anything helps."

"Those things can certainly be arranged," I confirmed. "When shall we begin?"

"I will require some time to set up an appropriate room for our lessons—and you need time to heal and rebuild your strength. Perhaps a few months, before we start your journey."

"And how long should we expect your company?" Aydan asked.

"Tradition states that a witch's training is complete after a year and a day of study."

"Very well," he said. "Anything you need, it shall be yours. Thank you, again, for the great risk you have taken."

"I think you'll find my vision is quite similar to yours, Your Majesty," said the witch. "I believe we will be strong allies." She turned her attention to me. "If you think you'll need it during the healing process, continue taking your sleep tonic for now. But I would like you to stop using it by the time your training begins." I nodded, suddenly exhausted.

"I would ask why, but I think I'd rather go take a dose and get some real rest," I said. Lyra smirked.

We bid one another farewell, and when Aydan and I moved to leave the room, Catchfly remained at my heels. Before the door, shut Lyra called out: "Oh, just one more thing." She approached the door and poked her head out. "Please tell your groundskeepers not to kill any snakes this week. My own familiar will be on his way."

"Noted," said Aydan, bowing his head once more. Lyra mirrored the action and shut the door herself. He took my hand and effuged us to the sitting room while Catchfly bounded down the stairs to join us.

"Well?" I said with a shrug. "What do you think?"

"I think she's . . . nice. If a bit abrupt."

"You once told me you had never heard of a witch with good intentions," I reminded him, thinking to that first night in Ayzelle. "Does that opinion still hold true?"

"With so few words exchanged, my love, I really can't say. But I can see she has taken an incredible risk in coming here, and for that I am grateful." His hand rested gently on my cheek. "Do you want to talk about what happened to you?" Aydan's thumb brushed over a bruise there. Despite the ache, I didn't flinch.

"I will, someday," I told him. "But for now I think I'd like to just go to sleep. I feel like I've been awake for weeks—" I stopped when the door opened and knew in an instant that I would not be sleeping just yet.

The look on Alastair's face when his eyes met mine from the doorway was that of pure relief. Injuries be damned, I crossed the room as quickly as I could and all but leapt into the general's arms, wrapping my own around his neck and burying my face in his armored shoulder.

"I came as soon as I heard you were here," he said. "Where's Hannele?"

"She's at the Hazelwren Estate," Aydan replied from a few feet away. Al set me on my feet before moving to hug Aydan as well. "She's going to be all right."

"Why Hazelwren?"

"It was the closest place with a healer that my new teacher could effuge us to," I said. His eyes widened slightly.

"So you were successful?" he asked.

"Yes," said Aydan. "Congratulations, you live next door to a witch." He pointed up the stairs. Al inhaled sharply and then huffed a small laugh.

"I'm very proud of you," he said, squeezing my hand.

"How was Nautia?" I asked.

"It—er, well, it was—wonderful," he stammered slightly. "I'll prepare a report for each of you and leave them in Aydan's study."

"Thank you." Aydan took my hand. "You need to get some rest." I heard Alastair agree with him before we effuged back to the bedroom, where he gave me a dose of my tincture and tucked me under the blankets. Catchfly scratched to be let in and he opened the door. She jumped up and curled in next to me, purring against my body while Aydan sat beside me on the edge of the bed.

"I'm going to check in on Hannele and arrange for a healer to come see you in the morning," he said softly as I felt my eyes begin to close. "I'll be back in half an hour."

"Thank Reyna for me as well," I said. "I left without saying anything."

"I will." Aydan kissed me again and effuged away, leaving me to submerge myself in darkness.

Chapter Forty-Seven

For the next few days, I was ordered to take things slowly. Several healers Priamos recommended came to see me the morning following my return, and all determined there was nothing to be done but rest. I'd set myself back further by using the last of my fire on Deimos. Now I could barely produce a single spark, whether I tried or not. The healers told me my magic would return as my physical strength recovered.

Aydan was reluctant to leave my side but, given the nature of my disappearance, needed to meet with the councils to explain where his Chief Advisor had been for almost two months. The Cabinet had all voted to continue keeping my abilities a secret from the extended councils for now, so Aydan and Gerridan fed them a story:

I had received a letter that warned of a plot against the king. Hannele and I rushed to meet with the supposed informant, only to be kidnapped by an unknown assailant and held captive until we were rescued by Lyra—a mortal, and the newest member of the king's household.

The councils believed the story with ease, especially once Gerridan altered their moods to be less skeptical. Lyra would remain under our protection for as long as necessary, and once I regained my strength, she would teach me to control and wield the witchcraft in my veins.

Aydan also took these council meetings as an opportunity to announce our engagement, which had come as a surprise to everyone, including Gerridan, who was of course both thrilled and disappointed that he had not predicted we would get engaged ten minutes after reuniting. Aydan told me later that, while Priamos looked delighted, he couldn't tell whose face was more shocked—Solandis's or Lord Declan's. Both, however, offered congratulations to Aydan and well-wishes to me, their future queen.

"*Anointed* queen," Aydan corrected himself as he filled me in on the meeting.

"I would be more than happy just being your consort, you know," I told him while I sat resting in bed. My copy of *Enchanted, Enchanting* lay face down on my lap while Aydan sat beside me.

"I know," he said, "but I told you a long time ago that if I was smart, I would accept nothing less than an anointed queen. I'll need you by my side to ensure I keep making smart decisions." I huffed a laugh. For now, at least, the thought of ruling by Aydan's side did not frighten me.

"Your Majesty . . . my lady?" Elise said from the doorway. Aydan turned his attention to her. "Lord Gerridan and Princess Hannele have arrived." Aydan thanked her and stood to help me from the bed. When Elise and Isolde had come to tend to me after I returned, Isolde had held back tears, telling me how worried she'd been. Elise simply looked me over, embraced me briefly, and announced that she would run me a bath. I had not yet been to visit Zale and Tory in the kitchens but was told they sent their love.

Aydan helped me to the sitting room, where Alastair and Kenna were already greeting Hannele, who clung to Gerridan. No announcements had been made, but none were necessary. The night we had returned, Aydan told me, Gerridan came home and immediately began moving all of her belongings to his bedroom, now theirs to share.

Hannele saw me over Alastair's shoulder as she hugged him, and a broad smile spread across her face. Slowly, I approached and wrapped her in my arms. When we pulled away, she looked into my eyes and said with deepest sincerity: "You look like shit." I laughed.

"You've had better days yourself, princess." We both were gaunt, still healing from our injuries, and waiting for our abilities to return to us.

"I told you he wouldn't fire you." Hannele smirked. I rolled my eyes.

"About that," Aydan chimed from beside me. I raised my brows.

"Oh?" I said. "Have I been removed from my position?"

"This should be good," Kenna murmured behind me. Alastair shushed her.

"Well, technically . . ."

"Keep talking, Aydan darling, I think I saw a flame on her fingertips." Gerridan grinned wickedly. I scowled at him.

"The anointed queen is its own position," Aydan finally said. "The Cabinet answers to the Crown. You cannot be your own Chief Advisor." Oh.

"Fair enough." I laughed. "I need to heal and start my lessons with Lyra anyway." Gerridan chuckled, enjoying the exchange.

"And I hope you won't mind, my love, that I've already selected our next Chief Advisor, effective immediately," said Aydan, turning toward our mischievous blond emissary. "Gerridan, I would be honored if you took the position."

The color drained from his face. "You're serious?"

"Very. Congratulations, Lord Advisor." Gerridan shook Aydan's extended hand, and the men grinned at one another. So did Hannele and I, though she was beginning to sway on her feet a bit, which Gerridan noticed right away.

"You should get to bed," he told her. She didn't argue, and allowed him to grip her hand and effuged them both to their bedroom.

"You should be getting back to bed too," Alastair noted from across the room.

"I'm fine," I started to lie before Aydan cut me off.

"No, he's right. The healers said no more than a few minutes at a time." I sighed and he effuged us back to bed once I'd waved goodbye to Kenna and Al.

Aydan helped me back under the covers, then crawled in himself. "It's midafternoon." I laughed. "Don't you have some meeting to attend?"

"Maybe." He pulled me in snugly. "This is much more urgent."

"Of course it is." I chuckled.

"Being close to my queen is the most important, urgent task I can fathom," he said, kissing the back of my neck.

"I'm not your queen yet," I joked, curling my body against his while he stroked my hair, and I felt myself starting to drift.

"No, you always have been."

My eyes darted open as I stood in darkness again, Lord Ronan's study in the distance. I approached, the curiosity overwhelming me. When I stepped inside, Ronan wasn't alone. Brina was there.

"This is where you . . . do it?" she asked, holding her arms across her body.

"Yes." Ronan's voice was hoarse. He glanced up in my direction, and I knew he saw me.

"*Why?*" she asked. "What on earth—"

"There are people. Here. With plots against Zathryan. They've utilized this knowledge already, in secret. Now they bide their time, waiting to strike—"

"Then why not tell the king? Why not tell the Crown Princess, the council—?"

"There is . . . so much to explain."

"I'm not sure I want to hear it," Brina said softly. She turned for the door.

"Brina, darling, please—"

"Your secret is safe with me, Ronan. But be careful. Please." She left.

Ronan sighed and ran his hands over his face, then over his long auburn hair. He looked no older than Aydan, until you looked deeper into his eyes and saw the weight of eight hundred years pressing upon them.

"She'll be okay," I offered gently after a few minutes of silence.

"Maybe it's better like this," he replied with a glance to the door. "I don't want her caught up in my mess."

"Making things work between sorcerers and mortals is difficult."

"I'm not worried about that, I just—" He chewed his cheek. I waited. Ronan looked me square in the face. "I think I need your help."

My eyes flew open and I sat up straight, gasping for air and clutching at my chest. In an instant, Aydan was sitting up beside me, wrapping his arms around me, reminding me of where I was. There were no flames, no wind, no ice tonight. No defenses that my body and magic could muster to protect against an invisible threat. Just me, and Aydan, and the dread in my stomach at my father's words, which still rang in my ears. Was any of it real?

As my breath settled, I listened to Catchfly's loud purr from the foot of the bed. I took comfort in knowing that my family filled the house, and I knew as I buried my face into Aydan's chest while he laid us back down upon the bed, that I was safe here. For now, I was home.

Thank you for reading!

The Wayward Prince is a dream come true and I hope you've enjoyed the journey so far. If you have, please consider leaving a review on Amazon! Reviews are the best way to help authors gain visibility, and every single one is truly appreciated.

For updates on what I'm working on, follow me on Twitter @NCHayesAuthor, or Instagram @nc.hayes, and be sure to keep an eye out for the next installment of The Redfern Legacy— *The Queen of Reckoning.*

Cheers,
N.C. Hayes

N.C. Hayes lives in Arizona with her husband, children, and the things that go bump in the night. *The Wayward Prince* is her first novel.

www.ingramcontent.com/pod-product-compliance
Lightning Source LLC
Chambersburg PA
CBHW030536310726
48979CB00010B/1932/J

* 9 7 8 1 9 5 6 5 5 0 0 6 1 *